THE ULVERSCROFT FOUNDATION
(registered UK charity number 264873)
was established in 1972 to provide funds for
research, diagnosis and treatment of eye diseases.
Examples of major projects funded by
the Ulverscroft Foundation are:-

- The Children's Eye Unit at Moorfields Eye Hospital, London
- The Ulverscroft Children's Eye Unit at Great Ormond Street Hospital for Sick Children
- Funding research into eye diseases and treatment at the Department of Ophthalmology, University of Leicester
- The Ulverscroft Vision Research Group, Institute of Child Health
- Twin operating theatres at the Western Ophthalmic Hospital, London
- The Chair of Ophthalmology at the Royal Australian College of Ophthalmologists

You can help further the work of the Foundation
by making a donation or leaving a legacy.
Every contribution is gratefully received. If you
would like to help support the Foundation or
require further information, please contact:

THE ULVERSCROFT FOUNDATION
The Green, Bradgate Road, Anstey
Leicester LE7 7FU, England
Tel: (0116) 236 4325

website: www.foundation.ulverscroft.com

Paul Mendelson began writing at school, wrote and directed on the London fringe theatre circuit, and in 1986 at the age of twenty-one became the then-youngest playwright to be performed at the National Theatre with *You're Quite Safe With Me* at the Cottesloe. A dalliance with TV writing resulted, including work on *The Bill*, followed by eleven non-fiction books about mind-sports such as bridge and poker, a weekly column in the *Financial Times*, many magazine articles, and numerous monologues and short pieces for the theatre. His first crime novel, *The First Rule of Survival*, was shortlisted for the CWA Golden Dagger Crime Novel of the Year in 2014, and its sequel, *The Serpentine Road*, was longlisted for the same prize the following year. Both have been translated into several languages, and a television adaptation is in preparation. Paul lives with Gareth and Katy in London and Cape Town.

You can discover more about the author at www.paulmendelson.co.uk

THE HISTORY OF BLOOD

When the South African Police Service receives a panicked call for help from the wayward daughter of a former Apartheid-era politician, they soon discover not only her body, but within it, a message that will take Colonel Vaughn de Vries and Don February of the Special Crimes Unit on a journey through their country — and its past. As organised crime grips South Africa, new players arrive in Cape Town, determined to exploit the poor and hopeless. While other government agencies snap impotently at the small fish, de Vries, linked by a personal connection, resolves to follow this trail to its source and take it down from the top. Soon decades-old webs of corruption and influence are exposed; and as the boundaries of morality blur, de Vries's decisions begin to impact on his friends, colleagues and family.

PAUL MENDELSON

THE HISTORY OF BLOOD

Complete and Unabridged

CHARNWOOD
Leicester

First published in Great Britain in 2016 by
Constable
an imprint of Little, Brown Book Group
London

First Charnwood Edition
published 2017
by arrangement with
Little, Brown Book Group
London

A catalogue record for this book is available
from the British Library.

ISBN 978–1–4448–3176–4

Published by
F. A. Thorpe (Publishing)
Anstey, Leicestershire

Set by Words & Graphics Ltd.
Anstey, Leicestershire
Printed and bound in Great Britain by
T. J. International Ltd., Padstow, Cornwall
This book is printed on acid-free paper

Author's Note

When Nelson Mandela became President of South Africa in 1994, the system of apartheid (literally, separation) was already being dismantled — officially. A minority of white South Africans, including Afrikaners, deeply resented the democratic elections, seeing them as nothing more than a giving away of power from the Nationalist Party (the Nats) to the ANC (African National Congress). Some continued to fight the changes both politically and with the threat of violence; others sought to form their own whites-only enclaves within the country.

One of the first decisions when reforming the police force was to remove the military-style rank structure yet, strangely, in 2010, it was controversially reintroduced, creating echoes of the repressive force of the apartheid era.

The Hawks are part of South Africa's new Directorate for Priority Crime Investigation, who are given control over major crime. In the general public's minds they are probably most thought of as a rapid-reaction force with special training and greater resources.

Paul Mendelson

Prologue

The men stand, sullen, tired, dishevelled, their uniforms crumpled, faded. They have sat in the courtroom for three days, listening to arguments about six years of their lives, their silence ordered by superiors, instructed by their attorney. Actions are analysed by men who were not there, who may never have feared death, fighting on hostile ground, many miles from their own country.

The judge advocate describes the witnesses' testimony as a tragic insight into the by-product of an armed struggle. He depicts the senior officers' statements as either wilfully vague or deliberately misleading. He looks across his basic courtroom at the four men, in front of a plain rectangular school table. He asks if any of them wish to make a statement before he issues his verdict. The attorney rises.

'We reserve our right to remain silent, sir.'

The judge advocate nods, glances down at his notes. The rustling of the papers seems to echo in the silent hall. The spectators in the small gallery shuffle.

'I wish to make a statement.' The voice is deep, coarse with the harsh Afrikaner accent.

The eyes of the court turn to the tallest of the four accused. After three days of silence, one will speak. The man is well over six feet tall, blond

1

hair brushed sharply back from a high forehead. Unlike his fellow soldiers, he stands straight.

The attorney stands again. 'Sir?' He takes two paces towards the defendants, addresses the tall man: a whispered admonishment. The man stares back at him, silent, defiant. The lawyer turns, meets the eyes of men in the gallery, sits.

'I wish to make a statement.'

The judge advocate nods. 'You others may sit. Proceed, Captain.'

'I was taught that to serve my country was my duty and my honour. I did not seek religious objection, or exile, to avoid my national service. I served with pride.' He looks down at the three other accused. 'All of us understood that we fight for the soul of our country and the future of the continent. It was in our blood. It was what we were taught and what motivated every action. Were it not for us, for those who fought in the century before us, our country would have been at the mercy of foreign lands, Communists and black terrorists. We sacrificed our lives for the very people who have given away everything we've fought for, for the people who betrayed us politically and now want to make us criminals for following their orders.' He stops, chest heaving, fists balled. He breathes deeply. '*Vir veertig jaar, het die weermag ons teen die rooigevaar beskerm, en nou —* '

'In English, Captain.'

He stares back at the judge advocate. 'In English,' he repeats bitterly. 'For forty years we fought the Border War to save us from the threat of the reds and the blacks. And now, to appease those who terrorized us, we have given them everything, and this court will punish us for our service.' He remains standing, staring ahead.

The judge advocate lays both palms on his desk. 'I have heard enough.'

PART 1

Cape Town, December 2015
He sees the enormous aircraft bank, its fuselage catching the intense white sun, the blinding light like a Biblical revelation. He grabs at the visor, slaps it down, changes gear, guns the accelerator. It is as if, subconsciously, he has decided to race it to the airport.

The freeway is quiet: no commuter traffic, no school runs, just a low mirage-filled haze beneath the thicker layer of dirty copper smog that settles daily over the townships and squatter camps on the Cape Flats. He has the air-con off, window open, his elbow and the glowing tip of his cigarette in the 120 k.p.h. breeze. His head is clear. For others today, there might be much anticipated excitement or reflection; for him, there is near-contented resolve.

He slows to drift towards Boucherds Quarry Road, glances at the car clock, stalled at seven thirty, tilts his wrist and sees that it is two hours later. He turns into the industrial estate adjoining the airport road, amid the warehouses, catering companies and offices that service Cape Town International. Between a huge low factory, manufacturing steel components, and the back of a garage car wash, the textured grey concrete façade of the DF Malan Motel sits defiantly among the modern minimalism of unadorned functionality. Until the new millennium, it had shared its name with the airport, which was named after the prime minister when it opened in 1954. The owner had refused to sell it to the new airport authority, persevering with his business despite its obsolescence. Previously, it might have provided on-the-spot accommodation for air-crew on a fast turnaround or passengers delayed overnight. Now those rooms not sold by the hour serve only truck and taxi drivers.

He drives across the kerb to the pot-holed car park, searches in vain for shade, settles on a space close to the covered portico, the bleached blood-red letters unlikely to entice passing trade. He winds up the window, steps out into the dry, still heat, slams and locks his door. To his right, he sees two SAPS patrol cars next to an ambulance. In the half-dozen steps to the entrance, he feels sweat gather at his armpits, around his neck, realizes there will be no air-conditioning inside to cool him. Hours will pass until he exits this building.

Colonel Vaughn de Vries sighs: this is what he hates; this is what he loves.

* * *

A uniformed officer ambles towards the glass doors as De Vries approaches, checks his ID, salutes lazily, thumbs towards the staircase. 'Room twenty-two, sir. Second floor. Lift isn't working.'

De Vries indicates the deserted reception desk to his left. 'Owner?'

'Up there, complaining.'

'Cooler outside, Constable. Stay there. I don't want anyone else through here until she's taken out.' He trots towards the staircase, takes the shallow treads two at a time, crosses from threadbare pink to pale blue carpet as he reaches the landing on the second floor. Static electricity hums around his shoes as he pushes through double doors to the corridor, finds a second officer leaning against the wall opposite room twenty-two.

'Anyone else in these rooms?'

Before the officer has time to answer, De Vries hears the double doors behind him smack back against the wall, turns to see a tall, middle-aged man, pale, hair thinning, yet just too long. 'Are you in charge?'

'I am.'

The man holds out a limp hand. 'Piet Grobbelaar. It's my place. Some woman tells me no new guests. How is that right?'

De Vries ignores the hand. 'You know what's in that room? Until I find out why she's there, how she died, your property is my crime scene. If you stay out of my way, I'll give you back your business. Bug me, and it may be weeks. All right?'

Grobbelaar balks. 'I have regulars. They expect service.'

De Vries says, 'If you turn them away once, I think they'll be back. Don't you?'

The owner stands silently, shows no sign of departing.

'Go stand in your car park. Tell them yourself.

9

You can't be here.' De Vries gestures towards the doors, waits until the man slouches through them, then says to the officer, 'He comes through those doors again, you warn him once, then you arrest him. *Ja?*' He turns away, then back again. 'In fact, stand by them. No one comes through without my permission.'

He watches the officer pigeon-step unhurriedly down the corridor. Everything is moving slowly in the static, stagnant air. He extracts two small packets from his jacket pocket, snaps on plastic overshoes, worms sweating fingers into clammy latex gloves, knocks at the door of room twenty-two, pushes it open.

The living turn to him. He meets their gaze briefly, then drops his eyes to the dark, sodden carpet, soaked bedcover and the bottom half of a skirt tie-dyed with blood. He cranes his neck to see around the end of the bed. The girl is face down. There is so much blood. 'I'm Colonel de Vries, Special Crimes Unit. You are?'

The woman answers: 'Warrant Officer Lee-Ann Heyns, sir. Rondebosch.'

De Vries frowns: Rondebosch is a leafy university suburb twenty kilometres away. Heyns is a slim, fit, dark-haired woman, perhaps in her late thirties. He pulls his gaze away from her to the two paramedics examining the body. One looks up, nods, the other stays low over the body.

De Vries turns back to Heyns. 'Who got here first?'

'Sergeant Pietersen of Langer station, plus the officer outside and the one in the foyer. I placed them there, sir. I asked Sergeant Pietersen to search all the rooms on this level and talk to the owner. Then I called your office.'

'Why did you do that?'

'Special Crimes Unit: high-profile murder, kidnap, robbery.'

'*Ja*, but why us?'

'The victim, sir. She's Chantal Adam.'

'How did you know?'

'She called the emergency number, identified herself. When I got here and saw her, I recognized her.'

'Before you saw her, Warrant. Why did you come here?'

'Because I'm the officer assigned to her disappearance. Her father contacted us.'

'Her uncle.'

'Uncle?'

'Her father was Willem Adam.'

Heyns frowns, shakes her head.

'Willem Fourie Adam was a politician in the last couple of National Party governments,' De Vries says. 'He pushed for free elections. He was murdered — assassinated — in spring 1994, after the elections.'

'It sounds familiar, but I didn't connect Charles and Willem Adam. What happened to Chantal's mother?'

'She was deemed incapable. Psychological issues. I don't remember how it went down, or what happened to her. I just know that Charles Adam brought up Chantal as his daughter. She was about three years old when it happened.'

'You've done your research, sir.'

'Not really. I know Charles Adam.'

She blinks. 'You do?'

'My daughters were at school with Chantal and Charles's own daughter.' He glances at the body, feeling a sudden illogical terror that the girl is actually one of his own. He looks back at Heyns. 'Go on, Warrant.'

'Mr Adam spoke with my CO — Captain Maart — to report that he had lost touch with his daughter, that no one had seen her, and requested our help. When I heard the call today, I thought the dispatcher mentioned the name. And the description sounded like her. I came out, and it is.'

'Listening to radio broadcasts?'

Lee-Ann Heyns opens her mouth, checks herself. 'Quiet day.'

De Vries nods, turns to the paramedics. 'What have you got for me, gentlemen?'

The white paramedic looks at his coloured colleague. 'Wrists slashed. Probably self-inflicted with the glass here.' He gestures above him to the broken window. 'Brutal, though. If she did this to herself, she was determined. I'm marking her time of death as between seven and seven thirty this morning, barely two hours ago.'

Heyns says, 'That fits the limited time-scale we have already, sir. There's debris here, glass obviously, but what looks like a cell phone too.' She indicates the pieces with a pen and moves between De Vries and the body. 'If you're going to kill yourself, why call the police?'

★　★　★

12

De Vries leaves the room, Heyns following. From the far end of the corridor, a man appears, attired in crime-scene overalls and a head-covering that resembles a cheap pink shower cap.

'This,' Heyns says, 'is Sergeant Pietersen.'

Pietersen looks first at Heyns, then De Vries. 'Nothing. All the rooms are locked. Owner says there's no one on this floor. I went down the fire-exit stairs, but the doors at the bottom are locked. No sign of blood or anything else. It's all just dirty.' He wipes his forehead with the sleeve of his overalls.

De Vries stares at him, then turns to Heyns. 'All right. Run me through what happened this morning.'

She takes a notebook from her pocket. 'At seven oh one, 112 get a call from a Chantal Adam. I haven't heard it myself, but that was how she identified herself.'

'Chantal Adam?'

'Yes, sir.' She waits. He shakes his head. 'She said she was a prisoner in the DF Malan Motel. She asked for immediate help. Langer station was contacted and a patrol car was dispatched containing Sergeant Pietersen and two other officers. Another car arrived, but left again when the scene was secured. I have the details.'

'And you?'

'I arrived twenty minutes after the Langer officers.'

Pietersen confirms, 'That's right, sir.'

De Vries spins his right hand to accelerate the flow of information.

'When we arrive,' Heyns says, 'there's an

13

argument with the owner about privacy, but we get past that, locate room twenty-two and approach. There is no answer to our calls so we gain entry using a pass key, find the scene. I enter alone, study the body for life-signs, but the girl is dead, bled out. I back out, seal the room.'

De Vries reflects that it will have been her eyes that confirmed the girl's death. The eyes are a window in life; in death, they take a final indecipherable photograph. His job is to find out what they saw.

'I instruct that the hotel entrance is guarded,' Heyns continues, 'and no guest is permitted to leave — I don't think there are any. Looks like mainly daytime trade. I place a constable on the corridor and ask Sergeant Pietersen to check each of the remaining rooms. The owner says they're empty, but we use the pass key to check.'

De Vries is impressed with her efficiency. She has followed procedure, ensured the integrity of the scene.

The white paramedic appears at the door, paperwork completed, preparing to leave. 'We're done.'

De Vries takes the paper, thanks them, turns back to Pietersen and Heyns. 'I want you all outside while I take another look at the room. When the crime-scene guys arrive, show them up here. *Ja?*' He reaches to open the door to room twenty-two, turns back, glibly gleeful. 'Forgot to say — Happy Christmas.'

★   ★   ★

14

He lets the door close slowly, snap shut. The room is strangely silent, despite the broken window, the relentless wind blowing against the opposite side of the motel buildings. Beyond the shattered pane, the factories and warehouses sparkle grimly in the bleached sunlight, the garage car-wash still and deserted.

He closes his eyes, takes a deep breath. Above the distant interference of traffic on the N2 freeway, he hears the mournful tune of a Christmas carol, 'In the Bleak Mid-winter'. His mouth smiles; he wipes perspiration from his forehead.

Chantal Adam's body lies almost at right angles around the end of the low bed, her head partially submerged in the thick bloody gruel which envelops her torso. He can see only one side of her face. He expects it to be a mask of agony, but finds it strangely relaxed, almost . . . accepting.

⋆　⋆　⋆

The camera flies low and fast over the water, a vast plain of silver-grey, topped by parallel lines of sparkling white foam. It angles up to show the Waterfront, the newly completed Green Point football stadium, the skyscrapers of Mouille Point. The angle widens to encompass the City Bowl, Signal Hill, the huge, dark, broad form of Table Mountain. It seems to climb the almost vertical slopes, following tiny hikers ascending the Platterkloof paths, the cable car rising, rotating, until the lens zooms in on the girl.

She wears a white lace dress, her hair blown back from her face, arms outstretched until she reaches into her pocket and brings out a Mountain Bar. As she bites into it, the music reaches a crescendo and the sun appears behind her, igniting an aura of gold around her body.

★　★　★

He looks down the grey corridor, polystyrene tiles hanging down at angles from the low ceiling. In a black and white photograph, it might be art.

He stands still in the stale, fetid air, remembering Chantal Adam only as a young teenager, a friend of his daughters, more perhaps of Kate, the elder. He remembers driving — he thinks both of them — to the Adam mansion in Constantia for an afternoon of sweets and cakes and games in the sunlit garden.

He recalls the later story of Chantal Adam. Her journey from teenage beauty in Cape Town, on the cover of magazines, for ever the Mountain Girl in the famed commercial, leaving for New York, the newspaper stories of parties and drugs, her return to Cape Town, the gleeful tabloid accounts of her demise, supposedly cast out by her family, her body shrunken, her face unrecognizable.

On the second-floor landing, he finds Heyns, Pietersen and another uniformed SAPS officer. He shrugs. 'Shit shift.'

They say nothing. De Vries has visited his two daughters in Johannesburg, exchanged modest gifts, even met up with his ex-wife. Now, for him, Christmas Day is like any other, except that his building is quiet, with fewer officers and technicians on duty than usual. He stares down at the car park through the tall, dirty window, imagines families sitting down for their Christmas meal. 'Better here than at home,' he tells them. 'The people you celebrate Christmas with, there's a reason you haven't seen them all year.'

★   ★   ★

The Local Criminal Records Centre, attached to Langer Township, dispatch a photographer. De Vries sends him away. The Special Crimes Unit use their own people. The stocky little man sighs heavily, muttering as he returns to his vehicle. De Vries wonders how many corpses he photographs, perplexed that he is disappointed to miss one.

The Forensic Task Team from the Special Crimes Unit takes over the scene. De Vries rings the tarnished brass bell on the front desk, does not wait for the manager to answer, but lets himself into the man's office. He finds Grobbelaar on the telephone. When he hangs up, De Vries sits opposite him. The room is hot and claustrophobic. 'Just you here today, sir?'

Grobbelaar lights a cigarette, inhales deeply, studies the tip. 'Only me on duty over the holiday period. It's quieter here for a few days.'

De Vries can scarcely imagine the DF Malan Motel, even on a good day, as a hive of activity. 'You sign people in?'

'*Ja.*' Grobbelaar swivels the plastic-bound register towards De Vries.

'I can't read that.'

He turns it back. 'Think that's the idea. Most of my guests come and go, stay anonymous.'

'What time did she arrive?'

'They. Her and a guy. This morning.' Grobbelaar wipes sweat from the ragged edge of his moustache. 'Maybe six thirty?'

'Any cameras?'

'No, man. That wouldn't work here. We're an old-fashioned kind of place. Low rates, no rules.'

De Vries sighs. 'You didn't recognize her?'

He shakes his head.

'They arrive together? As a couple?'

'I don't ask.'

'But I am asking you: they look like lovers? Brother and sister?'

Grobbelaar smiles. 'I don't know.'

De Vries leans across the desk. 'Start thinking, because right now you're giving me nothing and, trust me, this isn't my season of goodwill.'

'Okay. They didn't seem like lovebirds. Happy enough. She could have been a pro, maybe part-time. I didn't ask. He's white . . . tall . . . blondish hair, ponytail, thin face, skinny guy. T-shirt, jeans. Nothing special.'

'Keep thinking,' De Vries tells him. 'You'll be talking to a police artist. I want details: tattoos, watch, dark glasses. How did they arrive? Car?'

'I don't know. I didn't see a car. I was in here. The bell goes, I take their money.'

'Cash?'

'*Ja.*'

'I need it.'

'Need it?'

'It's evidence.'

'No, man. They paid.' He has his hands flat on the desk in front him, his body half out of the chair. De Vries sees the half-smoked cigarette between shaking fingers. 'It's my money. Anyway, it'll be lost with the rest in the till.'

'It'll be on top. Show me the till.'

Grobbelaar looks down, glances up to see De Vries following his gaze. He turns a key, opens a desk drawer to his right.

De Vries stands up, peers over him. The drawer contains less than a thousand rand, mainly in fifties and hundreds. 'How much?'

'Two fifty for a day room.' Grobbelaar reaches for the notes.

'Don't touch the money.'

De Vries puts a glove on his right hand, extracts the notes and drops them into an evidence bag, seals it. 'You'll get a receipt. The man handle the cash?'

A nod. De Vries sits down. 'The room key. You get it back?'

Grobbelaar pats his pockets impotently. 'No.'

'Any luggage?'

'No . . . Maybe, ja. A rucksack. On his back. Saw it when they went to the stairs.'

'What did it look like?'

Grobbelaar shrugs. 'I don't know, man. What does a rucksack look like?'

'Colour?'

He closes his eyes. 'I don't know.'

'Either of them say anything?'

'No. 'Morning', 'thanks' — that's it.'

'Exact money?'

'*Ja.*'

'The girl say anything?'

'No. Seemed a little nervous, maybe a bit wired. Not unusual.'

'No shit,' De Vries says.

★   ★   ★

'They call me. I come.'

'Sorry.'

'I'm on call. One Christmas out of every three. Not so bad.' The scene-of-crime supervisor looks up. 'Until you see her, of course. First signs are suicide.'

'There was a man in the room with her.'

'On second thoughts . . . '

De Vries smiles perfunctorily. 'You heard what happened? She calls us, says she's a prisoner. We find her like this.'

Dr Steve Ulton gestures around the room. 'There's not much, Vaughn. Room's pretty dirty, lot of traffic. Window was broken from the inside.' He gestures into the open air. 'Glass down there too probably. Got a guy taping it off. At least it's a small scene. We'll get everything, but it'll take some sifting through.'

'A struggle?'

'I'd say so.'

'You look at the bed?'

'Filthy. That duvet covers a multitude of sins. Literally. It'll all be looked at but, again, first impressions are not that this was a scene of passion — not sexual passion anyway.'

'What was it a scene of?'

Ulton shrugs.

De Vries says, 'Anyone downstairs today?' The mortuary for the Special Crimes Unit is in the basement of his building.

'No. But I'd wait. Think it's Doc Kleinman tomorrow. Be quicker than to go anywhere else.'

'Okay.' He tilts his head at Ulton. 'You don't recognize her?'

'No.'

'Chantal Adam?'

'Name rings a bell.'

'The 'Mountain Girl'?'

'At the top of Table Mountain?' He stares at her face. 'You sure?'

'*Ja.*'

'Is it?'

De Vries grimaces. 'When you're done, Steve, we'll take her there just now.'

'Give me thirty minutes.'

De Vries backs out of the room, stepping over a technician by the door to the tiny bathroom. In the corridor, he finds Warrant Officer Heyns. 'You draw the short straw today?'

She smiles. 'Single woman, no family. I volunteered.'

'You said you were called by her father — her adoptive father?'

'Yes, sir. Are we going to inform the family today?'

'I think so. No PM until tomorrow, crime-scene guys will be here most of the afternoon. We'll take her back to my building, then go on to

21

the family.' He stares down at her, not unhappy that she will be at his side today. 'Looks like you've earned yourself a brief secondment to the elite divisions, Warrant Officer. I'll be watching you very carefully.'

★ ★ ★

'You've been at Rondebosch how long?'

'Three years. Mainly working in Constantia.'

They are smoking, windows wide open, as they drive out from the centre of Cape Town towards the Southern Suburbs. The Langer officers have returned to their station, Chantal Adam's body is in the morgue, refrigerated. The Forensic Task Team are returning to their labs. It is, after all, just another day.

Lee-Ann Heyns says, 'It's not easy. I'm eight years overdue promotion. Should have made lieutenant by now, maybe even captain. But I'm bad news three ways: white, Afrikaner, woman. There's not a month goes by I don't get passed over.'

It's a story De Vries hears every time he speaks with white officers.

'I had to push myself forward to accompany our captain when Charles Adam asked him to call at the family house.'

'He's known by you guys?'

'There's been trouble before with Chantal, ever since she came back from America. Captain Maart's a snob. Adam is a rich, successful man.' She looks up at him. 'But I forgot, sir. You know the family.'

'Not well. Not for a while now.'

'Don't think anyone knows how he made his money, but he spends it so everyone can see — parties for politicians and celebrities, a new treatment centre for the hospital in Wynberg, projects on the Cape Flats. Now magazine had him on the cover last year. 'Charles Adam: Gentleman Philanthropist'. Something like that.'

'What did he say about his adopted daughter?'

'He has another daughter, and a son. Both older than Chantal.'

'What was she? Twenty-two, twenty-three?'

'Almost twenty-four. Her father told us that she didn't want anything to do with the family, or the money, or the house, anything. She dropped out of university, went her own way.'

'What made Charles Adam call your captain this time?'

'Apparently, she'd told him she was going to leave the country, never come back. He said she'd been seen with . . . I don't remember exactly how he put it — but the wrong people. He wanted us to be aware, keep a look out for her, maybe bring her home.'

'How could we do that?'

'It had been done before. I guess he thought we might come across her.'

'With the wrong people . . . '

'In the wrong places. And we have.'

'We have.'

'And she'd been in trouble in the past, here and in the States.'

De Vries shakes his head. 'Not this much trouble.'

★ ★ ★

The slate-tiled porch to the old Constantia mansion is lined with red poinsettias, the door wreathed in conifer and red ribbon. A black servant, dressed formally in a dark suit, shows them into a double-height hallway, panelled in oak. De Vries stares at the vast Christmas tree nestling in the crook of an elegant stone staircase, a Norway spruce, deep green and aromatic. Ahead of them, the double doors to the dining room are open, and they can see past the remnants of a Christmas lunch — empty crystal decanters, cheese plates, a pudding on its stand — to a broad lawn outside where a large group has gathered under an enormous oak.

They are led to their left. The servant knocks and enters, holding the door for them. 'Colonel de Vries, and Warrant Officer Heyns.'

'All right, Joseph.'

Charles Adam rises from a chintz sofa, offering his hand. 'Christmas Day, an officer of your rank . . . I already know the news is bad.' He gestures for them to sit opposite him, gazing at De Vries. 'I know this officer.' He glances at Heyns. 'But I feel I know you too.'

'Our daughters were at school together, sir,' De Vries says.

He squints at De Vries. 'My daughter, Chantal?'

'Yes. I had two daughters there, Kate and Lulu. Their grandmother had attended the same school. She sponsored them.'

'I think I remember them. The name Lulu

24

certainly. She came here perhaps?'

'For a birthday party. Maybe eight or nine years ago. I delivered and collected them.'

'Are they well?'

'They are, sir.'

Adam's face falls. 'But that's not why you're here.'

De Vries leans forward. 'I'm afraid, sir,' he says gently, 'that Chantal was found dead this morning.'

Charles Adam closes his eyes, breathes in slowly and very deeply. He stays frozen for several seconds. 'I see.'

'I regret I have no details for you. We believe that she may have taken her own life, but we also have reports that at least one other person was present. I will be leading the investigation and will report to you as soon as I have any information.'

Adam nods slowly. 'Can I see her?'

'I'm afraid not, sir. There will be a post-mortem examination tomorrow morning. After that, I'll do whatever I can to have her released to you.'

Adam bows his head. In the distance, they hear children laughing and screaming. 'All my children, my grandchildren, everyone is here. I wanted Chantal. I hoped she'd come back. Christmas in Cape Town is a rare treat for us. Usually, the family are all over the world. This year, for the first time in many, they're all here . . . '

He produces a white handkerchief from the pocket of his blazer, dabs his eyes. 'I tell them this and I destroy their Christmas . . . There should be one last little bit of magic, don't you think, before they grow up?'

De Vries says nothing.

'You'll know,' Adam says, 'as a father. So many things you don't share, to spare them. But it costs you, every day . . . '

'I need to ask you just a couple of questions, sir,' De Vries says. 'May I do that?'

Adam nods, frozen in position. De Vries knows that the turbulence of shock and grief is deep within him, withheld until a certain moment arrives. He will be gone before that time; must be gone.

'When Warrant Officer Heyns visited you recently, you told her that you feared Chantal was mixing in the wrong circles. Is that right?'

Adam faces him. 'Teenagers are often rebellious. They grow out of it, mature. Chantal didn't. She was blinded by the brightness of the light. She called me when she arrived in New York in May 2009 — she never spoke to me like that, like herself, ever again. After that, she was drunk or high. One day she would be so happy she couldn't stop laughing, the next, she was terrified there was an intruder in her apartment. Whatever those people did to her, it led to this. We saw the pictures of her in the magazines, and sometimes we didn't even recognize her. When she came home, she wouldn't see us, speak to us, have anything to do with the family. For the last six years, my beautiful Chantal has been my tragedy.'

He runs a hand through his thick silver hair.

'I'm not answering your question, I know. What can I say? I decided to employ a man to keep an eye on her and report back to me. A month or so ago, he told me she was staying in one of the hostels on Long Street, mixing with the backpackers, drinking, probably sleeping around. Then, about ten days ago, I asked him to check up on her again. He couldn't find her. The thing about Chantal — whatever she said about us, she never went far, and she usually left a trail, almost as if she wanted me to know where she was. I asked Captain Maart — down at Rondebosch, a good man I know well — to keep an ear open, to pass the message on to the City police to keep a lookout.' Suddenly Charles Adam seems disoriented. He looks around the room, seeming to focus on nothing. 'She's an adult. What can you do?'

'The man you employed to keep an eye on her. I'll need his name.'

'Of course.' He stands up. 'His details are in my study.'

Charles Adam walks unsteadily across the room, lets himself out into the entrance hall. De Vries and Lee-Ann Heyns exchange a glance. De Vries looks up to the ceiling where two huge wooden-bladed fans turn slowly; they produce no breeze.

The door reopens, and Adam sits down heavily. He holds out a sheet of thick paper, two lines written in turquoise ink. 'That's his name, mobile telephone number, office address. Tell him I gave them to you. If he checks in with me, I'll ask him to pass on everything he has.' He

27

looks around his plush drawing room. 'What do I do now?'

'I'll contact you tomorrow, sir, let you know what the situation is. Then you can make plans.'

'My family are Catholic, Colonel. There will be many plans ... ' He subsides, his head bobbing gently on his chest. He stills it, looks up again. 'Even with the love of Christ, how will we bear this?'

★   ★   ★

'He had someone watching her?' Heyns says. 'He never told us that before.'

'I doubt he would have wanted you to know.'

'Why?'

'It's an admission of weakness, one way or another. That he can't control his own daughter, that he feels she needs to be watched.'

They drive along the tree-lined roads, past the paddocks and lush pockets of forest in Upper Constantia, heading for the road towards Kirstenbosch Botanical Gardens.

'Are you all right?' Heyns asks.

'I'm thinking about Chantal Adam,' De Vries says. 'Remembering her from the party I took Lulu and Kate to, trying to match her with what we saw in the motel room this morning. I can't picture her alive.'

'Even I remember the advertisements.'

'It was just an image, though, what the company wanted to show. A beautiful girl at the top of Table Mountain eating a piece of chocolate. That wasn't her. I want to remember her.'

'Whoever she was, it's just another murder.'

De Vries checks the road, then turns to her. 'It's never 'just another murder'. Not for me.'

'I didn't mean — '

'Once I'm on a case, I'm there for the victim. I represent her now. Everyone else has to cope as they can.'

'I only meant . . . I find it harder if I think of them alive.'

'That's what you're taught. Stay objective. Don't become involved. It's not how I work.'

'That's rough.'

'Maybe. But she was the same age as my elder daughter. I think Kate had a cover picture of her from *Vogue* or some other glossy magazine in her room.' De Vries's memories of his girls' childhood are slowly fading. 'She left the school and went away. My girls couldn't believe that she was in America, modelling.'

Heyns pulls a cigarette out of her pocket, lights it, holds it out of the window. 'You're not smoking?'

'Out.'

She draws deeply, then leans over, places the cigarette between his lips. He inhales, flicks ash out of his window, drags again, passes it back to her.

'When she came back, she was different. Kate and Lulu were at uni in Jo'burg when Chantal returned to Cape Town. After the first rush of coverage, everyone seemed to forget about her. I heard that she was living with friends, seen on the street. I didn't really make the connection to the girl we knew . . . '

Ahead, at the top gate to Kirstenbosch, the massive southern slopes of Table Mountain are revealed, lushly forested, bathed in late-afternoon sunlight, as far as Devil's Peak.

'That view always gets me.' Heyns punches her chest with her left fist. 'Right here.'

De Vries smiles. He rarely notices views. His focus is on minutiae, not breadth. 'Christmas evening,' he muses. 'Any plans?'

'None.'

'You want a glass of wine?'

'All right. Where?'

'I live in Rosebank,' De Vries says.

★　★　★

Cape Town, Saturday, 26 December 2015
He wakes at six a.m., rolls out of bed, hears an ankle crack as he pads to the bathroom. He showers, shaves, re-enters his bedroom. Without moving, without opening her eyes, she says, 'Good morning.' He grunts. 'Not a morning person?'

'In so many ways.'

She sits up. 'Was I supposed to go?'

'No. Of course not.' He turns to face her as he dresses, manages not to look her in the eye. 'Too much wine, too little sleep.'

She is kneeling in front of him now, still naked, frowning. 'No regrets?'

He looks down at her. Sleep still hangs over her, yet she remains desirable. 'Never. You?'

'No.'

He stands in front of the full-length mirror in

30

the corner of the room to knot his tie. He looks ahead at her, inverted in the mirror. 'But I'm curious. Last night — why did you stay?'

'It was Christmas night.'

'A present?'

'Why do you think?'

'Twenty years ago, I might have had some idea.'

She smiles at him. 'Your rank.'

He laughs, but he studies her eyes in the glass. Her smile is a mask. He turns back to her. 'There had to be a reason.'

★ ★ ★

'I don't need to tell you,' Brigadier Henrik du Toit tells him, 'that the papers and celebrity magazines will soon latch on to this.'

'Is that why you're here, sir?'

Du Toit is the director of the Special Crimes Unit, a man who, like De Vries, has maintained his position in the South African Police Service despite all the changes of the past twenty years: the culls of white officers; the positive discrimination and accelerated promotion of black colleagues. He has spent that time seeking to banish all that was wrong with the apartheid-era police force, while maintaining its long-honed skills. He had brought De Vries with him, installed him as senior officer, defended him, sought to form and retain his unit of four elite teams of investigators. He gazes across his desk at the colonel. 'Charles Adam is a Cape Town face, but Chantal Adam, she was front-page news once.'

'I don't give a shit about her image. It's her as a person that interests me. Not him, not the family.'

'And that's why I came in, Vaughn. So you can get on with what you do. I'll keep everything ordered for the press and the prying eyes upstairs.'

'Drag you away from the festivities?'

'A day with my extended family is almost always ample.' He sits up. 'If it's suicide, wrap it up quickly. Get her body back to her family.'

'I knew her.'

Du Toit frowns. 'What?'

'Lulu and Kate did. I was just the chauffeur. She was at school with them. I went to the Adam house for some birthday party. Adam remembered me.'

'Top man. Good with faces.'

'Whenever a girl is killed I always think about my daughters. Do you do that?'

'Used to,' Du Toit says. 'Learned to disassociate myself. Only way I could cope. You should try it.'

De Vries knows that it is beyond him, that it is what makes him effective . . . He becomes aware of Du Toit's breathing. He forces himself to focus. 'We'll know more after the PM. Harry Kleinman says he'll reach her about ten a.m.' He glances at his watch. 'Maybe a couple of hours.'

'Which of your team do you have?'

'Until we know what's happening, I don't need them. Warrant February made a request for several days a few months back . . . '

'I imagine he deserves it.'

Warrant Officer Don February is De Vries's investigating assistant, one of the first university-educated black officers in the SAPS and, in De Vries's opinion, one of the best. He continues, 'Sergeants Thwala and Frazer are due back tomorrow. Adam employed a private investigator of some sort to keep an eye on his daughter. I need to talk with him, and we may get something from Forensics on the man who was with her at the motel. I want to hear the call she made yesterday morning. We don't have anything yet.'

'Except that she said she was a prisoner?'

'I haven't heard that. But if that's what she said, a simple suicide seems unlikely.'

Du Toit nods. 'Keep it tight, Vaughn. Keep me briefed.'

De Vries gets up.

'By the way,' Du Toit says, 'the woman in the squad room. Who is she?'

'Warrant Officer Heyns. She was the liaison with Charles Adam from Constantia. I'm letting her stay on so she can help with the family.'

Du Toit looks up at him. 'You know we're being watched from above.' He points upwards. 'It's a constant battle just to keep the department in business. We've had a decent year, proved our worth. There's the full SAPS review in March. Play it down the middle, report everything to me, and try, for God's sake, to be diplomatic. Don't hand them ammunition.'

★   ★   ★

33

Dr Harry Kleinman is alone in the mortuary. He has worked there since the elite units moved to the new building over a decade ago. His skin has taken on the pallor of the magnolia walls; under greying brows, his eyes are sad and dark. He is as close a friend as De Vries will admit to having among colleagues: a man who sees what he sees and tries to make sense of it.

Between the occasional zaps of the electric fly-killers, De Vries can hear the pathologist's pen scribbling on a clipboard. He passes two covered bodies atop bare metal tables, stops beside the pale, emaciated form of Chantal Adam.

'Look at us,' Kleinman says, smiling. 'An atheist and a Jew. It must be Christmas.'

'I hadn't noticed.'

Kleinman fiddles with his micro-recorder, begins preparing for the examination.

'Somehow, that doesn't surprise me . . . ' He points to an area around the girl's left eye. 'I spotted this immediately. This is an old bruise. Perhaps six to eight days ago. It presents like a punch to the face, but I can't be certain . . . ' He picks up a magnifying glass, examines her more intently. 'Yes . . . and there is a cut which has only just broken the skin.' He angles his fist towards her face. 'Consistent with a ring on, probably, the middle finger.'

De Vries opens his mouth, checks himself, speaks slowly. 'Considering her physical shape and size, would she bruise more easily than a more . . . normal physique?'

Kleinman looks up at him. 'That's an

34

intelligent question. She weighs about eighty-eight pounds, a little under six and half stone. Without medical records I can't be certain, but there is no trace of long-term drug addiction so I suspect she was suffering from bulimia nervosa or anorexia nervosa. More probably the latter, because of her previous profession, and because bulimics are not necessarily underweight.'

'And the injuries?'

'More pronounced generally, but primarily because she would be less able to defend herself, and there is less flesh to protect her.'

'Any other injuries?'

Kleinman points to the front of her shoulders, two faint but discernible dark patches. 'Pressure bruising, again several days old. If you look closely, I think we can be clear that she was held from behind with some degree of force.'

'Could these injuries be accidental?'

'I doubt it.'

'More recently?'

'Yes . . . ' He moves his scrutiny down the body, examining it with his hands. 'There are bruises and discolouring likely caused by slapping or punching, which would have been a matter of minutes before death. Evidence of some kind of restraint on her left wrist.'

'What about the fatal wounds?'

'I know what you want to know,' Kleinman says, picking up one of Chantal Adam's very thin arms, twisting it slightly to view the broad slash across her wrist. 'I can tell you that the angle of the cutting wound is not consistent with the victim taking a blade or shard of glass and cutting herself, that is to say, in the normal manner, using her opposite hand.'

'It's not?'

'No. However, neither is it consistent with an attack.' He examines her palms, up each arm, then down her torso. 'There are no indicators of self-defence, and the cuts themselves suggest she was not struggling.'

'So, what does that mean?'

'It means we don't know what happened. Yet.'

'There was a man with her.'

'So I understand. There's nothing on her to suggest his presence.'

'Nothing sexual?'

'I checked immediately. Not recently.'

'But she was sexually active?'

'Certainly.'

'Was it consensual?'

Kleinman looks up. 'We can't be certain about these things but I don't have any particular concerns there. If you're asking whether she has been raped then, again, I would say no.'

'No?'

Kleinman sighs. 'Not recently.'

As Kleinman begins the vertical cut down her chest, De Vries looks past Chantal Adam's body to a point on the far wall, listens to Kleinman but hears the music from the television commercial, almost feeling the wind at the summit of Table Mountain. He becomes aware of organs being removed and placed in containers. He doesn't look at them, yet his mind relays a vivid picture, ingrained in him from his first experience of a post-mortem.

'Vaughn?'

He follows Kleinman's stare down to a wide metal tray.

'Her stomach is distended, and full.'

Kleinman cuts into it, recoils as scores of tiny plastic packages covered within bloody bile spew into the tray.

De Vries shivers from an initial identification; at first, they seem like engorged white slugs. His brain reassures him that they are not moving, that their skin is plastic or rubber.

'I think,' Kleinman begins, picking up one of the lozenge-shaped items, 'we may have discovered what she was doing at that motel.'

De Vries's mind races. 'Where was she going?'

'In some countries the contents of these things demand a premium.'

'But why would she do this? The Adam family are worth millions.'

'The reasons why women end up carrying drugs is rarely simply economic.'

'Why do you say that?'

Kleinman shrugs. 'I've seen documentaries. There's usually coercion, often brutal. And the result is more akin to people-trafficking than simple drug-muling . . . '

'She said she was a prisoner,' De Vries muses. 'Then she kills herself. Why call us first?'

'That's what you have to find out.'

Kleinman examines her mouth, swabs her throat, holding up the bud in front of squinting eyes. He sniffs the tip. 'As I thought. This is probably a lubricant to aid the swallowing of the packages.'

'You'll get everything to Ulton's lab?'

'Of course. As soon as I've completed the examination.' He looks back at De Vries. 'Where is Don February?'

'Few days' leave. Parents-in-law. All the usual family shit.'

'Who's your bagman, then?'

'Working with a warrant officer from Rondebosch. She's been dealing with the family.'

'That okay?'

De Vries glances around the mortuary. 'I made a mistake, Harry. Last night, Christmas night, you know? We'd been working all day. I let something get out of hand.'

'Your dick?'

De Vries nods.

'She pretty?'

'Prettier than she should be, for me.'

'You're both adults.'

'Nah,' De Vries says. 'There's going to be come-back, I can feel it. She wants in on the case, some positive discrimination, you know what I mean? I've been honey-trapped, man.'

'Seems to happen to you a lot recently . . . '

'I'm a single man again. I have no self-control.'

Kleinman shakes his head. 'If you have her now, make the best of it. Hope it sorts itself out. Just hope she's good at what she does.'

'I can attest to that.'

⋆　⋆　⋆

Lee-Ann Heyns says, 'I've completed the docket to date, followed up Charles Adam's investigator,

Dale Rix. I arranged for him to come in at noon. What's the verdict?'

'Don't do that.'

Heyns frowns. 'What?'

'Don't ever warn a witness we want to question him.'

'A witness?'

'You don't know who he is yet.'

'But Charles Adam — '

'Charles Adam's word is nothing. Something kept Chantal Adam away from that house. For all you know, it was him.'

'I don't believe that.'

'What you believe is irrelevant, Warrant Officer.'

She swallows. 'All right.'

'We know where Dale Rix is. We pay him a visit when he isn't expecting us, isn't prepared for us. That's how I work.'

'I'm sorry.'

De Vries looks at his watch. 'Where's Rix based?'

'Woodstock.'

'We'll get to him before he leaves for us.' He turns.

'What was the news from the post-mortem?' Heyns asks.

'Tell you in the car.'

★   ★   ★

Dale Rix works from a tiny office in the cobbled courtyard at the back of a recently gentrified workers' cottage. Across the road, but still

39

looming over the residential side-street, there is one of the original factory buildings from the time Woodstock was a centre of garment-manufacturing, a coloured suburb under apartheid, working class to its core. Now, De Vries reflects as he crosses the yard, Main Road is full of art galleries, antiques shops and artisanal bakeries.

Rix is in his late forties, apparently fit, greying hair cropped, dressed in jeans and a polo shirt. When he rises, De Vries sees him grimace, but he stands straight and proffers his hand. 'I was preparing to come to you.'

'We were passing.'

Rix smiles momentarily. 'I doubt that.' He gestures for them to sit down at his cluttered desk.

De Vries glances around the small room — bookcases crammed with cheap paperbacks, some wooden masks, curled photographs of, perhaps, a cricket team, a handful of small gold plastic trophies. 'How long have you been at these premises, Mr Rix?'

Rix's face falls. 'Sorry. It's a bit of a mess.'

'Live above the shop?'

Rix nods.

'When did you start working for Charles Adam?'

'About four months ago.'

'What was your brief?'

'To locate Chantal Adam. Keep an eye on her, keep her out of trouble, if I could.'

'You did find her, then, two or three weeks back, you lost her. Is that right?'

'She disappeared,' Rix says sheepishly. 'She wasn't in any of her usual haunts. I asked around casually, but no one knew where she was.'

'Where was she before that?'

'She was staying in Sea Point, then I thought Green Point. She's been there before, on the floor with some of her friends . . . I say friends. I don't think she had many.'

'Where else did she stay?'

'While I was keeping tabs on her, Sea Point, Three Anchor Bay, around here in Woodstock, Salt River.'

De Vries gestures at the desk. 'The addresses are in the files you're going to give me?'

'*Ja.*'

'What do you know about Chantal Adam that we need to know?'

'You're familiar with her back story?'

'You tell us.'

'The daughter of Willem Adam, the politician. Adopted by her uncle after his brother's death. She was called the 'Mountain Girl' — from the advertisement shot on Table Mountain. She was seventeen when that was made. Modelled in South Africa for a year, got taken to New York — parties, drugs, boys, tabloids, more drugs. Some kind of breakdown, apparently. Came back here, wouldn't speak to her family. If she'd had any money, it was gone. Living — where I told you — with acquaintances and strangers, still drinking, still using. Coke mainly. If she had any real friends, they weren't around any more. I thought she was sad, pathetic. I feared for her.'

'That it?'

'Yes.'

'We knew that,' De Vries says blankly.

'The reports I prepared for her father are there.' He points to the bundle of papers he has pushed across the table towards them. 'What did I know? Not much, I suppose. Not enough to predict that she would kill herself.'

'Did you ever see her return to the family home in Constantia?'

'No. Mr Adam told me she wouldn't meet, wouldn't even talk on the phone. He told me he'd offered her a property wherever she wanted it, but she rejected him.'

'How did she support herself?'

'I don't know. I suspected she had some money as she never looked dirty, but if it wasn't from her father, then I don't know the source. People told me she used to have an old Volkswagen Beetle, but I never saw her in it since the beginning of August.'

'Did she have anyone, or any group, she'd return to?'

Rix shrugs. 'Not that I know about. She was rarely in the same place twice . . . ' He grimaces again. 'Actually, there was a woman in Sea Point she stayed with a few times. The address is in the folder.'

De Vries looks around the office. 'What is your usual type of work?'

'I'm an investigator. Nothing very exciting. Missing persons, grounds for divorce, that type of thing.'

'And before that?'

Rix frowns. 'Army for ten years. SAPS for a couple. My busted leg got worse. They put me on a desk. Couldn't take that. Started on the booze, dossed around, decided to pull myself together.'

De Vries picks up the file from the desk, tucks it under his arm, stands and offers his hand. Rix struggles out of his chair, shakes.

'How did you get the job?'

'What?'

De Vries says, 'How did you get the job, working for Charles Adam?'

Rix colours, averts his eyes. 'I was recommended.'

'By who?'

'A friend . . . A former colleague.'

'Who was that?'

'That's commercially sensitive information.'

'Even if I knew what that meant, I still want the name.'

'Why?'

'Because you're a small-time, low-rent amateur running his business out of his scruffy lounge, and Charles Adam can afford whoever he wants.'

Rix snorts. 'Thanks for not mentioning the drink.'

'I don't throw stones in glasshouses.'

'Wally Maart.'

Heyns says, 'Captain Maart?'

'We were together when I was in the SAPS. He tried to help me. He knows I'm dry and trying to get back on my feet. He said he'd recommend me.'

'That was nice of him,' De Vries says.

'There are some decent people around, Colonel. After what I went through, I'm trying to be one of them.'

'And this is your vocation?'

'Read my report and tell me I'm not professional. You'll find everything there. I haven't missed anything.'

De Vries turns away, mutters, 'I think you have.'

Rix is limping around his desk, following them towards the front door. 'I missed something?'

'Yes,' De Vries says.

★ ★ ★

'Let's be clear on this,' Brigadier du Toit announces. 'Charles Adam called Captain Maart at Rondebosch. He got through to General Thulani, so we're on his radar. Adam is a man who undoubtedly mixes with people who will listen to his opinion of us, and he needs to be kept informed.'

De Vries sighs. Deputy Assistant Provincial Commander Thulani oversees their building from an icy office on the top floor. From the same background and rank as Du Toit, since 1994 he has risen fast to the top, clearing away all remnants of the former police force, to which, in their early careers, Du Toit and De Vries belonged. The Special Crimes Unit is under constant threat.

'I told him yesterday that I would keep him informed.'

'Regardless, the man has lost his daughter. He wants information.'

'Niece.'

'Niece, daughter, whatever. He calls her his daughter, so that's what she is.'

He peers at the crime-scene supervisor, Steve Ulton, at Lee-Ann Heyns, then returns to De Vries, who says, 'Dr Ulton has produced a preliminary report.'

When no one speaks, Ulton says, 'Following Dr Kleinman's analysis of the wounds sustained by Chantal Adam, my team have tried to ascertain how her wrists were cut, since those wounds are the cause of death. We now believe that the victim — although this is far from certain or proven — used the broken glass still in the window to cut her wrists. Dr Kleinman concurs that the wound patterns would be consistent with that explanation. I have technicians back at the scene studying the window now. If necessary, we will retrieve it and bring it here for further analysis.'

Du Toit sighs. Every action impacts on his budget.

'Since Dr Kleinman reports that there were no signs of recent ante-mortem bruising on the back of her hands or wrists,' Ulton continues, 'it seems likely that these wounds were self-inflicted, before the victim fell to the floor, bleeding profusely.' He studies his notes. 'This is only a working theory. We may or may not be able to prove that this was the action taken.'

'What can you prove?'

'We have Chantal Adam's partial prints on

pieces of cell phone recovered from the scene. It was an old Nokia model, first issued in 2007. It's pay-as-you-go, unregistered.'

'In the tape of her call to 112,' De Vries says, 'she's whispering, sounds agitated and frightened, but she's also surprisingly concise and clear. She describes herself as a prisoner in the DF Malan Motel, in room twenty-two. We know from the post-mortem that she had injuries dating back several days, others maybe older, suggesting restraint. Based on the fact that she disappeared, certainly from the rather amateur Mr Rix's view, for almost a fortnight, we're assuming that she was held, then taken to the motel, possibly willingly, but more likely under duress, to swallow the drugs, and take a flight . . . ' He looks at Lee-Ann Heyns. 'Which, thanks to Warrant Officer Heyns, we now know was . . . '

'Pandan Air began a weekly service to Bangkok from Cape Town International in July. Chantal Adam was a no-show for the flight, which left at eleven a.m. on Christmas morning.'

'Thailand?' Du Toit says. 'Any other no-shows?'

'I asked, sir,' Heyns says. 'One elderly married couple in business class. There's no reason why whoever would have chaperoned her onto the flight would automatically take it too. We can't identify the man with Chantal Adam that way.'

Du Toit holds up his hand. 'We can talk about an investigation in due course.' To De Vries, he says, 'Is there any reason why we can't release Chantal Adam's body to her parents?'

De Vries looks at Steve Ulton. 'If Dr Kleinman has completed his report and Steve here doesn't need anything further then her body can be released.'

Du Toit nods. 'Good. That's what I wanted to know.' He smiles perfunctorily at Ulton and Heyns. 'It's a lesson. If we can say yes to members of the public, particularly in times of distress, then our reputation is enhanced.' He strides out of the office, across the squad room, into the long corridor that leads to the lifts.

De Vries turns to Ulton. 'If that was all he wanted, we could have saved our breath.'

'Maybe Chantal Adam wouldn't want to be given to Charles Adam.'

De Vries and Heyns stare at him.

'What did you find in Chantal Adam's blood?' De Vries asks.

'Residual levels of cocaine, cannabis. Some kind of Valium-like anti-anxiety prescription drug, with a high drowsiness level. We'll identify it precisely in due course.'

'So she was drugged, either self-medicated or otherwise?'

'She'd have been groggy. Probably like a hangover.'

'That's fine, Steve. Keep it to language I understand.'

Ulton smiles.

'Did you find anything that might identify the man with her?'

'We found lots of everything, Vaughn, but we don't have anything we can work on regarding a second person in the room that morning. There's

47

no SIM card from the cell phone. Either we haven't found it yet, or the other party took it with him. We'll pursue that if required. The place was filthy — there are prints everywhere. If instructed, we'll continue looking.'

'Keep looking.'

'If Chantal Adam's death is ruled suicide, aren't we out of the picture?'

'She wasn't there through choice. Someone threatened her, probably imprisoned her. That's coercion, perhaps kidnap.' He looks at Heyns and Ulton. 'Then she took her own life.'

They say nothing.

'Nobody's asking any questions?'

Neither speaks.

'She's accompanied by an unknown man — who subsequently disappears — and swallows a hundred and twenty grams of pure coke in condoms. She's booked on a flight to Bangkok, then slashes her wrists, and before doing that, she gets us to find her.'

'She decides she can't go through with it?' Heyns suggests.

'But she called us. She made contact. If she waits, we arrive and find her and then she doesn't have to do anything. She just tells us the story.'

'But we don't know . . . '

'We don't know because we need to find who was in that room with her.' He pauses. 'How much for a day room at that motel?'

Heyns shrugs. 'Not much.'

'But how much?'

'I don't know. I didn't see a sign, a tariff.'

'There wasn't one.'

'So, how much?'

'Two hundred and fifty rand.' He looks up at her. 'Ask me how I know that.'

Heyns folds her arms. 'Okay.'

'I asked.'

★   ★   ★

They travel to Cape Town International Airport in separate cars. In her Rondebosch patrol car, Heyns draws up next to De Vries a few seconds after he has turned off his engine. The car park at the DF Malan Motel contains half a dozen cars, none in the first flush of youth.

De Vries trots towards the main entrance, pushes open the doors to the tepid foyer, approaches the reception desk, scanning his surroundings. He walks behind it, into the back office.

Piet Grobbelaar jumps. He looks tired and frustrated. 'Now what?'

'More questions.' He gestures for Heyns to stand by the door. 'The man with Chantal Adam yesterday morning. What is his name?'

'I told you, I don't know.'

'You seen him before?'

'No.'

'I think you have,' De Vries says, 'probably with other women. In fact, I'd bet on it.' He steps minutely closer to him. 'I want to know what you know about this individual, or I'll close down your business and tie you up in so much bureaucracy, you'll be begging just to go bankrupt.'

Grobbelaar averts his bloodshot eyes from De Vries, who senses the man's hot, stale breath quicken.

'You have one chance, or you're coming with me to the station, now. Not in five minutes — immediately.'

Grobbelaar mutters, 'He never told me his name. I heard him answer his phone and say, 'Leon.' I don't know if that was him but, after, that's how I thought of him. I don't know what he's doing with the girls, but they're all adults, never kids.'

'All of them?'

'Seven or eight maybe . . . '

'Different girls?'

'Ja.'

'White? Coloured? Black?'

'White.'

'All of them?'

'Ja.'

'How often?'

Grobbelaar glances towards his empty foyer, then back to De Vries. 'I tell you things, you don't let anyone know, *ja*? I don't know who he is, but I don't like him. Whatever he's doing with the girls he takes up there, when they come down again, they look frightened and sick.'

'How often?'

'Every two weeks.'

'Same day?'

'Maybe . . . Friday. I don't know.'

'Yesterday morning, did he appear again after seven a.m.?'

'Maybe. I was in here. I thought maybe someone ran by, but I'm not certain.'

De Vries shakes his head.

'You've seen this guy seven or eight times. Give this officer a proper description.'

He beckons Heyns into the room, then goes out into the lobby towards the stairs. He climbs the first flight, turns right and walks the long dark corridor to the fire doors at the far end. He checks the fire-escape door. It is locked. He retraces his steps, hears moaning from beyond one of the flimsy bedroom doors, grimaces. He reaches the stairwell, climbs again and stands outside room twenty-two. There is still crime-scene tape across the door. De Vries looks around, wonders why whoever was with Chantal Adam would pick this room.

When he returns to the office, he says, 'He tell you which room he wanted?'

'No . . . Just on the top floor. Not many people go up there. They prefer ground or first. Always ground, if they're in a chair.'

De Vries looks curiously at Grobbelaar. 'A chair?'

'Guys in wheelchairs.'

De Vries sighs. 'So when 'Leon' arrives, he hands you the money, you give him a second-floor room and he takes a girl there?'

'Yes.'

'What car does he drive?' Grobbelaar shrugs. 'He's a regular guest. You must have seen one.'

The man squirms. 'He'll know it was me.'

'I know it's you. You know, and I want what you know. Stop whining and talk.'

'Maybe a Toyota. Red . . . maroon, with a black vinyl top.'

'You could have told me this yesterday. Instead, you wasted my time.' De Vries turns to Heyns. 'We get a proper description?'

Heyns nods.

'I'm going to send an officer to visit you, Mr Grobbelaar, in the next couple of weeks. If he finds your fire doors locked, he'll close you down on the spot. Understand?'

'If I leave them open, they just smuggle people in. I can't do that. Security.'

'That's your problem. Put alarms on them. Whatever. You keep them like that, this place is a death trap. 'Leon' turns up again, you get his car registration, you call us immediately. If I find you haven't, I'll charge you with being an accessory. And you wouldn't like the hotel I can send you to.'

★　★　★

As they walk to their cars, Heyns says, 'What made you think the manager had seen the guy before?'

'People like him always know more than they say. You should know that. There's no tariff displayed, no room rates anywhere on show. When I asked him before what they'd said when they checked in, he said nothing. They just handed over the cash and took the key. The man knew because he had been before. He had asked, and had found out.'

'You think Grobbelaar's involved?'

52

'No. He makes a point of not seeing anything, thinks discretion and integrity are the same thing.'

As they reach their cars, he says, 'What was the description?'

'I'll add it to the docket tomorrow morning.'

He walks around the boot of her car. 'You have to go back to duty in Rondebosch, Lee-Ann. The Chantal Adam case is closed. I have my own team who'll be coming in tomorrow. If we continue the investigation into the smuggling, into whoever was in the room with her, they'll take over.'

Heyns makes no move to pass him her notes. 'Captain Maart is happy for me to liaise with you for as long as you need me. One call to him tomorrow from you, he has to agree.'

De Vries studies her. Everyone he interacts with seems desperate: for their job, their freedom, their security. 'That's not the way these things work.'

'But it could be, couldn't it?'

'Not really.'

'But *you* could make it happen?'

De Vries feels his jaw tighten, forces himself to unlock his teeth. 'Let's get in the car a moment.'

Heyns unlocks the doors; De Vries sits in the passenger seat in the stifling heat. Even with the door open, the air doesn't move. She switches on the engine, then the air-conditioning. They close the doors and, slowly, the cabin begins to cool.

'I enjoyed yesterday,' De Vries says, staring ahead. 'Probably a bit impulsive. We'd both had a bit to drink. I don't want it to be a mistake.'

Heyns snorts. 'That has nothing to do with my request. Jesus, haven't you heard what I've been saying? Everywhere I go, I can't get a break. I'm better than these black guys. You know I am. I work twice as hard as those fat coloured fucks. I'm fit. I have some of the highest marks on the range. I sailed through the Lieutenants' Panel. Fuck it, I actually turn up for work every day. I do my job. If I work for you on this, it gives me some leverage.'

'I can't authorize a temporary transfer and, even if I could, it wouldn't work. You need to be trained, and there's no money to pay us properly, let alone take on more officers. In court, the defence could use the fact that you're not a regular member of my team to discredit evidence.'

'Vaughn . . . Sir. I thought you understood what it's like. If you don't help me, what chance do I have?'

'Same as the rest of us. It's a battle.' He meets her eyes. 'You handled the scene well yesterday. Your research is efficient. I like the way you work, but all I can do is tell you that if we have a vacancy, the budget to train some new people, I'll call for you.'

Heyns shakes her head, pouts. 'No.'

'What?'

'I'm not going back. There's fucking nothing but property crime, lost handbag dogs. Guys without a clue moving past me.'

'I don't think you have a choice.'

Heyns dips her head, grits her teeth. 'There's more than one way to recall last night.'

De Vries knows what is happening. He stays very calm. 'I hoped that you understood exactly what it was.'

'I understand . . . The elite units have their own internal investigation department. Would they approve of your use of rank as a means of securing sexual favours from a married woman?'

De Vries wonders what he had read in her, from the moment the ecstasy of orgasm subsided, that had told him they would reach this point. 'You have one chance to apologize for that comment, or it's over for you, Warrant.'

Heyns is staring at him, trying to read him. 'Please?'

'It's not happening. It's not in my gift and, even if it was — '

'I hear that Colonel Wertner is looking for anything to discredit you and your department.'

Anger rises in him. De Vries realizes he is trapped. Colonel David Wertner heads Internal Investigation. With a major review of the elite departments due in March, he knows he cannot risk Wertner and their mutual boss General Thulani — both of whom have been trying to disband Special Crimes, which they leeringly describe as the White Crime Unit — launching another inquiry into his behaviour.

'You're married?'

'Yep. To a cop.'

'You told me you were single and alone on Christmas night.'

'I was alone. He was on duty.'

De Vries turns away.

'Don't act disgusted,' Heyns says. 'People

55

know your reputation. So, you screwed a married woman. A lower-ranked officer. So what? But maybe not everyone sees it that way.'

De Vries stares out of the windscreen at the yellowing, sunbaked palms, the flaking grey of the motel walls. He feels the heat of the late afternoon pulsing on the other side of the windows. 'When you heard the call go out yesterday morning, you jumped on it, didn't you? Couldn't wait to be out of your station. You found your missing girl, then called the Special Crimes Unit and got me. Quite the Christmas present.'

'No.'

'I think so.'

'Forget what I said,' Heyns says, her tone suddenly lighter. 'You see what this job does to me? I'm committed. I'll give whatever it takes to succeed in my job. I just need a fucking chance.' She stares at De Vries. 'A few days, then I have something my captain can use to move me upwards.'

'You think I can trust you now?'

'This is about my career, my life. You know I'm good. You said so yourself.'

She waits in silence. 'I could be useful to you.'

'But not as useful as you think I could be to you.'

'Maybe that's the deal, Colonel.'

De Vries speaks quietly, calmly. 'When my warrant officer returns to duty, you go back to Rondebosch. No arguments, no threats. You ever threaten me again, you won't have a career. You understand?'

'Yes. Thank you, sir.'

De Vries climbs out, slams the door. Before he has reached his own car, Heyns starts to reverse out of the space. He waits for her to turn and accelerate onto the street. He listens until he can no longer hear her car.

★　★　★

It is the feeling of impotence that destroys his self-confidence. Events conspire to disempower him. Normally he would have sent her back to Rondebosch with a private warning to her CO. But, right now, his warrant officer, Don February, is on leave; he knows the slightest claim regarding his propriety would be seized on by his enemies within the SAPS. He has promised Du Toit not to provide them with ammunition and he has done exactly that, through his arrogance, through his weakness.

He resents Heyns, feels as if he has been assaulted. Yet, counter-intuitively, part of his brain appreciates that her actions are driven by overwhelming frustration with her career, a stifling stasis from which she, like so many white officers, feels unable to escape. What hope for the SAPS without good officers?

Each time he allows his sympathy for her to grow, it is checked by the belief that she would have fulfilled her threat.

He does not listen to the radio, watch television. He sits in silence, cannot understand why anyone would want music in the background. As a child, when he was sick and home

57

from school, he would hear the radio in another room, playing old songs, military tunes, tinny and distant. That sound repulses him now.

He sits in his armchair at the dining table where, during twenty years of marriage, he had sat as the head of his family. He thinks, and drinks. He likes the sound of the wine flowing from bottle to glass, likes the sensation of the liquid, discernibly thicker than water, entering his throat and trickling to his stomach. He appreciates being alone, drinking alone. To drink with others and be forced to talk is not sharing or sociable; it merely dilutes the pleasure.

Before sleep overtakes him in his chair, he trudges upstairs and lies, still clothed, on his bed. He finds himself almost asleep, his thoughts utterly dominated by a sense of helplessness and self-disgust so intense it makes him feel physically sick. The sheets are still soiled from the night before.

★ ★ ★

Cape Town, Sunday, 27 December 2015
At 9.25 a.m., De Vries parks next to an unmarked car he recognizes as belonging to one of his regular team, Sergeant Sally Frazer. He can see the imposing form of Sergeant Ben Thwala bent almost double beside her.

Out of the back door, Lee-Ann Heyns appears, walks over to him, opens his passenger door. 'Dr Ulton's team matched prints from the banknotes and inside the room to a man called Leon Barker.' She sits next to him, avoids eye

58

contact. 'He was in the system. Previously arrested for auto theft and shop lifting. Mug-shot pretty much matches the description Grobbelaar gave us.' She points her chin up the road towards an intersection between two narrow suburban streets. 'Look at the car.'

De Vries sees a maroon Toyota with a faded black vinyl roof. Although they are only a few hundred metres from Voortrekker Road, a major route through the townships to the industrial areas of Goodwood and Parow on to Bellville, the residential streets are quiet, almost deserted. The properties here are dilapidated single-storey houses on tiny plots, lacking any vegetation; just another layer in the strata of deprivation that begin at the edges of the City Bowl and end in the squatter camps of corrugated-iron shacks and cardboard boxes that crowd out the Cape Flats.

'How long have you been here?'

'Twenty minutes.'

'Any sign of movement from his address?'

'Nothing. Curtains are drawn. He's probably asleep.'

De Vries glances at her. His resentment has cooled. She is alert and efficient. He wonders how she marshalled Frazer and Thwala when she was unknown to them.

'Round the back?'

'High wall backing onto the next property. Only one exit — through the front.'

'Side windows?'

'*Ja*, but barred. If he can open them, he still can't escape.'

De Vries nods; his head throbs. 'All right.' He presses speed-dial on his cell phone, speaks to Frazer in the other car. They move off towards the property slowly. De Vries, Heyns and Thwala approach the house; Frazer blocks the road with her car, stands by it, weapon drawn.

De Vries knocks, calls Barker's name. There is no reply, no movement from inside. He calls again, then turns to Thwala, who launches a kick at the door with his heavy boot. The wooden front door bursts open on the first hit, hangs by a single hinge. Within, the iron-barred safety door is unlocked, tucked in against the inside wall.

The entrance leads straight into a kitchenette and living area. There is an acrid, chemical smell of burning hair, nails, flesh. He gestures to Heyns and Thwala to pass him. He walks around the stained sofa, sees a man's body sprawled on the floor, blood on the thin nylon carpet. He stops, waits for the others to report. Thwala moves through the kitchenette, towards the darkened bedroom, ducks inside the door, indicates all clear. Heyns follows him. They check the second bedroom and the bathroom at the back. De Vries squats next to the body, looks up when they join him. 'It's Barker.'

Heyns looks at the corpse. 'Shit.'

Leon Barker lies face up, topless, his neck angled impossibly at a deep wound; bubbling dark blood, treacle-thick, still glistens. The attack has almost severed his head.

'There's nylon ties in the second bedroom,' Heyns says. 'Looks like the bed's been slept in, or on. He could've held a girl there.'

60

'No personal belongings?'

'Not that we could see.'

De Vries points at Barker's chest. Where the flesh is not covered with blood, they can see small, circular burn marks. On the inside of his arms, from shoulder to wrist, there are fine cuts, bisecting faded tattoos, as if the tip of a knife has been dragged down their length, splitting the skin.

'Torture?'

He looks up at Heyns, who has not shrunk away from the appalling scene.

'*Ja*. Probably whoever lost their courier and a few hundred grand's worth of coke in that motel room. I think Mr Barker paid the price.'

He stands up. 'Back out of here. Seal it. We need Forensics. I want to know if he brought girls here, if there's any trace of them, and whatever we can find out about whoever did this.'

★   ★   ★

By the cars, in light that is blindingly bright, Ben Thwala contemplates the houses opposite them. 'She says she wants two hundred rand and to talk to the man in charge.'

De Vries laughs, coughs, drops his *stompie* in the gutter, looks over the road to the house on the corner. Behind metal bars at the front door, he can see an elderly coloured woman wearing a headscarf. She is staring in his direction. She starts to jab her finger at him.

'She says she saw them last night.'

61

De Vries says, 'All right. Just for the novelty of a willing witness . . . ' He crosses the street, walks up the six-metre path to her door. The weeds between the concrete slabs look more vibrant than the grass around the bungalow. At the security gate, she says, 'Two hundred rand to feed my granddaughter. I will tell you everything.'

De Vries smiles. 'One hundred rand, when I hear what you have to say.'

She seems to ponder, then unlocks the gate and gestures him in. She looks past him to Ben Thwala. 'Only you. The women you can't trust and he looks like he would eat me.'

He walks into a small but neat living area. The tiny kitchen is clean and ordered, a beaded net covering three apples in a dish in the middle of a watermarked dining table.

She sits on the velveteen sofa that faces a small television set. 'Who are you, then?'

'My name is Colonel de Vries. Vaughn de Vries.'

'Sit down there.' She points at a dining chair next to the sofa.

'What is your name?'

'Why do you need my name? It is better not to.' She leans forward. 'You have the cash?'

De Vries retrieves his wallet from his jacket pocket, finds a blue hundred-rand note, shows it to her and places it in his top pocket, like a handkerchief.

She smiles at him, as if this is really a game, but her eye does not leave his pocket. 'There are three of us. Me, my daughter and my granddaughter. Around here, you have to be very careful.'

De Vries doesn't envy them life in this neighbourhood. At night, even to venture into their front yard would be dangerous.

'So, I'll tell you. My granddaughter is seven. She sleeps with me. She has nightmares and we get up and check the house in the night, maybe have a sip of milk. Last night, I don't know when, I saw them outside that man's house . . . '

'Leon Barker?'

She shrugs. Bony shoulders click, crack. 'Maybe his name is Leon, yes. Three of them come. The woman in her sports car and the two men in a white van. I watch them go in. Then I hear shouting and screaming. I think it is him, Leon, but I do not know.' She pauses, narrows her eyes. 'Is he dead?'

De Vries nods.

'It sounded like someone was dying. I tried not to let my granddaughter hear. We went back to bed and I sang to her. When I came back, the woman was gone, and I saw the two men get in their *bakkie* and drive away.'

'You didn't call the cops?'

She smiles crookedly. 'Why? And have one of them tell those people it was me? Then they come for my daughter and my granddaughter. I say nothing.'

'You've seen the woman before?'

'Oh, yes. She arrives in her white Mercedes Benz SLK, and she thinks she is so smart, but that car is not so nice as she thinks. It is old, and the rust is terrible in the wheel arches.'

De Vries smiles openly.

She wags a thin, bent finger at him. 'My husband sold cars, mister. I have walked past that car of hers, and looked at the letters on the back and checked in her wheel arches. That car is like her. It looks okay on the surface, but underneath, it is rotten.'

'Why do you say that?'

'I see her arrive. She has a girl, a young woman — maybe twenty years old — in the car, and they go inside and then she comes out without the girl. I think she is a madam. She is a brothel-keeper and he is some kind of driver. I see him driving the girls around.'

'How many girls?'

'Many.'

'Three, six?'

'Many. I do not know.'

'White?'

'Ja, white. They all looked sad. Tired of life, you know? There are many poor white families all around Cape Town. It is not like when the Nats were in. At least then, the whites and us, we had the jobs. Now we have nothing, the Cape Coloureds least of all.'

'The woman in the sports car, what does she look like?'

'Like she has lived, this woman. Tight face, and mean. Blonde hair from the bottle, dark glasses. She is skinny, and not tall.'

'And the men?'

'I don't see them in the dark. I have not seen these men before. Just the woman and the girls.'

De Vries wishes he had a picture of Chantal

Adam to show her. 'Her car: you see the number plate?'

'I see it, but why would I remember it? I do not know I am doing a deal with the policemen.'

'You ever see anyone else go in and out of that house?'

'I see him in the street sometimes. He usually has a different girl in the car. He lives alone, apart from the girls — and that only began this last winter.'

'You see him on Christmas Eve, Christmas Day with a girl?'

'No.'

'A white girl with long hair, brown?'

'No . . . There was a girl yesterday. I saw her at the window over there. She was smoking a cigarette.'

'Yesterday? You're sure?'

'Yes.'

'Did you see what she looked like?'

'No. She was young, dark hair. It was only for a moment, then he came and they went into another room. Is she dead too?'

'No.'

De Vries's mind races. He pulls the note from his pocket and passes it to her.

'I earn my reward?'

'Yes.'

'You won't tell anyone it was me who spoke?'

'No.'

'Good. That is better. My friend Gertie tells me that, in places like here, the first rule of survival is to speak but say nothing.'

'I get that a lot,' De Vries says.

65

* * *

When De Vries has finished allocating tasks, Brigadier du Toit appears in the squad room, and De Vries invites him into his office. As he enters, Du Toit is lowering the new blinds on the glass windows that look onto the squad room.

'Close the door.'

De Vries waits to see at which side of his desk Du Toit will sit; he takes the visitor's chair. De Vries sits in his own seat, facing him.

'I need to know what's happening, Vaughn. You're running with this?'

'A man called Leon Barker took Chantal Adam to the DF Malan Motel, where I believe he compelled her to swallow forty packages of pure cocaine. He was planning to send her on her way to Bangkok. You know the penalty for smuggling there is thirty years in prison, minimum? Barker was not only killed, he was tortured first, presumably because he'd lost a valuable cargo. We have a description of a woman and two men who we're pretty certain attacked him. They're likely to be the next link in the chain. We have a chance to follow this link and find out where it leads.'

'This is what I thought, Vaughn. That is not our remit. We have enough on our plates already.'

'I have a witness who said she saw another girl in Barker's house yesterday. If that's right, then whoever killed Barker may be holding her. We can't just ignore it.'

'If, and maybe. This isn't for Special Crimes.'

De Vries hesitates, then says, 'I only know

what I read, sir, but for some years Nigerian organized crime has been grooming and sending black girls to Thailand. This is something different. These are white girls. They're being entrapped by white people, and it's possible it began as recently as last winter.'

'That is why this is a matter for Organized Crime and Drug.'

'Perhaps, but I think Chantal Adam called us for a reason. I think she suddenly realized what she'd become involved in, felt there was no escape and decided to kill herself. But she was leaving us a message, pointing us in the right direction to track these people.'

'You have no idea why she called us, Vaughn.'

'But there was a reason, and that is as good a guess as we've got.'

Du Toit sighs. He rarely wins a debate with De Vries without a direct order. Even then . . . 'What is that female officer doing here? I thought she was a liaison with Charles Adam.'

'I'm keeping her until Warrant February returns. She's proven capable. We have a small team right now. We can try to follow the leads we have or, if not, we can pass on what we know — but we have a head-start. All these operations work in tiers. They're so hard to crack because each layer is kept apart from the next. But we've found the first layer and we have leads to the second. This is about protecting vulnerable women, who may think that this idea offers them salvation. Before they know it, they're imprisoned and forced to risk everything. If this is a new set-up, we have a chance to get after them before they know what's hit them. We can't wait for it to be added to intelligence and sit for years.' He sees Du Toit is unconvinced. 'My daughter Kate and Chantal are the same age. Chantal was abused within the last few weeks, probably restrained. She was about to take the biggest risk of her life. I can't let girls like my daughter fall prey to these people.'

Du Toit is silent.

De Vries knows that Du Toit's children are barely older than his own. 'The whole idea of our unit,' he continues, 'is for us to be able to take over serious crime inquiries.'

'All right.' Du Toit holds up his palms. 'See what happens in the next forty-eight hours. If you want to check on the girl your witness may have seen, fair enough. But, Vaughn, if something comes along with our name on it, be prepared to move on. Agreed?'

De Vries watches Du Toit stand and move to the door. When he has gone, he rises, opens the blinds, walks out into the squad room. 'We have one chance,' he tells Frazer, Thwala and Heyns. 'By tomorrow, I want to know things.'

★   ★   ★

From the narrow road, John Marantz's house seems no more than a high white wall and a couple of garage roofs. Through the wood and metal gate, within a courtyard, you discover an angular concrete and glass building stepping down the forty-five-degree angle of the mountain slope, surrounded on three sides by a jungle of tree-ferns and trees. A long, narrow lap pool cantilevers out over the forest.

Marantz worked for the British government until his wife and daughter were taken, never seen again. He has hidden here since, mourning, fighting alcoholism, exiled from the service.

From the moment he met De Vries, they had liked one another, sharing an altruistic desire for justice; for Marantz, in vain. De Vries understands that his friend has walked as close to darkness as he, has stepped beyond. The shared knowledge of how far one must travel is a strong bond. Theirs is a dysfunctional but intensely symbiotic friendship. Neither man trusts the other, yet their loyalty is beyond question.

'Christmas,' Marantz says, as De Vries descends the wooden staircase, 'isn't my best time.'

'You spend it with friends?'

'It's fine. It's only another day.'

'I was working. Sorry.'

'I'd have been surprised if you weren't.'

De Vries walks into Marantz's kitchen, helps himself to a bottle of Merlot. He walks across the huge living area, through French doors four metres high into the terraced garden, where he sits in his usual seat. Marantz follows him with a cool drink for himself and a corkscrew, which he drops into De Vries's lap.

De Vries does a double-take on the bottle top. 'Thought it was a *scrouf-top*.'

He struggles to open the bottle, looks down as the tip of the screw meets the yielding cork, wonders when his hands forgot the ritual undertaken for so many years. He pours, leans back to admire the view down the valley over the narrow lap pool, across to the sprawling Cape Flats.

'What do you know about the drug-smuggling business from South Africa to the Far East?' Pleasantries are anathema.

'I read a book a couple of years back, called *Dead Cows for Piranhas*. An investigative journalist, I think for TV, tried to find out about the process.'

'Why's it called that?'

'If you're trying to cross a piranha-infested river,' Marantz says, 'you throw a dead cow into the water upstream. The piranhas all seek it out and you can cross safely. Apparently that's what these people do. They select the weakest girl, the one who can swallow fewest drugs or is most likely to give herself away, then tip off the Thai authorities. That girl is caught, the others get through. Cold business. She might serve thirty years in one of the harshest prisons in the world.'

'Jesus.'

'Sociopathic.'

'Nigerian underworld, sending girls out from Johannesburg to Thailand?'

'Sounds right. I can't remember exactly. The author likened it more to people-smuggling than drug-muling. The girls who make it through never come back. Not enough money to get home, no support from the South African consulate in Bangkok. They end up in the sex trade. It's grim. That was one of the major

70

themes: the SA government is abandoning them there, making no effort to get their citizens out of the brutal Thai jails and back here to serve out their sentences. I think she claimed it was in contravention of your Constitution.' He looks up. 'This what you're dealing with?'

'Something different. White girls. Seems like a new group, creating a territory.'

'Maybe white girls attract less attention at Customs.'

'That sounds right.'

'In fact,' Marantz continues, frowning, 'I think the suspicion was that the SA Drug Squad often knew they were carrying but let them board the planes and get captured. Trying to pass on the problem to keep down the prison population here.'

'Is there another country where everything, absolutely everything, is political?'

Marantz stands, walks to the side of the lap pool, sticks his hand into the narrow bed of flowering lavender, pulls out a long strand of invasive watergrass. He comes back, sits. 'Are you creating a territory, Vaughn? This isn't what you do.'

'Everyone knows organized crime is taking over Cape Town. If Organized and Drugs can't stop it, maybe I can take out a corner. These are people new to the scene. I want to cut them off now.'

'Be careful. They're sociopaths. They have no empathy for their fellow human beings. Believe me, I know.'

'I don't have a choice. I have information that

at least a dozen girls have been involved with these people. I can't let that continue.'

'Remember, you have a family.'

'I do remember, Johnnie.'

'Couriers are uneducated, desperate. They're seduced by promises of money, freedom. Why do white girls fall prey to them?'

De Vries smiles sadly. 'They're the new underclass. White working-class families are forgotten in our bright new country. I see it more and more. Both parents unemployed, terrible schools. The last twenty years, these are the people who have become desperate.'

De Vries pours himself more wine. It is hot even in the shade of the garden. In front of him, in the distance, the sprawling townships and squatter camps on the Cape Flats glitter in the sunlight beneath a low pall of copper smog. It is so ugly, so beautiful.

⋆ ⋆ ⋆

Cape Town, Monday, 28 December 2015
There are more white Mercedes Benz SLKs than he had hoped.

Sally Frazer is the best collator he has ever known. Every piece of information is put in order, documented, recalled on demand. De Vries has worked with her for almost three years, knows only that she is married, childless, living in Claremont, probably not two kilometres away from his own home. He has never seen the tight bun of dark hair released, heard her express an opinion on any subject outside work or seen her eyes smile at the same time as her mouth. The list on her screen runs to several pages.

'Discount anything less than, say, seven years old. Look for owners, maybe female, in the poorer neighbourhoods.'

He looks down the squad room at the giant parallelograms of sunlight projected onto the sandpaper carpet from the line of unprotected windows. Lee-Ann Heyns, her head bent low over paperwork, works intensely. Ben Thwala talks urgently on the telephone. Right now, they are all he has; he wonders what he is doing with two junior officers and a seconded warrant officer who has tried to blackmail him. In the SAPS, you make do. He turns back to Frazer's screen.

'There aren't that many old models registered.' She looks up at him. 'You know there's a good chance it isn't here?'

'*Ja*, but I have a feeling that she's the sort of woman who'll try to keep up appearances. I think she'd register her car, pay her taxes.'

Frazer hits a button, rises, walks to the printer. She swipes the sheet from the tray, scans it, passes it to De Vries. 'We're down to twenty-eight. We can try to eliminate according to majority racial make-up of the addresses.'

De Vries sits, runs a pen down the list, crosses out fifteen or sixteen, gets to his feet. 'There's a dozen we'll try first. Cross-check to see if any are in the system. If not, we'll do it the hard way.' He strides to his office. He doesn't think this way usually, but somehow he knows that the woman he seeks is on that list. He does not understand where this assurance comes from and fears it will betray him.

⋆ ⋆ ⋆

He drives with Lee-Ann Heyns to Brooklyn, a poor industrial suburb between Table Bay and the Ysterplaat military airbase, along quiet but polluted roads, stopped by repeating red lights. Diane Kemmel has appeared with a criminal record, her picture as close to Leon Barker's neighbour's description as they can hope for. Around them, pawn shops and pop-up stalls proliferate, but many other units are boarded up.

Heyns directs him down a narrow street into an estate bordered by two freeways and the Salt River as it prepares to hit the coast. The tired, dilapidated side-streets are lined with broken palms and simple bungalows, interspersed with builders' yards and small warehouses.

They drive down Shaddock Street, backs to the Mountain.

'Pull over here before the end.'

They reach a T-junction. To the left, De Vries can see that the side-road is a cul-de-sac; to the right, the road widens as it heads towards an industrial estate. Heyns studies the map. 'Eighteen should be at the end to the left.'

'How long is that road?'

'Not long.'

'If it's a cul-de-sac,' De Vries says, 'they'll see us coming.'

'I'll go. I can ring on the door of a neighbour's house, ask where a local street is.' She starts to

74

take off her blouse.

'What are you doing?'

'I walk down there dressed like this, it won't be very subtle. Give me your shirt.' She throws her blouse on the back seat. 'Come on.'

'It's pretty filthy.'

'Good. It'll look better. And so will you, if anybody passes. Man in a T-shirt looks casual.'

She struggles into his faded blue shirt, unlocks the passenger door, picks up her handbag, tips the contents onto the back seat. She scrabbles through the ephemera and shovels a few items back in. 'Light a cigarette. Look like you're dozing. Give me ten minutes.'

She slams the door, walks slowly to the corner, ruffles her hair, steps out of sight.

After fifteen minutes, his skin prickles. He wonders whether to get out, to follow her down the side-street. He lets his *stompie* drop to the hot, pale tarmac, suddenly sees her at the corner. She opens the door, slams it, lights a cigarette. She is sweating. 'It's a double-storey, iron gates across the front, with netting. Can't see much, but I saw the Merc — plates match the record — and a white *bakkie*, which could be your witness's van. I've got the number, but if that one's registered . . . There's at least one camera. She's got a yard at the back, razor wire down the sides. We can find out what's behind it but I'm guessing it's a warehouse yard, fenced, leading down to the canal.'

'You think there's access?'

'Don't know, but it should be easy enough to find out.'

De Vries checks in his mirror before driving back onto the main road. 'Sounds exactly what you'd expect. What did you do?'

'Knocked on a couple of neighbours' doors. No answer anywhere.'

'Not surprised.'

'Do we wait for her to come out?'

'If she's there. Any sign of movement?'

She shakes her head. 'You can't see in. Windows are curtained off. I couldn't hear anything.'

'It feels right.'

'The car's there.'

De Vries says, 'If it's the same white van, the guys who were in it could be there too. That doesn't sound good. Do we want to walk right up to the front and ring the bell, or close down the scene, protect escape routes around the back?'

Heyns has removed De Vries's shirt, retrieved her blouse and started buttoning it. 'There is an alternative.'

'What?'

'I go in.'

De Vries looks over at her, turns back to the road, brakes hard.

'Before you dismiss it, it makes sense.'

'Stop now. Listen to me. No one is going anywhere near that house until we've worked out what we have. If she has girls there, we could end up with a hostage situation.' He drifts towards traffic lights, checks that the lights are still red, turns again to her. 'What's the matter with you? That's a suicidal idea.'

'I can say I was living in the same squat as Chantal Adam, that she told me to follow her to Thailand, to come to the house.'

'You don't know Chantal Adam knew anything about this house and, even if she did, if she got a chance to tell anyone. In fact, their whole *modus operandi* is to stop any communication with the outside world. That's why Chantal Adam calling us caused such trouble.'

'If she called us, she could have called me.' She straightens the collar on her blouse, flips down the mirror in the sun visor, scrutinizes her face. 'They're one courier down. I don't know Chantal Adam never made it to the plane. I could provide them with a timely replacement.'

'For fuck's sake, Warrant, it's not happening. Do you understand? Don't even suggest it.'

Heyns snaps back the visor. 'We could send in the Hawks.'

'Whatever we do,' De Vries says, 'it'll be my decision.'

★ ★ ★

'Where are you?'

De Vries squints at his phone — he can't see the caller display now that he has answered it. 'Who is this?'

'Steve Ulton.'

'Sorry, Steve. I'm in the building, heading for the lift.'

'Want you to see something in the lab.'

'I'll be there just now.'

'I ran a detailed analysis: Chantal Adam had a rare blood type.' Steve Ulton looks up at De Vries. 'Do you know what antigens do?' He shakes his head. 'Simply, they're molecules within blood capable of triggering antibodies. Her already rare blood type, AB negative, also featured several missing antigens. That could be a reason why she deteriorated so fast in America. Her body may have been unable to protect itself from threat.'

'Does that help us with how or why she died?'

Ulton balks. 'It could increase the chance of mental disorders. It's interesting. You know, if she'd needed a transfusion, with her actual parents dead, there might not have been a donor in the country. Often harder to get blood over a border than it is a human being.'

'What did you want me to see?'

'The history of blood is fascinating.'

'Not now, Doctor.'

Ulton sighs, turns towards his section of the lab, leads De Vries towards the stainless-steel bench, which stretches the width of the room. Forty lozenges of raw cocaine are laid out in perfect symmetry. There is one smaller packet to the side, accompanied by a crumpled piece of paper. 'We started looking through each of the packets. Pretty standard, double-wrapped in condoms. We're seeing custom-made pellets too now, but this is still the most popular method. Swallow, pray for their integrity, shit them out the other end. The contents seem to be from the same batch. High quality, very pure. Then there's this.' He points to the smaller packet. 'You can see that this is different: a single condom containing no drugs, just this note.'

De Vries leans over the bench to the small piece of cheap paper torn from a larger sheet. He can make out some faint lines.

Ulton smiles. 'You're not going blind. This wasn't written in pen. Well, it was, but the pen didn't work, or had virtually no ink. There are ballpoint indentations.'

'What does it say?'

' 'I can't go back'.'

'What?'

'That's what it says. It could be just 'can't go back'. She attempted to write a vertical line several times before it, perhaps discovered that the pen didn't work. Looks like the letter *I* and the lower-case *c* suggests it wasn't the first word of a sentence.'

De Vries looks up. 'You know what this means?'

Ulton shrugs. 'Do you?'

'It means she never planned to be rescued . . . or knew she wouldn't be. She knew we'd discover this inside her body.'

'How does it help us? What does it mean?'

'This isn't just about drug-smuggling or abduction,' De Vries says. 'It's about what it's always about. The life of the victim before her death.'

★ ★ ★

'You're not going to like this,' Du Toit tells him. 'You're treading on toes. Organized and Drug called me, asked about the Chantal Adam case, told me the DF Malan Motel and Leon Barker are part of an ongoing investigation.'

'They're my investigation.'

'No, Vaughn. We've decided that Chantal Adam's death was self-inflicted. That was dealt with. Your investigation into Leon Barker was something else. They're dealing with it. Frankly, it's a relief. If General Thulani realized what was happening without us informing him, it would have been a misstep.'

De Vries snorts. 'A misstep?'

'Crossing the lines of departmental responsibility. We have a broad brief here, but that is beyond our remit.'

'Aren't you forgetting the torture and murder of Leon Barker?'

'I am not, and normally you would be free to continue your own inquiry, but if he features in their investigation, leave it to them.'

'If Barker and the motel were part of an investigation, how come Chantal Adam was allowed to enter that building and end up dead? In fact, how did Barker get away?'

'These aren't questions for us.'

'Well, I have a question for you, sir. What would you say if I told you that Dr Ulton's lab have just discovered a message, hidden inside Chantal Adam's body? A note. 'I can't go back'.'

'What?'

'She wrote it and swallowed it with, or after, forty individual packets of drugs she had

80

ingested. She called us and then she killed herself. Don't tell me there's nothing to investigate here.'

Du Toit bows his head, runs fingers through his thinning hair. De Vries can see his face contort.

'My God . . . '

'That's why this case is not closed, sir.'

'You just won't get it, will you? However many times I explain. This is the SAPS in 2015. We have remits, and we stay out of other people's areas of jurisdiction.'

'Fine, but Chantal Adam needs a voice. I want to arrest these people so this doesn't happen again — so that it stops.'

'You've suggested this may be more than narcotics smuggling, this could be Organized Crime. That is not our remit.'

'For Christ's sake, Henrik — sir. Stop saying 'remit'.'

'I wish that, just sometimes, you would let go. You have to make everything so personal.'

'It is personal. I met her. She was a friend of my daughters.'

'You met her once or twice, Vaughn, years ago. You saw her on TV and, like half the men in Cape Town, you wanted to know her. That's not the same thing.'

'You didn't see her body.'

'No, I didn't.' Du Toit sighs, a sound with which De Vries is familiar. 'Make your enquiries about Chantal Adam. Report to me, and I will make sure Charles Adam is satisfied. But this other stuff, pass on what you have to Organized and Drug and get back to work on what you do best.'

★ ★ ★

By 5.30 p.m., the squad room is empty. De Vries has sat in silence alone in his office for the past hour. He senses a shadow in his peripheral vision, sees Heyns walking towards him. She knocks and enters in one single movement.

'What?'

'I was waiting for you by your car.'

'Why?'

She sits in the chair opposite him. 'They won't do anything.'

'Who?'

'The Drug Squad guys.'

'Your opinion is irrelevant, Warrant, as is mine. It has been decided.'

'I thought you didn't give up so easily.'

De Vries sighs. 'I don't do politics. This is inter-departmental. You have to pick your battles.' He focuses on her. 'Why were you waiting for me by my car?'

'You want to eat?'

'If I want to eat, I eat alone. You should get home to your husband.'

'And back to my station?'

'Yes. There's nothing so conclusive as one of Director du Toit's pronouncements. I've kept my side of the bargain.'

'You were looking at me in the car when I took my blouse off. Why not admit it? You like me.'

'I don't like you.'

Heyns smiles. 'But you want me.'

'No.' De Vries regrets that his answer is not as absolute as he has tried to make it sound. He knows she has picked up on his confused intonation.

'I promise I will never say anything like that again. I'd never have done it. I want to be with you.'

'It was what it was, Lee-Ann. It's over.'

She tilts her head. 'Look after me tonight or I might do something stupid.'

De Vries stands. 'Go home, Warrant Officer. You almost redeemed yourself with some good work. Count that a result.'

Heyns rises. 'I always do good work. That's why it's so fucking Fascist that I'm still following orders and not giving them.'

'You've made your point. I can't do anything about that. Keep working hard, you may get lucky.' She opens her mouth to speak, but he continues, 'Your captain is expecting you tomorrow morning. Go home.'

Heyns stares at him for a moment longer, throws open his office door, strides away through the squad room.

* * *

De Vries eats at Barrister's restaurant in Newlands Village, watches the young couples and families around him, wonders why they would come out to eat when all they do is stare at cell phones, send SMS messages and update themselves on social media?.

He orders a 600g sirloin steak and a bottle of Merlot, mixes the blood from the rare meat with the wine in his mouth, leaves nothing.

He drives home slowly, through the archway of overhanging trees in Newlands Avenue, past the President's Cape Town residence, through Rondebosch to the common. As his gates close behind him, he switches off the engine, sits in the silence. He looks up at his big dark house, a family home once full of life. He realizes that all evening he has been thinking of nothing but Lee-Ann Heyns.

★ ★ ★

Cape Town, Tuesday, 29 December 2015
'Operational details are to remain within as small a circle as possible, for security. I am sure, sir, you have the same policy here?'

De Vries looks across his desk at Major Ade Ngcuka, commanding officer of the Drug Unit, Western Province. He had decided against visiting and now he has the man in his office. Ngcuka's physical neatness, his precise voice, his incanting of protocol, all of these things annoy him.

'Either your team, Major, were aware that Leon Barker was supervising the secretion of narcotics in girls at the DF Malan Motel prior to their dispatch to Thailand or they weren't. It's a simple question.'

'Brigadier du Toit informed me that you would be debriefing us on the information obtained during your inquiry. We could not agree to the

84

sharing of information.'

De Vries clenches his fists beneath his desk. 'Major, I am a senior officer, involved in the investigation of the death by suicide of one victim, the torture and murder of another. Sharing information with me can only assist that investigation. That is why I want it.'

'I understood that you were no longer interested in the murder of Leon Barker.'

'I'm extremely interested. What's more — '

'Brigadier du Toit told me clearly — '

De Vries sits forward. 'Listen to me, Major. I don't care what Brigadier du Toit told you. You're talking to me now. You're evading every question I ask you, and it makes me wonder why. What does your unit know about the connection between Leon Barker and Diane Kemmel?'

'I do not know who that woman is.'

'You deny knowledge of a woman called Diane Kemmel?'

'I do not recall seeing that name in the reports. I oversee numerous cases simulta-neously, but the name does not seem familiar.'

'How long have you been investigating the DF Malan Motel?'

'That is confidential.'

'Not to me. Answer the question, Major.'

Ngcuka hesitates. 'I do not know exactly . . . '

'A week? A month? Six months?'

'I don't know, sir.'

'Take an informed guess.'

'Perhaps . . . eight to ten weeks.'

'And in perhaps eight to ten weeks, what have your team established?'

'I cannot tell you if this was a matter they worked exclusively. They certainly had other investigations to work on.'

'What have they established, Major?'

Ngcuka shakes his head. 'I do not think I can answer that question, sir.'

'Since your team have spent at least eight weeks on this matter, and they — or you — seem unaware of the connection to Diane Kemmel, I would think that anything you say will not be news to me.'

'I cannot comment on that, sir.'

De Vries says quietly. 'Do you understand that this total lack of co-operation between departments is what holds the SAPS back? This is what gives the criminals an advantage over us.'

'I have rules I must abide by, Colonel.'

'And those rules are what is suffocating this force.'

'That is a political matter. That is beyond my remit.'

De Vries sits back, snorts, 'I thought you might say that.'

★ ★ ★

'What are you doing, Vaughn?'

De Vries closes his eyes, opens them, pastes a smile across his face. His office used to be a place of sanctuary. He dislikes Du Toit's new-found office mobility. 'Good afternoon, sir.'

'You know I don't trust you when you call me 'sir'.'

Du Toit closes De Vries's office door.

'Another meeting in my office. Is this a new policy of closer supervision?'

Du Toit sits. 'I feel more relaxed when I know exactly what you're doing. And so does General Thulani.'

'I passed the information to Major Ngcuka.'

'I gather that you were unhappy there was no quid pro quo?'

'I was, and I remain unhappy that a unit from the Drug Squad can survey the DF Malan Motel, follow Leon Barker, and still let Chantal Adam die. I'm unhappy that there may have been another girl with Barker, and that this Diane Kemmel may have taken her . . . And I'll tell you what I'm most unhappy about, sir: that, after ten weeks' work, they claim to know less than it took my ad hoc team of four to discover in forty-eight hours.'

'You are an unhappy man generally, then.'

'Don't patronize me, Henrik. If the Drug Unit were watching Leon Barker, how was the woman identified as Diane Kemmel and two other men allowed to enter his premises, torture him, kill him and possibly remove another girl?'

Du Toit opens his mouth.

'And don't tell me that this has nothing to do with us.'

'It doesn't.'

De Vries stares at Du Toit. 'Doesn't it interest you? Don't you wonder why the SAPS, as an institution, fails so much of the time? Surely this is why you fought to establish this unit.'

'Yes, and we have it. But to keep it, you have to play their game.'

'What — not be involved? Not stick our heads above the parapet? That's pathetic, and it results in nothing. Nothing at all.'

'I don't think what we achieve is pathetic.'

'You're like politicians. Hold beliefs, convictions, then turn them a hundred and eighty degrees just to get elected. What's the point? We have some degree of freedom. We must use that.'

'We achieve more by being prudent.'

'We've had this discussion so many times . . . ' De Vries feels the pulse in his neck throbbing, fights the rising pressure. 'The game prescribed from above is always the same: avoid confrontation, turn a blind eye to corruption. They do it because they think that if we expose corruption it reflects badly on them. You know that's the reverse of how it should be. Did you read the story in the *Argus* last week? The black warrant officer in Stellenbosch who turned up for work just twenty-three days in the year, then received automatic promotion to lieutenant. Are you surprised the public have lost all faith in us? That morale among the ranks is at an all-time low?'

'You of all people should know that you can't believe what you read in the papers. Most of these claims are racially motivated.'

'Is all criticism of non-whites racist now?'

'All right, Vaughn. You didn't like Major Ngcuka . . . '

'I didn't like that he claimed not to know anything. Either they're incompetent, or there's a reason why obvious links haven't been followed.'

'What reason?'

'It's an open secret that to operate at all, these

rings have to have police and immigration officers in their pockets. If the system worked properly, the smugglers would go somewhere else. They operate here because they're allowed to.'

Du Toit shakes his head. 'Don't do this . . . '

'Don't arrest the murderer, don't find the girl?'

'Don't interrupt me. Isn't life hard enough without volunteering for more grief?'

De Vries bangs his fist on his desk. 'For fuck's sake. What's the point if we give up before we even begin?'

Du Toit sighs. 'Just . . . just find the girl. And liaise, Vaughn. Follow protocol. I'll inform Major Ngcuka that we'll continue with our investigation until we are satisfied.'

'Thank you, sir.'

Du Toit stands. 'When is Warrant February due back?'

'Officially, the second of January.'

'Maybe see if he can return sooner. He's a calming influence on you.'

'Is he?'

'I think so. And he tells me what you're doing.'

De Vries laughs. 'He only tells you what I want him to tell you.'

'Nonetheless . . . '

'I'll call him just now.'

'And, Vaughn, I want to see you daily. I want to know what's happening. Don't make me come over here each time.'

De Vries watches Du Toit walk away, doesn't care that he is adding weight to the man's shoulders; knows that if weight isn't absorbed, isn't pushed back, it overwhelms.

* * *

'Warrant Officer Heyns? Do you still have her?'

De Vries swallows. He feels a pall instantly descend over him. He has dreaded such an enquiry, somehow expected it. 'No, Captain. I told you last night her secondment ended. She knew that she was expected with you this morning.'

Captain Maart says, 'There's no sign. Her cell phone's off. We've tried her home and I spoke with her husband. Not been seen.'

De Vries swallows, his mouth suddenly dry. 'What's her husband's name?'

'Immelman . . . Think his name's Marc. Lieutenant with the Drug Squad operating from town. They seem to work very different shifts. He said they've seen virtually nothing of one another the last few weeks.'

'Tough job when you're married.'

'Doubly so when you're both on the job. You'll let me know if she turns up, sir?'

'I will.' De Vries wonders whether to voice his suspicion. He finds the fewer who share his thoughts, the quieter his and their lives are. He ends the call.

* * *

De Vries sees the man's shoulders slump, knuckles tighten. Major Ngcuka does not even

90

straighten up as De Vries approaches the central table over which he stands. Ngcuka manages to avoid eye contact with him. 'I received the call from Brigadier du Toit,' Ngcuka says. 'It was a surprise. I am disappointed. This will certainly be referred upline.'

'You wriggle as much as you like. Meantime, I'm liaising with you, Major. I'm following protocol. Make the most of it.'

'Our position is still the same.'

'I don't give a shit about your position. Just listen to me. Whatever your team have been doing, my team linked Leon Barker to Diane Kemmel. I have a witness who places her and two unidentified men at Barker's house at the time he was tortured and murdered. The same witness saw another young girl inside his house that day. After the attack, she wasn't there. We believe Diane Kemmel may have taken her and could be holding her at her address in Brooklyn.'

'I told you. We don't know a Diane Kemmel.'

'Well, I do, Major, and now you do. I want her for questioning. I want the men who may have acted for her and, if she's there, I want the girl — plus who knows how many others — rescued, and questioned.'

'This is not part of our inquiry.'

De Vries smiles. 'No, it isn't, is it?' Ngcuka looks up at him. 'And it should be. It should have been several weeks ago. I need to find out why it's not and, if you're doing your job properly, Major, so should you.'

'That is not your concern.'

'It is now. First, it will accelerate your

investigations into the smuggling emanating from the DF Malan Motel. Second, I believe that an officer who briefly assisted me may have made an unauthorized approach on that property and may, as we speak, be in grave danger.'

'What officer?'

'Lee-Ann Heyns. Have you heard of her?'

Ngcuka nods. 'She is Marc Immelman's wife. What connection to this matter does she have?'

'She should have had no connection. Working from Rondebosch hub, she had been assigned as a liaison with Charles Adam, whose adopted daughter took her own life in the DF Malan Motel. She involved herself in the investigation into the girl's death, then remained with me while we confirmed that suicide was an accurate COD.'

'What makes you think she's inside the Kemmel property?'

'Because we found it. She reconnoitred it, suggested she try to enter the property under cover. I told her it was out of the question. However, Warrant Officer Heyns is headstrong, determined to make a name for herself.'

Ngcuka stares at him impassively. 'She is an impulsive officer. Lieutenant Immelman believes it is why her career has suffered.'

De Vries snorts silently to himself. Immelman would scarcely share his thoughts with Ngcuka as to why white officers were being held back.

'I must inform him immediately.'

'He's already aware that she is not at work. I need the men from one of the teams, and we need to work out a strategy to move on the Brooklyn property.'

'I hope you are not suggesting seconding my teams for this task?'

'That's exactly what I'm suggesting.'

'That is not acceptable.'

De Vries stands between Ngcuka and the door to the squad room. 'I'll tell you what isn't acceptable. I am your senior officer. I expect the respect that rank demands. You get the team that was assigned to the DF Malan Motel and Leon Barker and you have them here, at my disposal, within the hour, Major. I have a warrant in place. And I want you there, contributing to the briefing and supervising your men.'

Ngcuka stands silently.

'One hour, Major. Don't make me wait.'

★ ★ ★

De Vries appreciates the bonds of trust and routine upon which, for their very survival, small, close-knit teams, working in intensely stressful situations, come to rely. He finds this team negative and intransigent. He obtains blown-up aerial shots of the Kemmel compound, lays them on the central table in their squad room, challenges them to create a strategy to launch an armed assault on the property if, as he suspects, a standard approach from the front fails.

He steps into the corridor, taking Ngcuka with him. He looks back through the small safety-glass panels in the double doors to the squad room. The ceilings in this building are low, the air stale and humid with sweat. The lighting is old and oppressive, the room lit mostly by the austere glow from bulky computer monitors, exuding heat and radiation. De Vries turns to Ngcuka. 'Who is leading this team?'

'Lieutenant Esterhuysen.'

'Where is he?'

'He will be here shortly. He has a matter of urgency to conclude first.'

'This is a matter of urgency, Major. An officer's life may be at risk. Get him here immediately and stop wasting my time.'

Ngcuka stands his ground. 'With respect, sir, you should appreciate that this is an unprecedented situation. They do not know you, do not trust you.'

'I'm an old dog, Major, but when one of our people is in danger, I expect everyone to work together to assist. I don't understand their apparent lack of loyalty to a fellow officer.'

'That is not the case. You are imposing on one of their carefully established operations.'

'It isn't established. Neither you nor your team knew anything about Diane Kemmel.'

'Jack Esterhuysen is a meticulous unit leader. He will not commit his team to an operation until he is certain of the outcome.'

De Vries looks back through the panel. The men slouch over the desk, talking casually. 'There are many times when quick decisions must be made. Get Esterhuysen in there and teach him that to be proactive is not necessarily reckless.'

Ngcuka shrugs.

De Vries steps up to him. 'Don't shrug your shoulders at me, Major. That officer is under your command. Impress on him that this operation is happening imminently and I am looking for his total commitment.'

Ngcuka shudders. 'This entire matter will be reported in full to my superiors.'

'You can threaten me all you like. Get on with it.'

He watches Ngcuka saunter through the squad room doors, approach the group. They meet with expectation, as if he is about to announce the cancellation of the operation. De Vries's jaw is locked, teeth gritted. He questions his motivation for such determined action, wonders whether he is overplaying his rank or whether the safety of Lee-Ann Heyns has disproportionately affected his judgement. For a moment, he shivers, imagining her AWOL in some west-coast cottage belonging to some other lover, this mission ending in casualties and destroyed evidence.

He takes the fire-escape stairs to the ground floor, barges through the door, uncaring that an alarm may sound in some distant control room. In the *stompie*-strewn yard, he lights up, draws deeply on the filter, feels his hand shaking. He smokes two cigarettes, climbs the staircase heavily, re-enters the corridor. This time, he sees the men focused around a tall, taciturn man with a beard, piercing eyes scrutinizing each of them. He walks into the room, hears Esterhuysen outlining strategies, indicating areas on the plan, motivating his team. There is, De Vries thinks, passion in his voice.

★   ★   ★

It is dusk before five cars leave for the Brooklyn address. Esterhuysen leads the group, which will prevent escape from the back of the property and, if required, launch an ingress from the rear. Two further cars carry officers trained to storm buildings and counter armed resistance. De Vries travels in one of two marked vehicles with three uniformed officers. Ngcuka, who had suggested that he stay behind to co-ordinate efforts, has been made to occupy the other car. De Vries's team will approach the target from the front, attempt to serve the warrant and gain access.

Silhouetted against silver-grey sky above the sea on the horizon, backed by the almost purple Mountain behind them, the neighbourhood seems less tawdry, but the warm wind still blows ceaselessly; dust devils swirl in the flickering light of the street-lamp under which he stops. He lifts his radio, contacts Ngcuka.

'Two minutes until units in place.'

De Vries checks his watch. Esterhuysen has impressed him with his briefing and preparation. The man seems as disenchanted by Ngcuka as he is. He has assumed control of his unit, seemingly over and above his commanding officer.

De Vries says nothing to the uniformed officers who accompany him. As he waits for confirmation, he realizes he is nervous. If they

96

gain access to the property, he has no idea what might be waiting for them. Finally, Ngcuka confirms that all units are in position and on stand-by.

De Vries transmits: 'Unit One approaching target now. Stand by.'

He nods at the driver, who edges forward and turns left into the cul-de-sac. About fifty metres from the junction, a car is parked at the kerb. When his vehicle draws level, he says,

'Stop now. Stay in the road here.'

De Vries steps out of the car, accompanied by two uniformed officers, surprised by how hot the wind still seems. It dries his eyes, cracks his parched lips. The air smells thick, laced with chemicals and pollution. He strides up the middle of the road, trying to walk off his anxiety. He reaches the letterbox and, beside it, an entry-phone unit. He presses the button, hears an electronic chime.

Above the gates, he can see the barred and curtained windows on the first floor of the Kemmel property. All are closed. Between two towels hung over the far-right window, he can see yellow electric light. He rings again. At the base of the nylon mesh behind the iron railings guarding the property, flotsam has assembled until it is nearly half a metre high. It rustles over the dull roar of the distant roads. He puts his face up to the mesh, sees the white Mercedes SLK, to the right, the white *bakkie*. He wonders what they might be doing inside the property. He presses the bell again, speaks into the unit.

'This is the SAPS. Answer your door.'

He strains to detect any sound from the faded plastic unit, hears what, in a sea-shell, might be deemed the ocean but is nothing more than the ambient noise of distant factories and roads. The wind causes the nylon mesh to flap against the iron railings, rapping out a fast metallic chatter. He pulls out his radio.

'No answer at the front gate. Suspect's car and white van in place.'

The radio crackles in time with the wind. He hears Ngcuka say:

'Unit Four reports movement on first floor at rear of the building.'

De Vries hesitates for a moment, takes a deep breath over his pounding heart, says:

'This is Unit One, De Vries. Commence ingress on target building. Go, go, go.'

He gestures for the uniformed officers to follow him back to their car, watches the Unit Three car swerve around the corner of the cul-de-sac and roar past them up to the front gates of the property. The driver of his own car has reversed to the intersection and stopped just around the corner. De Vries instructs the officers to return to the car. He draws his weapon, ducks behind the parked car. As he does so, the door to the adjoining property opens.

'Close that door. Get back inside,' De Vries shouts.

A man stumbles onto the narrow path, barefoot, clutching a can of beer.

'What's happening, bro?'

De Vries raises his weapon.

'Turn around, go inside. Don't come out.'

The man stares at the pistol, smiles crookedly, spins on the spot, begins to sway back towards his door.

At that moment, there is an explosion from the Kemmel property; De Vries snaps back to the scene. He sees a small plume of black smoke rise from the gates. Drug Squad men, keeping low, squeeze through a gap in the railings towards the house. He becomes aware of the radio in his pocket, shouted commands, acknowledgements. Suddenly he hears gunfire, echoed over the radio, tinny and rapid. Instinctively, he runs towards the building, hearing the transmitted voices become high-pitched and urgent. A scream, which sounds distant in the night air, makes his pocket vibrate, skin tingle.

He reaches the gate, squeezes through the gap, drops to a knee, weapon primed. The front door is open. From within, he hears shouting, followed by two quick bursts of gunfire. He hears a woman's voice, loud and strident, followed by another scream. In the front-right top-floor window, he sees a shadow pass, hears shots, sees the towels drop, the window mist with black spatter, shatter, fall like ice onto the roof of the *bakkie* beneath it. The glass bounces onto the ground beside him, tinkles by his boots. Still, he hears a woman shouting. He eases himself upright, approaches the front door, clicks his radio. 'Unit One entering front door now.'

He checks around him, passes into the house.

On his left a narrow front room lit by a fluorescent tube is empty. To his right, an open door leads onto an empty garage space. The air is stale and hot, grey-tinged with gun-smoke. He moves on, aiming his gun up the staircase, then ahead of him. Above, he can hear pounding feet, men shouting all-clears. Ahead, he hears the screaming woman, coarse and hysterical. He runs into the wide back room.

The woman he assumes to be Diane Kemmel is at the rear of the room, sheltering behind a young girl. She has the girl's wrists in her grip, manipulating her, like a puppet. The girl is petrified, legs limp, crying, her head swaying loosely as she is thrown about. Two men face them, their weapons pointed at the women. Kemmel is screaming at them.

De Vries checks behind him, sees one of the men from the attack unit at the bottom of the staircase, gestures for him to wait, turns back to the room. 'Are the suspects armed?'

Neither man speaks.

'Are they armed?'

'Negative.'

He holsters his pistol. 'Lower your weapons.'

The officer in front obeys the order, tilting his gun downwards; the man behind remains unmoving. De Vries sees that it is Esterhuysen. 'Lieutenant. This is Colonel de Vries. Lower your weapon.'

Esterhuysen glances at him, follows the command.

De Vries steps level with the two men, addresses the women: 'Diane Kemmel. I am Colonel de Vries, SAPS. Release your hostage and no one will get hurt.'

He cannot see Diane Kemmel's face, only the whimpering, tear-stained one of the young girl. 'This property is under our control. Release your hostage now.'

The girl screams, begins to struggle, kicks behind her, gets one wrist free and tries to run. De Vries is focused on the women, does not see Esterhuysen raise his gun. He steps forward. 'Release the girl, Diane. Do it now.'

Suddenly the girl jolts forward, almost knocking De Vries over. He grabs her, spins and heads for the exit. As he does so, Esterhuysen screams, fires a shot towards Kemmel. De Vries pushes the girl through the door, turns back. Diane Kemmel is lying against the far wall, Esterhuysen's weapon pointing at her head.

De Vries freezes, says loudly, calmly, 'Lieutenant Esterhuysen. Lower your weapon.'

He sees Esterhuysen's grip on the trigger tighten. 'Lieutenant. This is a direct order. Lower your weapon.'

He sees the tall officer's chest heaving, sweat from his brow dripping down his face. The weapon wobbles in his hand. De Vries steps forward, puts his hand on Esterhuysen's shoulder. 'Stand down, Lieutenant. Scene is secured. Repeat: secured.' He leans down to the man's right ear. 'Get out of this room. Leave the building through the front. Do it now.'

He watches Diane Kemmel, senses Esterhuysen moving out of the room. He glances at the other officer, his weapon still pointing at Kemmel. De Vries nods to him, approaches Kemmel. He grabs her by the back of her collar.

'Ms Kemmel, you're coming with me.'

He marches her from the room, through the house, out of the front door to the yard. There, he hands her over to the uniformed officers who wait on the other side of the iron gates. He turns back, re-enters the house, walks to the bottom of the staircase. An officer says, 'Two armed white males dead, sir. Two women, one injured. Warrant Officer Heyns, sir . . . '

De Vries pushes past him, takes the steps two at a time to the landing, ducks into the first room to the left. There, he sees two male bodies, one by the broken, bloodied window, the other behind the bed. He turns, passes the bathroom, barges into the second room. On the first of two single beds, a young girl lies, attended to by one of the unit officers. She is whimpering quietly, holding her left arm. There is no blood. De Vries jumps around the bed to the next, looks beyond it, sees nothing. He backs out, runs to the room at the back of the house.

Lee-Ann Heyns lies on the bed. He takes in bindings around her ankles, wrists, her clothes ripped. He feels the breath stolen from him, bile rising. He forces himself to breathe, to swallow. He approaches the bed, sees beyond the dark blood oozing over her breasts, dripping in slow motion from her torso onto the bedding: deep, jagged gunshots. His brain counts black bullet-holes, reaches double figures, shuts down.

PART 2

'I ask you to do one thing for me,' Henrik du Toit says. 'To keep everything by the book until the end of the year and, now, we have this.'

De Vries is not aware of his surroundings, grateful that the single lamp on Du Toit's desk illuminates his office just dimly. His fingers and thumbs rub against one another. His leg twitches.

'If it wasn't for me, we wouldn't have anything.'

'An officer dead?'

De Vries places his hands on Du Toit's desk. 'You need to understand what I found before you pass judgement. Lee-Ann Heyns was tied to the bed. She was probably abused, possibly tortured. She was as good as dead the moment she went into that place — in contravention of my direct order.'

'It shouldn't even have been discussed.'

'It wasn't discussed. She was an officer out of control.'

'You are the officer out of control. You're like a mad dog. You need to slow down and calm yourself. You don't think logically when you're like this.'

'Warrant Heyns was probably dead before we arrived.'

'Probably?'

'Probably.'

'She was under your supervision.'

'No, sir. I discharged her yesterday evening,

105

confirmed to Captain Maart in Rondebosch that she would return to him. Warrant Officer Heyns had issues with being passed over for promotion and I think she was determined to make her mark.'

'What you think right now is irrelevant. There will be an inquiry. You have to convince them, not me.'

'Two young women were found in the building, including one who may have been present at Leon Barker's property. The two men we believe may have been responsible for Barker's torture and murder were involved in a fire-fight with our teams and were taken down.'

'I'm not hearing any certainty about these people's involvement.'

'The moment you release me, we'll interview Diane Kemmel about imprisoning those girls, her presence at Barker's house and her part in his death.'

Du Toit wipes his brow. 'Nothing is happening tonight, Vaughn. It's almost eleven p.m. If you think you are going to interview this suspect now, you'll be disappointed. Her attorney will delay questioning. Major Ngcuka has notified me that he is to make a formal complaint against you. I can't even guarantee that you will be allowed to continue in command.'

De Vries runs his hands over his head to the back of his neck. He is still charged from the raid, shaken by Heyns's death. He feels his energy begin to wane, fatigue and frustration at SAPS bureaucracy undermining his former determination.

'We have one girl in hospital, the other here for questioning. I have Diane Kemmel in the cells.'

'And she'll still be there in the morning. You need teams to sweep that house, find whatever they can, build a set of definite charges against her and the men who were killed by the assault team.'

'What is it with this job? We had definite intelligence that Diane Kemmel was involved, suspicion that our own officer was inside. They refused to answer the door to their fortified premises. It's just so clear.'

'To you.'

'And now I'll be delayed by Wertner. He wants me gone, and our unit disbanded. If you don't support me, that is what will happen.'

'Go home, Vaughn. I know you'll sit up all night, but go home. If you stay here, Wertner is more likely to have you removed officially. There's only so far any of us can go to protect you.'

★ ★ ★

Cape Town, Wednesday, 30 December 2015
De Vries wakes early, eyes, nose, mouth grainy at their edges, tongue glued to his palate. His ex-wife insisted on water at their bedside, but he has not retained this ritual. He swings his feet to the floor, stands up, staggers to the bathroom where he leans his full weight on the basin. He runs cold water almost to the top, plunges his head in, leaves it there to cool as the detritus of

sleep melts away. This, he thinks, is what happens when he avoids alcohol at night.

He pulls the curtains to reveal the overbearing triangular mass of Devil's Peak against a sky of intense blue, which he has seen nowhere but in his own country. White eyes and orange-winged starlings sing and hop in the pepper trees. Water still drips from his hair but he can sense the coming heat of another summer's day. He wonders why his system still favours ugliness over beauty, anxiety over respite.

★　★　★

As he drives over Hospital Bend onto the upper road into town — De Waal Drive — he sees the black scarring from yet another fire, knows that arson is the most likely cause. He despairs at the meaningless crime that sweeps the city, knows that in this he has no influence, no input: his work is crime premeditated and designed, the motive buried deep in the human psyche, fossilized in the continent's turbulent history or committed by desperate men who believe their only hope of redemption lies in evil.

The umbrella pines, with their thick, corky bark, still stand, charred but alive. The odour of wood-smoke sends his thoughts to Lee-Ann Heyns, to the sex, to her death. His breath catches. He coughs, shifts gear aggressively, hauls his car around the corner, down Roeland Street towards the middle of town.

★　★　★

His squad room is empty, Du Toit's office deserted. He overfills a new filter paper, switches on the coffee machine, heads back to the lifts.

The custody sergeant for the elite units is far less busy than those in regular police stations, yet De Vries finds him with his head on his desk. He has seen him before but does not know his name. 'Long night, Sergeant?'

The officer jolts, sits up, stands shakily. 'Boring, sir.'

'My prisoner?'

'Ms Kemmel? Slept like the dead until her first visitor.'

'Visitor?'

'Lieutenant Esterhuysen, Organized and Drug — '

'I know who he is. When was he here?'

The sergeant runs his thumb down the ledger. 'Seven twelve a.m.'

'What did he want?'

'To speak with Ms Kemmel.'

'You let him?'

He shrugs his shoulders. 'It's not unusual. Happens all the time.'

'With the officer in charge of the case, perhaps. Not visitors, Sergeant. Not with my prisoners.'

'He said he was assigned to the case. He is a lieutenant.'

'You remained outside the cell?'

'No, sir.'

'Why not?'

'I — I usually don't.'

'You hear anything that was said?'

'No, sir.'

'When did he leave?'

'Seven twenty-six, sir.'

De Vries feels muscles and tendons tighten. He rolls his shoulders, stretches his neck. He wonders what Jack Esterhuysen would be doing talking to his suspect, what, in those fourteen minutes, might have been discussed. 'Her *first* visitor?'

'Attorney arrived a few minutes ago . . . at seven fifty-one.'

'A lawyer in the cells before eight? Who is it?'

'Don't know him, sir. Calder. Mr Tim Calder.' He picks up a plain card, hands it to De Vries. 'Of Kriel, Calder. Address in Brie Street.'

De Vries glances at the minimalist lettering, weighs it in his hand. 'This is trouble,' he says. 'Heavier the card, pricier they are.'

⋆ ⋆ ⋆

He finds Du Toit seated at his desk, opposite Major Ngcuka and the Special Crimes Unit's own legal adviser, Norman Classon. Even before he has knocked, he is waved in.

'Heard you were in the building, Colonel,' Du Toit says cheerfully. 'No idea where, so we started talking this through.'

De Vries stands behind the chair he assumes is intended for him, gazes down at Ngcuka and Classon. 'Talking it through?'

'There are matters of jurisdiction, questions surrounding the raid last night. As you are aware, we must be ready with answers before the

110

questions are asked.'

'I have a question,' De Vries says quietly, mimicking the same casual tone Du Toit is affecting. 'Why did one of Major Ngcuka's officers visit my prisoner in her cell this morning without notifying me?'

Du Toit's calm joviality fades. He turns to Ngcuka. 'Major?'

Ngcuka steals a glance at De Vries, refocuses on Du Toit. 'I was not informed until after the event, sir.'

'Of what were you informed?'

'Lieutenant Esterhuysen told me that he had tried to persuade the suspect to confess readily to avoid prolonged interrogation and therefore seek a shorter sentence. It was a ploy, but he feels that it backfired.'

'That was a mistake,' Norman Classon says in his deep and, De Vries thinks, affected voice. 'If she relays this to her attorney, it could be used against us even before an interview has begun.'

'Major?'

Ngcuka shifts. 'Jack Esterhuysen is under great pressure. The wife of one his colleagues has been murdered.'

'And his unit,' De Vries says, 'had failed to make the most basic connections during their lengthy investigation into this criminal group.'

'That is not proven, sir,' Ngcuka says quickly, staring directly at Du Toit.

Du Toit turns to De Vries. 'Sit down, Vaughn.' He waits as De Vries walks around his chair and slowly sits. 'Our most pressing matters are the Independent Police Investigation Department, who are at the scene as we speak. They, and I, wish to know what happened to Warrant Officer Heyns, how the raid was planned and executed. Go about your work as usual, but remain aware that we're being watched.'

It seems to De Vries that he is always under scrutiny: whites watched as closely now as blacks were previously.

'Next is the interrogation of Diane Kemmel. We need to discuss who will be involved and in what capacity.'

De Vries looks at Du Toit, then at Classon. 'With respect, sir, all that requires discussion may be the nature of the approach we take towards this woman. This is our investigation and I will lead the interrogation with one of my officers.'

'I think,' Du Toit says, 'we should consider this a joint operation with Organized Crime and Drug.'

'This has nothing to do with them.'

'Colonel!' Du Toit holds up a palm. 'Every element of the SAPS must operate in harmony. We expect co-operation, and so does Major Ngcuka's unit.' He sees De Vries draw breath, raises his voice: 'As the senior officer heading this inquiry, naturally you will take the lead, but Major Ngcuka will be at your side, lending his expertise and knowledge to your questioning. This approach will be welcomed by those who supervise us. We all need to remember that.' He looks at each of them in turn, finishes at De Vries. He does not lower his eyes until he obtains a tiny acquiescent nod.

* * *

At 10.15 a.m., Diane Kemmel and Attorney Tim Calder are escorted to the main interview room. De Vries and Ngcuka sit across the table from them, knowing that, behind them, beyond the two-way mirror, Du Toit and Classon are observing them.

Ngcuka performs the legal requirements, begins the interview with standard questions of identity, address and other such details.

De Vries stares at Diane Kemmel. She seems older than her declared forty-eight years, her tanned skin stained and blotched, cheeks sagging, neck loose. She has no eyebrows, those previously painted on rubbed away, perhaps during troubled sleep. Without lipstick, her thin lips seem inward-curling, her teeth small and stained. Even her blonde hair seems jaded and dull. However, beyond this tired façade, De Vries reads a calm quite opposite to the anxiety and trepidation he expects to see in a suspect. He notes her body position, inclined slightly towards the attorney at her side.

He turns his gaze to Calder: small, wiry, no more than forty. He can imagine him at a Rondebosch Common Running Club meet after work, panting around the scorched grassland, talking about his body-mass index with fellow professionals over a quinoa salad and light beer in a café afterwards. He does not trust men who drink low-alcohol beer. His close-cut ginger hair and silver spectacles frame a narrow face, eyes pale but intense, focused on a legal pad covered

113

with closely written lines of tiny text.

Ngcuka says: 'What is your relationship to a man called Leon Barker?'

She glances at Calder, turns back. 'None.'

'Did you visit his address on Friday, the twenty-seventh of December?'

'Ja.'

'Why?'

'I was told to.'

'Who by?'

'Ray.'

'Who is Ray?'

'My ex.'

'Your ex-husband, Ray Rossouw?'

'Ja.'

'What did he tell you to do?'

'He didn't tell me, okay? He made me. That's the difference. Deliver the girl to him.'

'What girl?'

'Whichever girl it was that week.'

'What did these girls do?'

She shrugs. 'None of my business.'

'You don't know?'

She faces Ngcuka for the first time, meets his eye. 'Right, I don't know. I might have an idea, but that's only because I work stuff out, put two and two together.'

'What did you think they were doing?'

'Ray had stuff in the house. So they were selling it, carrying it. I don't know.'

'What stuff did Ray have in the house?'

'Drugs shit.'

'He kept drugs in your house?'

'My house? May say that somewhere, but Ray

114

moved back end of April. Not my house any more.'

'So, on the twenty-seventh of December, you delivered a girl to Leon Barker's address. What was her name?'

'Marie.'

'And her family name?'

Diane Kemmel sits up, leans in towards Ngcuka. 'Look, we have a rule. Only first names. They stay with me for two weeks tops, then they go. That's it. I don't know anything else.'

'You returned to Barker's house that night. Why did you do that?'

'Ray wanted her back.'

'Why?'

'Don't know.'

'What happened to Leon Barker?'

'Happened?' She shrugs, but the movement seems false, as if expected of her. 'I took the girl and went home. No idea what Ray and Jan did.'

'Who is Jan?'

'Friend of Ray's. Jan de Mueller. Known each other for ever. Always involved in some kind of shit.'

'Leon Barker was tortured and murdered. You see that happen?'

Kemmel's expression does not change. 'No.'

De Vries studies Diane Kemmel, listens to answers he knows have been prepared. Every question is one on which Calder would have briefed her. He can see the attorney nodding as she recites what he has told her to say; observes Kemmel grow in confidence as her lies begin to mesh together into a defensive position. He

115

wonders whether Ngcuka understands what is happening, or whether, for him, the route is to be marched, regardless that nothing is achieved.

'Where do these girls come from?'

Another shrug. 'All over.'

'How do you meet them?'

'Ray and Jan bring them.'

'And what did you do?'

'What I was told. Took them shopping, bought them clothes, haircuts, make-up. Made them feel like young ladies.'

'Why?'

Diane Kemmel smiles sourly at Ngcuka. 'Because I was told to.'

'Why were there three young women on your property yesterday evening?'

'Ray's property.'

'Okay.'

Kemmel says nothing, just stares blankly at Ngcuka.

'Who were the three women with you last night?'

'Marie, Suzie and some other one.'

'Who were they?'

'I told you. Ray's girls.'

'Two women were cuffed to their beds. Who did that?'

'Ray.'

'Ray?'

'Look. I did what he said or I would've been in their place. Simple.'

Ngcuka turns to De Vries, who gestures to him to continue. 'Describe the events at your property yesterday evening.'

116

'Ray's house.'

'The house is registered to you, Ms Kemmel. That is the law.'

'Lots of things the law says that Ray didn't care about.'

'Your explanation is noted. Last night?'

'We're going to eat. You arrive, burst in, shoot up the place, kill one of my girls, injure another. Don't know what happened to Marie. She alive? Know you shot Jan and Ray. Don't think I'm not grateful. Only way I was getting out was if something like that happened.' She smirks. 'Fucking Ray: used to put a gun in my mouth and tell me if I walked, he'd hunt me down and shoot my fucking head off.'

She looks back at Calder, still silent, still nodding.

Ngcuka waits. Kemmel looks around the room, back to him, realizes they are waiting for her. 'Didn't know what was happening. All that noise. I was terrified, feared for my life.' She emphasizes the last sentence, glares at both policemen, glances at Calder.

'Is that why you grabbed the girl called Marie in the back room and hid behind her?'

'Grabbed her? I didn't grab her. No. We were frightened. Stayed close. Ray's friends are fucking crazy. Didn't know it wasn't them till later. Can't think with guns pointing at you. Heard Suzie upstairs screaming like a banshee — scared me shitless.'

'How many girls have you had staying with you since Ray moved back in?'

'Fifteen, twenty? Lost count. When you do as

you're told, you just do it. You don't think.'

'You know where Ray got the drugs?'

'Was it drugs?'

Ngcuka nods.

'Asked about what he had back there once. Didn't make that mistake again.' She undoes three buttons of her blouse, pulls the top open roughly to reveal a narrow pale scar above her left breast.

'Did Ray do that?'

'That's what he's like.' She smiles again. 'Correction, Officer. What he *was* like — thanks to you.'

De Vries watches Ngcuka recoil minutely.

Suddenly Tim Calder speaks: 'Have you got any questions for my client, Colonel de Vries?'

Echoing Diane Kemmel, he shrugs.

* * *

'Tell me,' De Vries says, as he walks into Steve Ulton's laboratory, 'you have so much forensics on this place that a defence attorney will die of natural causes before he's read it all.'

Ulton smiles. 'There's a lot. Don't know how much helps.'

'Anything may do it.' De Vries looks around the lab. It is as busy as he has ever seen it. 'Any trouble from the Independent Police Investigation Department?'

'Nah. They'll take my results. Benefit of only elite units being involved. Two supervisors over there keeping an eye.'

They walk towards the other end of the lab.

118

'You know my first question?' De Vries asks.

'Who killed Lee-Ann Heyns?'

'*Ja.*'

'I think it's clear-cut. I'll show you in a moment. All the rounds bar one come from weapons belonging to the men shot in the compound. Ray Rossouw and . . . '

'Jan de Mueller.'

'*Ja,* those guys.'

'All but one?'

'It's too early to be certain but there's a round from an R5 rifle, almost certainly from the assault team. Angle of entry suggests it was a ricochet, and not fatal — if she wasn't dead already. We may be able to clarify that uncertainty.'

De Vries swallows. 'But she hadn't been dead long.'

'Judging by the estimates I've been given, no. Perhaps they shot her when they heard the assault.'

'That's not good.'

'She would have been in a bad way, Vaughn. There are high levels of drugs in her system, cuts and bruises, burn marks.'

'Jesus . . . '

'I'm sorry I can't be definite.'

'What about the girl, Suzie Rice?'

'Haven't had a chance to examine her. She was taken to hospital. Far as I know, she's still there.'

'But, first impressions, it looks like our boys are in the clear?'

Ulton turns to him. 'Was there any doubt?'

'Always doubt.'

'For Heyns, it looks that way.' He guides De Vries over to a long desk at the far end of his lab, covered with bagged evidence, docket reports, test results. 'You look at her car?'

'Whose?'

'Diane Kemmel's. It's in the vehicle bay.'

'What about it?'

Ulton laughs. 'She likes a smoke. Hundreds of butts — genuinely hundreds — in everything: ashtrays, but also glove compartment, cubbies, down the seats, all over the floor. She's an animal.'

'Nice.'

Ulton clears his throat, returns to the table in front of them. 'We have identified fingerprints and DNA belonging to Rossouw and De Mueller all over the utility area at the back of the house. We can link them to the drugs recovered, approximately a hundred grams of cocaine . . . very pure. On the street, it would be cut, maybe one part to twenty of filler.'

'I don't think they were selling here. Buying, more likely, then moving it on to Thailand. I don't like that there's so little.'

'A lot for local dealing, but for a big operation, international, agreed, it's not much, but that's all that was found. We still have people there.' He waits for De Vries to speak again, then continues, 'Two weapons they used to defend themselves at the scene. One weapon links to the shooting of Leon Barker — definite match.' He points to the far end of the bench. 'Full arsenal they had — handguns, three rifles,

120

two shotguns, something like thirty knives.'

'Any prints from others?'

'Not on the weapons. Looks like it was just those two.'

'What have you got on Diane Kemmel?'

'She's all over the house, obviously. Nothing on any of the weapons so far. We'll keep working.' He pulls an evidence bag forward. 'See these cuffs. These were found on Suzie Rice. They have partials from Diane Kemmel on them. She handled them, but whether she put them on the girl, I can't tell you.'

De Vries nods. 'That's all I need for now. I'll need more in due course. I want her kept here until we have everything.'

'Gather you didn't get much from her.'

'Is that what you heard?'

'Is it not right?'

'I didn't speak to her.'

Ulton frowns.

'Interdepartmental co-operation, Steve. Major Ngcuka from Organized and Drug ran through the preliminaries with her. She was very fluent.'

'Fluent?'

'Coached. Expensively.'

'Plenty of money in her business. What's she like?'

De Vries laughs. Ulton usually shows no curiosity in personality: his interests lie solely in suspects' excretions.

'Just as you'd expect. A real lady.'

★   ★   ★

De Vries sits in another chair, another office.

Sergeant Sally Frazer says, 'We've only had a casual chat with the two girls, Suzie Rice and Marie Smith. Suzie says Kemmel picked her up at the top of Long Street. We've found some footage of Kemmel, but she's just there, on the street.' She turns towards the monitors, which line one wall of the small technical booth. 'Marie Smith claims she's from Port Elizabeth. She's refused to give an address for her parents' house. It may be that they have no address, that they're living in a camp, but PE police have no criminal record for her or, if they exist, her parents.'

'When did she come to Cape Town?'

'She didn't come, she was brought. She was told that she would be given a lift on the thirteenth of December. She wouldn't tell me what happened, but whatever it was, it wasn't nice.'

'And then she falls into Kemmel's hands?'

'We have Diane Kemmel chaperoning other girls, but not Marie.' She leans over him, pointing at the three left-hand screens, displaying three different day and date readings. Constable Joey Morten who, to De Vries, exists nowhere but in this tiny room, surrounded by his horseshoe of screens, reels off the segments he has already documented.

'This confirms what she said in interview,' Frazer says, 'about taking the girls shopping, for make-overs, et cetera.'

De Vries looks up at her.

'Anything she said she did that wasn't illegal is true. Everything else is shit. That's how it works.'

'Look at this, then.'

Frazer nods to Morten. More shots of a mall appear on screen.

'Oh, shit,' De Vries says. 'This is depressing.'

Century City is a shopping and residential development on a grand but, ultimately, rather cheap scale, maybe twenty kilometres out of town. 'Since when did shopping become entertainment?'

Morten slows the action. Frazer leans forward, points at the screen. 'That is Diane Kemmel. She entered the mall alone twelve minutes earlier.'

De Vries squints at the tiny figures in front of him. 'I don't get it.'

'Watch her . . . and watch this girl here.' She indicates a second figure sitting on a bench looking over the busy corridor of shoppers. After a moment, the girl gets up, begins to follow an elderly woman, who is limping slowly across the concourse.

'Now look at Kemmel.'

He sees Diane Kemmel set off after the girl, getting closer. The girl approaches the older woman from behind, begins to tuck in next to her handbag, then trips and stumbles against it. De Vries cannot see what she does next, but her left hand is out of view behind, or within, the handbag. Whatever the girl is attempting is cut short by Diane Kemmel, who takes her right arm and pulls her away. The girl seems empty-handed. He watches Diane Kemmel walk her forcibly towards the camera and out of sight. He looks up at Morten, who presses some

123

buttons, then stares at the main screen. In front of him, looking from a reverse angle, De Vries can see Diane Kemmel and the girl talking; Kemmel gesticulates.

'Can we get closer?'

'Not without losing too much definition.'

'We have no idea what's going on.'

'Watch for a moment longer, sir.'

De Vries sees the women walk away to the exit. The screen goes blank, flashes, then illuminates with an even grainier black and white picture of the exit to the underground car parks. Morten zooms in on the occupants of a white Mercedes SLK: Kemmel and the girl.

'What this almost certainly shows,' Frazer says, as the screens freeze on the final shot of the two women, 'is that Diane Kemmel was not merely shopping and guarding these girls, she was actively recruiting them. The girl appears to be attempting to steal from the victim's handbag. We've looked back, followed her. She comes in early in the morning and, basically, scavenges. She's quite subtle, but that's what she's doing. She gets two guys to give her their half-full cigarette packet at an outside café, then finds a partially drunk coffee. She sits there for the best part of an hour, watching passers-by. We lose her again as she goes inside, but she's grifting one way or another. Kemmel spots her and pounces. Maybe threatens her, maybe just seduces her with whatever she has to offer, but that girl gets in her car and leaves with her.'

'Can you identify her?'

'If she's been reported missing, possibly.'

De Vries studies the pixelated face of the girl in the car, wonders where she is: in Thailand, a rich woman, or in jail? In a brothel, lying dead, bruised, cut and raped, in a ditch beside a palm-lined road? He does not know her, but he wants to save her. He looks up at Frazer, across to Joey Morten. 'That's really good.'

★　★　★

Marie Smith sprawls in De Vries's office, yawning, blinking, hands shaking. She has scarcely spoken since she was released from Diane Kemmel's compound. She has spent the night waiting at the hospital to be checked over, slept sporadically in the basic room provided for her when no home address was forthcoming.

De Vries reads fear in her, but also a brooding teenage disillusionment. He dismisses the officer who has escorted her. He sits next to her, smiles, says nothing while she sips from a mug of coffee, watches the tiny ripples across the surface of the tepid, scummy drink.

'Are you all right?'

She nods, eyes focused on the diminishing contents of the mug.

'I need your help, Marie. Can you help me?'

Her shoulder twitches. He sits back, looks at her painted toes wiggling in cheap sandals, her scratched white legs, light denim skirt, plain blue T-shirt, the crude tattoo of a red angel on her forearm. 'The clothes okay? We'll return the ones you were wearing when we've finished with them here.'

'I don't want them.'

Her voice is so quiet, head still angled down, that De Vries scarcely hears her.

'Where do you live? Do you have an address?'

She shakes her head again, but says, 'Live with my mum. Dad went. I wanted to go too.'

'Go where?'

'Anywhere.'

'Why?'

She looks up, stares past him, then her eyes fall again. 'Cos there's nothing there. No work, no chance.'

'Where?'

'PE.' She looks up at him. 'You been there?'

De Vries nods. Port Elizabeth is 750 kilometres along the south coast of Africa from Cape Town; maybe twenty years behind. 'Who recruited you?'

'There were three of us, but I don't know what happened to the other two. A woman called Leslie. I met her at the Boardwalk . . . '

'The casino?'

'Yeah. She was nice, at first. Got me some clothes I wasn't ashamed of. Clean, new. Told me she'd get me work, get me out of PE, maybe even travel. Said I was like her, but now she was doing well. She'd got her own place, a car, some money . . . ' She drains the mug, puts it down, rubs her eyes.

'What happened next?'

'Told my mum. She laughed at me, told me no one does anything for nothing.'

'You went back to this Leslie?'

'What else is there? Mum can't work. I've

126

tried for waitress jobs, kitchen, cleaning. There's nothing. We live in one room. One room all the time.'

'What did Leslie say you could do?'

'Delivering something to Thailand, maybe get a job there. Nothing fancy, but enough to save a little, come back.'

'Delivering what?'

'She didn't say, but once I got to Diane's house, I knew.'

'How did you travel to Diane's house?'

Marie Smith's shoulders slump, her eyes moisten. 'It was like a nightmare.'

Her voice is still tiny and shrill, as if her throat is constricted. It is, De Vries thinks, the voice of a child. He waits, stays silent until she has wiped away tears, pulled herself up. She stares ahead, says nothing.

'I need your help. I want the men and women who took you, who mistreated you. Can you remember how you got to Cape Town?'

He sees the pain in her face, hears her breath quicken, tighten.

'This guy comes to Leslie's house in an old car . . . I don't know what. I didn't like him, but I had no choice. I got in. We drove out of town, past the airport, onto the freeway, the N2, *ja*? He doesn't say anything until we get to this Engen garage on a side-road, tells me to get out, walks me to the toilets. He waits outside. When we get back to the car . . . I don't know . . . ' She starts to sob. 'He hits me . . . picks me up, pushes me into the boot, slams the lid. It's dark and hot and I can't breathe.'

De Vries wishes he had Sally Frazer with him, someone who might put an arm around her.

'Every time we stopped I screamed, but nothing happened . . . '

De Vries speaks quietly, gently. 'How long were you in there?'

'I don't know. I thought I was going to die. I was so hot. I thought I'd puke . . . '

'An hour? Two hours?'

She shrugs, her face drained. She stares at him and her head bows again. She whispers, not looking at him.

'Can I have a drink?'

'A cool drink?'

'*Ja.*'

De Vries shouts for the officer outside the door, asks what Marie would like, repeats it to the officer. As he turns, De Vries says, 'Leave the door open.'

Marie Smith looks up, stares at the open door.

'You remember anything about this man, the driver?'

She nods. 'White guy, with greasy hair, silvery, in a ponytail. He had veins on his face . . . and a tattoo on his chest, right here. A South African flag — an old one: orange, white and blue stripes.'

'Where did he drive you, Marie?'

'I don't know where. It was a warehouse or a garage. There were some wrecks, old cars, machinery. It seemed to be in the country but I could hear a road. Could have been anywhere.'

'Anything you remember?'

'I was tired. My whole body hurt. I was

bruised. They took me and handcuffed me to some metal pipes.'

De Vries hates making people recount torment. He empathizes with the victim when the prosecuting attorney makes them tell their story for the jury because it makes them suffer all over again but, without her information, he knows he cannot move on, cannot stop these people. 'You were there overnight?'

'I think they gave me something. I didn't feel right. Like I was drunk. In the night, some man came over to me, kissed me on the lips . . . then he . . . '

Behind cupped hands, De Vries sees her face convulse, the tears flow, her body shuddering. He finds himself drawn to this slight, desperate girl; finds himself emotionally caught up in her story.

'You want to talk to my female colleague, Sally?'

She shakes her head. 'He ripped my skirt. You saw it? He put his fingers in me. I tried to push him away but I had one hand tied and the other . . . felt so heavy.'

'You tell the doctor about this?'

She nods. 'The man pushed my head back . . . by my neck . . . ' She displays the light bruise line across her throat. 'He was so rough, so horrible. He had his hand on my mouth.'

De Vries holds up his hand. 'You don't have to tell me.'

'I do. I do. He raped me. He tied me up and raped me. He put all his weight on me so I couldn't move, couldn't escape, and then he

129

pushed my blouse over my face and he . . . raped me.' She says the words, then looks him in the eye. To say it out loud has strengthened her.

'Not the man who drove you?'

'No. He was there before. This was someone else. He was shorter, tattoos on his arms, like ivy. Green leaves. I couldn't see his face. When I was lying there afterwards, I tried to look at it.'

The officer knocks on the open door, hands Marie a can of Grapetiser and a plastic cup.

She cracks it open, drinks from the can.

When she puts it down, De Vries says, 'You stay in this warehouse more than one night?'

Marie shakes her head. 'They put a blindfold on me, tell me if I leave it on I can sit in the front. When we get close to Cape Town, he tells me I can take it off.'

'You remember him? Remember the car?'

'It was Leon. Old maroon car. He drove to Diane's house. I was so happy to see her, another woman, but she wouldn't listen. I told her I wanted to go, but she said it was too late now. She'd invested in me. I had to pay her back or she said Ray would fuck with me. She made me swallow some packets, but I couldn't. Kept gagging, throwing up. They said they'd find a way . . . '

De Vries thinks about dead cows, wonders whether Marie Smith was to have been their sacrifice to clear the way for other girls with bigger guts, a lifetime in a brutal Thai jail. A short life for a girl like this. 'You were there for, what? A week?'

She nods. 'I thought I was going soon. They

130

took me to Leon's house. He told me I'd be on my way. Then Diane and the men came and took me back. I tried to get out, but the whole place is locked down all the time. She handcuffed me to the bed in the room at night.' Her eyes redden, her arms start to shake, her hands claw at thin air. 'Ray and the other guy would come in . . . '

De Vries looks away, lets the silence stretch as she composes herself. He despises this time, when he feels nothing but shame in between each pulse in his wrist, his neck. It is so quiet, he can hear his blood inside his head.

'They undressed me and stared at me. They . . . '

'You don't have to say. They're dead, Marie. My men took them down. Diane Kemmel is in the cells. None of them will ever hurt you again.'

'I saw names in the warehouse on the wall. They did this before to more girls.'

'We know that now.'

'Ray and the other guy. I'm sure they hurt another girl. I heard her screaming. Lee-Ann? I was so frightened, I puked everywhere. I thought I was next. Then I heard gunshots.'

'Was this yesterday?'

She nods.

'She was screaming before the police arrived?'

'In the afternoon, again in the evening.'

'How long before we arrived?'

'Two hours, three?'

'You're safe now.'

She stares ahead blindly, the adrenalin wearing

131

off. De Vries sees her energy wane, the joy of even being alive pall, as her memories flood her brain.

'It was my fault. I was stupid.'

'No. You were looking for something better, but you found something worse.'

She says, determined, 'I can't go back.'

He opens his mouth to speak, finds his throat dry, checks himself.

'What did you say?' he finally says.

'I can't go back.'

'Where? Where can't you go back?'

'Home.'

De Vries wishes he had one thing to offer her, one fragment of hope, a tiny chance, but he has less than Diane Kemmel. He sits still and silent as self-disgust weighs down on him.

★   ★   ★

He is about to go into Director du Toit's office when his cell phone rings. He sees John Marantz's number displayed, silences the handset, knocks on the door, enters.

'I hope,' Du Toit says, 'that you have been busy.'

'Very.'

'To what end?'

'Building a case against Diane Kemmel, understanding her and her operation, how they recruited their girls, where they've ended up. We've identified a few of them from documents discovered in the Kemmel compound, matched two to missing-person reports. I'm waiting for information from the South African consulate in Bangkok.'

'What, then, was the point of this morning's interview?'

'It was a standard preliminary. It allowed Diane Kemmel to think she had answers to our questions.'

'Did she not?'

'She had answers to Ngcuka's questions. It also served to allow the Major to be involved.'

Du Toit sighs. 'That's not really the point, Vaughn. Ngcuka was pissed off with you already. Then you say nothing in the interview and stalk off. I am trying to persuade him to accept that this joint operation could reflect well on him and his department, to drop his complaints about you . . .'

'It'll reflect well on him if he stays out of it.'

'Listen to me,' Du Toit says. 'Ngcuka is involved whether you like it not. It plays well with General Thulani and it is keeping Wertner off your back, so live with it. Multiracial, interdepartmental co-operation. It couldn't be better.'

De Vries sighs. 'Yes, sir, you're right. It's Paradise.'

'When are you talking to Kemmel again?'

'Soon. When we have everything we need.'

'I want to know before she goes back into that interview room, and I want Ngcuka there. You understand?'

'You don't need to worry, sir,' De Vries says. 'I'm ready to play the game.'

★　★　★

133

He presses the dial button, hears ringing.

'Vaughn?' Marantz's voice is different. He cannot discern how.

'What is it?'

'They found them.'

'What?'

'They found them. Rosie, Caro.'

His wife, his daughter. Seven years gone.

'John?'

'They're dead.'

'I'm coming now.'

★　★　★

The huge double-doors are closed. De Vries walks across the room to Marantz, hears his footsteps echo through the house. 'What's happened?'

'They've found my wife. They've found my daughter.' Marantz's face is swollen, eyes bloodshot. His hands shake.

'Have you been drinking?'

'No.'

'What do you mean they've found them?'

'I don't know. No details. They've identified two bodies discovered in the ground near a house they'd been watching. It's them.' He seems out of breath.

'They're certain?'

'They say so.'

'I'm sorry, John.'

'We knew they were dead.'

'We almost knew.'

'I'm going to London. Tonight. I'm going in a few minutes.'

'Is that a good idea?'

'Of course it's a good idea. Of course it fucking is . . . because until I see them, until I know, it's not over. It's never been over.'

'Shit, John. You need to get to the airport?'

'Taxi. It's fine. I'm numb. Got a flat seat on the plane. I'm going to lie awake all night in comfort.'

'You have someone the other end?'

'They know I'm coming. I'll be chaperoned.'

De Vries sits opposite him. 'I'm sorry.'

'I need a favour.'

'Go on.'

'I need you to take Flynn.'

'I can't, John. I'm in the middle of something. I'm not even going home some nights.'

'It's okay. Leave him at your place. Just make sure there's water — lots of water. Leave him in the garden. He'll be okay. He knows your place.'

'It's not a good idea. Can you rather ask a neighbour?' Marantz shakes his head. 'Jesus, I don't even feed myself, let alone a dog.'

'Please, Vaughn. You're the only other person he knows.'

★ ★ ★

De Vries stays until Marantz's taxi has taken him. He checks each door and window in the house, sets the alarm, locks the front door with the spare key Marantz has given him. He calls the dog, watches it trot to the car, jump into the back while De Vries holds the door. By the time he is behind the wheel, the dog is sitting neatly

135

in the passenger seat, looking out of the windscreen expectantly, tongue out.

⋆　⋆　⋆

The traffic crawls out of a bleached city to the greener suburbs. Even in dark glasses with his visor down, the glare blinds him. His mind riffs on the hopelessness of Marantz's journey, his own plans for Diane Kemmel, what he will do to find all the people who have destroyed the lives of these girls.

He changes down a gear as he takes the sharp curves of De Waal Drive, sees that the queue out of town stretches right back to the raised section of Nelson Mandela Boulevard. Beyond it, the sea is shimmering black and white behind the sparkling ligaments of huge container cranes, scaffolds on unending developments, the enormous oil rig in dock for servicing.

⋆　⋆　⋆

De Vries sees him, outside his office, before he is seen. He does not know him, but he knows who he is. The inevitability of the moment smothers his fear. 'Lieutenant Immelman.'

The man jumps, spins towards him. 'Sir.'

'Come with me.'

De Vries knows without looking that the man is following him. He walks to the lifts, steps back into the one he has just left, waits until Immelman is beside him. They stand apart, in silence, for the long time it takes to descend a few floors. De Vries walks out into the foyer, across the expanse of grey linoleum.

In the street, he turns to Immelman. 'You drink?'

Immelman nods.

De Vries crosses two roads, strides up Long Street until he reaches Longmarket Street. He looks up at the ornate iron and glass lantern, weaves past hawkers wheeling their unsold wares to tiny lock-ups on old-fashioned carts, stolen porter's trolleys, supermarket trolleys, waits to cut across them into the entrance to a closed and empty restaurant. He walks past a security guard, up a long staircase. At the top, he turns right, enters the little rooftop bar.

He waves at the barman.

'We okay?'

The man squints at him, the recognition reluctant, nods.

'A beer, then. East Coast Ale.' He turns to Immelman. 'Beer?'

Immelman nods. They are in the eaves of a tall old building. At this hour, Tjing Tjing bar is deserted.

De Vries hands him his glass, takes the other, walks out onto the small terrace overlooking the fire escapes and air-conditioning vents of the surrounding buildings.

They sit across from one another, under a pergola, and drink without toasting.

De Vries says, 'They're closed until six.'

'I want to talk to you off the record.'

'That's why we're here.'

★ ★ ★

137

Marantz boards early, finds the first-class cabin empty, takes his seat: 1A. He calls the cabin-service director.

'My wife and daughter are dead. Tell them not to bring me alcohol, even if I beg.'

★ ★ ★

De Vries recounts everything that happened from the moment he arrived at the DF Malan Motel to the moment he saw Lee-Ann Heyns's body in the Kemmel house. He leaves out only his home, banks on Immelman not knowing where his wife slept that night.

Immelman says, 'You seconded her to your team. I talked to Captain Maart at Rondebosch. He spoke to you.'

'My warrant officer is on leave. She was good. She knew her job. It made sense.'

'She went fucking under cover and you left her there.'

'No.' De Vries lowers his voice, tries to appear calm. 'When we had confirmed the location, she suggested that to me. I've told you this. I would never put an officer in that situation. It was unknown and extremely dangerous. She left our building and I never saw or spoke to her again. I didn't know she was in that building. When she went AWOL, I suspected it. That's why we raided the compound when we did. Before we should have.'

He watches Immelman's face, knows that he is fighting what the man believes.

'You let her go. You let her walk into that

138

house.' A second beer has begun to loosen his reserve.

'I did not. Your wife was obsessed with her career, her rank, her ambition. She wanted to make a point, and it was the wrong decision.'

Immelman is breathing hard. He says nothing.

'Why call herself Heyns, not Immelman?'

'Because at work she wasn't my wife. She was a cop. That's how it was with her. Fucking feminist fucking shit.'

So much pain.

'She played you, didn't she?' Immelman says suddenly.

De Vries looks at him. 'What?'

'She's done it before, with other officers. She says she can't get a chance, never gets a hearing, so she finds a way to be involved.'

'She was at a scene. She claimed she heard the call-out.'

'Like I said, she played you. What did she do?'

De Vries feigns incomprehension.

'All right,' Immelman says. 'I'll tell you. She gets there ahead of you. She sets up a team. Does it perfectly, gets everyone motivated and working for her. And then you arrive and she's there, installed, and there's nothing you can do. Am I right?'

'More or less.'

'Ja. She was good, and nobody told her, nobody rewarded her. And I know why. She's a threat, so she gets rejected and then she turns it up a notch. That's what she did, didn't she?' Immelman studies him.

De Vries feels himself colour.

'She fuck you?'

'She fucked up.'

'You fucked her, didn't you?'

'No.'

He tilts forward, facing De Vries. 'I know you fucked her. And you know what? She probably fucking enjoyed it.'

'No.' De Vries hears himself repeat the same word, hears the conviction ebb from the single syllable.

Immelman empties his glass slowly, swallows, springs out of his chair and launches himself at De Vries, catches him on the right cheek with his fist, falls between the table and the bench. De Vries pulls himself up, ignores the searing pain in his cheek, pins Immelman to the decking floor beneath him. He glances up, sees the tall barman standing a few metres from him, shakes his head, watches the man lope back to the bar. Beneath him, Immelman lies still, breathing heavily. Beneath his feet, De Vries can feel his shuddering through the decking.

★ ★ ★

Third and fourth beers stand between them. Immelman has retaken his seat opposite De Vries, head bowed. De Vries waits silently until he looks up again.

'I'm not sorry.'

'But you're wrong.'

'You were responsible.'

'I was responsible until she was dismissed. I told you what she said: she was single, alone. We drank. I like women, but not other people's.'

Immelman snorts. 'Like I said, it wasn't the first time.'

'I'm sorry. I'm sorry for what happened afterwards too, but I can't control an officer after they've left work.'

There is a long silence. Then Immelman says, 'No.'

They drink wordlessly for a few minutes.

'I need to ask you about Major Ngcuka's unit.'

'What?'

'I need to talk to you about your unit.'

Immelman slams down his glass. 'No, you're not doing this. We talk about Lee-Ann for . . . what?' He twists his wrist, looks at his watch. 'For twenty fucking minutes. And then you want to question me. No fucking way.'

'If I could wait, I would. We're talking about the lives of young girls here.'

'No, we're talking about Lee-Ann here.'

'Lieutenant. For Christ's sake, let's make what Lee-Ann did worth something. Otherwise . . . Jesus, what's it all for?'

'How did they even know who she was?'

'These people have contacts everywhere. We're working up the line. We'll find them.'

'But she was good. They had to know.'

'That,' De Vries says quietly, 'is why I need to talk about your unit.'

★　★　★

He walks back to his building as dusk descends. Long Street illuminates, animates with the lights

141

and music of bars and restaurants. Tourists and locals in pre-New Year mood meander past the child grifters and shifty hawkers. On the Victorian wrought-iron terraces, students drink and smoke and laugh. Bars and cafés overflow onto the pavement, bikers congregate outside a neon-lit tattoo parlour while smart middle-aged couples duck down side-streets to tapas bars and pop-up supper clubs.

De Vries walks downhill blindly, relying on others to dodge him, thinks of nothing but what he is to do. He has forgotten Immelman and Lee-Ann Heyns, his lies, the pain in his face and chest. The pressure to drive forward suffocates him, charges him. He understands that he cannot make a mistake now, that everything before will parlay into everything to come. He hates feeling this way; he loves how he feels.

★ ★ ★

The small cell block for the Special Crimes Unit is quiet and dark. De Vries has fought against its use as an overflow for the Central Division: knows that if his unit's suspects are held among drunks and street criminals, the power of silent confinement is undermined.

The same custody sergeant sits behind his desk — alert this evening — accompanied by a young black constable.

'Just Kemmel?'

'Yes, sir.'

'She been fed and watered?'

'On schedule, to the minute.'

142

'Good, Sergeant. And, today, any more unexpected visitors?'

'No, sir. Her attorney left at . . . fifteen twenty-seven, reminded me to inform him the moment you intended any further questioning of his client.'

'I'm sure you won't forget.' He places a coffee in a plastic cup on the desk, leans over it, points to a small portable radio. 'Turn that on.' He straightens, feels for his cigarettes, puts one between his lips.

'Sir?'

'You haven't seen me, Sergeant.'

'The smoke alarms are very sensitive.'

'Then it's right we test them. Listen to your radio, gentlemen.'

He turns, picks up the coffee in one hand, a grey stacking plastic chair in the other, strolls towards the small cell block, through the unlocked main barred door, into the thick scent of disinfectant towards the end cell. The perished rubber feet of the chair caterwaul as they scrape along the linoleum floor.

Diane Kemmel is sitting on the concrete bench, head back against the wall, eyes squeezed shut.

'Awake?'

Her n-shaped lips smile bitterly for a split second, revert. 'Give me a cigarette?'

Amid a stream of blue smoke: 'No smoking in here.'

She sniffs, repositions her head.

'Of course,' De Vries says, positioning the chair, sitting, 'if we were chatting, maybe we

143

could share a cigarette . . . '

'Fuck off.'

De Vries sits back, lifts the coffee onto a flat horizontal cell bar at knee height, smokes slowly. When the ash has grown, he takes an empty plastic cup from his pocket, places it beside him, taps into it. When he has finished the first, he lights a second cigarette with a match, gently blows the sulphurous smoke towards her. He smiles when she looks up, empathizes with the desire a struck match can ignite: the sound, the smell.

She slides along the bench until she is sitting at right angles to her previous position, facing him.

'Coffee's for you.'

She stares at it, pouts, reaches over to take it.

'Sugar?'

'Three.'

She sips, sips again.

'Who pays your legal bills, Diane?'

'Don't know.'

'You called them.'

'Had a card in my bag.'

'Who gave it to you?'

'Don't remember.'

'Lawyers can only work with what they're given. You're on film recruiting girls in Century City. Your prints are on the cuffs used to imprison them. There are statements from the two women discovered in your compound — they told me what you did and when . . . '

'They didn't see anything. Drugged anyway.'

'By you . . . '

'By Ray and Jan. Not me.'

'Details. Witnesses placing you at the scene of the torture and murder of Leon Barker.'

Diane Kemmel chews imaginary gum. 'At the scene . . . collecting Marie. Not doing anything.'

'Fingerprints on cuffs and other restraints, in the rooms where the girls were kept, on videotape, Diane . . . '

'Duress.'

'Good word. No one to testify to that. Your word, your record. They don't mean much. Anyway, you have to get to court first.'

He watches her blank face, observes the formation of a tiny frown, knows that Diane Kemmel is aware of South African procedure: suspects awaiting trial go to prison — maximum security prison — until fully processed. Some are dead in a day.

She sits frozen but for her right arm, lifting the cup to her lips.

'What did Lieutenant Esterhuysen say to you this morning?'

'Who?'

'The officer who spoke to you before your lawyer arrived.'

'Nothing.'

'For fourteen minutes?'

'*Ja.*'

'You sure?'

'Wanted a deal.'

'What deal?'

'Give up what I knew, maybe cut my time.'

'That's what friends are for.'

'You people aren't my friends.'

'I am.'

Kemmel laughs hoarsely. 'Course you are.'

He hands her the remains of his cigarette. She takes it, draws deeply, holds the smoke inside her, exhales only a thin, pale stream of dirty breath. She looks down at the stub, reckons there is no more than a burning filter, flicks it out of her cell on to the floor of the corridor.

One hot tip, rich and sticky — totally unsatisfying.

He lights another. Still no alarm. He smiles to himself. 'Listen to me carefully. You're about to choose between life and death. Your life, your death.' She looks away.

He stays silent until she tilts her head, waits until her eyes meet his. 'One week from now, either you'll look back at this moment and realize you made the right decision, or you'll be dead. I promise you: one or the other.'

'Right.' She nods to herself, smiles half-heartedly, starts tapping her right foot, looking around the cell. After maybe two minutes, she turns back to him. 'What?'

'If you haven't been told about me, then I'll tell you now. I don't small-talk, I don't bullshit. What I say I'll do, I always do. You fuck about with me, and you'll be remanded to Pollsmoor Prison — don't think your expensive attorney will swing it because he won't — and everyone will know who you are and what you do. Everyone will know you've talked, even if you don't — maybe they'll hear it's young kids, not women — and all that will happen will be a race to fuck you up. You want to know the figures

146

— the rapes, the injuries, the murders? I can guarantee your safety or . . . ' He lowers his voice, cups his hand around his mouth, 'I can guarantee your death.'

Kemmel swallows. 'Maybe I'll ask my attorney.'

'Ask him and the offer's gone. I'll save you if you give up what you know. You don't, you're dead.'

Her eyes widen minutely. He sees the pulse in her neck quicken.

'Give me another cigarette.'

'No.'

'I'm not talking.'

De Vries stands. 'Then you're not talking ever again.'

He turns. He has witnessed her expression change in the last few moments, hopelessness dull her eyes. In the silence, he knows now what he will hear. He takes a first step, a second.

'Wait.'

He does not move. He pulls a cigarette from his pocket, lights it.

'Maybe I'll talk to you.'

He turns around. 'Maybe?'

'Give me a cigarette.'

He passes the end of his cigarette through the bars, puts the fresh one between his lips.

'You're a mean cunt.'

'I am.'

★   ★   ★

'You wanted to be informed, sir.'

Henrik du Toit stands in beige chinos and a

147

checked shirt. He smells of *braai* smoke. 'What made her change her mind?'

'Process.'

'Process?'

'What lies ahead if she doesn't co-operate.'

'Her attorney may not feel that is inevitable.'

'I made it clear I thought it was. She seemed to believe me.'

'I'm assuming this was off the record?'

'Off the record, just like the conversation she had with the leader of the Drug Squad unit.'

'Stay away from that, Vaughn. You have enough on your plate.'

'Coffee and nicotine . . . '

'And Ngcuka?'

'On his way. I don't want her sleeping on it and changing her mind.'

'Her attorney will object.'

'She waived her rights. She doesn't want him.'

Du Toit shakes his head very slowly. 'You'd better make damn certain that's one hundred per cent clear. You know what a defence attorney can do with that?'

'*Ja.*'

'When?'

'Now. Right now. That's the point. The moment Ngcuka arrives.'

'Why does nothing ever seem quite right with you?'

'Because when it feels right, it's not being done right.'

'General Thulani thinks you're a dangerous liability.'

'And what do you think, sir?'

★ ★ ★

Diane Kemmel sits straight, hands clasped tightly on the table. Ngcuka sits forward nervously. De Vries runs through the textbook preliminaries, emphasizes that she is happy to proceed without her attorney.

'You have agreed to answer my questions in full and to pass on to me any and all information on your activities with Ray Rossouw and Jan de Mueller?

'Yes.'

De Vries nods. 'How did you become involved in the procurement and imprisoning of women prior to their carrying narcotics to foreign countries?'

'I told you before. Ray came back. You people dealt with him in the past. Look at his record. My ex-husband doesn't discuss things. He just does what he wants. Always has. I didn't have a choice. Couldn't pay the bond on the house, couldn't sell it. I would've had nothing. He said we could use it together, pay off the bond, make some money for a new start. Knew it would be *crook*, but what can you do?'

'How did you choose the girls?'

'They wanted white girls . . . '

'Why?'

'I don't know. How many blacks fly to Thailand?'

'How did you choose the girls?'

'They chose me.' She flares her nostrils, tilts her head backwards in pride. 'You think there aren't plenty who want to get away? You're probably from the Southern Suburbs — it's not like that further out. I could have found a thousand in Brooklyn alone, but he said he wanted girls with a bit of class. Up in town, Century City — city's full of 'em. Pretending they're something. But they're not. We're not. These days, we're the ones living in the fucking squatter camps.' She juts her chin at Ngcuka.

'Just in Cape Town?'

'Anywhere we wanted.'

'Durban, Port Elizabeth, Pretoria . . . ?'

'Not Jo'burg or Pretoria — Ray said another group had Gauteng.'

'What did you do?'

'Talk to them. Convince them. That's all I did. Any nasty stuff is down to Ray and his sick little friend.'

'Jan de Mueller?'

'Ja.'

'They ever come back? The girls?'

'Not yet. They've got people in Bangkok. Don't know what they do with them there.'

'Don't care?'

'Live like us for a few years,' Kemmel says bitterly. 'See if you care.'

'Who's they?'

'They?'

'The people in Bangkok. Who are they?'

'Friends of Ray's? Whoever's idea this is. We're just part of it.'

'Never met them? Spoken to them?'

'No.'

'Where do the drugs come from?'

'Don't know.'

'Are they delivered? Did Ray bring them?'

'Ray and Jan,' Kemmel says. 'Every couple of months. Got tanked up, went out at night, came back, locked something away. Probably drugs. I didn't ask.'

'Where did they go?'

'Don't know.'

'How long were they gone?'

'Few hours, overnight sometimes. Heard them saying never the same place twice. Ray's always been careful.'

'I need more.'

'There isn't more.'

'What did they say?'

'Nothing.'

De Vries forces his brain to process what he has learned. 'There were a hundred grams in your house. Why so little?'

Kemmel ponders. 'We were low. They were talking about a collection. Something about the Yacht Club and fireworks.'

'The Yacht Club?'

'Just what they said . . . Meeting in Jo'burg afterwards.'

'They go to Jo'burg often?'

'I told you: no.'

'Never?'

She shrugs her shoulders. 'Not since they've been at my place.'

'Tell me about the girl, Lee-Ann.'

'She claimed she knew a girl, Chantal. Said she wanted in, wanted to follow her out to Thailand.'

'Who's Chantal?'

'Girl we were sending. Fucking slit her wrists when she was with that fucker Leon.'

'What happened to Leon?'

'We went to get the next girl back . . . Marie. Ray was going to fuck Leon up for not doing his job. I took the girl, they stayed behind. That's all I know.'

'They told you they were going to 'fuck Leon up'?'

'Yeah.'

'What happened to Lee-Ann?'

'Why do you care?'

De Vries feels Ngcuka turn, ignores him. 'Everyone should care. They're girls. Just poor, desperate girls.'

'She wasn't.'

'What do you mean?'

'Something about her. Was she one of yours?'

'No.'

'Ray thought she was. That's why he did her and nearly me too.'

'Ray killed her?'

'Ray and Jan. More likely Ray.'

'You saw Ray and Jan go to her room?'

'I saw them. Didn't wait for them to see me.'

De Vries feels Ngcuka relax. He shifts in his chair. De Vries wills him to keep still, to stay focused on Diane Kemmel. 'Who got Ray into this?'

'Don't know. Didn't ask.'

'He mention any names? Any locations?'

Kemmel affects to think. 'You promised no prison. I stay in the cells here, yeah?'

'You'll be detained in these cells, yes.'

She gurns. 'The lawyer. Ray gave me the card — said his mate, Carl, gave it to him, told him if we get in trouble we call the number.'

'Who's Carl?'

'Don't know. That's what Ray said. I gave you a name. Full cooperation. That's the name.'

'When did he meet Carl?'

'I told you, I don't know.'

'Carl set him up in the business? Supplied the drugs?'

Kemmel purses her lips, turns her head away from them.

De Vries says quietly: 'I need Carl.'

'I can't give you him.'

'Can't?'

'Can't give you what I don't know.'

'He meet up with Carl while he was staying at your place?'

Kemmel thinks, shrugs. 'Not when I was there.'

'He go to visit him?'

She trances momentarily, stays silent. De Vries stares at her.

'What?'

'We don't finish till you tell me what I want to know.'

'I'm telling you about Ray and Jan cos they're dead. I tell you what I know — even what I think — about these men while they're still around, I'm dead.'

'Many ways to die, Diane.'

He sees her jaw lock, her eyeballs slide to the right of their sockets. This, De Vries has been told, indicates that a suspect is utilizing the

153

imaginative side of the brain. He does not know whether he believes this.

'You ever meet this Carl?'

'No.'

'But you know where he stays, *ja*?'

'No.'

'You like to know everything, Diane.'

She sighs, her exhalation long and heavy. The room is airless and hot, the ceiling low, the light grey, insipid, tiring, the rhythms of the interview relentless. De Vries sees that she wants to close her eyes, lay her head down — as if she has been trapped in the middle of a row in an economy seat on a flight that has no end.

'Ray said something about Mossel Bay. Heard him talking to Jan about cars . . . '

'What kind of cars?'

'Old cars . . . classic cars . . . ' She wets her dry lips. 'They were gone a day, to Mossel Bay . . . ' She pushes herself back, away from the table, her chair vibrating, grating.

De Vries stares at her. 'That's it?'

'That's it.'

De Vries glances at Ngcuka, who is motionless. 'For now.'

★ ★ ★

'What did you do, Colonel? You offered her deals in return for her evidence?' Ngcuka is standing between De Vries and the end of the corridor.

'We got what we wanted.'

'That's what the SAPS did with the evidence

154

against Shereen Dewani. Remember what happened there?'

De Vries laughs. 'Major. Whatever Diane Kemmel told us about her involvement is irrelevant. There's witness and forensic evidence to convict.'

'The questions about Warrant Officer Heyns. She places the two dead men in her room. You compromise everything.'

'You said it. The men are dead. I compromised nothing.'

'So the point of your interview?'

'Was to see what we could learn about whoever lies further up the chain.'

'I do not understand you. This is a complex investigation. It takes time and hard work to peel away each layer . . . '

'That,' De Vries says, 'is why every investigation stalls. You fuck around watching them, trailing them, writing reports, telling everyone how complex it is. By then they probably know you're coming. We have a chance. We're going up the line so fast they're not going to know what's hit them.'

'We are?'

'You heard Kemmel. Yacht Club, fireworks. Put it together. Something's happening tomorrow night — New Year's Eve. A delivery, a meeting, at the Yacht Club while the Waterfront is in chaos, the city's jammed. Everybody's looking at the sky.'

Ngcuka shakes his head. 'You are mad . . . I want nothing to do with this. You have already got one officer killed.'

155

De Vries's hand shoots out at Ngcuka, pushes him back against the wall. He hears a crack, takes one stride forward, pins the smaller man.

'Colonel!'

De Vries freezes, lowers his arm, steps back.

Brigadier du Toit approaches them. 'Get in my office. Both of you. Now.'

★ ★ ★

De Vries stands in front of Du Toit's desk, while Ngcuka has been told to wait in a neighbouring office.

'My God, you don't let up, do you?'

'Everything I've done has been proactive and in the pursuit of justice.'

Du Toit waves away his words. 'You cannot operate like this. You have half a team. You refuse to co-operate, refuse to compromise.'

'That little shit has tried to play me from the word go. He struts around like he has the fucking rank, and there's a point when these black fuckers have to — '

'Enough. Don't say another word. Calm right down and think carefully.'

De Vries takes a breath, holds it, waits. 'Nothing gets done — '

'Colonel. Shut up. Just shut up. You're sleepwalking into a disciplinary discharge. You'll drag me and everyone else down with you.'

De Vries breathes deeply, concentrates on modulating his voice. 'He told me I had got Warrant Heyns killed. That is wrong.'

'That is wrong. But you left yourself open to

attack with your stupidity.' He scrutinizes De Vries.

De Vries knows that he knows. He shakes his head. 'We're drowning in crime,' he says quietly. 'Not just in the townships and squatter camps. Everywhere. We're fighting on fronts we can never win, just for the show of it. I thought the whole point of what we're doing here is to do it differently, more freely, to bypass all the shit and get the job done.'

'But we must be seen to be doing it right.'

'Being seen to do something isn't the same as doing it. Ngcuka's team had been watching Leon Barker at the motel. They'd been on it for weeks. They knew nothing about Kemmel. They let Chantal Adam go in and come out dead. It took me a day to link Kemmel in. What were they doing?'

'We've talked about this before . . . '

'We've identified maybe half the girls they sent. We've stopped them. Now, we have a lead to a possible delivery, information on another suspect further up the line.'

'I don't think what that woman claims to have overheard qualifies as a lead. Besides, you incentivized her to give you information. That doesn't mean it's apposite.'

De Vries squeezes his fists behind his back, straightens each knee, keeps trying to breathe slowly. 'Even if it's nothing — and I don't think it is — it's a chance. For whatever reason, Ngcuka isn't interested.'

'Ngcuka is rock solid. I made enquiries, Vaughn. Leave the man alone. He has a wife and

157

children and he's trying to do his job so he still has one this time next week. Sit down.'

De Vries lowers himself into the chair opposite Du Toit.

'He's an overseer, not involved in operations. Probably hasn't done any real policing in the last five years.' He lowers his voice. 'Up there, they like him. He's educated, erudite and, whether we like it or not, he is the future.'

'Black.'

'That's irrelevant.'

'This country is so corrupt, you want to get anything done, you trust only your friends. This is what we are for.'

'You can't work like that.'

'Do you know what happens to these girls? They can't eat for thirty-six hours because of stomach acid. If they make it through without the condoms exploding or breaking down and the drugs killing them, you heard Kemmel: none of them come back. They're sold into one kind of slavery or another. They're the lucky ones. The ones who get caught, they face thirty years of living death. The women's prisons in Thailand are gruesome . . . '

'I don't need a Wikipedia lecture.'

'They starve, they get sick, they're raped by the guards. They make our prisons look civilized. For Christ's sake. I'm looking at the cost. That girl Marie, she couldn't swallow the packets. You know what they do with girls like her? They set them up. A word to the Thai authorities, she gets caught, the others walk away.'

'All right.'

'We've stopped these people for a week or two. Someone else will be sent to take Kemmel's place. I'll stop that.'

Du Toit sighs deeply, feels ridiculous in his checked shirt, wishes he had the protection of his full uniform or, at the very least, a suit and tie. 'You are a dedicated man, Vaughn. But you'll get us all fired or killed.'

'You're talking about the future, Henrik. That's inevitable.'

★ ★ ★

London, Thursday, 31 December 2015

The city is grey and dark. Orange veins pulse with static traffic. The air seems thick, the River Thames cow-shit dirty. Rain is squeezed from the porthole windows. Marantz sits upright, swallows nausea.

As he touches down, a shiver passes through his body; his teeth chatter. The plane stills, engines die, stress-inducing soothing tunes saturate the cabin. He sits, immobile, as his fellow travellers retrieve coats, wait to be passed luggage. When he senses that the door is open, he rises, sleepwalks to the exit, steps onto the aerial walkway.

'Mr Marantz?'

A serious young man in a shapeless suit, a lanyard around his neck, stands in front of him.

He nods.

'I'm here to look after you.'

He gestures to Marantz to head down the walkway. Where it meets the soulless fluorescent

159

tube-lit corridor, he beckons to Marantz to follow him in the opposite direction from the rest of the passengers, into a restricted area. He follows the man blindly.

In the car, the man says, 'Rush-hour. It's going to be slow.'

Everything is slow.

★ ★ ★

'Couldn't wait till next year?'

Don February smiles. 'New Year's Eve, sir. New directive: we all have to be seen.'

De Vries looks around the squad room. Sally Frazer, Ben Thwala and two other officers are talking at the far end. He looks down at his warrant officer. 'I don't want you here, Don. Join another team for a few weeks. You've missed too much.'

'Brigadier du Toit has already spoken to me. I am to review the information to follow through the case from the beginning, try to liaise with the embassy in Bangkok, find out if the girls were sent to different destinations. I think he does not expect you to be doing this.'

'Good. Stay in the office. You know anything about any of this?'

'No.'

'You're not going to like it.'

'Brigadier du Toit said you were a man on a crusade.'

De Vries snorts. 'Someone has to be.'

★ ★ ★

160

'Major Ngcuka has returned to his unit,' Du Toit says. 'He's happy to be out of it. I've impressed on him that this is still a live operation and therefore totally confidential.'

De Vries rolls his eyes.

'Vaughn. You have no choice but to trust him.'

'We may still need one of his units.'

'Nothing is decided but, if we proceed, we have access to our own unit.'

'We do?'

'If General Thulani deems it appropriate.'

'Thulani?'

'No choice. That's the deal.'

He has known Henrik du Toit for twenty years. He is deliberate, political, media-aware — all things that De Vries dislikes and resents — but, crucially, he is trustworthy.

'Politically,' Du Toit continues, 'our leader may regard this as an opportunity. Changes are coming to Western Province and he doesn't want to be one of them. Just let me play the game.'

'I hate games.'

'Which you have made quite clear. I have sought to free you up to do what you do, but there are parameters.'

De Vries looks at his watch. 'We have maybe twelve hours to get in place. I need to know what resources I have.'

'Draft a plan, bring it to me. I'll go to General Thulani and see what can be done. We need to be sure that Harbour Police and Ngcuka's people know what we're doing.'

De Vries smacks his forehead with the palm of his hand. 'No! No, sir. That is the point. Don't let them know anything. The only reason these gangs can operate at all is because they have inside information. I keep telling you.'

'That's not the way it works.'

'For fuck's sake — it doesn't work. How many times . . . '

Du Toit looks across his desk at him, knows that, to an extent, what De Vries says is right. He fights the need to comply with the new directives, the new order, to live a quiet life where he ends his career with honour and a decent pension. 'This can all be referred to General Thulani. If he agrees with you, so be it.'

'When have you ever known Thulani to agree with me?'

'General Thulani . . . has taken a more moderate view towards you lately.'

De Vries scoffs at Du Toit's carefully chosen words, wonders how much more effort his boss puts into sentences than him.

'He likes your results.'

'But he dislikes my methods and mistrusts me personally.'

'We are the old guard. History travels with us, like body odour. You, of all people, should understand that.'

'Do we have to discard everything from that time, everything we learned?'

'The answer to that is simple, Vaughn.'

'Yes?'

'Yes.'

★   ★   ★

John Marantz stumbles through the doors of the building in which he worked almost from his first day of paid employment. The glass doors reflect only the heavy grey sky. They part swiftly, silently to reveal a grey foyer, grey-uniformed security personnel manning X-ray and scanning systems. He is still shaking. He passes through the checks, is issued with a lanyard, follows his still nameless escort to the lifts.

Aiden Wright's office overlooks the river. Rows of leafless trees line the riverbank as far as the next gridlocked bridge. Beyond that, the Houses of Parliament and Big Ben sit on a horizon of grey pollution and misty rain.

His former boss stands behind his desk, sombre and uncertain, hand extended, other arm half encouraging an embrace. Marantz shoves his hand into Wright's, shakes once, disengages. Behind him, the door closes, his chaperone dismissed.

'Where are they?'

Wright recoils minutely; a man usually fond of candour momentarily dumbstruck. He gestures towards a chair. 'John, sit down a moment.'

'I came to see them, not talk to you.'

'All in good time.'

Marantz sits; Wright follows.

'I won't waste your time, but I haven't seen you for six years.'

Marantz stares at him. He is more stooped than before, shorter in his chair. His spectacles' lenses are thicker, eyes sadder.

'You look well.'

'How do you know it's them? How do you

know it's Caroline and Rosie?'

Wright sighs, opens a drawer in his desk, retrieves two small polythene evidence bags. 'DNA. Multiple samples, indisputable matches. What was left of their clothes matches the description you gave at the time. And these . . . ' He pushes the bags across the desk to Marantz. 'They were found on the bodies.'

Marantz pulls them towards him. He sees his wife's wedding ring, remembers when they chose it together, the expression on her face. He tears open the packet, retrieves the simple gold band, plays with it in his fingers, lifts it to his nose, hoping that some distant scent might reach him. He cannot raise his head.

His daughter had worn a simple silver chain with a St Christopher medal — a gift from her mother — and, even now, he harbours the tiniest grain of disapproval. Yet it is hers. There is no more doubt. He takes this too in his hands, ripped free of its confinement. The two metallic items are cupped tightly, safely, between his sweating palms.

He knows that Aiden Wright is watching him cry, his body shaking with spasms of grief, but he is without pride. Every tiny doubt he manifested during his grief for the last seven years is being released now. When he has exhausted himself, he raises his head, repeats, 'Where are they?'

⋆   ⋆   ⋆

De Vries borrows a black blazer from a colleague, removes his tie, undoes the top button

164

of his shirt. The drive from his building to the dock area is slow and hot, the late-morning sun blasting the buildings, the light breeze suffocating.

He passes through the Christiaan Barnard security gate into the docks, passes the massive expanse of stacked containers, the slip-roads to the oil-rig servicing warehouses and yacht-refurbishment companies, parks on Duncan Road a hundred yards from the unprepossessing entrance to the Royal Cape Yacht Club. Without needing to show his ID, he saunters past the barrier to the car park unchallenged, to a coded security gate, follows a middle-aged couple into the compound at the cost of a smile.

Beneath beige sail canopies, families and groups of deeply tanned men drink and eat lunch overlooking the crowded marina, the clanking of rigging against masts a background rhythm. He paces the deck, which runs as far as another heavy iron gate, leading to boatsheds, beached dinghies and what look to him like fishing boats, being painted, welded, hosed down.

He retraces his steps, enters the clubhouse, nodding in greeting at anyone who acknowledges him. Down a narrow corridor at the back of the building he finds a door marked 'Club Manager', knocks, is invited in.

The man in the small, warm office rises. 'Yes, sir. What can I do for you?'

* * *

Outside the laboratories, Aiden Wright says, 'You understand our agreement?'

'I do.' Marantz nods.

A security card is swiped, the door clicks open; Wright leads the way. More doors follow; desks and benches at which faceless men and women work without glancing up. They reach an anteroom, with a long rectangular window.

'I'm going to ask you again,' Wright says quietly, 'because I think this is a mistake.'

'Seven years. This is the end.'

A white-coated man enters the room beyond the window. Lights dimly illuminate two benches, two forms, one large, one small; they are covered with light-green sheets. Marantz's heart pumps, falters and returns to its rhythm. He closes his eyes, opens them. The man stares at the window. Wright nods.

The technician pulls back the sheet from the larger form, walks slowly to the next bench. Two brown skeletons lie with their skulls closest to the window, stretching away from Marantz. He fights back bile, stumbles forward, places palms on the glass, leans his face to it. These things are not his wife and child. Unknown to him, the disparity in size would be disturbing in itself, the sight of a child's body harrowing and scarring. But, attached to his memories of a life lost long ago, the images overwhelm him. He feels his legs weaken, his head throb, the hardness of the nylon carpet on his knees . . .

★   ★   ★

166

His meeting with the Yacht Club's management concluded, De Vries has returned to his building, the promised outline plan delivered, his agreement with Du Toit fulfilled.

'You will have four men, small arms only, undercover at the Yacht Club. Frazer, Thwala and February, plus you. Eight, that's it.'

'That's all we need.'

'Discretion, Vaughn,' Du Toit says. 'If this amounts to nothing, we want no one to notice. If something happens, no collateral damage. The suspects must be followed, contained and brought in.'

'That is the intention.'

'The men from the reaction unit will arrive at six p.m. to be briefed.' Du Toit sits down. 'You realize that the freeway will be solid, access roads blocked and closed. You couldn't pick a worse night.'

'Shall we ask them to pick another?'

'You know what I mean. And, be aware, the city is full of tourists. New Year's Eve is a huge night. I'm telling you now, better to let a suspect go than risk a fire-fight or possible injury to bystanders. Clear?'

'Yes.'

'You have any information on who Jan de Mueller and Ray Rossouw might have been meeting tonight?'

'No.'

'This 'Carl' man?'

'Possibly. Kemmel claims she never met him.'

'So, you have nothing. How will you identify a suspect?'

De Vries taps his nose. Du Toit frowns.

'My bet,' De Vries says, 'is that all of this originates outside South Africa. Produce is brought in, perhaps by boat, by road, the girls are primed and dispatched from here. The more we look into it, the more widespread this type of operation seems to be, not just from South Africa. What we knew existed in South Africa is based out of Jo'burg but, as I've said all along, this is something new, and we want to take it down fast, send a message.'

'You questioned Kemmel about Jo'burg?'

'There's no record of Ray Rossouw or Jan de Mueller flying to Jo'burg, under their own names, anyway. They might have driven or taken the train, but Diane Kemmel seemed adamant that they hadn't visited recently. It seems odd, that's all.'

'All right,' Du Toit says. 'I'll see you at your briefing.'

De Vries smiles. 'Keeping an eye on me, Henrik?'

'Like I said, playing the game.'

★ ★ ★

Marantz finds himself back in Aiden Wright's office, lying on a sofa, shoes off. He pulls himself up, eyes gritty. For a half-dozen seconds, he is innocent. Then he sees them again. A dull pain invades his stomach, his chest. He breathes slowly, tries to calm himself.

When he finally gets up, the door opens. 'You're up?' Wright says. 'The MO said it was

168

exhaustion and shock. Have you eaten?'

'Aeroplane food.'

'Not good. Got you a place, not far from here. Fridge full of good stuff. Stay as long as you need.'

'Why?'

'To make whatever decisions you have to make.'

'I'm not coming back.'

Wright smiles. 'No, you're not.'

Marantz nods.

'Everything still stands. Everything you signed. Don't forget that.'

'I won't.'

'Maybe we'll keep in touch. You never know.'

'Putting me to sleep?'

'Deep sleep. Pension will be paid. You let me know where.'

'That it?'

'I've said it before, John. I'm sorry. I'm sorry we couldn't find them, and I'm sorry we know who they are, as far as the group is concerned, but we can't get to them. Our contact tells me those involved were not acting under orders. They're probably long dead.'

'But we won't know.'

'Free-thinkers don't last long among these people.'

'You get anything from them?'

Wright is silent.

'That all you have to say?'

Wright stares at him.

★ ★ ★

Table Mountain stands before a sky of pelargonium pink, a pure black silhouette against a seemingly unnatural colour. On the hard shoulder of the freeway, he can see drivers out of their cars, snapping the view.

As the sun falls, the colour fades quickly to grey. Even now, the air is warm. Being driven towards Table Bay, De Vries feels the heat leaching off the concrete buildings, the tarmac streets. He hasn't eaten, and a dull, persistent flow of adrenalin is taking over from the last of his coffee rush.

Cars are double-parked already as revellers arrive at restaurants and clubs in town. Four lanes into the Waterfront, Greenpoint and Mouille Point on Nelson Mandela Boulevard are jammed solid as far back as the Woodstock slip-road. De Vries looks up at them as he passes beneath the freeway, heading towards the docks. Even here, the vehicles crawl. 'What is it with us,' he says, 'that we all want to be in the same place together?'

Don February assumes, initially, that his boss's questions are rhetorical.

After another moment, in a different tone, De Vries says, 'You up-to-date on where we are?'

'I hope so, sir.'

'What do you think?'

Don waits until he applies the footbrake again. 'I think that this is not what we usually do.'

'And?'

'If we are going to do it, then this is a chance we have to take. Unless Ms Kemmel is holding back on us, this, and the name 'Carl', are the last pieces of information we are likely to have.'

'Exactly.'

'But we are assuming many things, sir. That Ms Kemmel's evidence is reliable, that she heard correctly, that this is the yacht club she was referring to. The fireworks reference strongly suggests tonight, but even so . . . '

'It's what we have.'

They edge forward. The traffic lights change against them. De Vries is restless. He taps his foot, opens his window, lights a cigarette.

'This case, sir. I wondered why it's become so important to you.'

De Vries holds his cigarette outside. 'I met Chantal Adam, seven, eight years ago. My daughters, Lulu and Kate, went to a birthday party at her father's house. They were at school together. Now, Lulu's doing her master's, living in Jo'burg, preparing for her adult life. Chantal Adam called us, left a desperate message, smashed a window. Then she walked over to it and slit her wrists on the broken glass. She did it for a reason.'

He turns back, brings in his hand, draws deeply on the cigarette, drops the butt on the tarmac. 'I didn't remember her, but I won't forget her now.'

'And because of Warrant Officer Heyns?'

De Vries nods. 'Yes, her too.'

Don stares at him; turns back to the road, moves forwards slowly, crosses the junction, waits in line for the security check into the docks.

'What did Frazer and Thwala tell you about

171

me and Warrant Heyns?'
  'Nothing.'
  'So who told you?'
  'No one, sir. Until now.'

★ ★ ★

The gala dinner has begun by the time De Vries
and his teams arrive at the Royal Cape Yacht
Club. They disembark from unmarked cars, walk
briskly but casually towards the low buildings.
Each has been prescribed individual positions.
Two will be on the long, broad flat roof, two on
the jetties. Sally Frazer and Ben Thwala will be
by the gates at either end of the Yacht Club
compound. De Vries positions himself close to
the entrance to the club from the car park,
through which all legitimate entries and exits
must be made. Don February covers the car
park, monitoring vehicles entering and leaving.
They affect various covers to blend in. De Vries
calculates that alcohol consumed will be their
best disguise.

★ ★ ★

At 11.50 p.m., the already crowded decks facing
the marina and, beyond, Table Bay fill to
capacity with diners from within the clubhouse.
No one has left the party. No officers report
sightings of individuals or groups arousing
suspicion at the extremities of the compound.
The volume of the band increases as the dining
room empties. New Year's Eve traditions follow:

'Auld Lang Syne' is mouthed, a few revellers join hands. Before it has ended, and before the advertised countdown, the crowd gasps at the first burst of aerial mortars as the vast display begins in the distance above them. De Vries studies the party-goers. Everyone looks skywards, exchanges the occasional word with friends; a few raise glasses.

De Vries's radio crackles.

'Alpha Team, jetty four. Party of . . . five adults walking towards clubhouse. Correction. Six. Six adults.'

De Vries repositions himself, looks towards the gate where the jetty meets the main gangplank up to the land. In the distance, he sees them, laughing, stopping and turning to see the display. The women carry handbags, one man holds a pair of bottle boxes. He clicks his radio. 'De Vries: where did they come from?' He waits. 'Jetty four. This is De Vries: where did they come from?'

The radio squeals.

'From a boat, sir.'

Even through the distortion De Vries senses the inaccuracy of the response, surmises that the officer has been watching the fireworks. The group have climbed up to the deck, are edging their way through the tightly packed crowd, towards the clubhouse.

The band are playing 'Party Like It's 1999'; the firework explosions echo back hard from the walls of buildings. De Vries ducks, clicks his radio. 'Don. Pedestrian front entrance. What can you see?' He waits.

'Five adults . . . '

'Five?'

'Six. Guy just followed them out.'

De Vries freezes, mind racing.

'Don. Follow them.' He begins to stride along the pathway, passes through into the car park, trots around the clubhouse buildings to the front.

'Alpha Unit, roof. Survey Duncan Road.'

He accelerates his pace, runs under the car barrier, past a security guard sitting in a doorway, onto Duncan Road. Ahead of him, he counts five figures walking in the direction of the Waterfront, perhaps towards a parked vehicle. He catches up with Don February, who is walking at a distance behind them. 'Well?'

'Two men, three women. I did not see the other man.'

The pyrotechnic explosions intensify. De Vries shouts, 'Where did he go?'

'I did not see.'

'Keep after them.'

De Vries follows, pats his holster, checks he has his pistol. The roar from the raised freeway has dulled; the fireworks still glitter above the vast form of the oil rig. The sound of the explosions follows belatedly, echoing from the dense concrete pylons. He jogs to the far side of Duncan Road, studies the perimeter fences. Suddenly, he sees a figure in the scrubby buddleia next to a small concrete shed. He runs towards him. The man does not move, his back to De Vries. As De Vries approaches, pistol drawn, the man turns, sees him, struggles with

174

his fly, holds up one, then both hands.

'What are you doing?'

The man looks down at his trousers. 'Urinating.'

De Vries is panting. 'Why?'

The man laughs. 'I needed a piss.'

'You on your own?'

'I'm with those guys.' He turns and points at the group of five, who have stopped a couple of hundred metres away, car doors open. 'Party to get to.'

De Vries lowers his weapon. 'All right.'

'I can go?'

'Ja.'

'Happy New Year.'

De Vries nods minutely, head full; frustration floods his body. 'Ja.'

★ ★ ★

By the time De Vries has checked that everyone has maintained position, and he has crossed the car park to the main gate, some guests are leaving. Reluctant grandparents have taken the end of the firework display as their cue to demand return to their beds, families begin to drift away into the car park and beyond the gates. De Vries watches them, head down, eyes closed. The moment, he knows, has passed.

He wonders about Diane Kemmel's information, whether he was hoodwinked by her performance, realizes that, even if Ray Rossouw and Jan de Mueller had planned to come to the docks tonight, their contact might already have

175

found out about their raid, cancelled the rendezvous, rerouted everything. He shakes his head bitterly, wonders whether any evidence remains which can keep him on the trail.

Suddenly, he thinks of Kemmel's words and a realization clicks into place. He looks up at the blank, clear sky, presses a speed-dial on his cell phone.

'Don. I want a lift into town. You drive.'

'We finished here?'

'*Ja.* I need to get to Long Street.'

'I can try, but the roads are closed or gridlocked.'

'I need to get there now, Don. Meet me at the car-park entrance.'

He jogs past more party-goers, wondering how many will drive home intoxicated and incapable. When he reaches the gate, he finds Don February is waiting.

'I have called for a motorbike, sir. From Harbour Police. He is coming just now.'

'Good.' De Vries does not like motorcycles, has seen too many accidents, too many mangled bodies, to be able to relax, especially riding pillion.

They hear the powerful bike approach down Duncan Road, pull up by the slip-road to the Yacht Club. De Vries leans in towards the rider's helmet. 'Top of Long Street, fast. But, Constable, if I have to die this year, it's not going to be tonight. *Ja?*'

The man nods, reaches into one of the side panniers and produces a spare helmet. De Vries pushes it on to his head, gets astride the bike, taps the driver's shoulder, grabs the hand-holds.

He keeps his head down behind the driver's back, tries to lean into corners. His back spasms as they cross the railway lines out of the secure dock area onto Christiaan Barnard Street, around the wide circle with its fountains full of kids. As they hit the city centre, the roads become chaotic: pedestrians dancing and singing obstruct junctions, illegal parking blocks side-roads and shortcuts; the traffic is static on Adderley Street. The driver weaves around the vehicles, and De Vries finds himself tossed one way, the other, jolted forwards as the officer brakes hard to avoid another zigzagging motor-cycle. Finally, he breaks through, accelerates up the middle of Strand Street, turns hard left onto Long Street. Of all the thoroughfares in Cape Town, this party street is the busiest, pedestrians taking up one lane in each direction. Halfway to the top, De Vries grabs the man's shoulder and, when the bike stops, he jumps off. 'Good work.'

He returns the helmet, stretches his back and neck, begins to force his way through the revellers on the pavement, stepping onto the street between double-parked vehicles.

Opposite Kennedy's Irish Bar, he sees them: two small bars, conjoined. To the left, with its silhouetted skyline banner, is 'Pretoria'; to the right, painted bright red, its huge swirling writing glittering above the small bar: 'Jo'burg'.

He pushes through people forming a tight barrier of sweat and cigarette smoke, feels the heat hit him as he enters the small, packed space. To his left is a crowded bar, ahead a tiny

177

dance-floor with flashing coloured lights and a disco ball. Beyond that, there is a back room, which usually houses a pool-table, but tonight it has been moved away to allow for more revellers. He glances inside, loosens his jacket, turns back to the bar. As he waits with a hundred-rand note in his hand, he seems the epitome of the minority: old, white and sober.

He takes a beer, scans the front bar, moves towards the back room. He checks the fire exit, whether it can be opened from outside, stands with his back to it, surveys the room, trying to nod to any rhythm he can discern from the deafening rap music.

He looks down at his tan leather jacket and jeans, decides he does not look too out of place. He grabs the edge of a bench when a girl gets up; he sits down, stares over the rim of his glass at anyone who peers into the room. Within minutes, his head is throbbing. He orders a second beer, using the long wait to observe everyone. He sees no one he recognizes. He takes the beer out front, lights a cigarette, mingles with the crowd. Resolving to spend only ten minutes more, he ducks back inside, makes for the rear, grits his teeth against the noise. The edge of the bench where he sat previously is still free. He sinks onto it, bows his head. Fatigue and disappointment hit him, pull him down. He feels submerged in the cacophony of sound, alien to this elite atmosphere of happiness.

He looks up, freezes. A man at the corner of the corridor sees him, disappears. De Vries drops his beer, pulls himself forward and up, chases

178

him down the corridor. Ahead of him, he sees people stumbling backwards, arms raised among the smoking barricade. He follows the commotion, pushes through the angry group, stares up and down Long Street, across the road. The figure has gone, unsurprisingly invisible amidst the surging, chaotic flow of merry revellers, embracing friends, stumbling drunks.

He is panting, bent double, hands on knees. His head spins. Nothing to eat all day, too much adrenalin, too much alcohol, too many battles fought, just to lose the war. Yet, he knows what he saw, who he saw, knows that it is no coincidence. Checking for a rendezvous, apprehensive and, when seen, panicked: Jack Esterhuysen.

★ ★ ★

John Marantz leans his forehead against the wide window of the dark apartment; through scattered, clattered raindrops and damp, sticky eyes, he stares at the Houses of Parliament, Westminster Bridge crammed with spectators, the seemingly static hands of Big Ben, paused just before midnight. He cannot hear the legendary chimes, which lead to the moment; does not observe the big hand finally eclipse the small. He sees, without watching, the first of the huge mortars rise and break above the river, repeating down its length towards the South Bank and beyond. In the furthest distance, he discerns the explosions.

All his thoughts are memories of eight years of

marriage, five years of fatherhood. Only during the last had his daughter learned to love fireworks. Before, she would recoil, push her head into the crook of his arm or against his chest. But on that last fifth of November, the sparklers, hot sausages and burgers eaten outside, the spectacular explosions which emanated from a tiny speck flying skywards, they had finally entranced her.

He remembers watching her, smiling at his wife, acknowledging that their baby had become a little girl. He imagines how she might be now, at twelve, feels himself shaking, feels the pain course through him. He goes to the bed, sits, concentrates on breathing slowly, calmly. He does not know when he lies back, or when unconsciousness takes him. He knows only that in the fearful crevasse between sleep and waking, he sees the bloodless skeletons of their bodies laid out against an emotionless background of nothing.

He strives to form an image of those who took his family. He has none. Associates of a man whom the British government had detained, whom he was charged with interrogating, breaking, had destroyed his life. The man had never given up the associates, never shown remorse or provided any clues. Without an image on which to focus, his revenge becomes indiscriminate: anyone who defies, contradicts, disagrees with him, he will cut down. Amid his darkest fantasies, he finds acceptance that they are gone, his family and their murderers. He wonders how he can live.

★ ★ ★

Cape Town, Friday, 1 January 2016
New Year dawns a second time for De Vries at 7.30 a.m. He is still dressed, legs caught in jeans half down his legs, one arm in a shirtsleeve, the other hanging loose by his head, scalp almost on the floor. He hauls himself back to horizontal from his contortion, torso twisted out of the side of his bed, right hand levering his spasming back onto the mattress, his locked neck onto the cold, soft pillow.

Five hours previously, he had all but commandeered a taxi to bring him home. He sprawls, lost in dreams fuelled by an exhausted inebriation at his dining-room table where, in his silent house, he sits to think. Half conscious, he reflects on Lee-Ann Heyns, Chantal Adam, the building pressure to get Ngcuka's team to co-operate and perform, the adrenalin and frustration at his wasted operation at the Yacht Club, his sighting of Jack Esterhuysen: however many times he considers it, that is a man somewhere who had no reason, no right, to be there. His attempt to follow him has shattered what little confidence he retained: his unwieldiness allowed Esterhuysen to escape, leaving him becalmed amidst the saturation of human bodies, their smell, their clichéd drunken bonhomie, their viscosity, as he stumbled between them, back down Long Street, uncertain of Esterhuysen, mistrusting of himself, desperate for the night, his old year, to end.

181

By 9 a.m, he is in his office, looking out over a deserted squad room. He pushes away two empty paper cups, previously containing triple espressos; feels wired and antsy. He sits up, pushes himself into his desk until its edge bites into his swollen stomach. His head spins: he can recall every detail of the pointless operation the previous night, nothing of his journey to work this morning, but for the sudden, panicked swerve as the slip-road he takes each day surprised him by its sudden proximity.

At the flicker of movement from the squad room, he looks up to see Don February walking towards his office. His warrant officer knocks, enters. 'Happy New Year, sir.'

'To you too, Don.'

He must concentrate to form such words.

'We were concerned when we heard nothing more from you, sir. You weren't answering your cell phone?'

'Couldn't hear, didn't notice. Sorry.'

'What did you do?'

'Jo'burg. The bar in Long Street, not the city. I think that's where Ray Rossouw and Jan de Mueller would have met someone after they'd collected their supply. Maybe another deal, I don't know. I went there, but there was nothing . . . '

He has already decided not tell anyone about Esterhuysen, wants none of his team implicated if he is wrong.

'So, where is the investigation now?'

De Vries waves him in, to the guest chair. 'There's more than one investigation. We still have Diane Kemmel. She provided another name, and I'll follow that. I want the people who set this up, who think that these girls are commodities, who encourage them to sacrifice their lives for nothing.' He lets out his breath through pursed lips, brow furrowed. The pain is intensifying.

'More than one investigation?'

De Vries nods, regrets it. 'I want you, Frazer, Thwala, whoever else, to investigate what happened to Chantal Adam, how she ended up in the DF Malan Motel, why she called us, then took her own life.'

February frowns. 'Is that a job for our department?'

'If I say so.'

'I am thinking only of what I will say to Brigadier du Toit, if you are not here and I report to him.'

'You tell him you are following my order. That girl is my daughter's age. Every time I think about Kate, I want to know where she is, what she's doing, who she's with. So did Charles Adam. And, Don, you didn't see Chantal's body in that motel. That was no place for anyone on Christmas Day.'

Don nods.

'You've seen the notes from the private investigator Charles Adam employed?'

'I know we have them, but I have not read them.'

'I'll leave it to you. You're in charge. And,

Don, keep what you find to yourself and to official reports. Don't release them to anyone but Director du Toit. If anyone else wants them, ask me first.'

'There is a problem?'

De Vries lowers his voice, counts on his fingers. 'We have Internal Affairs and General Thulani watching us. We're on their agenda and they want us off it altogether. So do the Police Ministry and any number of political factions seeking influence and control, including Organized Crime and Drug, which, through negligence or corruption, let Diane Kemmel and her cronies flourish. So, most places along the line, we have a problem. This is modern policing in the bright new South Africa.'

'It was not like this where I was before.'

'This is what we do. The crimes, the people behind them, aren't mindless. They're backed, connected and protected. You can't come at these people head on. I keep trying to tell Du Toit.'

'But Chantal Adam?'

'A victim. Work it like you were taught, like we do together . . . And, Don, find those women in Bangkok. I want every one we know about accounted for.'

★ ★ ★

He spends the morning writing his report on the failed operation at the Yacht Club, then takes the lift down to the lobby, walks out onto the street.

There is a certain calm to the city this morning, the air cool, but promising heat later. The streets are devoid of workers, the bars and restaurants quiet, mostly closed. A few pink-eyed tourists amble aimlessly up and down the hillside streets, keeping their heads still as they walk, seeking coffee, browsing darkened windows.

De Vries takes Dorp Street, crosses Buitengracht Street and walks up into Bo Kaap. Formerly known as the Malay Quarter, many of the narrow streets climb the lower slopes of Signal Hill, cobbled, lined with tiny, brightly painted cottages. Close to the nineteenth-century mosque, there is a permanent hawker's stand, selling paper cups of strong, muddy coffee. He buys one, swallows the thick liquid in one go, crosses diagonally down to a little café on a distorted crossroads of cobbled and potholed streets, sits in the corner, places his briefcase on his lap.

He orders potato and vegetable samosas with chutneys, produces his old work laptop. Online research is almost entirely delegated, but his daughters have taught him the basic operations. He types a search into Google and, while the page slowly opens, a waitress brings him a can of Appletiser and a milky Duralex tumbler with three tiny lozenges of ice. He tips the room temperature contents into the glass, agitates it to impart coolness. He takes a sip. Bo Kaap is good for him: no alcohol.

He looks down at the screen, squints at the small images displayed at the top of the page, clicks on the result indicating a Mossel Bay address, waits for the N2 Classics website to open.

Even to De Vries, the site seems dated: a medieval-style font describes the Western Cape's biggest selection of classic cars. The illustrated stock-list runs to several sections. At the bottom is a customer-enquiry address: carl@n2classics.co.za.

He scrolls back to the top of the page, discovers that the business will be open on Saturday, 2 January, with holiday offers, closed again on Sunday and Monday.

De Vries spends the next few minutes searching for any reference to Carl's surname. He finds a Carl Hertzog and his wife, living in a house close to the beach just up the coast from Mossel Bay. He cannot establish a link with the classic-car dealership, but thinks it more than possible the two are one and the same.

When his food arrives, he sits back, drains his soft drink and calls for another, asking for more ice. He dips the first of the samosas into a tomato relish, stares out at a group of young Muslim boys sitting on cardboard boxes, smoking under a ragged tree, thinks that Saturday will suit him well: weekends are just like any other day. He smiles to himself, begins to eat.

★ ★ ★

'I spoke with our embassy in Bangkok,' Ben Thwala tells Don February. 'I alerted them to the arrival of my email regarding the girls from the Kemmel operation, asked them to make it a priority as it concerned a current investigation, but they did not seem very interested. They told me that they may not be able to help.'

Don looks at Thwala from his low-backed swivel chair at his desk in the corner of the squad room. 'Did they give a reason?'

'No, sir.'

'If we do not receive a reply in forty-eight hours, I will ask Brigadier du Toit to arrange contact with the ambassador.' Thwala nods. 'Why would they wish not to liaise with us?'

* * *

De Vries stares at the display on his phone, number withheld. Usually, he would let it go to voicemail, listen to the message, decide whether or not to return the call. Today he answers it. He listens, frowns, describes the position of the café in Bo Kaap, says, 'I want to talk to you too.'

* * *

Charles Adam's private investigator, Dale Rix, has produced a mixture of printed reports and handwritten notes. The reports are efficient and precise, stating only facts. The notes, which are far more extensive, are of a different tone. It takes Don February a while to become used to the heavily slanted, closely spaced wording, but eventually he can read fluently.

The notes document a far wider timescale than suggested in the reports, comment on

187

Chantal Adam's appearance, what she is doing, with whom she is spending time. Each person is identified, their characteristics noted. The description of Chantal is detailed, at times intimate, and Don senses a bond between Rix and his subject. When she disappears on 14 December, Rix seems to work all night trying to locate her, spending the following two days revisiting all the places she has stayed. According to the notes, he speaks to many of the people with whom she has been seen, asking them about her likely movements. At this point, any secrecy is blown. On two occasions, Rix notes that he tells the person he is a private investigator for Charles Adam and needs to find Chantal urgently.

The collection of photographs includes a file of fashion and publicity shots from 2010, when she returned from the United States. There are several paparazzi shots of her in bars and clubs in Cape Town, showing her emaciated, without make-up, her hair matted and dirty, face and body thin and pale. Then, there are distance shots, presumably taken by Rix himself, showing Chantal Adam in the street, several properties in various states of disrepair with handwritten notes on the reverse stating the address itself and the dates when she was staying there, a few pictures of other subjects, again with notes on the reverse.

Clearly Rix has spent many more hours trailing Chantal than the hours for which he was charging Charles Adam. Within the notes, Don interprets panic when she disappears, anxiety

188

when he cannot locate her and, in his last few sentences on the day before Christmas Eve, almost an emotional attachment: 'Revisited Long Street and the Rucksack Rooms. Still no sight of her or any reports. Christmas two days away. C has made no contact with anyone, has not been seen. The longest she was out of contact before was three days. This is nine days. Fear she may be weak or ill or high in some hot bedsit. Not the Christmas either of us wanted . . . '

★ ★ ★

Jack Esterhuysen is dressed in shorts, T-shirt, sandals. Unshaven, seemingly relaxed, he appears quite different from the sullen, intense officer mesmerized by Diane Kemmel.

De Vries gestures for him to sit at his corner table, back to the street, while he moves a little to one side, allowing a clear view of the entrance. They order more cool drinks. 'You're off duty, Lieutenant?'

'Yes, sir.'

'No family?'

'I needed to speak with you, sir.'

De Vries says nothing. It disturbs him that he cannot anticipate what Esterhuysen wants to say.

'Can I speak off the record with you?'

'That's why I agreed to meet you here.'

They lean back from the middle of the table as the waitress delivers cans and glasses. Esterhuysen takes his, but does not open it.

'Right now, my team are working nine different cases, some involving surveillance, others just intelligence. We hadn't been watching the DF Malan Motel because two weeks previously the two assigned officers reported that they had been spotted. We were aware that Leon Barker was escorting girls to the motel and leaving with them later. We knew only subsequently that this was connected to the drug trade and then we were pulled back from the investigation.'

'Pulled back? By who?'

'Major Ngcuka, sir.'

'What reason did he give for standing you down?'

'He called it 'a matter of priorities'.'

'That sounds familiar.'

'Sir?'

'Administrators and their criteria for decisions. Good corporate practice, bad policing.'

Esterhuysen smiles grimly. 'When I discovered in the Kemmel house that Lee-Ann — Warrant Officer Heyns — was dead and that Diane Kemmel was responsible, I was angry and confused. I apologize that you had to repeat your order to me, sir. It won't happen again.'

'Shooting Kemmel would have achieved nothing.'

'No.' Esterhuysen does not meet De Vries's eye. He seems to scrutinize the furthest corners of the room. He opens the can, drinks. He pushes away the glass.

'You come here often, sir?'

★   ★   ★

190

'Don't you people ever give warning that you're coming?'

'Not when we need to speak to you immediately, sir.'

Dale Rix stands but remains behind his desk. He gestures to Don February and Sally Frazer to take a seat. 'What can be so urgent?'

'In the SAPS, we work an inquiry full time. We cannot wait. I need to ask you about your enquiries. Is our visit inconvenient?'

Rix sighs, glances at Frazer, then back to Don. 'No.'

'We have been reading your reports. You were very thorough, sir. I was wondering why you devoted so much time to this one case?'

'I gave you everything so that you could know what I knew, even my personal notes.' He straightens in his seat. 'I remembered Chantal Adam on the top of that mountain, hair billowing behind her, that music. It was an iconic image. I read about her being snapped up by the Americans and how she left everything and everyone, chased her dream and, when it all went wrong, came back and no one cared. I suppose I thought I knew her so, when this job came up, I made it my business to do it as well as I could. And, frankly, despite all of this . . . ' He sweeps his hand over the desk. 'There isn't much else happening for me.'

'Did you meet Miss Adam personally?'

Rix swallows. 'I spoke with her a couple of times.'

'You did not say that before. It is not in your notes.'

'No. It wasn't professional and I regret it now. It makes her death more disturbing. When I saw her, I couldn't believe she was the same girl. Did you see the pictures I took of her in Cape Town? I asked her if she needed help, if she wanted to see someone who could help her. She said no. She was polite, but firm. She walked away from me.'

'When was the last time you actually spoke to her?'

'Late November. I saw her again on the street. She didn't recognize me. I don't think she could even see that well. Her eyes seemed bad — red, infected, maybe. I asked her if she needed a doctor, or money, but she just kept walking.'

'You did not report to Mr Adam that her physical condition seemed to be worsening?'

'I sent him the pictures, reported on what I saw. I suggested that he might intervene, have her taken into hospital or some kind of protective care, but he said that she wouldn't allow that.'

'Did that seem strange to you?'

'Mr Adam said that when she left he'd promised her that he wouldn't interfere in her life. He was fulfilling his promise.'

'But he was not, was he, sir? He was having her watched and followed.'

'Discreetly, yes.'

Don watches him for a few moments, senses a pall fall over him, his shoulders slump. He seems tired, defeated.

'What else are you working on now?'

Rix looks up.

'A few things. It's quiet this time of year.'

Don consults his own notes. 'You state that, before she disappeared on the fourteenth of December, you heard from a third party that she had been spotted in a hostel off Long Street. Did you see her there yourself?'

'The Rucksack Rooms, just off Long Street, *ja*. No, I never went in there until she was gone. I asked for several days, but there was no sign of her.'

'But she was not staying there herself?'

'No, I don't think so. There was a group of Australians. The manager said she had spent a few days with, he thought, one of them particularly, and socialized on the deck with them in the afternoons. She came back a couple of days later and he told me she seemed surprised, disappointed that they had gone without leaving word. She returned to the hostel the following day and asked again, but he had no information for her.'

'How did she react to that?'

'The manager said she seemed upset.'

Don scribbles in his notebook. 'And, before that, she was staying at the apartment in Seapoint owned by . . . '

'A woman called Angela Cole.'

'You recount your interview with her in your report, but did you ask her if Miss Adam had indicated that she was leaving?'

'Yes. She said Chantal hadn't. She had left belongings behind.'

'They are still there?'

'As far as I know. Angela Cole may have

thrown them out. I got the impression that she wasn't sorry to see the back of Chantal.'

'I need to ask you, sir. Why do you think Mr Adam employed you?'

'I told the other officer, the colonel. I was recommended.'

'I meant, sir,' Don continues quietly, 'do you have any idea why Chantal Adam would refuse to return to the Adam house? There was a family feud, a disagreement?'

'Mr Adam never told me officially why his daughter was estranged from the family, just that she refused to return home and rejected any money from her father.'

'What about her mother?'

'I scarcely met her. It's like . . . she is always in the background.'

'She did not seem concerned for her adopted daughter?'

Rix hesitates, then: 'I don't think she was interested in Chantal. She had her own children. I got the impression she couldn't care less.'

'Really?'

'Wouldn't you, as a parent, show concern? I never saw any from her.'

Don writes quietly, makes no attempt to speak.

'In any case, as I said, Chantal would rebuff any attempt to help or support her.' He waits for Don February to speak. When there is only silence, he clears his throat. 'They're never together, Charles Adam and his wife. Whether it is just because he was dealing with me, I don't know, but there seemed to be a distance between

194

them ... I got the feeling that he felt guilty about what had happened, that he was trying to make amends, whereas his wife — it was as if she bore a grudge.'

'Go on, sir.'

Rix folds his arms. 'That's it. I don't know why Charles Adam felt guilty. I suppose that, as a Catholic, guilt was an emotion he was used to.'

'You think he felt he had sinned?'

'I have no idea.'

'But you are a religious man, a Christian. Yes?'

Rix shifts in his chair. 'What makes you say that?'

'You are wearing a crucifix, sir ... in your photograph.' Don points to a long, low shelf at the base of the cluttered bookcases. At the far end is a black and white photograph in a simple ebony frame. Rix squints at it. From where he is sitting, he can scarcely identify himself among the group of men, mostly topless, wearing shorts, posing around a *braai*, beers in hand. 'That was taken years ago.'

'A team you were in?'

'Kind of ... '

'I am only asking, sir, because, if that is the case, you would be alert to such an influence.'

'Influence?'

'You mentioned guilt. That Charles Adam might want to make amends. I am asking you: what for?'

Rix takes a sip from a tall plastic glass of water, keeps the beaker to his lips for a long while. He sips again.

'It was just my impression. I have nothing to

195

back it up. Why don't you ask Charles Adam?'

'Every piece of information is important, and we will talk to Mr Adam, sir. Maybe he has secrets he is keeping from us too.'

* * *

'What isn't Rix telling us?' Sally Frazer says.

'People like secrets. It makes them feel stronger,' Don says. 'I think that Mr Rix has much he would like to say but he feels that if he did he would be in a weaker position.' He brakes abruptly to avoid a taxi-van pulling out without signalling into the crowded road, with its ramshackle architecture of warehouses, Victorian terraces and modern developments. The sun seems to drain the colour from the scene, making it all gradations of grey. They drive into the shadow of the broad overpass of Nelson Mandela Boulevard. Two seconds later, the sun envelops the car once more.

'But you think he'll tell us eventually?'

Don glances at her. 'If we do not ask, yes.'

* * *

Dale Rix struggles to his feet, limps stiffly around his desk, stretches his back, hobbles across the room to the photograph. He picks it up, takes it to the light of the side window and studies it. He is standing, on two good legs, with men from his unit. They are in Angola, having a few days' leave after months without respite. Within six months, he will have been shot twice

196

in his lower leg. He looks more closely, studying the faces of men he has not seen for two decades. He recognizes the crucifix he had worn from his teenage years until his first injury. When he was lying on the hot ground, leaching blood, the pebbles like flames, waiting for what seemed like hours for his unit to come back for him, he had prayed.

He could not remember what had happened to the crucifix and the silver chain on which it hung; wonders whether it was taken by one of the medics; realizes that, until today, he had not thought about it. He remembers that in answer to his prayers, as he lay in agony, there was nothing.

★   ★   ★

De Vries has not shifted his gaze. 'You visited my prisoner in the cells at seven twelve in the morning. Why?'

Esterhuysen swallows, rubbing his jaw. 'That's what I came to explain.' He leans towards De Vries. 'I understood that Major Ngcuka was to lead the interrogation with you. At that point, I wasn't aware of your . . . standing. I felt uncertain that Major Ngcuka would obtain the information required to continue the investigation. He is sometimes . . . ' Esterhuysen gesticulates, seemingly hunting for words, 'more interested in closing a case than in discovering the truth.'

'What did you say to her?'

'I suggested that if she told me off the record

197

about her contacts, where she obtained the product, the names of those involved, we could do a deal.'

'You had no authority to offer her a deal.'

'That's the point, sir. I knew that Major Ngcuka would never approach witnesses with a deal, would never accept one. Since he became CO of our units, we've become less successful because paid informants, deals over charges, sentencing have been cut back dramatically. He says that justice must be seen to be done.'

'And you think?'

'That we have to operate beneath the radar, especially with organized crime and drugs. It may not be precisely to the book, but it achieves more.'

De Vries agrees with Esterhuysen's philosophy — he, too, found Ngcuka's staid, unimaginative methods frustrating and ineffective — yet there is something about Esterhuysen he finds perplexing. 'Why are you telling me this?'

'Because Major Ngcuka has instructed us that the case is completed and closed.'

'But you think otherwise?'

'Kemmel, Leon Barker, Ray Rossouw, Jan de Mueller: they were all small-time. Someone set up the process. Two girls every week from Cape Town to Bangkok, carrying product. None of these girls have come back. That wasn't their idea. This is a new operation and, if we don't find who's behind it, it'll just start all over again.'

'You were in Jo'burg Bar on Long Street at twelve thirty-five last night. Why?'

Esterhuysen sits up, smiles. 'I didn't expect to see you there, sir.'

'I don't care. Why were you there?'

'There was a group of us up the road, guys from the units, having a few beers. I'd read the interview transcript. The bit about meeting in Jo'burg didn't make sense and then, after a few beers, I thought about the place on Long Street. I needed to walk off the alcohol, so I went there, in case I recognized anybody.' He pauses. 'You thought the same, sir?'

'*Ja.* But whoever Rossouw and De Mueller were supposed to meet didn't show up and, obviously, neither did they.'

Esterhuysen sits back. 'We can work together to find who killed . . . To find who's behind this gang?'

'I don't think the SAPS is set up to co-operate, Lieutenant. Besides, you have your own duties.'

De Vries sees Esterhuysen's jaw tighten, arms flex.

'I have to do this. I want those people — and now is our chance. Everything in the SAPS is *crook*. Nothing happens . . . '

De Vries hears his own voice in the other man yet something bothers him. He waits to see if Esterhuysen will continue.

The door to the café opens and a large Muslim family enters. It is mid-afternoon. They order mint tea and food. The quiet café is transformed by children's questions and arguments, both waitresses scurrying. From the tiny kitchen at the rear, De Vries hears sizzling, smells

199

pungent spices. The door opens again, a single elderly man enters, walks to the counter, perches on one of the tattered stools.

Esterhuysen has sat back, is tapping his armrest, downing the last of his drink.

'Why were you late for the initial meeting of your unit for the raid?' De Vries asks.

'I had a call to make.'

'More important than the safety of one of your colleagues?'

'Major Ngcuka told me that it was Lee-Ann.'

'You knew her through Marc Immelman?'

'Ja.'

De Vries is watching his eyes. 'How well did you know her?'

A pan clatters in the kitchen. Customers jump, laugh. De Vries stays locked on Esterhuysen. 'Lieutenant?'

He is suddenly still. He breathes out, looks beyond De Vries. 'I knew her . . . ' he speaks almost without moving his lips, his voice low, 'quite well.' He bows his head, raises it again, meets De Vries's eye. 'We were together. I know it wasn't right, but these things happen. She wasn't happy with Marc. Unsatisfied.'

'You were conducting an affair with Lee-Ann?'

'Kind of. Maybe more a relationship. We spent time together, committed, loyal. It wasn't just sex.'

'That's why you wanted to kill Kemmel?'

'That fucking bitch, Kemmel. Her and those guys. They fucking tied her up and tortured her. You know that?'

'I saw her.'

'We had no choice, with those two men. They were shooting. We returned fire.'

'Are you saying that for me, or for yourself?'

'I'm telling you. It was shoot or be shot.'

'I'm not arguing. But if you'd killed Kemmel, we would have had nothing.' De Vries leans across the table. 'You want justice for Lee-Ann, keep your head down and let me get on with the job. If I need help, I'll call you.' He sits back, realizing that if he could read infatuation in Esterhuysen's face, then his own might betray him too.

'I'm leaving now. Keep what you've told me to yourself, or there'll be comeback.' He gets up, pushes the table into Esterhuysen's midriff, edges his way out. 'Stay here a few minutes. Thanks for the drinks.'

In the glass door, he sees Esterhuysen faintly reflected, hand in the air, calling for the bill.

★   ★   ★

He walks back to his station in a daze of reflection, grateful that the streets are quieter, that no one scrutinizes his introspection. Any marginal hope he harboured is lost: Lee-Ann Heyns had wanted him for no other reason than what she had admitted: his rank, his influence. He clings to the thought that, only just afloat on turbulent water himself, perhaps she had seen him as a rescuer, perhaps a rock. He smiles to himself wanly. He is almost drowning.

★   ★   ★

The landlady identified by Dale Rix, Angela Cole, lives in a huge development of 1970s apartments called Bordeaux on Beach. Her flat does not overlook the main road, promenade, shallow beach and vast, flat expanse of blue South Atlantic but, instead, a face-brick and concrete block, even less attractive than her own, across the narrow street.

Driving from town, Don February discovers that Oliver Road is one way, forcing him to drive two streets further on, take a turn down Worcester Road, then along Beach Road before turning back towards Cole's home. Sea Point is a suburb of the city he does not often frequent. Main Road is bustling, packed with shops, bars and restaurants, but the beaches are poor for sunbathing or games, the water ice cold. He once brought his wife to the revolving restaurant at the top of the Ritz Hotel, but the evening was not a success.

Forewarned by a call from Sally Frazer, Angela Cole opens the door to them enthusiastically, inviting them into the compact apartment. She sits them on a low sofa, offers coffee, sits opposite. She is wearing an orange-patterned headscarf, white blouse and black slacks — which Don observes are unbuttoned around her bulging waist — along with a pair of oversized sunglasses, which, despite the dim interior and heavy net curtains, she shows no inclination to remove.

'Suddenly, everybody wants to know about Chantal Adam again.'

'Everybody?'

She studies Don a moment, turns her head to Frazer. 'Five years ago, she was just a schoolgirl who became the Mountain Girl and got taken to America. Every schoolgirl in the country wanted to be her. She was a dream. Her whole life was a dream. But, when she came back, no one wanted to know. The press are so fickle, so cruel. If you're beautiful, you're it, and when you're not, you're not.'

Don watches her expansive hand gestures, her painted eyebrows rising and falling, the pleasure she seems to take in her own performance.

'When did you first meet?' Frazer asks.

'About two, two and half years ago. I was having lunch with a girlfriend at the old Cape Quarter. You remember, the original courtyard? And she was there, looking wretched, sitting at an empty table outside Andiamos. I excused myself and I went right up to her and said, 'I know who you are, Chantal. Can I help you?' And she looked at me, and I think she saw someone she could trust, someone who had some experience, you know, and she said that she needed somewhere to stay for a while.'

'You took her in?'

'It wasn't like she was a stranger. You feel you know a girl you've seen on television and in the magazines.'

'And she came to live here?'

'Only to stay for a few days. Then she went. But she came back. I told her, 'If you get in trouble and you need a place to stay, you come.''

'Did you talk much with her?'

'She was a quiet girl, and when I saw her, she

203

was tired. I don't know if it was because she was taking drugs or going to parties or just sleeping on the street but, when she was here, she'd usually just sleep.'

Don listens, knows that he has been excluded. There are, as De Vries has told him, many moments when the lead officer must step back because a colleague can do a better job. Sally Frazer has established a rapport with this witness, and that is good. Angela Cole starts to recount conversations about the New York fashion scene. He glances around the apartment. It is unusual but, he thinks, it has some style. There is an old gramophone player in one corner, a folded screen covered with a collage of glamour shots of women from the 1950s or 1960s. The furniture is futuristic fifties, even the wall clock, with its golden spikes marking out five-minute intervals, is in period.

'How many times did she come to stay in total?'

'I don't know. Maybe a dozen. She would come and go. I didn't give her a key because I worried that it might end up in the wrong hands, but I'm usually here in the mornings, and Chantal knew that.'

'Did you give her money?'

'A little, a couple of times.'

'And the last time you saw her?'

Cole's shoulder twitches. 'About the tenth of December.'

'And she seemed okay?'

'Yes . . . '

'But you had a fight?'

204

Cole turns to February. 'Why do you say that?'

'Chantal was being watched by a man her father had sent to check on her safety. He reported that he saw her leave your apartment looking upset, crying.'

'No wonder the poor girl was upset, if she was being stalked.'

Don smiles gently, leans forward in his seat.

'She was not being stalked. She was being watched by a private investigator. Those are two different things. Did you argue that day?'

She looks away from Don February towards Sally Frazer, who says nothing, just gazes at her enquiringly.

'She wanted money for drugs. She didn't say that. She said she owed some people. It was coming up to Christmas, money's tight, and I had lent her enough. I mean, enough is enough, isn't it?'

'So, you wouldn't give her money?'

'She had the spare room if she needed it. I couldn't do more.'

'Did she leave her belongings behind?'

Cole speaks to Frazer. 'They're still in her room. You can look. It isn't much, but I have a feeling it's all she had.'

Frazer rises, as does Cole, who leads the way out of the living room, across the small, square hallway, to the back of the apartment.

Don smiles to himself. He knows that he is unassuming, and he is used to being unnoticed but, in the last couple of days, being the lead detective, he had expected something different, something more.

Don gets to his feet, wanders around the room. On the shelf under the pale-wood oval coffee table, he sees old editions of *Vogue*. As he pushes a copy back into the pile, a rectangular card drops to the floor. He glances at the writing: 'Dominique — Style Editor — SA *Event* Magazine'. Underneath, there are some numbers and an email address in tiny print. He studies the plain white card, replaces it inside the magazine.

He stands again when Angela Cole and Sally Frazer return. His eye meets Frazer's: she shakes her head gently.

'You have talked to other people about Chantal Adam, madam?'

'A few people. People who knew her to say hello.'

'A journalist?'

She looks at him suspiciously. 'If you know the answer to a question, why do you ask?'

'If I knew the answer, I would not ask,' Don says quietly.

The woman says nothing, arms folded in defence.

Frazer says, 'Did you get the impression that Chantal Adam would consider taking her own life?'

Cole turns back to her, hands falling to her sides. 'With artists and performers you never know what is going on here.' She touches her head and then the left side of her chest. 'I think she was becoming desperate. Not for money, or for companionship, but for something.' She turns to Don February. 'I don't know what.'

⋆ ⋆ ⋆

As he drives out of town towards Rosebank, De Vries sees the cloud forming over Devil's Peak, thick and dark over Newlands. Atop Hospital Bend, the sun disappears, the air cools.

When he reaches his gates, he sees Marantz's dog, Flynn, waiting for him. As the gates swing open and De Vries drives in, Flynn jumps up at the door, tail wagging. De Vries has left the dog alone almost since Marantz flew to London. He gets out of the car, squats on the driveway, strokes the dog behind its ears. Then, he calls Flynn to follow him, lets them into the house, goes to the kitchen. There is a large tin of corned beef in the cupboard. De Vries decants it onto a side-plate, places it on the floor. Within moments, the meat is gone.

De Vries opens the French doors to his overgrown, untended garden, the pool green, fallen branches everywhere from the heavy rain a few weeks' back. He sits at his table, pours himself a glass of Merlot.

He sends an SMS to Marantz. He usually replies to text messages instantly.

He has already decided to travel to Mossel Bay to meet Carl Hertzog. Everything Marie Smith said about being taken from Port Elizabeth fits with her midway destination being close to Mossel Bay, even her mention of old cars in the warehouse where she was kept overnight. He has run through the reports of what was found at Leon Barker's house, and there is nothing to tie him to an address in that area, but De Vries

207

senses that the information is coming together, that Diane Kemmel has given up her contact in the hope of a break for herself.

He opens a second bottle of wine, cuts himself two thick slices of seed loaf, spreads them thickly with butter and apricot jam. He looks down at Flynn, glances at his silent phone, wonders where Marantz might be. Marantz has always lived with the unknown, a tiny vestige of hope left for his family. Although he talked about his conviction that they were dead, De Vries knows how the human mind clings to hope, however tenuous; now, despite so many years of grieving, there is more to come. De Vries has seen it before: in parents of abduction victims, husbands of murdered wives, in a community destroyed by seemingly inexplicable violence.

As dusk settles, he wonders whether to call Jack Esterhuysen; decides against it. Something about the officer bothers him, but he still can't work out what it is. Many remember the famous Chantal Adam; few cared about her once she had fallen, and now she is just another murder in a country full of death.

The dog is snoring quietly, wrapped around the table leg. De Vries has enjoyed being responsible for nothing at home for two years; alone, independent, free to run his life as he chooses.

It is, he reflects, a prosaic realization so patently true; he wonders how he has hidden years of overt denial even from himself: you cannot function as a homicide detective and also run a family. You cannot be a husband and a father. You know that, at any moment, you may be gone, for days, or weeks, or for ever. If you stay, sooner or later, you will start lying and, like a gambler, like a psychopath, you will never stop.

He sends a text message to his rarely seen friends, Robert and Tania, who already have two dogs, asking if he can leave Flynn with them for a few days.

He drains his glass, replaces it on the table too heavily, fatigue still weighing on him. He checks that the doors and windows are locked, returns to the dining room. He sees the display on his phone light up, wonders whether Marantz has replied, but it is Robert confirming that one more dog amid their menagerie will be no problem. He smiles. He must be rid of everyone, everything close to him; only then does he feel free.

⋆ ⋆ ⋆

Overberg, Mossel Bay, Saturday, 2 January 2016
Dog deposited, De Vries drives past the airport, through the congested multiple junctions beside Strand and Somerset West, up over Sir Lowry's Pass, down into the Overberg. The road from the plateau offers a breathtaking panorama, vast, rolling hills extending as far as the horizon on every side, clouds kilometres long casting fast-moving shadow over arable crops, grazing sheep, bucolic farmsteads. He stops at a farm stall just short of Caledon, buys coffee and pastries, eats as he drives.

The N2 highway runs parallel to the southern

209

coast of Africa between the sea and the mountain ranges that separate the burned-out sandy Karoo from the verdant agricultural land that gives its name to the 'Garden Route'. Past Mossel Bay, some of the road runs beside the sea, offering views of endless dune-fringed white beaches, washed by elongated strands of silver surf. The journey from Cape Town to Mossel Bay is almost entirely inland, the vastness of the scenery numbing to those more used to a view across a street, or from the side of one house to the next.

He refuels in Riviersonderend, a quiet agricultural town, dusty and faded, its wide main street deserted but for a few coloured children sprawled under the canopy of the town's Superette.

He speeds through Stormsvlei, then slowly through the dead still, sweltering air of the old-established country town of Swellendam, set in the crook of tall, sheltering mountains, on to Heidelberg and Riversdale, before beginning to converge with the coast as he approaches Mossel Bay. When he glances at the clock in the car, he is surprised by the speed at which he has driven, perplexed by an impetus within him he does not understand. The traffic has remained light; he has travelled nearly five hundred kilometres in little over four hours.

He moves off the freeway onto the R102 into Mossel Bay. This road is smaller but busier, leading towards the sea, slow with holiday traffic, although, for De Vries, Mossel Bay would not qualify as a holiday destination. The town is

210

densely constructed with low, unattractive residences scattered among industrial estates, all on ground sloping towards the developed beach areas.

He turns ninety degrees, the sea on his right, the N2 freeway running parallel with him to the left. As he passes a golf driving range, he sees a sign advertising 'N2 Classics'. After three hundred metres, he pulls into the customer car park. The garage is on a large plot, with parking to one side of a courtyard, the main showroom facing the road. Beyond that, under a series of canopies, classic cars stretch out for two hundred metres. A few motorists have pulled over to look through the chain-link fencing at the rows of old Jaguars, Rolls-Royces and Bentleys. In the far section, American classics and muscle cars sit in front of a short row of rusting Minis.

De Vries pushes through the heavy glass door to the showroom, expecting air-conditioning, but finding only the same hot, dusty air as outside. It smells of old leather and damp carpet. Of the half-dozen or so cars inside, one is being polished unenthusiastically by a thin coloured man; a 1970s Triumph Stag has a white couple sitting inside it, feeling the seats and fiddling with the switchgear. A white guy in his mid-thirties, wearing a pale blue nylon shirt stands over them, bored. De Vries studies the cars, glances up at the little office at the rear of the showroom, sees a middle-aged white man at the desk, arms big, tattoos protruding from tight short sleeves. He turns away, walks outside to the canopied area, paces along the lines of classic cars. On closer inspection, the stock seems in poor condition: dented body panels, rusting scrapes, perished tyres, sagging exhausts . . .

He walks to the end of the line, then behind the Minis and back up the row. Beyond the showroom, behind a deserted cracked-concrete car park, there is a low warehouse and several sheds in disrepair. He looks around, strolls towards them. In the middle of the courtyard, he can hear only the road. He turns to the first of two large sets of wooden double doors. There is a hefty padlock. He studies it without touching it — it is in regular use. He moves to the second set of doors, listens, but hears nothing from within. These doors also feature a padlock, but this one is open, hanging loosely off the right-hand door. He takes a tissue from his pocket, pulls on the handle to open the door.

'Hey!'

The voice is coarse, echoing over the sun-bleached concrete. De Vries turns slowly.

The man walks quickly towards him. 'That's private in there.'

'I was looking for cars you didn't have out. You know, new stock.'

'No cars in there. Just our workshops.' The man points him back the way he has come, towards the canopied section of the business.

De Vries walks swiftly away, does not turn to look at the man. He moves towards a group of Mercedes Benz cars from the 1970s — they remind him of Marantz's old car. He wonders what has happened to Marantz, checks his phone to see if he has responded to his SMS. Nothing.

He looks back towards the courtyard and warehouses. The man has gone. De Vries snorts. The man had silver hair in a thick ponytail, face reddened by exposure to the sun and too much alcohol. He has no doubt that he is Marie Smith's driver and jailer.

He checks himself, as he vowed to Henrik du Toit he would. After studying the cars outside for a further ten minutes or so, he returns to his own, turns back towards town, taking a road to the left towards the sea until he reaches the car park for the Santos Express Train Lodge. Eight years previously, he had brought his family here on the way to their holiday in Plettenberg Bay. The lodge is a series of old train carriages on tracks beside the beach, offering modest accommodation in the carriage compartments, a wide deck overlooking the sea, where meals are served all day.

The deck is busy with tourists. He finds a table in the corner under the shade of a parasol, faces into the cool air blowing in from the ocean, orders a full cooked breakfast and a lemonade.

What he has seen at the garage convinces him that this was the stop-off point for Marie Smith. The name Carl and the description of the man with silver hair is, to his mind, conclusive. He has still not formulated his plan. His instinct is to bypass the local police, to survey the classic car garage perhaps after it has closed for the evening, assemble evidence and pump the man named Carl for further information. He has no qualms about using force if necessary to discover the source of the drugs, the names of the people in Port Elizabeth and those higher up, giving the orders, collecting the profits.

He considers his colleague of over twenty years, Henrik du Toit, the man's relentless quest for assimilation, both for black officers joining the SAPS and older white officers to remain in it. From the beginning, twenty years ago, to the stresses endured each week, the tensions are almost unsustainable.

He drinks half of the icy lemonade, starts on his hefty breakfast. He has decided that, even if he involves the local cops, his plans are fluid because he is here alone.

★ ★ ★

Refuelled, he gets back into the car, retraces his route.

George Road is a dual carriageway, with old streetlamps, low bushes and dying conifers planted in the central reservation. The SAPS station is a collection of low, pink-tiled buildings, fronted by a grassy bank of agaves and startling red hibiscus bushes. He parks in one of the spaces outside, walks into the public reception area. He flashes his ID at the desk officer, is buzzed into the administrative unit, invited to sit in a small, humid waiting room.

After a short interval, Captain Trevor Josephs salutes De Vries, shakes his hand, ushers him into his office. 'What brings you to Mossel Bay, sir?'

De Vries studies him: a slim coloured man, nervous, enthusiastic, impressed by De Vries's rank. He smiles to himself: Josephs is the perfect officer for what he requires.

'This is confidential, Captain, an extension to an investigation out of Cape Town, linking to towns between the Mother City and Port Elizabeth. We have reason to believe that suspects may be based in, or close to, Mossel Bay.'

Josephs nods encouragingly. 'It will not surprise you to know that we are short-staffed, backs to the wall, but we will offer you any assistance we can.'

De Vries observes the orderliness of the simple office, the notices neatly displayed, the Captain's desk clear of dockets and post-it notes, the simple photograph of the man and his family. So many local police stations are chaotic, lacking basic security, basic order.

'I may need you, three or four more officers. I will also need a forensics team. You think that is possible?'

'When, sir?'

'Now.'

Josephs balks. 'I'll see what I can do. May I ask the nature of your enquiries here?'

'In due course. We may require warrants. I assume you have a route to obtain these quickly?'

Josephs frowns. 'It would have been easier, sir, if we could have prepared for this.'

De Vries leans over the man's desk. 'Captain, I prefer to bypass official channels, especially when my information is sensitive, but even I have to answer to those upstairs and they want this

215

done correctly. Co-operation and synergy. I rely on you to assist me. You understand?'

Josephs nods. 'The addresses for the warrants required, sir?'

'You will deal with the warrant application personally, Captain. I don't want news of my interest to leave this room.'

'Yes, sir.'

'N2 Classics.'

'The classic-car garage?'

'*Ja*. The manager, or owner, Carl. You know him?'

'No, sir.'

'You can find out about him? I believe his name is Hertzog. Carl Hertzog.'

'I know an officer with an interest in old cars who has been there. He doesn't speak highly of the business.'

'He's on duty?'

'Yes. I can call him now.'

De Vries waits as Josephs makes the call. Within a minute, there is a knock on the door. Sergeant Daniels stands straight as he speaks. 'The owner's name is Carl Hertzog, sir. His family are from Germany. They came to live in Mossel Bay back in the nineteen fifties.'

'He owns the business?'

'I believe so. I have two old Mercedes cars, sir. I work on them when I have time. I visited the garage on three or four occasions, maybe a year back, for spare parts I couldn't find elsewhere. Mr Hertzog was not in any way helpful. He has stock there he cannot possibly sell on, but he was unwilling to assist me. I looked at the stock

216

carefully. Most of it is in very poor condition. I don't understand how he keeps his business going.'

'You see another man?' De Vries describes the burly older man with silver hair and tattoos.

'No, sir.'

'He's there today. I saw him when I pulled into the car park before lunch. He doesn't sound familiar?'

Both men shake their heads.

'We'll need the home address of Carl Hertzog.'

'I already know where he lives.'

'You do?'

'After I had visited his garage for the last time,' Daniels says, 'I discovered that he lived on Muller Street, about ten kilometres up the coast. A big house, right on the beach.'

'Why did you find that out?'

Daniels shifts his weight, glances at Josephs.

Josephs says, 'Sergeant Daniels suspected that the garage was being used for illegal activities. He came to me, but I told him that, without evidence, we could not proceed. We have enough work already.'

De Vries turns to Daniels, quietly impressed by the tall, broad officer, narrow threads of beard and moustache delineating the features of his face.

'Your suspicion may be correct.' He looks back to Josephs. 'But your captain was right to wait. I believe that we will find evidence of serious crimes on this man's premises ... With your permission, Captain, let us include Sergeant

Daniels here, with two or three more officers. I'll brief you and your team when we have completed and obtained the relevant warrants.'

* * *

De Vries hears shouting, slurred voices arguing, the sound of a struggle or fight. A hot Saturday afternoon in a working seaside town. He has not left Josephs's office. Part of him is congratulating himself on taking the official route, consulting with the local force, involving them in a traditional, scripted operation, yet he fears he has taken an unnecessary risk that, despite warnings of strict secrecy, Josephs or Daniels may tell colleagues of their plans and, somehow, the information will leak to Carl Hertzog.

By 5 p.m., the warrants have been issued, Josephs has assembled a team of four officers plus himself, and all have listened to what De Vries has told them. As they drive to the N2 Classics garage, De Vries reflects that it was harder to work with a trained team of Drug officers from Cape Town than a group of motivated ordinary police from Mossel Bay. He hopes that Captain Josephs will do nothing to dent his favourable impression.

* * *

De Vries is pleased to see the car park empty, the showroom seemingly locked. He leads two marked police cars into the rear of the property, dispatches two officers to check the showroom

218

area. As he turns to the sheds, the door of the warehouse opens and the silver-haired man appears. He sees the patrol cars, ducks back inside the unit. Three officers chase after him, two run behind it as the other shakes the now locked door at the front. De Vries stands calmly with Josephs. He hears officers shouting a warning from behind the sheds, then sees them appear with the silver-haired guy in cuffs, marching across the courtyard.

The man stares at De Vries, tilts his chin at him. 'I smelt fucking cop pig on you.'

'*Ja?* I smelt pathetic loser on you.'

They lead the man away to a secure van.

'You check if he had a phone?'

One of the officers produces an old-model cell phone. De Vries puts on gloves, switches it on, checks recent calls. None made or received for the last two hours. A battered wallet reveals an ID card bearing the name Kevin Coetzee.

The officers return from their search of the showrooms and canopied areas to report that no one else is present. De Vries signals to Josephs, who calls for Forensics to attend the scene.

Kevin Coetzee is locked into the back of a police van and De Vries follows the forensics team into the main warehouse.

Josephs says, 'We have missed Carl Hertzog.'

'We know where he is,' De Vries says, 'and we know that Coetzee hasn't contacted him. He won't know we're here.'

The interior is hot and muggy, thick with the smell of oil and petrol. Above them, the underside of the tin roof is clearly visible;

219

beneath their feet the concrete floor is dirty and warm, gritty with metal shavings, screws and plastic debris. All the surfaces of the building exude the heat of the day. De Vries feels sweat at his collar, his face greasy and hot from a day in the car and now inside the sweltering building.

The main area is large and open. The left-hand side has a workbench littered with tools and small car parts. To their right, two cars have been partially dismantled. Ahead, there is an exit, now open, allowing the early-evening air to drive a cool path from front to back of the building.

De Vries paces the inner perimeter, head bowed, gently moving debris with the toe of his shoe. There is an atmosphere inside the giant shed which unnerves him, as if it were a place where fear had been experienced, evil had manifested itself.

In the far-left corner, he squats down to examine a group of items, feels his fingers tingle. On the ground there are two large concrete blocks with iron hoops sunk into them, like parts of an old bicycle rack. A set of handcuffs is locked to each hoop. He tries to move one of the blocks but it is too heavy. He imagines the girls cuffed here, left in the shed overnight, alone, frightened, probably drugged.

After one of the forensics team has photographed the area, he pulls three wooden crates away from the corner, placing them carefully to one side. Behind them, low on the wall, he sees shallow scratches in the concrete sections making up the structure of the building. He

220

stands up, lets the team move in to process the scene. He indicates the cuffs. He steps back, peers over their bowed heads, tries to make out the letters scratched on the surface. He deciphers two girls' names: Mary and Anna. Under Anna's name, there are two more words. When he makes them out, he swallows. 'Help me.'

He struggles to recall if the names Anna and Mary appeared on the list of girls they have so far identified as being sent to Thailand. His brain is scrambled. Seeing the scene in the shed has brought Marie Smith's story to life. It appals him.

De Vries returns to the front entrance of the shed, where he finds Josephs. 'The girls I told you about were kept here. If the forensics team can pick up DNA, we may be able to find out who and how many.'

'We had no idea.'

'No reason you should. The classic-car business was a perfect cover. Cars come in, go out, travel around.'

'You want to go to this Carl Hertzog?'

De Vries wants to tell Josephs nothing, to walk to his car and continue his business alone. He feels he owes him a truth of sorts. He gestures for Josephs to follow him away from the sheds, towards the garage showroom. 'I need to speak to Hertzog off the record and before he's arrested.'

'I don't understand.'

'Once he gets into the system, lawyers up, starts official proceedings, it'll be too late. He, or his attorney, can warn people higher up in the chain. I can't let that happen. I need to know about the victims, how they were chosen, who his contact is, where the drugs come from, who works for him in Port Elizabeth.'

'We can find that out through questioning.'

'Captain, I'm showing you the respect you deserve, and I'm ensuring that you are not implicated. There are situations in which procedure doesn't work. I want you to leave me to operate as I see fit. Stay here, then I need you back at your station, preparing to interview Coetzee.'

'You do not trust me to work with you?'

'If I didn't trust you, I would have done this alone. You've vindicated my decision to involve you. But I won't compromise your position. Turn away from me, Captain.'

Josephs says, 'Take Sergeant Daniels with you.'

'I don't think that's a good idea — for him.'

Josephs lowers his voice. 'Dan Daniels is a good officer. He is wasted here. He was suspicious about this place a year ago. I stopped him. He'll back you up, and he'll keep what happens to himself.'

'All right. Send him over. And, Captain, I was right about you.'

* * *

De Vries and Daniels drive in convoy along the now quiet N2 freeway, east along the southern coastline. As they reach the turn to the Bothastrand and Glentana Estates, dusk falls quickly when the sun disappears behind the black pencil line of the horizon. The dunes turn a dusty turquoise, the sea an inky blue.

They drive down Kus Street, well-tended, deserted, sand blown across the surface, gathering in the gutters. A few lights from the houses to the left of the road mark out the residential side as it leads to a prominent hill. They drive past a parking area for the beach to their right, join Steenbras Street, climb the side of the hill. De Vries orders Daniels to wait at the beginning of the single-track section of the road, pleased that the officer is with him. He drives on, pulls over a few metres past the house identified as belonging to Carl Hertzog.

The ground-floor windows are illuminated, the door answered quickly by a short blonde woman, identifying herself as Hertzog's wife. De Vries does not show his ID or state who he is, merely says that he is looking for Carl. She studies De Vries with eyes he decides are innocent of her husband's crimes. She points down the street to a walkway onto the beach, explains that Carl is walking the dog, as he does every evening.

De Vries trots the hundred or so metres to the end of the road, steps off the tarmac surface to a sandy path, out onto the broad, flat beach. Beyond this point, there is only a narrow track leading, he assumes, to a further property at the top of the shrubby hill. He calls Daniels, instructs him to move his car up to where he has sight of the path to the beach, to look out for anyone else walking on or off the sand.

Ahead, the beach becomes narrower as grassy dunes replace man-made development. A few hundred metres further on, the rocky haunch of the dark hill crumbles onto the beach, disintegrating into stones and shingle in the sea. There, waves hit land, burst into matt-white spray.

★ ★ ★

The light is muted, glowing faintly above the cold sea. To his right, the sandy beach stretches as far as he can see back towards Mossel Bay, its land boundary illuminated by the occasional house or street light. There are a few people in the far distance. To his left, where the beach narrows, he sees a single figure and, next to it, a large dog, chasing a ball or stick into the waves, running back out again. De Vries begins to walk along the beach towards them. At sea, a few dim lights glimmer on boats, to his left, the land is dark, the sky low, milky with cloud.

He thinks that the tide must be at its highest as the beach becomes narrower and the sound of the waves engulfs him. Amid the cacophony he thinks of Marie Smith, the scratched autographs in the concrete. He increases his pace, breathing more deeply. The man he believes to be Carl Hertzog is sauntering towards him. When they are about a hundred and fifty metres apart, the man stops. Although he cannot hear him, De Vries assumes that he is calling his dog. The animal bounds in from the sea towards its master, runs to him, curls around his legs, stands facing De Vries. De Vries continues walking until he hears the voice.

'Who are you? This is a private beach.'

De Vries waves, smiles. At the same time, he looks to his left, wonders if there is anywhere to run for cover if the dog comes for him.

'Stop there.'

De Vries stops. The dog is bigger than he had anticipated: a Rhodesian Ridgeback with powerful hind legs and a big jaw. It has pushed its front paws forward in the sand, the hanging tongue replaced by curled lips and a row of top teeth. 'I'm looking for Carl Hertzog.'

'Who are you?'

'Are you Carl Hertzog?'

They are less than twenty meteres apart, but the conversation is shouted against the crash of waves rolling onto the beach. There is little more than a stiff breeze, but it still whips the sounds from their mouths.

De Vries steps closer.

'Stay where you are. Who are you?'

'Police. There has been an incident at your place of business.'

Hertzog makes no move towards him or to calm his dog. The animal has its eyes locked on De Vries. 'What incident?'

De Vries steps closer, hears the dog growling over the waves hitting the hard grey sand. At fifteen metres, De Vries sees Hertzog reach into his pocket. He takes out his pistol. The dog has started to bark. De Vries can see the tension in the dog's limbs, imagines the damage an attack could cause him. The animal could take him down, kill him.

'Hold your dog or I fire.'

Hertzog raises his hands, empty.

'Hold your dog.'

Suddenly, Hertzog turns, runs. The dog yelps, jumps towards De Vries, kicking sand behind it. De Vries aims his gun, fires one shot in front of the dog, prepares to shoot again at it. At the crack of the pistol, the dog stops, almost falling over itself. Its eyes reflect the blank grey-blue of the sky, seeming to flash in the gloom. De Vries does not want to shoot the animal. He despises Hertzog for sending it towards him. In the split second their eyes meet, De Vries wills it to turn away. The dog's mouth hangs open. Its tongue appears. It spins round, runs after Hertzog. De Vries follows, gun out, sees Hertzog up ahead on all fours. He has fallen, is trying to drag himself upright.

As De Vries approaches him, the dog takes up position next to its master. The tongue disappears, replaced by the threatening snarl.

'Stay away.'

Hertzog's voice is strained. As he struggles to stand, his left leg gives way and he sinks down onto the other knee.

De Vries walks closer, his gun still trained on the animal. 'Hold your dog by its collar. Do it now.'

Hertzog looks first at De Vries, then beyond him. De Vries trusts that Daniels has guarded the entrance to the beach, stays focused on Hertzog. The man reaches into his loose jacket pocket.

'Wait.'

He moves slowly, producing a metal link lead. As he draws his arm back, De Vries sees the bright green tattoo, the trailing tendrils and spiky leaves.

'He's guarding me. Leave the dog alone.' He snaps the lead onto the dog, drags it towards a jutting piece of rock, loops the lead around it.

'That had better be secure. The dog attacks, it's dead.'

'It's secure.'

De Vries approaches Hertzog, who has fallen back to his knees, pats him down, takes his phone. He glances behind him, sees nothing in the deep gloom, hears only the relentless crashing of the surf. 'You know why I'm here?'

Hertzog stares up at him. 'No.'

'I want the names of the people you collect the girls from in Port Elizabeth. I want to know the source of the drug shipments, the name of your contact above you.'

'I don't know what you mean.'

De Vries lashes out at Hertzog's face, waist high, unmoved by the fact that the man is on his knees. He feels the smack of his knuckles against the man's skin, the thud of the pistol barrel on his cheekbone. Hertzog howls; the dog barks and squeals.

'I'm not here to talk. I want what you know. You give it to me, or I shoot your dog.'

'No.' Hertzog is panting, shocked by the assault on his face.

De Vries registers no compassion. He feels his vision tunnelled by the darkness. He needs only the information. The dog's incessant barking makes him impatient to finish his job.

'I tell you anything, I'm dead.'

'You raped those girls, then sent them to their deaths. Right now, you have one chance of living.'

De Vries stands over him, sees the blood from Hertzog's nose drip onto the sand, enunciates slowly and clearly, his eyes never leaving Hertzog's pathetic upward stare. 'I will kill your dog. I will kill you. I will kill your wife. If you have children, I'll find them. Whatever they've threatened you with, I'm worse.'

'Who are you?'

'No one is coming. I have colleagues up at your house now. I give the signal, they kill your wife.'

He sees Hertzog frozen, shocked and unfocused. He smacks him on the top of his head with the butt of his pistol, sees him keel over onto the sand, the side of his head almost bouncing on a partially submerged rock. Hertzog screams, claws at the sand with his hands. His dog yelps and howls. De Vries gets on his knees, his gun pushed into the side of Hertzog's face.

Hertzog is snorting gobs of phlegm and blood, his entire body shaking.

'What — what do you want?'

'The names of the people in Port Elizabeth.' De Vries's voice is like rock on rock, staccato, uncompromising.

Hertzog mumbles something..

'The suppliers, where you collect the product, where you store it before delivery to Cape Town. Talk now.'

He hears slurred sentences, names, addresses. His mind will retain every detail.

'Who runs the operation?'

'Don't know.'

'Your contact?'

Hertzog groans, feigns unconsciousness. De Vries kicks him, pulls his head up by his hair. He hears nothing but waves, hysterical barking, Hertzog's moans, his own breathing, as if refracted back from the side of the black hill collapsing into the beach. He smacks Hertzog's head back down onto the rock, raises it again. The man's face is contorted, featureless in the darkness, but glistening with black, tar-like blood, encrusted with sand. It is almost no longer a face. 'Your contact?'

Hertzog coughs blood, eyes squeezed shut. He draws a breath, shouts at De Vries. 'Uys — Tony Uys . . . Bweha Bweha.'

De Vries drops Hertzog's head. In the split second he stands straight, he acknowledges what he has done. Intense guilt sweeps over him, like a wave, but it dissipates on the shore as he remembers Chantal Adam, Marie Smith, the names of the girls scratched onto the wall, molested in their beds at Diane Kemmel's house, sent to lives of slavery or jail in Thailand.

He walks briskly away, guided only by the luminosity of the grey sky and the lights in the houses overlooking the perfectly beautiful beach.

PART 3

Cape Town, Monday, 4 January 2016
'Two more girls identified, a section of the pipeline severed. Two suspects in custody. A further connection up the chain of command. In Port Elizabeth we've raided two addresses, evidence of girls being lured, almost abducted, into the operation in the Boardwalk Casino environs.'

'Were you involved in the arrests at Mossel Bay?'

De Vries looks at Henrik du Toit, smiles. 'Let the locals take the credit. Co-operation, just as you prescribed.'

'One suspect was badly beaten. The medical examiner's report suggested a considerable struggle.'

'Well, sir. These people aren't very nice.'

Du Toit stares at him. 'Be careful, Vaughn. Your rank can protect you only so far.'

'Don't you tire of always being reactive, Henrik? Don't you believe in your own project any more? We intervene to break up criminal conspiracy, cut through bureaucracy, catch these people before they've embedded themselves in government, or the SAPS, or organized crime.'

'We have this conversation every time. We share the same ideals. I just work within the constraints of the law and the service and you . . . let's put it politely: strain the rules to their limits.'

'At least we get somewhere.'

'Yes,' Du Toit says. 'That is why we are tolerated, so far. Don't think for a moment that General Thulani won't dispose of us immediately if we give him reason. A whole generation of South African society — black, white and coloured — believe there is no place for the last vestiges of the apartheid regime. And that, whether you like it or not, is how we're still seen.'

'I met motivated, hard-working officers in Mossel Bay. Maybe just a small cross-section, but they're there. They were willing to act quickly to achieve justice.'

'I suspect a little bit of elite unit glitter rubbed off on them.'

'I've commended the station CO, Captain Josephs, and a Sergeant Daniels.'

Du Toit pulls himself up. 'I doubt that a commendation from you is really what those men need.'

'We all need a little praise, sir. Just sometimes.'

★   ★   ★

Don February says, 'I have searched throughout the Internet. The only reference to 'Bweha Bweha' is as a private game reserve on the south-western border of the Kruger Park.'

'Who owns it?'

'I don't know that, sir, but there is something interesting about the property.' He looks up at De Vries.

'Go on.'

'Bweha Bweha was bought eleven years ago

from its original owners. Since then, it has ceased to be a traditional tourist reserve, but instead concentrates on trophy hunting. It has registered with the appropriate bodies but, if you look on the Internet, there is quite a lot of material relating to it.'

'What kind of material?'

'Allegations of the mistreatment of animals, unlicensed removal of horn and tusk, the disappearance of stock from annual migrations across the unfenced reserves around Bweha Bweha.'

'I don't understand.'

'The concessions for big-game hunting are closely controlled. Game is not shot at random. Animals are usually brought into the vicinity, rangers guide the hunters to their quarry and ensure that the kill is made humanely. They use animals that would otherwise be culled because of sickness or overpopulation. A few voices claim that Bweha Bweha does not comply with regulations.'

'What about the name Tony Uys?'

'Tony, or Anthony, Uys is not listed on any of the material I could find on Bweha Bweha. He is not in the SAPS system but, sir, as you know, that does not mean he has not had dealings with us.'

'You can't locate anyone by that name connected to Bweha Bweha?'

'No. As far as I could discover, there is no one registered in that name in that area of Kruger Park.'

'All right, Don. Thanks. How's your part of the investigation going?'

'It is slow work. Chantal Adam did not stay in

any one place for long, especially in the weeks prior to her death. We will build up a picture of her movements.'

'Good.'

'You do not require the team to assist you?'

'No.'

De Vries looks down at Don February, all his notes neatly handwritten in front of him, impressed by his quiet warrant officer's careful order, his ability to fulfil De Vries's demands and continue his own investigation.

'Somewhere along the line,' he says, 'what we're doing is going to meet. Then, we'll know why Chantal Adam died.'

★ ★ ★

De Vries spends most of the morning reading Don February's research into the Bweha Bweha reserve, finding no reason to link it to the girls' abduction and trafficking. He even considers that Hertzog may have sold him a story unconnected with his contacts up the line in the process, yet when he reflects upon Hertzog's face, what he saw in the man's eyes, he feels confident that he told him the truth. As the sun hits the apex of its arc, its rays are reflected from the windows of the building opposite. De Vries's office warms rapidly. He looks out towards Signal Hill, glances down through the Christmas decorations, old and faded even before they were installed for another year, the streets busy with tourists, the New Year lull in business over, the season back in full swing. He knows that his knowledge of crime in the Western Cape casts a heavy pall over everything he sees: behind the façade, inhumanity thrives.

He turns back to the reports, agitates his mouse, Googles a name that has recurred numerous times.

Richard Dow is a former deputy chief ranger from Gogoswana, the game reserve adjoining Bweha Bweha. His is an impressive CV of previous appointments and experience. For the past two years, he has written to newspapers and magazines, and produced articles and blogs, claiming that those at Bweha Bweha are mistreating their wildlife and accusing them of smuggling ivory and rhino horn off their reserve to sell on the black market. Only when De Vries reaches the end of the piece does he suddenly make a connection.

He squints at the screen, scrolls down the page, finds an email address to which he can send an enquiry. He asks if he can speak to Richard Dow, either online or by phone. He sends the message, sits back . . .

When he wakes, his mouth is dry, sweaty hands sticky on the plastic leather armrest of his chair. He leans into the screen, but there are no emails for him.

He stumbles up, his chair sliding away from him as he levers himself up from his desk. His squad room is quiet, the coffee-machine jug full. He has tried to avoid the office coffee as it gives him heartburn, but the thought of the hot walk to one of his favourite coffee-shops persuades him to compromise. He returns to his office with a mug, lays it down, sits, already despondent at the lack of information, the absence of a decent drink.

★ ★ ★

A little before three o'clock, he notices messages in his inbox. Several are junk but the subject line of one runs: 'Re: Richard Dow'. He clicks on it and reads:

Colonel de Vries.

Richard Dow was killed seven weeks ago. He was in a car accident on a road near White River. The police here ruled the crash an accident. They have closed the case. For the past few years, Richard had been critical of the owners of the reserve next to his workplace. Both SANParks and the local police made cursory enquiries and gave the place a clean bill of health, but Richard received many threats to our wellbeing and to his life. My husband knew the roads around here well. It is too much of a coincidence that his 'accident' occurred when it did, but nobody will listen.

If you can help me, I will speak to you, but if you dismiss our claims, there is no point. I am returning to my home town in the Northern Cape on Saturday, the 9th, but I am available to meet you near Bushbuckridge before then.

Jane Dow

De Vries stares at the screen. The message changes his view of a connection between Bweha Bweha and his own investigation. He clicks to reply but his fingers hover over the keyboard and he withdraws them. From experience, he knows how unsafe email can be. He is certain that the elite units' Internal Investigation Department, headed by David Wertner, has hacked him, and everyone else, is probably still doing so.

He stands up, grabs his briefcase, heads for the lifts.

★　★　★

Dominique is not, as Don February had anticipated, a woman. He is a very tall, very black slim man, head shaved smooth, diamond studs in both ears. His skin shines, smells of oranges. He wears a black suit with a zebra-skin waistcoat.

'It's *faux*,' he tells Don. He sits up eagerly, invites the officer to join him on a pair of bright red chairs shaped like lips. The SA *Event* magazine offices are bright, every wall hung with blown-up covers, celebrities from South Africa, the United States, the UK smiling down at them, their faces perfect, without blemish.

'What is your surname, sir?'

'It's Dominique. Just Dominique.' His voice is high and soft. His hands stroke his thighs, smoothing invisible creases.

'You wrote an article for this magazine about Chantal Adam. Is that right?'

'Yes. Well, you say one, but I wrote more than

239

one . . . The original article was about the 'Mountain Girl' and her big adventure to America.'

His accent, Don thinks, is Mozambican; precise and slightly French. He finds Dominique intimidating in his camp self-confidence; he is conscious of his own old suit. Even the offices, with their table-tennis table and café, he finds alien; he wonders how much work is actually done here. 'Did you speak with her personally?'

'Oh, yes. When she was eighteen, she was happy to talk to anyone, especially a magazine like *Event*. She was at the start of a big career. This was exposure, and that's what it's all about, right?'

'Did you ask her about leaving home? About being away from home in America?'

'She couldn't wait to get out. Like any other teenager, she wanted freedom.' He elongates the last word, long fingers forming palm fronds. He lowers his voice. 'You know they're not her real parents, don't you?'

'Yes, sir.'

He spreads his thin arms along the back of the wide chair. 'Whatever they gave her — the house by the sea, the education, the allowance — she was happy just to be on her way.'

'Do you know why?'

'Why do we all want to get away? To do what we want, when we want, with whom we want. To be ourselves.'

Don's brain stalls briefly. He sits up, says: 'You do not think she was happy at home?'

'I don't know.' He stretches his neck right

240

back, exposing his Adam's apple, rests first one cheek, then the other against the corresponding shoulder, rights himself. 'I don't think her step-daddy wanted her to go. He was quite against it, but I don't think anything would have stopped her. She was eighteen.'

'What happened in America?'

'It's not an uncommon story. She went to New York naïve, innocent, got overtaken by the lights, the music, the drugs. I don't know if this is true, but I was told she had an affair with the guy who managed her out there. When that broke up, so did her career.'

'And she got ill?'

'She did what the other girls did, but she couldn't cope. It's almost a cliché. In the pictures of her, you could see she was on something . . . probably lots of things. But her weight, my God, it went into freefall, and all of a sudden that sun-kissed, perfect skin, beautiful hair, eyes, they were all dull and grey. That was it.'

'Did you see her when she returned to Cape Town?'

'I saw her, sure. Did I interview her? No. Why would I? We're not that sort of magazine.'

'But you're writing about her now?'

'Yes.' He pouts. 'It's the end of the story. A short story. A prosaic story. It is what the readers want.'

'Did you speak to a lady called Angela Cole?'

'In Sea Point? Yes. Why?'

'How did you know she knew Chantal Adam?'

'I didn't. She came to me. Called the office. I

went, but she was just a landlady, a lonely woman seeking a corner of the limelight. When you are me, you're surrounded by them.'

'May I see your article, sir?'

'No. It isn't written. It's all in here.' He touches his head with a flourish. 'But the original article is on my website. Here . . . ' He proffers the same card that Don saw at Angela Cole's house.

'You will report that she committed suicide?' Don asks.

'Is that not correct?'

'Do you have a theory as to why she might have killed herself?'

'Not a theory, just a feeling. She has come from way up there, and now she is so low, it is almost impossible to go lower. When she was famous, she had all these friends telling her how beautiful she was, how talented she was. Everyone recognized her. Now, there is none of that. She is on her own, she is not well, she has no money. She is desperate . . . '

'So why not go home?'

'Maybe she feels it is not really her home. She is an orphan who had everything, and now she has nothing. You think of it like that, and perhaps it is no surprise she wanted to end it all.'

★   ★   ★

De Vries buys coffee, uses the café Wi-Fi to send a message to Jane Dow from his own private email account, suggesting a meeting. As he walks back to his building, he recognizes Jack

242

Esterhuysen coming towards him.

'Can we talk?' Esterhuysen is dishevelled, agitated.

De Vries nods, retraces his path to the café, takes him to the back. The L-shaped layout affords him cover from the street, yet enables him to see who enters in the long mirror down the side wall. He buys two more strong coffees, lays them down. 'What is it, Lieutenant?'

'What's happening?'

'What's happening with what?'

'I thought we had a deal that we would work together to crack these people.'

'You thought wrong. I told you I'd call you if I needed you.'

Esterhuysen shuts his eyes, his breathing heavy. 'Mark Immelman — Lee-Ann's husband — has been off sick since she died. I am concerned for his wellbeing. This has caused more repercussions than you know. What happened in Mossel Bay?'

'Two men were arrested. They led us to several addresses in Port Elizabeth.' He studies Esterhuysen. 'Why aren't you at work?'

'Because . . . ' Esterhuysen almost shouts, then lowers his voice, 'because I've taken leave owed to me. I want to help on this — need to help. You found links up the line?'

'Possibilities only.'

'Where? Who are they?'

'I don't know.' De Vries is concerned that Esterhuysen is somehow obsessed with the case, his grief for Lee-Ann Heyns distorting his professional judgement. He fears that, left out,

Esterhuysen could go to Du Toit, even David Wertner, report how the original events have escalated. 'I may be going north tomorrow, another lead — something that may be nothing or may be a source of all this. Go home, pack a bag. I'll book a flight for you too. I'll SMS you when I know times.'

'Where to?'

'Kruger Park. Place called Bushbuckridge. We may be going hunting.'

★ ★ ★

Gauteng and Mpumalanga Provinces,
Tuesday, 5 January 2016
De Vries and Esterhuysen scarcely exchange a complete sentence on the two-hour flight from Cape Town to Johannesburg. O. R. Tambo International Airport is busy, resolutely non-smoking. De Vries is dry-mouthed, frustrated. They reach the car-hire desk to find the queue stretching beyond the faded navy blue velvet rope and worn carpet intended to cherish the customer.

They wait wordlessly, take pigeon steps towards the desks. When Esterhuysen turns from him, De Vries studies the back of his head, observes tension in his shoulders, monitors the fast-beating pulse in his neck. What drives him remains obscure, unless Lee-Ann Heyns meant more to him than he to her. Whatever it is, right now, he is happy enough to have him at his side.

There is a protracted argument at the desks. De Vries looks at his watch again. He hopes his effort will not be wasted, that Jane Dow will not refuse to speak to him unless he offers some unsustainable undertaking. He dismisses such negativity. In the in-flight magazine, he had read the words of Desmond Tutu: 'Find in everything frustrating a little oasis of calm.' De Vries sighs deeply, taps his foot, wishes he could find a little oasis where he is permitted to smoke.

He tells Esterhuysen to remain in the queue, seeks an exit into the fresh air, goes outside. Within five seconds, he has lit up, inhaled a joyous first draught of nicotine.

* * *

Almost ninety minutes after landing, they locate the car in its underground space. De Vries kicks the rear tyre of the low-grade, cut-price vehicle, ordered in line with departmental regulations. He swings open the door, feels flimsy metal flex, curses the need to penny-pinch every last cent.

As they reach daylight, he opens his window onto the oppressive, aviation-fuel-soaked air, pulls open the ashtray, laughs as it comes off in his hand. He says, 'I am a little oasis of calm.'

Esterhuysen navigates out of town on the busy N12, then the N4 towards Nelspruit or, as the new signs insist, Mbombela. Road and town names are changing, the old familiar map of South Africa suddenly more African, almost alien.

De Vries has eaten nothing since a snatched supermarket pasta dish the previous evening. He pulls into the first decent-looking service station, buys two pepper steak pies, two cheese and bacon twists, two extra-large coffees. Esterhuysen nods silently as he takes the supplies. He tries to fit the cups into the tiny plastic holders, but ends up holding one in each hand.

They pass through burned-out landscape under a low, heavy sky, so different from the rolling expanses of the Cape, with its massive cloud formations bathing the land in shadows the size of islands. Here, the distance between land and sky seems shallow; the air smells of electricity.

As they turn off the freeway onto the R40 to Hazyview, the landscape broadens, low mountains border their route, the feeling of weight above them recedes. The air seems warmer and, reluctantly, De Vries winds up his window until it jams just short of closure, guns the whining air-con, focuses on the uneven surface of the narrower roads.

Jane Dow has instructed him to meet her at a resort called Milner's Lodge, off the road between Bushbuckridge and Graskop.

By five o'clock, they reach Hoof Street in Graskop, finding the long, low concrete-and-wood Graskop Hotel at the end of the main drag. De Vries sees a sign to a SAPS station on the parallel Monument Street only a few metres from the hotel, wonders whether they can remain incognito, even for the short time he intends to stay. They park on the street, directly outside the hotel, check into their executive twin room.

De Vries has already told Esterhuysen that he

will meet Jane Dow alone: he fears that more than one person might intimidate, inhibit her. He sends Esterhuysen away, showers, changes his clothes, gets back into the car, heads out on the R533. The winding road cuts through huge forests of gum trees, wide agricultural land and the occasional farmstead. When the sun appears through the matt grey cloud, it is low, intensely orange.

He spots a hand-painted sign indicating the turn to the resort, takes the gravel track down into a shallow valley, finds a busy car park in front of an original Victorian hunting lodge, surrounded by modern chalets and cottages built in a thatched vernacular style. He parks, unfurls himself from the car, walks quickly to the reception, where he is greeted by a smiling black woman. When he asks for Jane Dow, her expression darkens and she calls for another member of staff from the back office. A slender German woman examines him, and his ID, over a pair of narrow frameless glasses, then escorts him through the old building into a converted barn, out onto a small terrace overlooking gardens and a wide circular swimming-pool. De Vries walks slowly towards a middle-aged woman sitting at the only occupied table, looks back as the metal-framed door onto the terrace is closed behind him.

'Mrs Dow?'

She is already standing, her hand proffered. Her face is marked by grief, tight with stress, smile forced. 'Mr de Vries.'

He sits next to her, watches as she pours a

247

glass of water from a jug, places it in front of him. She is deeply tanned, lined and world-weary, but she has the look of someone happy to have spent her life out of doors. Her dark hair is styled up and back from her face.

'Thank you for coming all this way. How was your journey?'

De Vries drinks the water, grateful for any refreshment. 'Tedious.' He looks around him. 'But this is a nice place. Not where you lived, surely?'

'No. I moved out of our house. My friends felt it wasn't safe, especially as I'm on my own now.'

'I'm sorry.'

'Kamilla, the woman who greeted you, is an old friend of ours. She insisted I stay here while I arranged the move home.'

'Who do you think is threatening you?'

'The men who killed Richard.'

'And they are . . . ?'

'The people from Bweha Bweha.'

De Vries shakes his head. 'We need to start from the beginning, Mrs Dow.'

'You don't waste time.'

'There's none to waste.'

She scrapes the metal chair back on the stone terrace, crosses her ankles, but sits open and relaxed. 'Richard worked in the Kruger for the last thirty years. I met him, married him and moved here. His most recent position was as a ranger trainer and naturalist at Gogoswana Reserve. He was highly regarded by everyone in his field.' She takes a sip of water, sighs. 'About six years ago, the land next to the reserve was granted a licence as a hunting concession. They had been seeking it for a while, and our attempts to prevent it failed. They opened only a few months later as Bweha Bweha. I can't tell you that we were surprised it obtained its licence because, even though it is located amongst conservation reserves that have taken down the fences, allowing free movement of game within the Kruger, that is unimportant. Here, it is only who you know, and what influence you can exert.'

'This is Africa.'

A slight, sad smile flashes across her face. 'Almost immediately Richard became aware of disturbances to migration paths, groups of animals diminishing, and a high number of hunters arriving by helicopter and car, disturbing the ecosystem. He and others reported to the game protection agencies, like the National Wildlife Reaction Unit, the National Biodiversity Investigators Forum, SANParks, but, after cursory investigations, their concerns were dismissed and Bweha Bweha continued.'

'I read a little of the Internet discussions.'

'I'll keep it brief. Richard suspected that Bweha Bweha was far exceeding its quota on big game. He thought it was possibly being used as a cover for ivory and rhino horn smuggling — I'm sure you've read about that. It's a multi-million-dollar business. The moment he made those views public, the trouble started.'

De Vries rubs his hand down his face. The evening is humid; he can hear the distant rumbling of thunder. He stands, takes off his jacket, hangs it on the back of his seat. 'How are people allowed to hunt big game at all?'

'It's not really hunting. The trophy hunting concessions buy in game from elsewhere and set it up to be killed by their very rich customers. Old and injured animals are used, those which would be culled anyway because of overpopulation or illness. Even so, the business should be very closely monitored. Richard felt that, for whatever reason, Bweha Bweha was escaping proper supervision.'

'He suspected some kind of conspiracy?'

'Yes.'

'What happened leading up to his alleged accident?'

She looks at him, silently challenging his choice of words. He estimates that she must be approaching sixty, but she is slim and strong; the life behind her eyes speaks of an alert mind, a woman capable of passing judgement accurately. He is apprehensive of such women.

'Complaints, not just from Richard but also from reputable conservation bodies, were consistently rejected. A tracker from Bweha Bweha gave evidence against his employers. A week later, he had disappeared. They said he had returned home, but he was never found. Richard called a contact of his, a journalist in Jo'burg. He rolled up there posing as a guest, a hunter. All of a sudden, he's dead. Accident. You can look it up — May of last year. His name was Bryan Voetes. We wait to see what will happen, but the police here, they investigate and say, 'Accident — that's what it was.' Now no one wants to get involved.

250

Not the police, not the papers. Everyone around here just keeps quiet.'

'And you are leaving?'

'There's nothing left.'

De Vries hesitates, distracted by the increasingly strident sounds from the bush now that dusk has fallen. 'I haven't been to the Kruger for twenty years . . . '

'That's sad.'

'At Bweha Bweha, is there a man called Tony, or Anthony, Uys?'

'Tony Uys. Yes. Why?'

'I told you that I am investigating a serious crime in the Western Cape. I have a possible connection to a Tony Uys at Bweha Bweha Reserve.'

'It wouldn't surprise me if he's involved in bad things. We all call him the White Mamba.' She chuckles at De Vries's expression. 'It's a joke. The most feared snake in the Kruger is the Black Mamba. Tony Uys is a white guy, and he is feared — there's no doubt of that — so that's what we call him.'

'Why feared?'

'He has a malevolent presence. You get the feeling that, if what they do at Bweha Bweha is criticized, he is the one they wheel out.'

'What's his role, officially?'

She leans forward, almost conspiratorially. 'I should tell you, as a conservationist, that the Black Mamba is not as much trouble as the Puff Adder. It just plays on its reputation.' She smiles. 'I don't know what he does. I only visited Bweha Bweha once. I didn't want to go back.' She stares out at the darkening gardens and beyond, to the edge of a broad gum-tree plantation. The crickets drown out other natural sounds. 'In fact,' she continues, 'I think Richard said he arranged and transported the foreign guests.'

'Do you know who these guests are?'

She smiles at him sadly.

'You ask the right questions. Many hunters are Americans, but Bweha Bweha specialises in guests from the Far East: Thailand and Vietnam particularly.'

Something clicks in his brain. 'Is that unusual?'

'There are Far Eastern trophy hunters out here but never women. At least, if there are women, they're not interested in the game. One man might bring three or four women with him, stay a few days and then go home again. That way, they can legally take trophies out of the country — for each of them. That equates to a lot of contraband. Guess where the two major markets for stolen ivory and horn are located?'

'Thailand?'

'Thailand for ivory, Vietnam for rhino horn. It's worth more than gold. A real status symbol. But it's no more than keratin. These people might as well be snorting toenail clippings.' She looks up at De Vries, evidently expecting a reaction to what she is saying. 'Are you listening to me?'

'Yes.'

'What are you thinking?'

'Snorting? They snort the horn?'

'They treat it like cocaine. They pile it up in

252

little mountains on their coffee-tables to impress their guests.'

He shakes his head. 'Piles of nail clip-pings . . . '

'Exactly the same.'

'Did you tell anyone I was coming?'

'Only Kamilla. What are you going to do?'

'Leave your forwarding address with your friend here. If I have news after you've gone home, I'll leave a message for Kamilla to pass on to you.'

'What are you going to do?'

'Speak to people at Bweha Bweha. Obtain a warrant if necessary to investigate further.'

'The last officer who tried to get a warrant was refused by the local magistrate. A few days later, he was transferred to the Eastern Cape. Everything that happens here gets passed on to the people at Bweha Bweha. You need to be careful.'

'I will be.'

She looks at him, waits, nods to herself. 'I didn't expect you to help to find Richard's killers, but whatever you're doing is dangerous. Are you sure that what you want is worth the risk to you?'

'Tony Uys may be behind more than the smuggling of contraband,' De Vries says quietly. 'He may be dealing in human beings too. If he is, he has the blood of many women on his hands.'

She looks away from him, and he sees her swallow. Just the right side of her face is illuminated by the storm lantern on the table. He imagines that, in a different situation, Jane

Dow would be a strong, striking woman, dynamic and not fearful.

'That is frightening. I can tell you that, here in the Kruger, it would surprise no one if there's blood on his hands.'

'Then he must not go unchallenged.'

'That is a commendable attitude, but I want you to remember that my husband challenged him. He never mentioned Uys's name, not as such, but Uys still came after him. I'm positive of that. I'm moving thousands of kilometres away and still I'm not certain that I will feel safe.'

'Then you should welcome my intervention.'

'It won't bring Richard back to me.' She sits up. 'But I'm being selfish. I suppose you meet a lot of people when they are at their lowest ebb. The victims of attacks, the widows, the families . . . How does that not taint everything you do?'

'I think all of us,' De Vries says calmly, 'have a well of pain within us. I just seem to bring it to the surface.'

★ ★ ★

The drive back to Graskop is very dark, the road lit by neither man nor heavens, the moon below the tree-line. Occasionally, his headlights reflect scarlet in the eyes of a wild animal staring at the oncoming vehicle, and he swerves several times to avoid small game, tortoises crossing leisurely.

The top of Hoof Street is crowded with workers and locals, but the end where the Graskop Hotel sits is quiet, almost deserted. As he parks in the same space as before, he hears a

254

crackling sound. He gets out of the car, looks above him. On the lamp post, there is the thin neon outline of a Christmas bell. It flashes languidly, fizzing with each illumination. He turns, looks back up the street; five more non-religious symbols are casting tiny pools of insipid light on the dusty pavement.

Inside, Jack Esterhuysen sits at the bar. De Vries orders a beer, suggests they eat immediately. The recommendation is the hotel's own pancake restaurant, Harrie's. The greeter tries to seat them amid the other guests, but De Vries asks to be shown to a table at the far end of the restaurant. He orders a pancake filled with biltong and mozzarella cheese; Esterhuysen decides to have the same. 'What have you been doing, Jack, while I was meeting Mrs Dow?'

Esterhuysen looks at the table. 'Stayed here. When it got to nine o'clock, I went to the bar for a beer.'

De Vries studies him, unable to decipher what the man is thinking. He does not trust his statements, yet none promise or deny anything of importance. He has met many introverted, sullen policemen in his time, but Esterhuysen's enigmatic behaviour is frustrating. When he works with a colleague, he needs to be able to relate to them, but in this officer, there is nothing. De Vries recounts what Jane Dow told him, pausing only for the arrival of two beers.

When he finishes, Esterhuysen says, 'Every time you say her name, I think of Jane Doe.' De Vries frowns. 'That's what American cops call an unidentified female body,' Esterhuysen clarifies.

'You get that from a crime novel?'

'I like crime novels.'

Their food arrives and both eat without speaking, except to order more beers.

'So, what do we do?' Esterhuysen says eventually. 'Try to get a warrant from the magistrate here?'

'No. The last time an officer tried to do that, he was transferred, far away. It's quite possible that the magistrate, or someone working for him, would warn the people at the reserve. We don't even need a warrant if we suspect that evidence might be removed while we apply.'

'So, we just drive into Bweha Bweha and ask for Tony Uys?'

'That's what I'm going to do,' De Vries says. 'I have other plans for you.'

★   ★   ★

Mpumalanga Province, Wednesday,
6 January 2016
When De Vries wakes the next morning at six thirty, Esterhuysen is not in the room. His bed is neatly made, bag packed. When De Vries looks at his nightstand, he sees that the car keys are missing.

He showers, wonders what Esterhuysen is doing, unease making him tense before he has even left the bedroom, a pervasive feeling that he is a thousand kilometeres from home, up against a powerful force, alone.

When he enters the dining room at seven, he sees Esterhuysen sitting on the opposite side of the room from the one other occupied table. They nod at one another.

'You sleep?' De Vries asks.

'Not well.'

'Where did you go?'

'I took the car to the local garage — it's just at the top of the road. Filled up, checked levels, bought a new map of the area.'

'All right.'

'I don't like having an underpowered vehicle,' Esterhuysen says. 'If we need to move fast, we can't. At least I now know exactly where we're going. There are a few options if we need to get away fast.'

De Vries nods. 'Major Ngcuka told me you were very thorough.'

'I'm risking — we're risking our lives here. You are the detective. My job is to get us back safely.'

'Good.'

'According to the online brochure for Bweha Bweha, guests who are there for game viewing — not hunting — take a drive between oh five hundred and oh nine hundred hours. If we arrive just after that time, people will be returning from the viewing and eating breakfast. That means there will be witnesses to your arrival. You should ensure that you're seen. It will make it harder for them to treat you as anything other than a guest.'

De Vries nods, impressed that Esterhuysen has done his research, that he considers his role to ensure their safety.

'Whoever these people are, whatever they're doing, they've managed to frighten a lot of people around here. If what Jane Dow told you is accurate, they retaliate quickly if you cross them. We need to be careful.'

'How long will it take us to get there?'

'Assuming a clear run, about forty-five minutes. We should leave at eight ten.'

De Vries glances at his watch, orders a full cooked breakfast from the waitress, a second pot of coffee.

★　★　★

The journey is fast and smooth, the roads almost empty. They pass the gates to Gogoswana, drive along a curved road for several kilometres before passing the tall, ostentatious gates to Bweha Bweha. De Vries pulls over to the side of the road a few hundred metres further on.

'When you enter, there will be a security gate.'

De Vries turns to Esterhuysen. 'How do you know?'

Esterhuysen smiles. 'Google Earth. The gate is likely manned twenty-four seven. The hotel and game lodges are approximately two kilometres further on.'

'You going on foot?'

'Ja.'

'What about the game?'

'They'll be more scared of me than I of them.'

Esterhuysen opens the door, closes it quietly. Without another word, he strides into the tall grass by the side of the road, heading towards the fence some hundred metres away.

De Vries swings the car around, retraces their path to the main gates, drives on to the property.

The security gate is only fifty metres inside. He brakes harshly. A quasi-military uniformed guard appears with a clipboard, salutes, questions him about his reservation. De Vries claims to want to discuss the possibility of game hunting, calling himself Henry van de Merwe. The guard makes a phone call, then directs him to the lodge in the far distance. He drives down the dirt track slowly, glancing in his mirrors out into the bush, looking for any sign of Esterhuysen. He sees only the neck and head of a giraffe, the backs of some unidentifiable buck and, in the distance, a herd of buffalo. The lodge building is huge: beige concrete and vast triangular plains of thatch, broad sliding glass doors on every side. When he reaches the car park, a young blond man trots down the steps to open his car door.

'Welcome to Bweha Bweha, sir. I am Simon Boucher, the marketing manager here.'

He has, De Vries thinks, a salesman's smile.

Boucher leads him inside the air-conditioned modern lodge, provides a quick tour of the slick but soulless premises, emphasizes the gaudy bar area, hung with trophy heads, with its contemporary take on a *boma* and permanent fire. In the dining room, De Vries sees two large tables of elderly guests, deep in intense conversation. He makes a point of walking inside the room, staring out at the view from the vast open windows, nodding at the pensioners. From there, he is led to a chilly meeting room overlooking the car park, where he accepts the offer of coffee. Boucher swings out of the room. While he is gone, De Vries studies the walls, which are

259

adorned with photographs of proud hunters holding up the sagging heads of slaughtered animals — a lioness, a wildebeest, a glamorous woman astride a dead rhinoceros. The humans are all Caucasian, not one Asian face. De Vries spent his early childhood on a farm, so he is not averse to shooting for the pot, but there is something smug about the people in these pictures, a pitiful desperation in their false pride, which makes him uneasy.

The door to the meeting room opens and De Vries turns. A man is entering, very tall with silver hair swept back from his deeply tanned forehead, a small white moustache above narrow lips. De Vries takes him for ex-military, immediately dislikes the atmosphere he brings with him.

He marches up to De Vries, too close. 'Sit down.'

'Who are you?'

'Who the fuck are you?' His voice is deep, the Afrikaner accent thick.

De Vries indicates the table. 'I was having a meeting with your marketing manager.'

'That meeting is cancelled.'

'Why?'

'Because you are not Henry van der Merwe.' The man walks forward again.

De Vries tries to resist stepping back but feels compelled to retreat. 'I'm here to bring you business. I expected a warmer welcome.'

The man laughs, eyes fixed on De Vries, a confining stare. 'The only business you plan to bring is trouble, Colonel.'

De Vries's heart begins to thud. 'Colonel?'

'Colonel Vaughn de Vries, SAPS.'

'I know you?'

He points his chin towards the window, out to the car park. 'Your car. Only one Jo'burg firm hires those.'

'Is that right?'

'Piece of shit. You've probably worked that out by now. Not a car you bring to the bush.'

'You traced me back to a car-hire firm?' The man nods slowly. 'Why would you do that?'

'At Bweha Bweha we like to know who our clients are . . . '

'I bet you do.'

'And then we tailor what we provide, very carefully.'

'Why is that?'

'We charge a great deal for our services. We're the best there is. We have the most experienced trackers, professional hunters. Our clients get exactly what they want.'

'I'm sure.'

'What do you want, Colonel, so far from home? You under cover? You want to come here without an invitation, get yourself a warrant.'

'I don't need a warrant. I have reason to believe there is evidence of a crime on these premises. I can enter them, search them and you, close you down for as long as I like.'

The man laughs. 'You're out of your jurisdiction and out of your depth.'

'You want to test that theory, sir?'

'You have been fed misinformation, gossip, rumour. Around here, there is nothing to do, so

261

all people have is speculation. You've probably spoken with the widow Dow. She and her late husband were conspiracy theorists, convinced that we were poaching big game. All the authorities confirmed that was not so. Like them, you are wasting your time and mine. My advice is to go home now, while you still can.'

'I don't take advice from the public or any notice of threats. That is the benefit of rank.'

The man moves away from De Vries towards the door. 'Your rank means nothing here.'

De Vries snorts. 'You may intimidate the locals, but it's not working on me. I want to see your official ID. Now.'

The man stands still, does not move his hands, does not change his facial expression.

De Vries says, 'I think you are Tony Uys, friend and associate of Carl Hertzog of Mossel Bay.'

'You are on my land. Private land. What you think is irrelevant.'

'Nonetheless, I will see your ID, and I will find the answers I'm looking for.'

'You're deluded, Colonel. When your superiors hear that you are in the Kruger, on a fishing trip for information, threatening me without any evidence, you will find that no one supports you . . . ' A smile forms slowly on his dry lips. 'And then there is your highly strung colleague waving his gun around in the bush, thinking he is some kind of commando. It took my men less than five minutes to shut him down.'

De Vries feels his heart thump, bile rising.

'I'm giving you a chance to leave with your head held high. Take your man with you and leave the Kruger right now.'

'And if I don't?'

'There will be considerable disruption to your career, your safety and that of your family. We always prefer to work with the co-operation of law enforcement and monitoring agencies, but we are not afraid of . . . a little friction.'

De Vries sees in the man nothing to make him doubt his words. He has been misguided, arrogant to consider that he, with Esterhuysen, could walk into this place and seize control. His limbs feel weak, his head heavy.

'When I have warrants in place, I'll visit you again.'

'Those are two things that won't happen.' The man has opened the door. De Vries does not move. 'You're an injured animal, Colonel, and so is your colleague. Find a dark hole and hide there.'

★ ★ ★

As he passes the main dining area, still busy with breakfasting guests, he is aware of Simon Boucher at his side, smiling, his hand just short of the small of De Vries's back. 'Your colleague,' he says quietly, 'is already back at your vehicle. I hope you have a safe journey home.'

De Vries stops by the main entrance, looks behind him, sees only Boucher.

'You happy in your work, Simon?'

'Yes, thank you, sir. It's been a pleasure to show you around Bweha Bweha.'

'Nice place to work?' He is staring at the

marketing man now.

'Bweha Bweha is an exceptional property. Who wouldn't want to build his career here?'

De Vries holds his stare for a few moments. Boucher is good, his smile consistent, matched by the brightness in his eyes. But De Vries sees something else also: tension behind the smile. For a split second, he registers what he interprets as a small wave of emotions breaking through the taut façade: regret, resignation . . . fear.

★   ★   ★

De Vries walks across the dirt towards his car. Only when he is beside it does he see Jack Esterhuysen. He lies across the rear seats, legs jammed behind the driver's seat. His temple is cut, oozing blood. De Vries opens his door, leans in. 'Jack? You okay?'

Esterhuysen raises his head a little, waves with the fingers of his left hand.

'Yeah. Sorry, sorry.' He is dazed, his body struggling against the shock. They have dispensed a beating, both warning and punishment.

De Vries gets in, drives in a wide circle around the car park, glancing up at the lodge, towards the windows of the conference room. No one is visible, apart from an armed guard at the corner of the building. He aims the car back onto the track towards the main gates, driving slowly over the rutted surface. In the back, Esterhuysen flinches and groans.

De Vries looks at him in the mirror. 'What did they do?'

'I don't know. I was one minute over the fence, and they were on me. Rifle-butt to the head, kicking me on the ground.' He coughs hoarsely. 'Sorry.'

In the distance, behind Esterhuysen's head, something catches De Vries's eye in the rear-view mirror. He brakes, turns to peer through the gap between the front seats out of the back windscreen. Beyond the lodge buildings, a small propeller plane is low over the hills, preparing to land. He watches it until it falls below the horizon.

'What is it?' Esterhuysen, his body now almost at forty-five degrees, is propped against one of the rear doors.

'Prop plane, landing close by.'

'Shit. They have a private army, thousands of hectares. What you saying now? Landing strip too?'

'Maybe.' De Vries continues to drive towards the exit. The air in the car smells of copper, sweat and blood; his pulse is still racing. 'I don't know who these people have in their pocket, but they knew who we were, where we were from and when we were coming — that's three things too many.'

★   ★   ★

The SAPS station at Skukusa is of the veldt, at a meeting point of tracks and roads, boasting thatched rondavels as well as low modern buildings. De Vries pulls up, badges the guard on duty, parks right outside the main building, his flimsy car looking incongruous next to mud-spattered four-by-fours and dusty vans.

He waits nearly fifteen minutes in a spartan, hot waiting room. His phone buzzes. He squints at it: soon he must abandon pride and buy reading glasses. It's an SMS from John Marantz:

It's over. In Jo'burg, meeting a poker buddy. CT tomorrow. You and Flynn come for a beer. J.

He sits, staring at the screen, a few minutes' silence for the memory of Marantz's wife and daughter he never met. He wonders how Marantz will cope now, whether he might be freed to emerge from his sleepless, joyless existence, to live again? His fingers hover over the keypad, but he can think of nothing to say.

A few minutes later, he is led into the station commander's cool, empty office, lit by cold fluorescent tubes. Captain Molewa is a physically big man, with a hangdog gait, a heavily scarred, moon-shaped face. The smile of greeting he produces has, to De Vries at least, the opposite effect.

'It seems, sir,' Molewa begins, as he motions for De Vries to sit down, 'that you impressed my desk officer with your rank. He came running into my meeting, thought that the whole world must stop for you.' He smiles, reaches under his desk, appears to open a door, retrieves two small bottles of water, throws one at De Vries, who only just catches it.

'Normally, for an officer to conduct SAPS business here, it is customary for my department to be informed. So that there is no . . . misunderstanding.' He speaks slowly, in a deep voice, his English heavily accented. 'But that is no longer my concern. Instead, it is your safety that worries me.'

'My safety?'

'It is not easy for an officer to come from a big city and adapt to the bushveld. Things here move slowly, in their own unique way, in their own time. Sometimes much patience is required.'

De Vries shakes his head. 'I'm not worried about my safety, Captain.'

'Nevertheless, I wish you had followed protocol and reported your presence here in the first place.'

'And who would you have reported to?'

Molewa frowns ostentatiously. 'I do not understand that question.'

'Sometimes protocol must be adjusted to cater for a nervous witness.'

'A nervous witness?'

'One who did fear for her safety. Jane Dow.'

Molewa nods sagely. 'Yes. I can understand why that lady might be afraid. But, if I may ask, why is a senior officer from Cape Town speaking to Mrs Dow about her concerns?'

'Perhaps she and I share concerns.'

Molewa shrugs. 'I do not know what to say . . .'

'She said I should not trust anybody.'

'And you think that includes my department?'

'Tell me about the accident her husband was involved in.'

'I can only tell you what the official report said. I was not personally involved. Richard Dow's car was travelling at close to a hundred and forty k.p.h. It was dark, the road was damp.

267

He veered off the road at a bend into the woods. The scene was investigated thoroughly.'

'Was there any evidence of a second vehicle?'

'No . . . Apparently not.'

'Why do you say that?'

Molewa shifts in his chair and looks over De Vries's shoulder. 'Threats had been made against Mr Dow.'

'By who?'

'I think you know that, sir, or you would not be here.'

'What can you tell me about Bweha Bweha?'

Molewa tilts his head. 'I see, sir, that you know exactly which direction this conversation is moving.'

'Bweha Bweha?'

'It is a private estate, owned, I think, by foreign investors. There is talk of the Far East, but if in doubt, these days, my money is on the Chinese. Always the Chinese. The claims that Bweha Bweha is not following conservation rules have been tested by the authorities. They have told me there is no case to answer.'

'You know all the owners of these reserves, Captain?'

Molewa waves a big hand inelegantly. 'We meet everybody. Despite the size of the land, it is a small place.'

'What about Tony Uys?'

Molewa's face darkens. 'Not so much. I do not think Mr Uys is the owner of the property and, besides, he is not a permanent fixture there. Sometimes no one sees him for weeks.'

'Are there any checks made on operators here?'

'What kind of checks?'

'Criminal checks.'

'There are rumours that some of the money behind these operations is not . . . what shall I say? Whiter than white . . . ' Molewa smiles broadly. 'But the bush is always full of rumours. We have to deal in facts and evidence.'

'And there is no evidence that Bweha Bweha are breaking the rules?'

'None at all. SANParks and the conservation officers here have investigated fully. There was nothing. They have helicopters flying over the reserves, checking for poaching and illegal activity. If that had been happening, we would have seen it.' He leans across his desk, his weight causing it to wobble. 'But you have not yet told me why you are here, Colonel. I am confused.'

'When I visited Bweha Bweha, I did not receive a warm welcome.'

Molewa's eyes widen. 'You have been to Bweha Bweha?'

'Is that a problem?'

'Whatever you are doing, Colonel, I urge you to be careful. The men at Bweha Bweha guard their privacy with great force.'

'I know they do.'

'I wish you had spoken to me first. This will cause trouble for us here.' The big man's frown deepens.

'What kind of trouble?'

Molewa shuffles papers on his desk. 'I cannot say. There are certain pressures which we all face. It is better if the cause of this trouble is left undisturbed.'

'Is Tony Uys threatening you, Captain?'

The man freezes. De Vries sees his right arm quiver, his Adam's apple bob. 'It is not only a matter of threat to me and my family. I have my men and female officers to consider.'

'And perhaps the magistrates. Maybe even the accident investigators.'

Molewa chugs on his bottled water. 'You come here to see me. Why? You have done what you pleased anyway. Now, you bring me only bad news. What do you want from me?'

'Did you call Uys when they told you I was at the front desk?'

'I . . . No.'

'No?'

Molewa sits rigid, his breathing heavy. He stares past De Vries, his eyes glazed, focusing and refocusing.

'Captain?'

'I have no choice, Colonel de Vries. You are not from here.'

'Who?'

'I spoke to another man, out of Bushbuck-ridge.'

'What man?'

'I don't know his name. Anything concerned with investigators, SAPS from outside the district, any mention of Bweha Bweha, I call him and . . . I tell him.' All the confidence has drained from the man. His eyes dart from side to side, blinking rapidly.

'What are you afraid of, Captain?'

'I have two young children, sir. A boy and a girl. There have been accidents, disappearances.

It has been made clear to me that if I do not co-operate . . . But it has not been illegal activity. I will not cross that line.'

'The line has already been crossed.' De Vries stares at Molewa. 'But I'm not here to pressure you. Quite the opposite. I merely require co-operation.'

'That demands much, sir.'

'Just your duty.'

'We are all compromised by fear, by a great weight upon us. We are used to threats here, to rituals of life and death, but not like this.'

'Then you have only one choice,' De Vries says. 'It is time to hide information, to corrupt it, mislead those who demand it. It is time for you to decide on which side of the line you will stand.'

Molewa shakes his head. 'You arrive here and think you can save us. It will not be so easy.'

'Keep what we have discussed in this meeting private, Captain. For your own good.' De Vries stands. 'If I can help you, I will. Meantime, fight quietly. We may yet prevail.'

Molewa's mouth opens and closes again. He shakes De Vries's hand, unwilling to meet his eye, sits down heavily, watches him leave his office.

★ ★ ★

The hire-car smells of liquid disinfectant, which Esterhuysen has applied liberally to his open wounds. De Vries has bought this and painkillers from the first pharmacy they passed in

271

Bushbuckridge. From there, De Vries travelled to Skukuza, believing that the SAPS outpost in the Kruger Park itself was most likely to be aware of the rumours and undercurrents there. As the gateway for many of the park's visitors, there is also an airport with regular flights to and from Johannesburg. De Vries has even considered travelling by air, but the planes out of Skukuza are full. While he has been with Captain Molewa, Esterhuysen stayed in the car, parked under a dense tree, windows open, the passenger seat reclined for him to rest.

The drive from Skukuza to Johannesburg seems longer than the outward journey. Esterhuysen sleeps occasionally, groaning in his slumber. The car radio offers little more than distant music above a roar of static. The air-conditioning struggles to keep the cabin habitable and, on the main road, De Vries finds that, if he turns it off, the little car seems to have more power. Throughout the journey, he reflects on his decision to make the visit. He has found nothing that directly links Tony Uys to anyone else, less still any evidence that could be used against him. Yet he has discovered a SAPS district under severe pressure, private landowners running the area as their own fiefdom, complete with threats and accidents; all classic symptoms of a community subjugated by organized crime.

At the airport, De Vries returns the car, carries Esterhuysen's rucksack along with his own, walks slowly beside his colleague, who limps uneasily towards the escalators. They check in, move towards the departure gate, still ninety minutes to go until their flight is due to depart. Esterhuysen heads for the washrooms, while De Vries buys himself a beer from the bar, gulps it, orders a second. His phone rings and he answers without studying the caller display.

'Colonel de Vries?' The voice is male, a thick Gauteng accent.

'Who is this?'

There is a pause. The background noise on the line harsh, not unlike the clatter within his tinny car.

'Do you know where your children are?' The voice sounds menacing.

'Who is this? Identify yourself.'

'Would you like to speak with your daughter?'

'What do you want?'

'I think she would like to speak to you.'

The background noise grows. De Vries feels his heart thumping in his chest, his skin cold and clammy. He presses the phone to his ear.

'Daddy?'

The single word is sufficient for recognition.

'Lu? Is that you?'

'Ja.'

'Where are you? What's happening?' He hears his daughter panting, swallowing.

'I was walking to lunch. These guys got me. I'm in a car.'

'What car? Lu, what car?' The line is silent but for the noise of the vehicle. 'Lulu?'

The man's voice is even, very controlled. 'This is a private warning, Colonel de Vries. Go back to Cape Town, report that your trail is dead. You have caused enough trouble already.'

'Listen to me — '

Even before he speaks, he has heard the line go dead, yet in his head, he still hears his daughter whispering, frightened, cowed. He scrabbles with the small buttons to see if a number is displayed in the call history, but it has been blocked. He is shaking, the beer forcing its way up from his stomach.

He pushes away the remnants of the second drink, grabs the bags, jogs to the restrooms. There are three men at urinals, two more at basins, the cubicles all seem occupied. De Vries shouts, 'Jack! Emergency. I have to go. I'm leaving your bag here. Take the flight.'

He hears shuffling from one of the cubicles. Esterhuysen shouts, 'What is it?'

De Vries senses that everyone in the washroom is listening. 'I'll tell you later. Take the flight.'

He drops Esterhuysen's rucksack, slings his own over his shoulder, runs out of the washroom, crashing into on oncoming passenger. He pushes through the crowds, searching for the exit, for taxis. He is on the wrong level. He runs for the escalators, his heart still racing, throat filled with acid. He stumbles off, almost missing the last moving step, spots the signs for taxis, sprints outside, past a uniformed security guard, onto the walkway. He fumbles for his ID, flashes it to the long queue at the taxi rank, chooses the most modern vehicle, shouts instructions at the driver.

As he sits back, he realizes he has been shouting almost hysterically. He mutters an

274

apology to the driver, scrolls through his contacts to find his ex-wife's number, is about to press call but thinks better of it. Instead, he phones a colleague at Johannesburg Central SAPS, Major Johan Bekker, finds him in the station, tells him what has happened. When he hangs up, buoyed by his colleague's eagerness to assist, he reflects that he has no knowledge of where Lulu was taken, what vehicle she may be in or where they are taking her. He grimaces at the pain in his chest, the burning in his oesophagus.

He calls his elder daughter, Kate. She senses panic in his apparent calm, tells him that she was due to meet her sister in a café called Canteen on Fox Street, a few blocks south of Ellis Park rugby stadium. Lulu is late, not answering her phone. He tells her he will meet her there in half an hour — to wait for him, that he will explain his concern when he sees her. He calls back his SAPS colleague, explains the likely area from which she was taken. He hangs up, meets the driver's gaze in the rear-view mirror. He holds on to the armrest in the passenger door.

'Fox Street, Arts on Main. Drive faster.'

★　★　★

As they slow in the mid-afternoon traffic, he remembers Marantz, presses the speed-dial. 'I'm not back till tomorrow.'

'Where are you now?'

'I told you. Stopover for a meeting in Jo'burg.'

'Where?'

'I'm at the university, Wits, Braamfontein.'

275

'That near Maboneng? Arts on Main area?'
'Couple of Ks. Why? You here?'
'I need your help. Can you get to a place called Canteen on Fox Street?'
'What's the matter, Vaughn?'
'My daughter, Lulu. I think she's been taken.'
'Taken?'
'Ja. I think so. It's fucked up.'
'I'm leaving now.'
The call ends.

* * *

Two SAPS patrol cars are parked outside Canteen on Fox Street, blocking the narrow road, lights flashing. De Vries pays his driver, tipping him generously, stumbles out of the cab, finds Marantz beside the gates to the Arts on Main centre. He waves, gestures with his finger for the SAPS officers to wait for him, runs through the gravelled Mediterranean garden inside the bare-brick walled restaurant, finds Kate by the door, talking to a waiter, phone in hand. She looks up, smiles, sees her father's expression, runs to him. 'What's happening? Why are you here?'

'I was at the airport. Work. Got a call from Lu. She said some guys had pushed her into a car.'

'They took her off the street?'

'I don't know.'

'Oh, God, Daddy. Have you told Mum?'

'No. Listen, just wait. We don't know what this is. If we know, we call her. Otherwise it could be a mistake, might be nothing.' He takes her hand.

276

'Come out with me. There are officers outside I need to talk to.' He pulls her out of the restaurant, through the garden, to the entrance. On the street, a small crowd has gathered. De Vries pushes through it to Johan Bekker, his SAPS colleague.

'Johan.' They shake hands.

'No word?'

'No.' De Vries holds up his phone, tilts it against the sunlight. 'Nothing.'

'No description of the vehicle?'

'She didn't say. They took the phone off her. Can you trace anything? Her phone, whoever called me?'

'Not incoming if it was blocked. Not fast. Give me Lulu's number.'

De Vries reads it. Bekker writes it down, repeats it into the phone to another colleague, hangs up. He turns, taking De Vries with him. 'You have any idea who these guys are?'

De Vries is sweating, the air humid and dirty, his head tight. 'I was in the Kruger, trailing some kind of pipeline for drugs, people smuggling, maybe rhino horn and ivory smuggling too. There were threats but . . . that was this morning . . . '

'This morning?'

'*Ja*, but if this is the same group, this has been going since Christmas. The guy shouting the odds was called Tony Uys, out of a place called Bweha Bweha, a few Ks on from Bushbuck-ridge.'

'Tony Uys?'

'Familiar?'

Johan Bekker holds up his hand, dials a number, turns away. De Vries can hear him speaking Afrikaans to someone, cannot follow the quickly whispered voice over the distant passing traffic, hears the words 'Tony Uys'. He feels dizzy, looks around him at the uniformed officers standing against their cars, at Kate and a small group of women talking, eyes wide, Marantz standing still, hands by his sides, watching. He spins back around. Bekker pockets his phone.

'Johan?'

Bekker shakes his head. 'Nothing. No word yet.'

De Vries turns away, walks over to Kate. 'You trying her number?'

'Every couple of minutes. It's not even her voicemail. It's just dead.' She stares up at De Vries. 'I have to call Mum.'

He nods, joins Marantz, holds out his hand. 'You all right?'

'Tell me what's happening, quickly.'

De Vries swallows; his eyes clench shut. He feels enclosed by the heavy afternoon air. 'Group of guys smuggling drugs, women. I've been on them since Christmas. There's intimidation, threats. Against me, my family, today.'

'What do they want?'

'For us to back off, I suppose. I don't know.'

'Did Lulu call you? Was that it?'

'She was in a car. They just wanted me to hear her, then they took the phone off her.'

'They say anything, Vaughn?' De Vries nods. 'What were the words?'

'I can't remember. 'Go back to Cape Town. Stop the inquiry. This is a warning' — something like that.'

'A warning?'

'Ja.'

Marantz trances for a few moments, looks up at him.

'They're not going to harm her . . . '

'No?' He is shouting, checks himself. 'You know that how?'

Marantz is very calm, his eyes scanning the scene beyond De Vries's shoulder. He looks back at him.

'If this is a warning and they want you to back off, back to Cape Town, they're not going to hold her. They do that, they have the entire Gauteng SAPS on their backs.'

De Vries frowns, unconvinced.

'If they're pros,' Marantz says, 'they'll dump her somewhere it'll take her time to make contact. They'll get far away, maybe torch the car. That way, they've sent the message, but you're not motivated to follow them.'

De Vries is nodding now, still absorbing the logic of Marantz's words. He wants to believe it, but can't. His heart thumps fast and deep, like the bass is turned up high in his chest. He wanders across the pavement towards Johan Bekker, feels his vision blur, darkness encroach from the outer edges of his eyes, feels pain sharp in his head, sickness deep in his stomach; feels himself falling.

He neither feels nor hears the thud as his body folds, hits the hot pink brick pavement.

Dale Rix sits back in his chair, his good leg propped on his desk. His eyes are closing, sleep overcoming him. He snaps to, shakes his head, flips the page of the newspaper, squints to focus on the print. Towards the bottom, there is an update on the police investigation into the death of Chantal Adam. He scans it for his name.

Cape Times, Wednesday, 6 January 2016
'MOUNTAIN GIRL': POLICE ENQUIRY WIDENS TO MOSSEL BAY AND P.E.

SAPS in Cape Town yesterday confirmed that their inquiry into the suspected suicide of former model Chantal Adam has been extended outside the city. Police say that they are pursuing leads on the criminal gang who had abducted Adam and planned to force her to carry pure cocaine on the Pandan Air flight on Christmas Day last year. Up to thirty other girls are thought to have already been dispatched to Thailand, and police are liaising with authorities in Bangkok.

The Special Crimes Unit, part of the SAPS elite divisions based in Cape Town CBD, have already named Ray Rossouw, 48, and Jan de Mueller, 47, as complicit in the conspiracy, and confirmed that they were killed by police during a raid on a property in Brooklyn where Chantal Adam had been held. Two other girls were also discovered. Both claimed they had been abducted and molested by the men. Police have also confirmed the arrest of a woman in Cape Town, two men in Mossel Bay and a series of connected raids in Port Elizabeth.

Although Chantal Adam's death was quickly ruled a suicide, police enquiries continue, raising the spectre that there is more to her death than police have so far revealed.

Rix fights for breath, eyes wide. He lays the paper down, feeling feverish. After a few moments, he picks it up, folds it to the article, reads it again. The names are there. One, possibly a coincidence; both, together, a certainty. He stares straight ahead, unseeing, his mind replaying events long past, deeply repressed, but, however hard he may wish them away, still vivid.

* * *

De Vries wakes propped against the wall of the arts complex, legs splayed across the burning pavement. Across from him, the redeveloped warehouses and factories reflect the sun, blinding him. He turns away, towards the flyover that still runs through the formerly dilapidated industrial area of the city. Nausea hits him and he bows his head. He is aware of Kate talking to him. He opens his eyes, sees a black hand on his arm. He pulls his shoulder away.

'I think you're all right, sir. When did you last eat?'

'This morning.'

'You are dehydrated and your blood sugar is low. Just rest. We've called the paramedics.'

De Vries puts his palms flat on the hot pavement, tries to lever himself up. With Kate's arm, he gets to his feet, still shaky. 'No doctors, no paramedics.'

'You must drink water, eat something, then rest.'

He nods at the police officer, thanks him, shuffles around the corner into the courtyard, sits on an empty chair under one of the olive trees. Water is brought to him; he forces himself to drink all of it. A sandwich appears. The sight of it makes him feel hungry. He picks it up, bites into it, chews slowly.

Kate sits next to him, puts her hand on his. 'Are you all right?'

'What's happening?'

'You fainted.'

'Not me. Lu. Any news?'

'Your friend, the English guy. He asked me where Lu was coming from. He's gone with some officers to Main Road — I guess she must have been walking.'

However gentrified, however trendy the pockets of fashionable redevelopment, Johannesburg is a dangerous city. De Vries wishes his girls were back in Cape Town. He longs to see Lulu and Kate together, smiling at him. He looks down at his still shaking hand holding the disintegrating sandwich, its filling scattering on the plate. He feels pathetic. 'Where's your mum?'

'She's coming.'

He closes his eyes, feels the weight of the events of the last twenty-four hours heavy on him. Kate's phone rings. She squints at the caller display, answers it. She listens silently for a moment. As he looks up at her, he sees her smile.

'Lu? Are you all right? What happened?'

'Where is she?'

'She's safe. She's in Soweto.' She pushes the phone to her ear, holds up her hand. 'Thokoza Park. She's with a teacher. It's his phone.'

* * *

They drive along main freeways, west across the city towards the agglomeration of Soweto. Johan Bekker is in the front seat, a coloured officer drives fast and accurately, sirens blaring. De Vries sits in the back, dazed, weak but charged with adrenalin. In the seconds after the call, he persuaded Kate to wait for her mother at the arts complex, then to go back to her apartment.

They reach Lali Street, find Lulu with a group of black men and women, standing outside a tiny bungalow next to a minimart. He tries to open the back door, finds it locked, struggles with the switch, is eventually let out by the driver. He hugs his daughter, will not let go. Finally, he steps back, scrutinizes her. She has been crying, but she seems unharmed, her clothes still clean and intact.

'This is the man who rescued me.' She pulls on the shirt of a tall thin man, wearing circular glasses, his sparse hair receding from his forehead.

De Vries turns to him. 'Thank you.'

'I was leaving my house and saw her lying on the edge of the park there. We do not see many white girls in the park.'

'He let me call Kate on his cell phone.'

De Vries shakes Peter's hand, thanks him again. He turns back to Lulu.

'You have all your things?'

'*Ja*. Just not my phone. They smashed it, tossed it out of the car window. But they left my wallet. I don't know what they wanted.' Johan Bekker and three other officers have been talking to the group. No one else knows anything. All were in the park or walking down the street. No one has seen the car from which Lulu de Vries was dumped. Bekker takes her to the other side of the road. She sits on the low white iron fence that divides the pavement from the edge of the park. De Vries stands dazed in the early evening sunshine, phones his other daughter. He hears her pass on the news to his ex-wife; Suzanne crying, Kate crying. He feels tears well, grits his teeth.

He leans against the chain-link fence of the teacher's house, looks out across the lush park amid the basic bungalows, the overhead telephone lines, piles of building materials, the disintegrating road. He recalls taking his young daughters onto the Mountain at Newlands Forest, seeing them playing hide and seek among the tall gum trees and rocky, fern-lined streams. He remembers Lulu hiding from them all, not coming out when she was called, the family's amusement transmuting to concern. They all called and there was silence. Suddenly, he was gripped by fear — and then Lulu ran out of her hiding place, giggling and screaming, chased by a dog that was trying to lick her.

He looks over the narrow street at his twenty-three-year-old daughter. As her father, he is only ever moments away from paralysing terror. That is the deal you accept; that is the sentence you serve.

⋆ ⋆ ⋆

They eat as a family in the twentieth-floor apartment of his ex-wife, Suzanne. For twenty years they lived together in Cape Town, seeing increasingly little of one another. It was not only his career that pulled them apart. As an overtly ambitious television journalist, she, too, answered calls in the early hours, travelled to remote locations. Their daughters saw their parents less and less; Vaughn and Suzanne began to miss them, not each other. Once the girls were at university, Suzanne had taken an anchorwoman's job in Johannesburg; he had stayed in Cape Town. There was no animosity, no remorse. Their separation was as natural as falling in love.

When he had visited before Christmas, they had sat by the tree exchanging presents after dinner in town, but now, he assumes, the meal around the table is down to a mother's instinct, in times of crisis, to draw her family together. It is agreed that the girls will spend the night here; he has no idea where he will go or what he will do. He eats well, drinks moderately but, as the evening passes, his anxiety grows. He waits until the girls drift off to the living room. He tops up Suzanne's wine, his own.

'I'm sorry.'

'Do you know who did this?'

He gazes past her at the nightscape of Johannesburg, the towers and skyscrapers illuminated against a glowing blue-grey sky. He finds the urban view beautiful, but cold, not reassuring.

'Not for certain. We're following a group we think are smuggling drugs, people, rhino horn, who knows what else? They're uncompromising and they're trying to get us off their backs.'

'I'm not worried about your back.' She snorts, pats his arm. 'Of course I am . . . but Jozi isn't an easy place to live, not here in town. I worry about the girls staying where they do.'

He shrugs.

'They'll make their own decisions soon enough.' He takes a deep breath. 'When are you going to your mother's?'

'On the fourteenth. I can't get away earlier, and the flights to Windhoek are still so busy. The schedules are set weeks in advance.'

'Let's get the girls out. Tomorrow. Find them some seats, whatever it costs. Just get them out of here while I do what I have to do.'

'You think they're in danger?'

'I think we all are.'

She scowls. 'I'll call Mum in the morning . . . How can this happen, Vaughn? How can you be fifteen hundred kilometres away and still these people come after us?'

The lights above the table are dimmed, the appliances in the kitchen glow. The muted sound of the television in the living room competes with the music emanating from the speakers in the kitchen-diner. They are all home together again.

'That wasn't a rhetorical question.'

He smiles grimly. He has heard Suzanne say just that to tongue-tied, evasive, obtuse politicians on her news programme.

'I don't know. Maybe we've stepped on some toes. Maybe they've been protected up till now, but the evidence took us up the line, and they're not nice. They're really not nice. They treat women, girls of Kate and Lu's age, like animals. Worse, like they're worthless.'

She gets up, swings around the kitchen island, switches on the coffee machine. 'You have to sort this. I can't go to work each day and worry that Kate and Lu could just disappear. This was one of the reasons it didn't work. You brought your job home. I get it — Jesus, I do it myself — but not the girls.'

Suzanne had been threatened, attacked, when she worked as a reporter. Her experience mitigated the tension and unease that, almost without knowing, he brought home with him each evening but, ultimately, she always moved on. He became obsessed, stagnated.

'I can talk to the guys who did the documentary about rhino horn poaching, if you like? See what they know.'

'No. These people, their tail's on fire. They're going to be running around snapping at everyone. Say nothing. Keep your head down. And go to Windhoek as soon as you can.'

She looks at him disparagingly. He is grateful that it is not worse.

'Even now,' he says quietly, 'when it was supposed to be over for you, I'm still bringing shit down on you.'

★ ★ ★

He wakes in the early hours, establishes that he is on the sofa in Suzanne's living room. The apartment is silent, the three women sleeping. He had not imagined he would be allowed to stay on the sofa. He would like to think they are happy to have him there as protection, but he does not delude himself. Suzanne has reacted more calmly than he anticipated. He attributes this to Lulu being unharmed, making contact within a short time of Suzanne being informed. Even now, he shivers at the thought of his daughter trapped in a car with strangers.

His thoughts turn to Marantz, his ice-calm analysis of her abduction, how he traced her route and persuaded police officers to follow him to the area to question possible witnesses. De Vries has exchanged four words, literally, by SMS with him since then, has no idea where Marantz is now, what his mental state may be.

Above everything, De Vries feels emasculated and weak. His collapse on the street; his helplessness, not only in seeking Lulu but also when confronted by Tony Uys, his police credentials worthless away from home territory.

Within thirty minutes of finding Lulu, he sensed that the Jo'burg SAPS had downgraded the case. She is safe and well, returned to her family. Seemingly, there were no witnesses to her abduction or release. It is this that convinces him of what he already knows. He is alone. The threat is against him and his family; a threat he must face down. At 4 a.m. on a still Johannesburg night, it seems pervasive, unending, unstoppable.

★ ★ ★

The Jeppe SAPS is located on a small rhomboid between railways, flyovers, side-roads and the main Albertina Sisulu Road in central Johannesburg. The complex includes what is described as a client service centre, the magistrates and regional courts. It is less than a dozen blocks from Fox Street, hence the rapid response to De Vries's call the previous day.

Major Johan Bekker meets him at the reception, leads him to a side building and into a small cube of an office, poorly ventilated, lit by oppressive fluorescent tubing. A civilian assistant brings two mugs of coffee.

Bekker is older than De Vries, his face long and sallow, hair cropped, eyes pale blue. For four years, they worked together in Cape Town, until 1996, when Bekker was presented with a choice: transfer or leave. He took the move to Jo'burg in his stride, rebuilt his career in the centre of the city.

He listens silently as De Vries describes the

elements of his investigation since Christmas morning, snorts in disbelief as he is told of his visit to the Bweha Bweha and his reception there. 'I know what you're going to say,' he says. 'But after we got you all home, I spent some time working on what we do and don't know about Bweha Bweha.'

'And what don't we know?'

Bekker smiles. 'More than we know, *ja*?'

'So?'

'Tony Uys isn't in the system. We both know that criminal records go missing, for one reason or another, so I can't tell you whether he was there, just that he isn't now. I've studied the licences and reports from the National Wildlife Reaction Unit and there's nothing. There's the SANParks reports and the National Biodiversity Investigators Forum. They've been there but, apart from a warning about overdevelopment of the natural bushveld, they've given it a clean bill of health.'

'What does overdevelopment mean?'

Bekker holds up his hands. 'I don't know. What I gathered is that Bweha Bweha were building waterholes, hides, tree-houses, and the conservation bodies thought it was too much. When you run a hunting concession, which also offers limited game viewing, I guess you're kind of catering to two different sets of clients.'

'That concession caters for Thai and Vietnamese hunters, which links with the drugs going to Bangkok.'

Bekker shrugs. 'Thailand is a magnet for these people. Must be dozens of outfits in Gauteng alone sending stuff there.'

'So, there's nothing?'

'I know what you want,' Bekker says. 'To go into Bweha Bweha, find evidence.'

'*Ja.*'

'I don't think that's going to happen.'

'Why not?'

'It's from the top. If the official bodies give a place a clean bill, we stay out of the way. We don't have the resources or the manpower. We have to let them police their own territory.'

'These people took my daughter, Johan, a few hours after I visited, hundreds of kilometres away. I can't leave them be.'

'You can't prove who it was, Vaughn. We've got zero witnesses. You said yourself it seemed too quick. You see them in the morning and by two o'clock, they've kidnapped your daughter. It doesn't sound right. It assumes the people you suspect have a network extending to Jo'burg.'

'What about the call? You process it?'

'Untraceable. Even if it tells us it came from Central Jo'burg, we know that.'

'So you can't do anything?'

'Tell me what, Vaughn. Tell me and I'll move.'

Bekker opens his palms. De Vries stares at him.

'I can't do anything, man,' Bekker says. 'Don't look at me like that.'

★　★　★

De Vries is back in Cape Town by three o'clock. He has spent the cramped flight reflecting on his meeting with Johan Bekker, his colleague's responses to his questions. He understands budgetary restraints, provincial jurisdiction, pressure of work, but something inside him knows that Bekker has been evasive. He ponders the reason, finds all the options unpalatable. As the plane powers down its engines, he sends an SMS to Joey Morten in the technology department, requesting urgent research. No one is better, he has discovered, at finding out what really lurks in old files and records.

Within the hour, he has reached his building. In the lift, he receives a message from Morten. He presses the button for the correct floor, steps out, strides towards Morten's office.

'Before you say anything, tell me that no one can trace what you've done.'

Morten frowns. 'There's a problem?'

'These people seem to have eyes everywhere.'

'I understood your warning, sir. There's no trail, not even the times the files were accessed.'

'Good.'

'By the way, in some cases, I don't think the records have ever been accessed. They were transcribed onto computer systems at the very beginning. We're talking really basic technology.'

'But there's something there?'

Morten nods. 'Very definitely.'

'Tell me.'

Morten pushes his chair back from the desk and the bank of screens above it. He taps his keyboard and two screens show copies of handwritten reports; a third is typed.

'Right. First up, he's not in any criminal

system that I could find, but his name does appear, and it's flagged. After 'ninety-four, when the Border War ended, and they began disbanding the army, Uys joined the police force in North-West Province. This is odd because, if you look here,' he points to the left-hand screen, 'there's reference to him standing trial in a military court for insubordination and war crimes. There's nothing on what the court found, but those records often went missing. He lasted less than a year in the SAPS but was entered on the list of informants by a Major Morne Smit, who stayed in as the new SAPS came about. If you look there, you can see that Smit notes Tony Uys joined Afrikaner Weerstandsbeweging — the Afrikaner Resistance Movement — in 'ninety-five. But that's it. No detail on information received, but payments were made for almost eight years.'

'Is Smit still around?'

'I can't confirm it, but I think he's dead.' De Vries opens his mouth, but Morten continues. 'I tell you what I did find, though. In April 2011, there was a one-year anniversary gathering for the death of Eugene Terreblanche up at Ventersdorp. You remember?' De Vries nods. 'Guess who's identified in one of the lead cars?' He presses a button on the keyboard and a pixilated black and white photograph appears, showing a parade of cars, with groups of men in quasi-military attire, parading down a street.

'Shit. So he was still associating, prominently, as recently as 2011?'

'Yes.'

De Vries gets up, reaches the door, turns back. 'This is good. Get rid of it now, *ja*?' He opens the door, closes it again. 'Tell me this: how easy was it to find that information?'

'The reports, you have to know the system, where to look, but the Afrikaner Weerstandsbeweging stuff is in the public domain.'

'Right.'

★ ★ ★

Henrik du Toit balances the weight of his head on two fingers, listens silently to De Vries.

'I never know with you, Vaughn,' he says, 'whether I am impressed by your rigour, or appalled by your lack of process.'

'It's the combination that makes me irresistible.'

Du Toit smiles, opens his palms over his desk. 'We have a handful of men with Afrikaner names, one with links to . . . an undesirable faction. But, hell, Vaughn, you and I have Afrikaner names . . . '

'We do, but these guys are a similar age. They feel connected — they are connected, at least in their present actions.'

There is a sharp knock at the door. Norman Classon, the department's consultant attorney, enters. As ever, he is dressed in a sharply cut suit, an expensive, perfectly pressed shirt, a silk tie.

'Take a seat, Norman.'

Classon places his briefcase neatly to the side of the chair, sits slowly, nods at De Vries.

'Don't keep us waiting,' De Vries says. 'What did you find out?'

Classon glances at Du Toit, unfolds a page from his pocket, lays it on the desk, flattens it.

'Kriel, Calder, the attorneys who represent Diane Kemmel, is a relatively small law practice, but it has offices in Johannesburg, Cape Town, a satellite office in Port Elizabeth. But . . . ' He looks at De Vries. 'You were right, there is a connection with more than one of your suspects. Carl Hertzog is represented by the same attorney who sat with Diane Kemmel, Tim Calder. Calder joined the practice in 2005 and was made partner five years later, returning to Cape Town to open the office here.'

'Calder was efficient in coaching Kemmel,' De Vries says, 'but he didn't win her confidence.'

'I spoke to a couple of my colleagues. He has a reputation for being very aggressive in court, sometimes to the detriment of his position. He seems to treat his clients as if they all have to fight like dogs to be acquitted.'

'Is Calder linked only to Kemmel and Hertzog?' Du Toit asks. 'Because, if so, that's worthless. Kemmel admitted that his card had been passed to Ray Rossouw and then to her.'

'The two arrested and accused of abduction of girls in Port Elizabeth applied to Kriel for legal representation. An attorney was dispatched from the Jo'burg office.'

'Of course they're linked,' De Vries says. 'We just didn't know whether it was an ad hoc arrangement or something longer-standing. Now, it looks like the latter. Who is Kriel?'

'This is interesting. Rudi Kriel used to work for the Public Prosecutor's Office under the Nationalist Party, pre-1994. Doesn't undertake court work any more. He must be in his seventies, maybe older.'

'We arrest Tony Uys, I wonder whether he'd come out of the woodwork.'

'I don't think you'd want to test that unless what you have is watertight. The man is encyclopedic on the law, even under the new Constitution.'

'What we have,' Du Toit says, 'is a possible connection via their choice of attorney and, I agree, that seems linked to an Afrikaner background. What we don't know is what brought them together in the first place.'

'Ray Rossouw was a career criminal,' De Vries says. 'We don't know any more about Jan de Mueller than his record. He wasn't based down here. Hertzog ran his car business for the last eleven years and, as I have just discovered, Tony Uys was one of us for a year, then appeared on an official informant list for eight years. They were in different parts of the country, doing different things.'

'I suppose it's not surprising,' Classon says casually. 'There are criminal groups within every sector of society.'

'That's true,' De Vries says, 'but these are very different men. If we're going to tie Uys to this, we have to know where they met before, or why they came together now.'

Classon nods.

Du Toit says, 'If Tony Uys, or someone above

him, is the ringleader, tread carefully. I know you want him for what happened in Jo'burg to your daughter, Vaughn, I understand that, but be careful you don't compromise the overall case by overstretching to get him. If you find the evidence, we will take him down.' He clears his throat. 'All right, Vaughn. I need to talk to Norman a moment.' De Vries rises. 'How is Warrant February progressing?'

'You know Don, sir. Calm surface, much kicking below.'

'An admirable trait.'

De Vries rolls his eyes. 'They say bottling up emotion causes strokes. Did you know that, sir?'

He leaves the office.

Du Toit and Classon smile.

'You have to admit,' Classon says, 'he reaches parts other policemen don't.'

'Yes.'

'Are perhaps better off not finding.'

'How much influence do men like Rudi Kriel still exert? Isn't their time past?'

Classon undoes his jacket buttons, leans back in his chair. 'I'm not sure that 'influence' is quite right. Twenty years of democracy — for want of a better word — has seen to that. But there are plenty of Afrikaners who still believe that power was ceded unnecessarily, that the perceived failings of the ANC prove they were right. And we know they have a small, but loyal, network of contacts throughout the civil service, the police — yes — and almost every area of operation in modern South African society. So, it is possible that a criminal group could be protected from

297

within. And, as I said, why should we be surprised that those from within a group that seeks to define itself as separate should form allegiances in any aspect of life, including criminality?'

'You think De Vries is right to see a connection?'

'The problem with De Vries,' Classon says quietly, 'is that he polices by instinct — and his instincts are good, there's no doubt about that. He just sometimes lacks an element rather important to my end — hard evidence.'

'There are,' Du Toit says slowly, 'two ways of reaching a conclusion. Evidence leading to suspicion, and suspicion leading to evidence. I've just never liked the latter very much.'

★ ★ ★

Don February has brought Sally Frazer with him to Charles Adam's house in Constantia. The reason is entirely racial: he believes Adam will be more relaxed if he doesn't have two black police officers facing him. There, he acknowledges, is an irony.

The butler, Joseph, opens the door, studies them, leads them across the hallway into Adam's study. The square room is painted deep maroon, heavy velvet curtains hang at either side of the tall, elegant window. Adam sits behind a leather-topped desk, partially obscured by a pile of leatherbound books and highly polished silver desk accessories. He does not stand, but gestures for them both to sit down.

'Sir, my name is Warrant Officer Donald February, and this is Sergeant Sally Frazer. We are colleagues of Colonel de Vries, who you met on Christmas Day.'

Adam nods. 'I knew Colonel de Vries long before that.'

'Yes, sir.'

'I understand you have some more questions to ask me about Chantal. I thought this deeply unfortunate business was concluded.'

'Almost, sir. We like to have a clear picture of events to be sure that we have not missed anything.'

'I'm sure you haven't.'

'Thank you.' He looks down at his notebook. 'I just need to confirm how you came to employ Mr Dale Rix.'

'Why would that be of any concern to you?'

Don smiles calmly. 'Much of our information regarding Miss Adam's movements over the last weeks of her life have relied on Mr Rix's investigations.'

'He was recommended by a trusted source, I assure you. One of your people.'

'Captain Maart?'

Adam says nothing, just looks ahead.

'Our problem, sir,' Don continues, 'is that you employed Mr Rix to keep watch on your daughter, but she disappeared. If he had done his job properly, perhaps the incident could have been avoided.'

'I don't know what you hope to gain by these questions, Warrant Officer, but Dale Rix was employed occasionally to watch out for Chantal.

She made it clear to me that she wanted to be independent, and I respected that, up to a point.'

'Why did Miss Adam refuse your help?'

Adam's expression locks. 'All families have their problems. Chantal was not an easy teenager. You have children?' He looks first to Don, then to Frazer; both shake their heads. 'Then you wouldn't know. Children who were once reliant upon you, looked up to you, suddenly crave independence, resent your advice, disagree with every opinion, decide that you exist simply to thwart their every desire. I have two older children and they went through similar, if not quite so extreme, phases.'

'But even when she returned from America . . .'

'My relationship with my daughter is not up for discussion. I offered her every support. I took a back seat, but maintained my promise that I would always look after her. That she rejected my help is deeply regrettable.'

'Your wife,' Frazer says. 'Had she spoken to Chantal since her return to Cape Town?'

'Chantal took against my wife. Theirs was never a close relationship. I'm afraid there was jealousy because Lillian was a very loving mother to our own two children. To be compelled to look after her niece from the age of three was difficult. She did a fine job until Chantal reached puberty, when the trouble started.'

'Would it be possible to talk to your wife, sir?'

Adam stares at Frazer. 'No. I can't allow that. The last fortnight has been truly terrible. Enough is enough. Colonel de Vries told me that Chantal was ill, on drugs, had fallen in with a group of heartless people intent on exploiting her and, in her confused and unhappy state, took her own life. That is a tragedy. There is a limit to the amount of pain we can endure.'

Don nods. 'May I ask you, sir, was there any one incident that triggered — '

Adam holds up his hand. 'No. You may not. My family is not on trial. I do not wish to continue this meeting.' He stands, waits while Frazer and Don also rise. 'I have already complimented the police on the way they have handled this matter but, as far as I am concerned, it is closed. Do you understand?'

'Yes, sir.'

He reaches under his desk, appears to press something. In the distance, Don hears a low bell ring. 'Joseph will show you out.' He waits until the door opens, sits, looks down at his desk.

As he leaves, Don glances back through the closing door, realizes, in that second, that Charles Adam's eyes are unfocused, that he is looking at nothing.

★ ★ ★

Joseph opens the heavy front door.

'Goodbye.'

Don stops on the step. 'Would you walk to our car with us, please?'

Joseph looks perplexed, bows, follows the two officers onto the driveway, towards their vehicle. Frazer strides ahead but Don drops back to walk beside the servant.

'How long have you worked here, sir?'

'Sixteen years, sir.'

'You don't have to call me 'sir'. I serve you.'

Joseph seems uncomprehending.

'Do you remember Chantal?'

'Yes.'

'Was she a happy girl?'

Joseph stops. Don turns to face him. 'The family is private. I am not allowed to say, sir.'

'Was there a moment when she wasn't happy any more?'

Joseph hesitates. 'I can't say.'

'I won't tell anyone what you say. I just want to know.'

'No . . . sir.'

'That is a shame.'

'I would like to help you, sir.'

Don holds out his hands, palms open, waits. Joseph stares at them, at him, does not move. He looks behind him, back towards the house. Don smiles at him, feels that he has gained his confidence, that he will reveal a truth.

Joseph leans towards him, his voice low, mouth small.

'Just because you think we are the same, does not mean that I will dishonour my master and mistress. You be a traitor, man. Not me.' He turns on the spot, walks briskly back towards the residence.

Don swallows, turns towards the car.

'Anything?' Frazer asks.

Don slides into the passenger seat, turns to her. 'I think they say, a wake-up call.'

There is no answer when De Vries rings the bell on the video intercom outside John Marantz's house. He speed-dials his number, hears ringing. Marantz does not have voicemail. He walks down the slope on the road to the far side of the property, peers into the garages between the slatted heavy wooden doors, sees Marantz's old Mercedes in place.

He walks back up to the entry-phone, pushes again. As he waits, he is aware of a figure. He looks up, sees Marantz's neighbour's gardener, Lucky, looking back at him.

'He is in the garden, sir. At the bottom. He is looking at the *donga*. And he was digging. He won't hear you.'

De Vries knows that Lucky has seen him before, thanks him. Lucky beckons him with grass-stained hands.

'You can get in through our garden. My mistress is not here.' De Vries follows him onto the adjoining property, down a rough stairway, cut out of rock and soil. After a while, Lucky gestures towards a dip in the ground between the *erven*, and a low wire fence. De Vries walks beneath the thick canopy of trees dividing Marantz's plot from his neighbour's, gingerly clambers over the low fence, into his garden. He calls out, hears nothing back, begins to descend the steep dirt path.

The side of the Mountain has been planted with indigenous trees. When he first visited this house, they were mostly saplings, none taller than Marantz himself. Now some are ten metres high and, below them, there are newly planted ferns and tree-ferns. As he climbs lower, he begins to hear the rush of the brook, which marks the lower boundary of the plot. He calls again.

'Vaughn?'

'Ja. Lucky let me in.'

'Come down then. Be careful.'

De Vries holds onto the tree trunks to steady himself, comes out in a clearing overlooking the collapsed sides of the brook. Although it is midsummer, there is still some water flowing off the Mountain, through the Southern Suburbs, into the rivers and canals.

'Did you ring?'

'Door and phone.'

'I wasn't expecting guests.'

De Vries looks to his side, sees two deep holes, a spade stuck in the hard red ground. Marantz is sweating, his hands dirty, trousers stained orange from the dust.

'They're for Caro and Rosie.' He sees De Vries's bemused expression. 'For trees. A remembrance. Caro never wanted us to live in a flat. She said we had to have a house, with a garden. She wanted Rosie in her pram under the trees so she could look up at the sky through bright green leaves. One day I'll come and sit under their branches, look up, remember my wife and daughter.'

'That's very nice, John.'

'It's all I have of them now.'

'As long as you move on, John. Not now . . . Of course not now, but sometime.'

'I am moving on,' Marantz says, 'and maybe

there will be other people in my life. But I can never forget.'

Flynn sits near the holes, his coat dripping. The dog's tail wags gently at De Vries.

'Has he forgiven me?'

'When I picked him up from your friends — Robert and Tania — he was lying down, being licked by a small bitch on either side of him.'

'It's a long-held fantasy of mine.'

Marantz smiles.

De Vries thinks that he sees that smile so rarely. He wonders what life will be like for his friend now that he is left with no doubt.

Marantz calls Flynn; he immediately bounds into the undergrowth. 'Thanks for taking him.'

They walk between the holes, the two large piles of earth and rock, to the other side of the garden, up the steps and under the house, coming out by the concrete stairs that lead up to the pool terrace.

'I've never been down there before.'

'You're not usually in a fit state.'

De Vries snorts. He fell into the swimming pool on one occasion, late at night. Marantz had laughed until he choked, promised not to remind De Vries of the event too often.

'You want a drink?'

'If you're not busy.'

'Help yourself. I'm going to swim.'

De Vries walks into the house through the tall, narrow doors, towards the kitchen. He hears a splash as Marantz dives into his pool. He opens a bottle of Merlot with a corkscrew, wonders how a recovering alcoholic can keep a house full of

305

alcohol and not touch it. Marantz is stronger, mentally, than him.

By the time he steps back onto the pool terrace, Marantz is sitting with a towel wrapped around himself, his dog by his side. 'How's Lulu?'

'Shaken, shocked, tired . . . '

'But safe. You've got them away from Jo'burg?'

De Vries is exhausted, the stresses of the previous forty-eight hours weighing heavy on him. 'In Windhoek, with her grandmother. Kate too.'

'And Suzanne?'

'Going next week. Can't or won't go earlier. You know these jealous TV types.' He flops in his usual chair in the terraced garden, looking down the length of the narrow lap pool, over the wooded slopes of the Mountain, out onto the Cape Flats. He pours a second glass of wine and turns to Marantz.

'I don't even know how to ask . . . ?'

'About what?'

'London.'

'London is cold and dark and miserable. Everything's the same. Left with no family, came back with no family.'

'Take your time.'

Marantz looks up. 'You know what? Time's up. I just have to stop dreaming of torturing the men who took them. Caro and Rosie are gone. They're not.' He leans down, picks up his customary joint, brings it to his lips and inhales deeply. When he blows out the smoke, it slowly drifts up into the trees on the border of his plot.

'Who took your daughter?'

'Don't know. They were efficient. No witnesses found at pickup or drop-off. How did you know?'

'About what?'

'That they'd let her go?'

Marantz leans back in his chair. 'Gangs work in different ways. They can use pervasive influence, blackmail, fear, strong-arm, even shock and awe. The fact that they've stayed under the radar suggests they've opted for discreet influence to build a network of informants, using blackmail and fear to create psychological walls that protect them, but they've steered clear of confrontation. To hurt your daughter would have been counter-productive.'

'They have hurt her. She's terrified. She's in a different fucking country.'

'You know what I mean, Vaughn.'

De Vries empties his glass, pours again, lights another cigarette from the end of his last. 'Everyone is afraid of stepping on other people's toes. No one will make a move. I talked to my contact in Jo'burg. Either he didn't want to know, or he deliberately misled me about intelligence. My guys found links back to the early days of the new SAPS, the judiciary. If I nose around, I'm going to be seen, and that puts everyone in danger. I feel constricted, worrying about Suzanne and Kate and Lu.'

'All the right people in the right places.'

'There's a link back to the Afrikaner Resistance Movement too. This man, Tony Uys, was involved at some level. I don't know about the others — Carl Hertzog, Ray Rossouw, the people in Port Elizabeth. I just don't have a handle to get inside Bweha Bweha, get hold of Uys.'

'There are other ways.'

'There are always other ways, John. But you're not involved. You have enough on your plate.'

'I've been officially fired. I'm retired. Nothing to do all day.'

'Get into women again.'

'Soon, Vaughn. Soon.'

De Vries tips the last of the bottle into his glass, knocks it back. 'Warm evening . . .'

'Don't change the subject,' Marantz says quietly. 'You can't leave it like this. Do nothing, and your family will never be safe. I didn't even know mine were in danger and they disappeared. You've been warned.'

De Vries gets up with the bottle, swings it by its neck as he ambles inside for the next. He pauses at the tall doorway.

'I know.'

★ ★ ★

Don February lies awake next to his quietly snoring wife. Getting to sleep is becoming harder: his wife wakes him in the night when she hears the neighbour's dog barking. He is more tired now than he has ever been. The pressure of being in an elite unit seems to grow slowly, steadily, month after month. Even in a comparatively safe suburb, like Pinelands, where they live in a house he can scarcely afford, the local press is full of stories about crime and, now, his wife receives a daily email update from the Neighbourhood Watch co-ordinator, outlining every incident in the vicinity. He has tried to explain that the forums are sponsored by the security companies — that anything which consolidates unease, stokes fear, is good business — but his wife believes anything in print.

Despite his days of work, he feels he knows little more about the last weeks of Chantal Adam's life than he did when he started. Two things concern him. Charles Adam's overly defensive stance regarding the cause of Chantal's alienation from her adoptive parents: he hears Adam's self-assured voice describing his wife as having been 'compelled to look after her niece'. This is not a description of a loving start to a mother — daughter relationship. There are many servants at the Adam house; Don wonders how much of her new mother the young Chantal saw.

What bothers him more is his interview with Dale Rix. It is as if the man had been obsessed with Chantal Adam, such was the extensive observation noted in his reports. Yet, despite their detail, he is convinced that the man has withheld information and, since he paid more attention to her than anyone else, it might prove crucial to the inquiry.

Outside, he hears the gentle ticking rumble of a diesel engine idling. The LED numbers on his alarm clock say 01:52. He wonders whether he should get up to look out of the window. He sighs, trying to relax. It is Wednesday night, the midweek night when Capetonians go out. It will only be party-goers returning home late. He closes his eyes.

Cape Town, Thursday, 7 January 2016
'Ray Rossouw, Jan de Mueller, Carl Hertzog, Kevin Coetzee, Tony Uys, Rudi Kriel . . . ' De Vries addresses his team in front of the central table in the squad room. 'We know there are contemporary connections between the first three. We need to find out if they were linked historically and, importantly, whether there is evidence leading to Tony Uys. Carl Hertzog told me that Uys was his contact up the line. He was under duress at the time, but I still feel the information is good.' He casts his gaze over each of them. 'We have to be careful. You heard what happened to my daughter. I don't want that pressure coming anywhere near you, so don't use SAPS contacts, even trusted ones. Use the Internet, historical files, whatever else you can to find out more about each of these men. Don't leave a trail. We need sufficient evidence to go back to Bweha Bweha without them having advance warning of our arrival. Whatever is going on there, they're doing their best to keep it secret.' He nods at them. 'We'll see where we are late afternoon.'

★ ★ ★

De Vries opens his window — an illegal action in itself — pokes his head out, peers down to the street below. People stroll the pavements, seeming to know where they are going — a sensation with which he cannot empathize.

310

Investigations used to take their course through logical progression but now, working as he does, nothing seems as ordered or regimental, as familiar, as it once was.

Control is important to him. It does not matter that he ventures so close to the line between control and being out of control, only that he remains on the right side at the crucial moments.

What afflicts him is an all-consuming obsession for justice for his victim and, still worse, if he fails, for the victims to come. He appreciates the need for impartiality, a cool head, an ability to distance himself but, in the moment, he is overcome.

Perhaps these emotions give him energy, a force channelled for good — perhaps they make him a better policeman — but to him, today especially, they make him weak, vulnerable and emasculated.

When he sits back down, he finds himself frustrated, impatient, his pulse throbbing at his wrists. He dislikes delegation, resents having to wait for information from disparate sources. He wants to attack from the front, to be clear, to be right.

★   ★   ★

Don February takes Ben Thwala to Woodstock. If Sally Frazer is meant to reassure, Thwala should induce the opposite reaction. He is half a metre taller than Don, broad and fit.

It is still the holiday season and the roads,

although busy, are quieter than at other times of the year; fewer taxi-buses, more shiny white tourist hire-cars, Gauteng registrations, coaches. Don observes kids on skateboards, scooters, older hawkers, beggars, even a group of middle-aged women, peering in through the darkened windows, scrutinising backseats for expensive purchases. The shops and markets are re-opening; black and coloured Capetonians fill the pavements, whites the edgy cafés adjoining happening art galleries. Thwala turns down the side-street towards Dale Rix's home, parks directly outside. It is still only nine thirty. Don rings the bell and, when nothing inside stirs, he knocks firmly. He squats down in front of the door, peers through the letterbox. Inside the little house it is dark, curtains drawn in the living room. Don gives his eyes a moment to adjust to the gloom, sees furniture upended, papers scattered on the floor.

'We need to open this door.'

Thwala looks at him.

'Now?'

Don nods.

Thwala pushes at it with his big hands, thumps it in the corners, next to the locks, stands back, kicks. It shudders but does not move. He kicks again. This time the wood around the lock cracks, splinters and, on the third attempt, the door flies open. Don, still outside, shouts, 'Mr Rix. This is the police. Are you home?'

When there is no answer, he steps in, Thwala following. The hot air in the living room smells

312

of alcohol and stale sweat. As he emerges from the narrow corridor running from doorway to living room, Don sees Rix on the floor by his desk. He runs to him, squats at his side. 'He is breathing.'

Thwala checks each of the other rooms in the small house, returns. Don pulls Rix upright. 'He is drunk. He told Colonel de Vries that he is an alcoholic.'

Rix has opened his eyes. They are bloodshot; the muscles around his sockets spasm as he tries to focus.

'What the fuck are you . . . ?'

'I need to talk with you.'

'I'm done talking.' He reaches for the edge of his desk, tries to pull himself up, but his hand slips and he falls back against the wall.

Thwala hauls him to his feet, manhandles him into a worn armchair at the side of the room.

'Get a towel and some water,' Don says. He glances around the room. The surface of the old desk is almost clear, papers and photographs cover the floor. The cupboards under the bookcases are open. There are piles of books on chairs, under tables.

Thwala comes back from the tiny kitchen, towel over his arm. He walks up to Rix, throws the beaker of water in his face. Rix starts. 'Shit.'

Don frowns. 'I meant for Mr Rix to drink. Give him the towel.'

Thwala grins, returns to the kitchen.

'That isn't even funny,' Rix says. 'How did you get in?'

'We rang and knocked, sir, but there was no

answer. When I looked through your letterbox, I was concerned there might have been a break-in.'

'So you broke in instead?'

'We entered your premises to check on your wellbeing.'

Rix coughs. 'My wellbeing isn't so great, man.'

'What happened?'

Rix sits back, stomach distended, breathing heavily.

Thwala brings him a glass of water, holds it out to him. Rix recoils, gingerly holds out his hand, takes it, sips.

'My wellbeing doesn't matter now. It can't.'

Don pulls a chair upright, sits opposite Rix; Ben Thwala stands back.

'What does that mean, sir?'

Rix scratches his head hard, lank hair parting to reveal pale scalp.

'Been dry for four years . . . ' He sips at the water again, ducks his head. After a moment or two, Don hears him splutter, clear his throat, wipe his eyes. He looks back up.

'Why are you here again?'

'Because I need your help. I need to under-stand why Chantal Adam took her own life.'

'You ever been desperate?'

'Not like that, sir. Not so that I would give up my life.'

'Good for you. Some of us have.'

'You, sir?'

'*Ja*, me. Me many times . . . '

Don waits, senses that Rix is working up the courage to say something.

'I talk to you now, I'm taking my own life.'

'Why? Why does talking to us threaten you?'

'Because I know . . . ' He closes his eyes; keeps them closed. 'I know what happened.'

'Whatever it is, sir, we can protect you.'

Rix snorts. 'A secret never goes away. If it's a secret about a bad thing, it festers. It infects everything, everyone who has been in contact with it.'

'What secret, sir?' His voice is gentle. The house is almost silent, the ambient noise from the main road whisked away on the summer breeze. In the distance, Don hears the honking of a taxi-van.

'I can't tell you.' Rix bows his head again. This time, he does not hide his face. Tears drip down his nose, spatter on the papers at his feet.

Don folds his hands over his stomach, sits still.

Rix looks up, sees him calmly waiting. 'I want you to leave.'

'I would not be doing my duty if I left, sir.'

'I can't tell you.'

'That is all right,' Don says. 'I will wait.'

Rix frowns, confused. He looks nauseous. 'I have waited . . . '

'For what, sir?'

Rix sighs. 'One moment of peace.'

The room is very quiet. Don hears Thwala shift his weight from one foot to the other, a long, slow squeak of leather.

'You know who Ray Rossouw is?' Don asks. 'He was holding girls prisoner, sending them to Thailand with drugs. Chantal Adam may have been in his house.'

315

'He dead?'

'Yes, and his accomplice.'

'Jan de Mueller?'

'You know these men, Mr Rix? Did you see them take Chantal Adam?'

Rix swings his head up, laughs loudly. 'No . . . You have no idea.'

'Tell me, then. Tell me what I need to know.'

'Bring me a drink. Is there any? Maybe in the kitchen. In the fridge. A beer.'

'We'll take a look.' Don nods towards Thwala. 'But you need to tell me what you know about these men.'

Rix sits upright, his eyes finally open, focused. He is still swaying gently.

'I know all about Ray Rossouw and Jan de Mueller.'

'How?'

'They were my friends once, long ago.' He eyes Don up and down. 'You're too young even to remember. Us guys, when we were eighteen, we did national service. I stayed on with my unit, so did Rossouw and De Mueller. We fought in Angola, all along the border, for nearly five years.'

'You served together in the army?'

'That's what I'm telling you. I should be telling your boss, De Vries. He'd understand. He'd have an idea what I'm saying.'

'I can call him.'

'No. No . . . Doesn't matter. You'll have heard it before, you can hear it again. It won't go away, so you'd better get used to it.'

'Get used to what?'

316

'In 1990 they released Mandela. We knew what would happen even before then, but we didn't think . . . We didn't think we'd give it all away. Everything . . . I saw four of my unit killed. They didn't just go. I was there. I watched them bleed and scream and beg for life. I watched my friend take his last breath. We were fighting to stop everything we'd worked for, everything we'd built, being taken away, run down, left to fail — just like everywhere else in Africa. Then Mandela's out, and everything changes. If it wasn't for us, we could have been a Soviet satellite, a Communist state. We fought and we saved this country.'

'That was a long time ago now,' Don says quietly. 'When did you last see Ray Rossouw and Jan de Mueller?'

'We're not there yet, Officer. We're not even close.'

'The photograph,' Don says. 'The picture I pointed out to you the last time I was here. Was that a picture of you with your comrades in the army?'

'Ja. We were on leave.'

'Where is it, sir?'

He looks around him, at his office strewn with debris.

'I put it away.'

'Why was that?'

'Because it shouldn't have been on show. But I wanted to be able to see it, to prove to myself where I came from; that once, a long time ago, I had been strong, and principled, and loyal.'

'Who else was in the picture?'

317

'Just my friends. The people who used to be friends.'

'Why did they not stay your friends?'

'Because I failed . . . I didn't do what they wanted. They wanted me to prove myself, to become one of them properly, and I couldn't do it.'

Ben Thwala appears in the doorway, a small can of Amstel lager in his hand. Rix gestures for him to bring it over. Don watches him take the can, crack it open, drink deeply.

'Do we need to search for the picture, sir? Or do you know where it is?'

'What is it with the picture?' His voice breaks. 'It's just a photograph of some men, tired and scarred and . . . proud of what we did, our service to our country.'

'Who else was there?'

Rix looks at him at moment, glances down to the can in his hand, raises it to his lips, tips it back down his throat. Then, he stumbles up, almost falls onto his desk, edges around it to the drawers, pulls one out. He rummages under other papers, extracts the faded black and white picture, slaps it on the desk. Don recognizes it as the photograph he had observed previously. Rix retreats around the desk backwards. Don gets up, guides Rix onto his office chair, stands next to him. Rix puts his hand on the picture, drags it towards him, then puts his shaking thumb on the man to the furthest left of the picture.

'That's Jan.' He moves his thumb, the picture sticking to it, moving sideways too. Don puts his forefinger on the other side of the print; Rix unsticks himself, points at the next man. 'Kevin . . . '

'Coetzee? Jan de Mueller and Kevin Coetzee?'

'Ja. Kevin Coetzee. How did you know that?'

'His is a name I recognize, sir.' He looks back at the picture. 'That is you, with the crucifix?'

'Yes . . . Ray Rossouw, Tony, Carl and Stuart.'

Don's palms are damp, his mouth dry. He tries to remain calm, to seem disinterested. 'They were your unit?'

'My team, part of the unit.'

'You all survive?'

'One way or another, ja.'

'But you do not see your colleagues any more?'

'No. Haven't seen any of them for . . . twenty years. Twenty-one this year.'

'Who are the others, to the right there?'

'Carl Hertzog, Stuart Lanchester, Tony Uys . . . He did all right for himself. Bought a place on Zanzibar, lay on the sand, fucked a different girl every afternoon.'

Don feels his heart beat faster, adrenalin flooding through him. He looks back at Ben Thwala, whose expression is pat, eyes blank, as if nothing he has heard is of interest to him. Don desperately wants to take Dale Rix back to the station, to have De Vries talk to him, have everything he says recorded and videoed, yet to move him from his own home in his still disorientated, intoxicated state would be a risk. The station might spook him. On the other hand, increased sobriety might render him wary and silent.

319

'Why did you not keep in contact with them after you left the army?'

Rix is slumped in the chair, staring vacantly at the picture, his thumb still on Tony Uys. 'When we were disbanded, Stuart went to the authorities, told them about some of the things we had done. It was a fucking war. He saw our guys go down, but he had some righteous itch which wouldn't ever stop. He betrayed all of us.'

'What did he say you did?' Don studies his face. In the man's glazed eyes, he sees a great sadness, a weight on him that seems to pin him down, leave him almost hopeless.

'There were things . . . We needed information. We got it one way or another. Tony and Carl mainly. We were just young guys. We saw our friends bleeding to death and we wanted revenge. Jan was a maniac — he'd kill anything that moved. He'd shoot corpses just to hear the bullet rip through a man's flesh. I couldn't stop them. These guys watch your back. They were all I had.'

'What happened?'

'We were arrested. Tony knew people. We had top attorneys. There was some kind of military hearing. Jan and Ray got time in military prison. I was only on lesser charges. They tried to get me to testify against the others but I wouldn't. Carl and Tony and me, we walked away. I think Tony bribed the judge. He was an Afrikaner and he hated the trial just as much as we did. He gave Jan and Ray minimum sentences.'

'So, you moved on.'

'No. You make it sound like we walked out of

the trial, travelled to wherever we wanted, set up a new life, and it was like nothing had ever happened. But when you fight and watch your friends die, you don't move on. It scars you in ways other people can't see. You look normal, but you're not. Not when you've been there . . . '

'Why did you not stay friends?'

Rix's head is heavy on his neck, his chin approaching his chest slowly.

'Not when you have seen what they did to us, and we did to them.'

In the distance, there is a sound like a gunshot. Don jumps, but the other two men do not move. A taxi-van backfiring, a kid banging a metal barrel with a metal stick?

Rix straightens in the chair, fixes his eyes on Don. 'There was a man called Willem Adam . . . '

'The politician?'

'Yes. He was a politician with the Nats. Once the election was done in 'ninety-four, even though there was a transitional power-sharing government, he stood down. He was one of the architects of the capitulation, one of the men who gave away everything we had. Tony and Carl said that he was the one, the actual man who persuaded De Klerk that apartheid was doomed, to give it all away — centuries of blood and toil and work.'

'He was assassinated.'

'I know,' Dale Rix says. 'I was there.'

★ ★ ★

'We have nothing,' Captain Josephs tells De Vries. 'Kevin Coetzee didn't speak for four days. He's locked away now until trial. Our guys in PE say that, once their lawyers arrived, none of them would talk either. They're shutting down everything tight, sir.'

'Carl Hertzog?'

'Attorney called Calder arrived, started threatening complaints and investigations about his client's state of health, but nothing's happened. We questioned Hertzog and he said he knew nothing about any of it, that this must be down to Coetzee, who he says came to work for him a few years back. It's bullshit, but that's his line.'

'All right, Captain. If there's any comeback over Hertzog towards Sergeant Daniels, let me know. He's in the clear.'

'He said you had quite a fight on the beach. There was the dog involved too.'

'Nasty business,' De Vries says. 'These people will do anything to escape justice.'

★　★　★

Durban, 14 October 1994
The rain arrives, tropical, drops the size of peanuts. Thunder rolls in from the sea, lightning illuminates dark clouds.

In the shadow of the low, bent trees, Dale Rix stands behind Tony Uys as he picks an old padlock securing a gate into the residential park. The trees above them drip water, leaves and blossom on their heads, the liquid flowing down their backs, soaking them entirely. Above

322

the sound of the rain, he hears the tinny clink as the lock hits the pavement. Uys bends down, pockets it, pushes open the gate, enters the park, Rix following, hobbling after him. He closes the gate, walks behind Uys for, maybe, a hundred metres, until he turns, pushes his way through the shrubs and trees at the side of the park, comes out by the chain-link fence, overlooking a narrow lane and the imposing detached house. The road surface is rutted, small craters filled with bubbling water; crooked telephone poles running parallel into a strangely concertinaed perspective. A single streetlight casts an unfocused yellow glow over the gates to the residence, the light reflected by precipitation so solid as to seem a plain of yellow metal, diagonal and impenetrable. Uys checks his watch, steps back from the fence, unslings the pack off his back, takes out the Smith & Wesson .44 revolver.

Eight hours previously, Rix sat awaiting the departure of Uys and Hertzog on another of their occasional missions, their aims, as ever, occluded from him. He understands that they will be away for one night. He is to clean the small, shared house, guard it from any who might threaten to break in, await their return. A few moments before departure, Tony Uys calls for him, informs him that he will be travelling with him, that Hertzog will stay behind.

'Why?'

'Because,' Uys tells him, 'the time has come for you to make a stand. You have to prove who you are. You have to stand up and be one of us.

We have no room for men we can't trust, dead wood.'

'I backed you against Lanchester,' Rix says. 'I stood up in court and told them what I was told to say. I refuted every claim Lanchester made.'

'You did, but that was then.'

'I'd do the same now.'

Uys stands tall over him. He slicks back his hair from his face, straightens his shoulders.

'There's no argument, boy. You come with me now, or you leave for good.'

Rix sees the expression on Hertzog's face: this is a challenge Hertzog believes Rix will fail. He seems pleased.

Rix hears himself say: 'I've proved myself before.'

Through his black gloves, Uys primes the revolver. He leans in to Rix to whisper in his ear, his voice clipped, harsh. 'Remember the training. Keep your head still and don't force it. Count on one shot. Take more if you have to. No one will hear. The storm will do our work for us.' He passes Rix the weapon.

Already, Rix can feel his bare, cold hands shaking. He lowers the weapon, aligns his finger along the barrel, steps through the bushes, rests the end of the barrel, neck high, on one of the plastic-coated strands of fence. He holds the gun with a straight arm, his left hand gripping his forearm.

Ahead, he sees light in the doorway of the house. Two black servants appear, holding umbrellas, and then a man Rix assumes to be Willem Adam is ushered to the driver's seat of

324

the car that is parked outside. Rix looks down the length of his arm, sees it shaking, the gun barrel grinding against the wire of the fence. He steps back.

'I can't do it.'

'You can. Get back in position.'

'My arm is shaking.' He sees his breath condense in the cool evening air, the rain smack it down. Uys physically moves him back into position, whispers, 'You fuck this up, we may not get another chance. Take the fucking shot.'

As he positions the barrel once more, he sees the iron gates to the residence opening. The car's headlights switch on, two almost solid beams cutting through the saturated air. Suddenly, a vehicle accelerates from left to right across his line of vision. He jumps, the barrel slips from the fencing. Spooked, dry-mouthed, sweat mingling with rain in his eyes.

'I can't. I can't see.' He is panting, spitting water from his mouth.

Uys's eyes narrow. Rix can see his jaw tighten, nostrils flare. He takes the weapon, steps forward, aligns the shot and waits. Rix steps back, the rain still pounding him. He feels feverish and overcome. He sees the headlights illuminate the fence, Uys suddenly silhouetted against the thrashing silver rain. He hears two shots, senses, rather than sees, the casings fly, the almost imperceptible hiss as the rain hits the scalding metal.

Uys turns back, pushes Rix away. 'Where are the shells?'

Rix gapes.

'You're a useless fucker, Dale. You're not one of us. You don't deserve to be.' He points the gun, shoots into Rix's calf, watches him fall, screaming, to the ground, leans down.

'Your prints are on the gun, boy. Remember that.'

He kicks him hard in the gut, steps over him, strides across the park. Rix watches him go, his leg on fire, his brain bursting. Tony Uys seems to take no more than three steps before he disappears into blackness.

★   ★   ★

'What happened to you?'

Dale Rix stares at Don February, his breathing shallow and quick. His eyes seem empty. 'I fell into a pit . . . fifteen years deep.'

'But you got away? From the scene?'

'I ran away, as much as I could. I was bleeding but the rain washed everything away. In the far corner of the park, the fence was split. I got through, stole a car, drove south to where I had cousins. One of them worked at the city hospital. He took out the bullet, patched me up. I still have it. The bullet from that gun. It's here . . . ' He looks around the office. 'I watched the news each night and there was nothing. They found nothing, did nothing, and you know why? Because an apartheid politician gunned down, that wasn't news any more. It wasn't prioritized. It went away.'

'And Chantal Adam was in the car?'

'Last few days . . . last night . . . I thought

326

about what I saw. Two men with umbrellas walking from the house to the car. She probably walked herself, held their hands, got into the back of the car.'

'You did not shoot that weapon?'

'I told you what happened. And I told you why I could never speak of it. Uys will have that gun. He'll have kept it. It imprisons me.'

Don frowns. 'I do not understand, sir, how you knew that Ray Rossouw and Jan de Mueller had entrapped Chantal Adam. Did you see them take her?'

Rix looks back up at him, aghast, his mouth almost smiling.

'Knew? I didn't know until I read it in the papers. The girl I was supposed to be protecting, because I knew her, because I understood what she had experienced, to be so nearly killed, and to see her father die, to be something and then nothing, to live her life because of us. Because if there was any justice for her, any honour for me, I had to save her. She had been taken by those people, by those men. If I had known, I would have killed them myself, taken her back and sheltered her. That's why I told you what I did. To stop them now, Hertzog and Coetzee and Tony fucking Uys.'

PART 4

'It was not,' Norman Classon pronounces, 'a heyday for crime-fighting.' He looks at Du Toit, De Vries, Don February. 'I'm sure you can appreciate that there was much resentment and suspicion still hanging over police officers from the apartheid era. After the ANC government gained control of the force and set to turning it into the SAPS we know today, many cases fell out of focus in much the same way that the white officers heading them up did. The newly promoted black officers were less motivated to investigate old crimes. Instead they were predisposed to tackle crime hitherto largely ignored within townships and squatter camps. The SAPS was undergoing rapid transformation, and positive-discrimination policies often meant that crimes were not fully investigated and unsolved cases were ignored.'

Don wonders whether this was strictly true, does not know enough to comment. He is aware that he is of a different generation, a different culture, from the others in Brigadier du Toit's office.

'In fact, it was suspected for some time that Willem Adam had been assassinated by a black terror unit.'

Don's brain registers a notch of understanding: 'black terror unit' is not a phrase he is used to hearing.

'I suppose we should contact the authorities in Port Elizabeth and request evidence retained and the dockets on the original case?'

'No, sir.'

Du Toit turns to De Vries. 'No?'

'Throughout this investigation, we know that Tony Uys and possibly his peers have been informed of our interest in advance. Since there was a unit operating out of PE, entrapping and transporting girls to Cape Town, I think we should reject any direct approach.'

'Isn't that being over-sensitive?'

'Not at all. Uys's people have tied down everyone in the Kruger area. It's perfectly reasonable to expect that they have contacts reporting back to him from his other areas of operation. In fact, it would make sense.'

'An approach independent of this investigation could be made, the material obtained,' Classon says.

'It has to be fast.'

'We can do that.'

De Vries glances at Classon. 'We have the bullet removed from Dale Rix's leg. Steve Ulton's lab have confirmed that it comes from a .44 Smith & Wesson. It's damaged, but he says that if the two bullets fired into Willem Adam's car have been retained, it should be possible to conclude positively that they came from the same weapon.'

'But all that proves,' Classon says, 'if you discover the weapon during your raids, is that Tony Uys has the gun that shot Willem Adam. If what Rix says is true, only his fingerprints may remain on the weapon. It's more likely that a prosecution of Dale Rix would result.'

Don puts up his hand. Du Toit nods at him. 'I think, sir,' he says quietly, 'that Mr Rix is fully prepared to testify against Tony Uys. At the very least, it is a claim that should be investigated.'

'Exactly,' De Vries says. 'It's our way in. Once we have Uys, there are numerous lines of questioning for him. We may even be able to pressure Carl Hertzog or Kevin Coetzee to testify.'

'Whatever else it is, gentlemen, it is a breakthrough in a murder case twenty-two years old. You are to be congratulated, Warrant February.'

Don bows minutely.

'Let's move forward, Norman,' Du Toit continues, 'to obtaining the dockets and evidence from Port Elizabeth discreetly, and preparing a way to obtain warrants and a force to bring in Tony Uys.' He stands up. The other men turn to leave.

'Colonel . . . a word.'

Classon and Don February leave the office, closing the door behind them. De Vries sits down again. Du Toit lowers his voice. 'Uys and his compatriots control a criminal organization encompassing people-trafficking, drugs, rhino horn and ivory. If you prove that Uys killed Willem Adam, you will implicate many others who may have been manipulated into co-operating with him in his criminal activities.'

'That is the nature of organized crime.'

'With the web of contacts and informants that

333

exists in industry, politics and the judiciary, several other Afrikaners may find themselves in untenable positions . . . '

'That's irrelevant.'

'I'm not suggesting anything, Vaughn, just considering repercussions — that is part of what I have to do. We live amidst a volatile social combination of races and attitudes.' He takes a deep breath, struggles to find a method of description. 'If it becomes publicly known that Afrikaners in public life and positions of influence — God knows there are few — have been backing a criminal organization, one responsible for the murder of a Nationalist Party politician who proposed the abolition of the system, it will discredit all of them . . . ' He looks up at De Vries 'All of *us*.'

'I didn't know you identified yourself as a supporter of the Afrikaner cause.'

'You don't have to identify,' Du Toit snaps. 'Your name brands you. History divided us, and that history is not soon forgotten. We've worked too hard to give up what we've achieved.'

De Vries shrugs. 'I don't know what you're asking me to do.'

'I'm not asking anything, Vaughn. I'm discussing how Uys's network can be dismantled without tarnishing those of us remaining in public office. You've intimated that policemen, attorneys, magistrates, members of the public are protecting Uys and his group. Whether they're acting under duress or merely in support of what the man stands for is irrelevant. It will make for very poor press.'

'I've always told you that my investigations are colour-blind, and that has to work both ways. Whatever they may think, or pretend to be, these people aren't political. They're exploitative, greedy, merciless. Dale Rix can talk all day long about how they're all scarred by war, betrayed by their leaders, but you and I, Henrik, we did our national service and we served our time. I saw men die in front of me and, at the time, I certainly wasn't sure that relinquishing power was the right way to go. But I didn't turn to rape and torture and murder.'

'No.'

'And you know how these things work. It's no use breaking a few teeth. They have to come out by the root, or the wounds fester. Worse still, the teeth may grow back . . . ' De Vries trails off.

'What?'

'You know I keep up with colleagues from the old days. A professional, social group. I wonder whether . . . ' He sits up, jaw tight. 'You're right. We have to do our jobs. Just as we always do.'

* * *

'I thought you'd want to know,' Steve Ulton tells De Vries. 'Evidence in Port Elizabeth, the dockets from storage, they're sending an officer by plane this evening to collect them. Apparently, General Thulani authorized the fast-track.'

'Discreetly, I hope?'

'The request came from my lab, asking for firearms evidence from a certain time-frame for research purposes. If you stop to think about it,

335

it may seem peculiar but, in my experience, people rarely stop to think.'

De Vries smiles. 'Something for which I'm regularly grateful. You find out if the bullets had been found and retained?'

'We followed instruction and didn't draw attention, but we know that there is ammunition within the evidence from the Willem Adam case so, unless something's happened to it, it should be there for us.'

'Then it'll be down to you, Steve.'

'I've already decided to work on them as soon as they get here. Nights are best for getting stuff done anyway. Fewer distractions.' He turns. 'You be here? Will I send the dockets to you?'

'*Ja*. Scarcely worth going home. Anyway, if Dale Rix's story is supported by the evidence, we have to move fast, maybe even tomorrow.'

'I'll come find you, Vaughn, if I have anything.'

'You don't get stick from your wife?'

'My wife videos *soapies*, hours of the bloody things. Loves it when I don't come home.'

De Vries snorts. 'Isn't it good not to be wanted?'

★ ★ ★

Cape Town, Friday, 8 January 2016
Henrik du Toit's office is full, its blinds down. General Thulani sits on an armchair to one side, his thighs bulging out of its sides. He is fanning himself with a small sheaf of papers. Du Toit and De Vries stand against the side wall, to which are pinned several maps and photographs. Steve Ulton,

336

Don February, Sally Frazer and Ben Thwala stand; Norman Classon and an unnamed officer, short and muscular, sit at the back.

Du Toit clears his throat, addresses Deputy Assistant Provincial Commander Thulani. 'Sir, as reported to you, we have completed the forensic testing of the ammunition used in the murder of Willem Fourie Adam in October 1994 in Durban.' He looks at Steve Ulton. 'Dr Ulton?'

Steve Ulton glances around the room, but faces General Thulani. 'We have compared the .44 bullet provided for us by Dale Rix, which he claims was shot into him by Tony Uys, with the bullet and bullet fragments retrieved from Willem Adam and his vehicle when he was killed in 'ninety-four, allegedly by Tony Uys. The striations on the complete bullet retrieved from the upholstery of the vehicle Willem Adam was driving precisely match those observed in the bullet taken out of Dale Rix's leg. However, the sample area is restricted. The bullet remained inside Rix's leg because of the leather and metal strapping he wore following his first injury. In effect, the bullet compacted and ricocheted within his leg. In court the findings might be open to the sowing of some small degree of doubt, but I am certain in my own mind that they are a one hundred per cent match.'

'Dale Rix,' Du Toit says, 'has provided a written statement detailing not only the events of October 1994, but those during his time in the army as part of the unit including Tony Uys and Carl Hertzog, who he claims are the leaders of the group, as well as Ray Rossouw, Jan de

337

Mueller, Kevin Coetzee and an additional man, now deceased, Stuart Lanchester.' He gestures to Thwala. 'Sergeant Thwala.'

'There are no court reports or detail of the military hearing that tried these men but, according to Dale Rix, one of their group, Stuart Lanchester, testified that they had been involved in the torture of enemy combatants, the burglary of ammunition and arms, and the sexual assault of Angolan women. The case resulted in the imprisonment for six months of Rossouw and De Mueller, but the other defendants walked free. Rix claims that the judge was sympathetic. When prompted, he recalled that the defence attorney was a man called Rudi Kriel, whose firm, Kriel, Calder, represents those arrested during the current investigation. No physical evidence, or the dockets from the case, can be located by the Johannesburg SAPS.'

'Dale Rix,' De Vries says, 'claims that Stuart Lanchester was almost certainly murdered by Uys and Hertzog at some point after the trial. When pressed, Hertzog gave up the name Tony Uys as his contact up-line, and directed me towards the Bweha Bweha concession on the borders of Kruger Park. I approached Uys directly and received no co-operation from him. I also discovered that the station commander at Skukusa was under threat from Uys and his men to pass on to them any enquiries regarding Bweha Bweha. He stated that many people in the area had been threatened and were acting as informants for Uys, including local magistrates, who had rejected requests for warrants, or who

338

had granted them only after forewarning Uys. Within the past year, a renowned conservationist, a man named Richard Dow, who had been raising concerns about activities at Bweha Bweha, was allegedly driven off the road to his death. Also, a journalist and two workers at Bweha Bweha, who had tried to speak to the authorities, have also been killed or have disappeared. There is considerable suspicion that the trophy-hunting concession is a cover for rhino horn and ivory smuggling, probably to Thailand and Vietnam.'

'On the basis of this evidence,' Du Toit says, 'and after consultation with the Directorate for Priority Crime Investigation, it has been decided that a raid on Bweha Bweha will be undertaken by officers from the Special Crimes Unit and members of the Hawks, who will command the operation. Their unit leader is here, Major Lwazi Ntuli.' The muscular officer stands up, bows to the group. 'He will brief those of you directly involved, with his team, after this meeting. As previously discussed, no other officers will be informed, including local officers, judiciary and civil service. Tony Uys and his employees will be brought back here, to Cape Town, for questioning and charges.'

There is a moment's silence. People glance around for the next speaker, wondering whether the meeting is at an end.

General Thulani speaks from his chair: 'This is an opportunity for the Special Crimes Unit to bring to justice a gang of men with no regard for human life or suffering, and to solve a murder case that has remained open for over twenty years. Follow your orders well, gentlemen, because there must be no mistakes. This is an extraordinary operation in effectively foreign jurisdiction. Its success or failure rests on all our heads.'

Thulani rises, stomps across the room, with officers stepping back to clear a route.

The others begin to move away to their pre-ordained places, leaving Du Toit, De Vries and Norman Classon behind.

Classon closes the office door. 'If Dale Rix is discredited, you have very little evidence. I want to be clear on that. If you cannot prove what you allege, Uys will walk, and he won't go quietly. It may also contradict evidence you think you have in your prosecution of arrested suspects.'

De Vries glances at him, then looks straight at Du Toit. 'Everything is fitting together, sir. We will obtain further physical evidence and personal testimony. Even General Thulani supports this operation.'

'You are relying heavily on the testimony of a man implicated in misdeeds during his service in the army, a lapsed alcoholic who had an unnatural connection to his charge, who ended up dead. As it stands, he is not a convincing witness.'

'No witness is perfect. His information rings true, and it connects a criminal conspiracy today to at least one murder twenty years ago. If that isn't a prize worth chasing, I don't know what is.'

'You don't have to convince me,' Du Toit says. 'You just have to deliver. If this turns out to be one very expensive, extremely controversial fishing trip, none of us is going to come out of it well. And I'm telling you now, if Thulani goes down, we all do.'

★ ★ ★

Mpumalanga Province, Friday, 8 January 2016
The small plane makes a steep approach into Skukusa airport, the surrounding veldt a dusty grey-green in the blurring dusk light. Already, the landscape seems flat and featureless, broken only by the occasional dwelling showing lights. The last commercial flight has departed, the airport shutting down for the night. The plane taxis to the private area towards the end of the runway. Hangar doors open; low light guides them in. Engines stall and decelerate. The cabin is silent as the door opens, steps fold down. Each of the dozen passengers takes their rucksacks and weapons; they parade out into the now closed hangar area.

De Vries is charged, but wary. He is not as fit as he was, is aware that, as the oldest officer in the group, he will be considered a liability, not an asset, an extra responsibility for the true professionals. He has Ben Thwala at his side. His decision to exclude Don February and Sally Frazer sits easily on him; he has no wish to put his officers in danger.

To the rear of the hangar, a dirt track leads to the air-side gate and out beyond the public areas towards the main connecting roads and the bush itself. The guards at the air-side gate will be

341

monitored to ensure that they cannot communicate with anyone while the vehicles head out towards Bweha Bweha. Even as he stands waiting in the hangar, De Vries feels hemmed in by the strong smell from the aeroplane's engines, heat still emanating from them, the men around him standing silently, or communicating in low voices and hand gestures. He looks for Ben Thwala, sees him chatting casually with one of the Hawks, another tall, well-built black guy. He wonders whether Thwala secretly harbours greater ambitions than his unit. Ultimately, he knows he is change-averse. He wants to establish a team he trusts, can rely on, then keep it, just as it is, permanently.

Signals are exchanged, men move out towards four vehicles: two Land Rovers, a bigger off-road vehicle with camouflage livery, and an old Toyota Land Cruiser. Each leaves at a different time, the convoy spread out to avoid attracting attention. The briefing from Major Lwazi Ntuli back in Cape Town has been replayed during the flight. De Vries is impressed both with Ntuli and his men, is aware that he and Thwala are outsiders. They travel in the last of the vehicles, De Vries in the passenger seat, Thwala and another officer in the back.

With the windows sealed, despite the air-conditioning, the vehicle interior soon heats up, the glass warm to the touch. The sky is a very dark blue, glowing phosphorescently, speckled with stars.

The driver is fast and accurate, the landscape blurring both from lack of light and rate of velocity, the shrubby woodland at either side of them forming a compressing tunnel as they proceed along deserted roads. He reflects on Richard Dow's untimely road accident, hopes that no one is waiting for them at the next corner. He fears that the guards who discovered and immobilised Jack Esterhuysen will be waiting. He feels his stomach tense as they reach the straight section of road leading to the gates of the Bweha Bweha estate. He has not seen another car, including one of their own team's vehicles, for the previous twenty kilometres. When they approach the gateway, the driver slows for the turn, accelerates down the drive. De Vries glimpses two uniformed guards on their knees inside the sentry gate, hands bound behind their backs, one of the Hawks standing over them with a pistol.

They cross the road hump beyond the gate, accelerate down the driveway. The back windows are open: Ben Thwala and the Hawk have automatic weapons pointing to either side. Ahead, between groups of low, long-thorned acacia trees underlit, De Vries can see the triangular plains of the main lodge, illuminated by spotlights around the imposing stone chimney; beneath, he sees rapid, jerky movement beyond the broad expanse of glass, almost senses the sound of gunfire before he sees a fleeting muzzle flash. The vehicle stops at the end of the driveway on the low bridge that spans the now dry stream, blocking any easy escape by car. The Hawks jump out, crouch, move forward.

De Vries looks away for a moment and they

are gone. He turns back to Thwala.

'Ready?'

'Yes, sir.'

They exit the off-roader, opening windows and both doors on each side, crouching between them, scanning backwards and forwards, weapons primed. Ahead, to the side of the main lodge, De Vries sees a line of what he assumes to be guests being led away from the lodge towards the residential rondavels beyond. He strains to focus on the scene through the glass of the main dining room, thinks he sees men and women on the floor, guarded by the Hawks. In the distance, he hears gunfire exchanged: two blasts reverberate against the far walls of the building, illuminating the sky above with a golden glow. Stun or smoke grenades, he suspects. There is something magical about the scene, distant enough to allow appreciation to dominate threat.

The sticky heat of the night air, the tension in his limbs, his churning stomach take him back to his years in Angola, during national service. A cold shiver pulses down his back, his calves ache. He saw too much blood, too much senseless and counter-productive action. That time had convinced him of the need to pick your physical battles carefully, to wait and outwit your enemy. He questions what has made this investigation develop from the cerebral to the violent so quickly: from the raid on Diane Kemmel's compound to the fight on the beach at Mossel Bay and, now, his second visit to Bweha Bweha. These are not cerebral people: these are soldiers and mercenaries, resistant to the sanctity of life,

344

motivated only by an all-consuming greed.

He swallows thick, hot saliva, urging it to travel through him more quickly, rechecks his position, scanning as close to 180 degrees as he can. 'Thwala? You all right?'

'All clear, sir.'

'Stay tight.'

'Yes, sir.'

De Vries hears distant shouting, but it sounds ordered, not panicked. Within moments, signalled from the entrance to the lodge, they see their cue to approach. They scan their surroundings once more, close the doors to the vehicle, begin to make their way towards the expanse of gravel in front of the lodge. As he stands almost straight, something catches De Vries's eye beyond the low roof of the veranda running along the side elevation of the lodge. Two red lights bouncing away from him. He draws binoculars to his eyes, finds it is impossible to identify the vehicle. He rechecks his recollection of the briefing: neither the men, nor the vehicles, were to leave their stipulated areas.

Ben Thwala looks back at De Vries.

'Something's wrong. Reach your position. I'm taking the car.'

Thwala seems confused, contemplates retracing his steps, freezes, hears the engine fire, ducks down as De Vries accelerates towards the main building, jerking right to find a track to follow in the direction of the rogue lights.

De Vries accelerates along the relatively flat surface that passes the side of the lodge, finds the road dipping sharply, dividing into two separate tracks. He picks the one that takes him to the right, struggling with the heavy steering to guide the huge vehicle down the gully, over the deeply rutted track where tyre marks from a time when the ground was wet have solidified into vicious grooves.

Even with headlights on full beam, his progress is slowed by the unfamiliar terrain and overhanging vegetation, often sharp and resistant. As he climbs a sharp incline and crests the top, he sees the lights from the vehicle ahead, is not certain that they are on the same road but senses that he is making up ground. Just from glancing ahead, eyes off the road for a few seconds, he has mispositioned the car on the narrow track, the front wheels scraping against a curb of compacted, hardened mud, the almost visceral squealing of coarse thorny shrub against glass. He brakes, adjusts position on the track, accelerates again, the strong torque of the Land Cruiser pulling him faster up the hill until he flies over the top of the incline, bounces on landing, misses the road altogether and hurtles across rough, scrubby veldt, the car jolting, sending him out of his seat, his head crashing against the ceiling of the car. He rejoins the track as it bends into his path, guns the engine hard, skidding in the dusty grooves. Ahead, he sees the vehicle not more than a hundred metres away, thinks he glimpses white hair on the driver, wonders whether it could be Tony Uys.

Jamming himself back into the seat, he presses harder on the accelerator, gripping the steering wheel to steady himself. The car in front has increased speed: it seems to De Vries to be pulling away from him along a meandering track traversing a gentle hillside. He changes down to first gear, stamps on the accelerator, feels the gear jolt into position and pull the car screaming along the road. The lights of the car in front disappear around a bend bearing right, circling the hill. De Vries prepares to brake, bracing himself for the force which will hit him, finds that the apex of the corner is upon him, skids to maintain control.

Within the single second of the manoeuvre, as the car spins to face exactly where he intends to travel, he is aware of the sensation of control lost, the vehicle overriding him, the turn, the track; the sense that the road has run out yet the car still travels. He braces himself, feels the jolt as the front tyres hit a raised bank, then the vehicle itself seems to leave the surface and smash into the ground. Around him, the windows scratch and squeal; beneath, metal grates and, suddenly, the velocity ceases. He flies forward, the crown of his head smashes the windscreen, his chest compressed against the steering wheel.

The engine still runs, idling quietly. De Vries is aware of blood on his face, his chest savagely aching. He tests his limbs, finds movement, checks his breathing: unimpaired. He sniffs the air, cannot detect leaking fuel. He pulls the door handle, expecting resistance, finds that it clicks open, the door falling away from him fast. He pulls himself out of the cockpit, realizes that he can stand. He steps up onto the running board, heaves himself onto the roof, struggles to stand straight.

Beyond, he sees only the dimly glowing night sky, the quiet and empty veldt. He slides into a sitting position on the roof, finds himself sliding off the convex surface, jams himself up there with one boot against the open driver's door, breathes deeply the hot, heavy air. He wipes the blood from his brow, picks rhomboid chunks of glass from his hair, brushes them away. He looks up at the sky ahead of him, sees the breadth of the Milky Way extending diagonally across his field of vision; beautiful and uncomprehendingly vast. He sits panting, fighting for moisture in his mouth and on his lips, looks down at the car, which has saved his life, engine still calmly ticking over.

Already, he is assessing how far from the lodge he has travelled, whether he can get the car out of the ditch in which it is stuck, whether he can find a signal on his cell phone to call for help. He bows his head, realizes again that his impulsive reaction to make chase was foolish and dangerous, scolds himself, but knows that his instincts, however often proven wrong, are resistant to change.

He slips from the roof, comprehends that the sounds of veldt have taken over from the low rhythmic grumble of the engine. He sits on the edge of the driver's seat, searches for his cell phone in his jeans, feels nothing in his pockets. Suddenly, a shot pierces his eardrums, thumps into the metal of the front wing. He scrambles wholly inside the car, struggles over the drive-train bulge between the seats, scrabbles on the scruffy leather upholstery for purchase to pull himself into cover. A second shot reverberates from the rocky incline of the hill, glass shattering. De Vries searches in the darkness for his weapon — cannot see it, cannot find it.

'De Vries!'

The voice is unmistakable, deep and gruff, tone sneering, accent thick.

'I bet my house it's you.'

De Vries pulls the handle of the passenger door, feels the locking mechanism release, the door unmoving. The realization of being unarmed, Tony Uys outside approaching, hits him hard. He fights for breath, uses his right hand to feel between the seats for any kind of weapon he can use in his defence.

'You're going to die here, Colonel.' The voice is closer now. 'When you're gone, I'll find your wife and your pretty daughters and, when they are looking into my eyes, they will know just how badly you fucked up.'

Straining to keep his torso still, he twists and wriggles his shoulders to stretch his arms further under the seats, into pockets and corners, under carpets. The fingertips of his right hand feel metal. He cannot stretch any further. He tries to judge how far away Uys might be. Perhaps Uys cannot see him from where he is, cannot be certain whether or not he is in the car or beyond it, dead, or fatally injured, or alive. He strains to hear over the crickets and animal calls, receives nothing he can discern. He braces himself, twists his body, keeping as low as he can, grapples with

349

the barrel of the pistol lodged at the edge of the carpeting in the passenger footwell.

Finally, he has it. He pulls it towards him, feels for the safety, knows that it must be loaded and primed. In his current position, he cannot find an angle to get off a shot. Uys has fallen silent. De Vries realizes that he could be skirting the vehicle from a distance, approaching it from any side. He wants to shout out to Uys, to illicit a reply to gauge his distance and position, but his silence buys him time and sows uncertainty. It is all he has to protect himself.

He uncurls almost horizontally across the front seats, his right hip grinding against the protruding division between the seats, his stomach exposed as he twists. Finally, he finds himself able to grab the inner door handle on the driver's side. He pulls himself slowly up, keeping his head and shoulders low. The shattered windows, fragmented windscreen, all allow sounds to enter the cabin, but he can hear only the ceaseless, pervasive whine of crickets. He finds the heat has made his body slick with sweat, glass fragments adhering to his bloodied skin, hands slippery. Tension builds inside him as he waits for any sign of Uys's position; he knows that he cannot wait to be discovered when he might have his back to his predator. He takes a deep breath, rises up in the seat, fires off four shots, twisting to aim through each window. The noise refracts from the cabin, blasts his eardrums.

Almost immediately, three shots hit the car, thumping into the bodywork with the sound of penetration deep and intense. He twists to his right; he knows that Uys is within a triangular sector from the point of impact. He raises his pistol, fires off a further shot.

The silence frightens him. The empty seconds that elapse allow time for terror to seep into him, for panic to build. He finds it hard to breathe, struggles to believe that he can still move. The sweat on him feels like a fever, an excretion of blood from every pore of his body. Suddenly, he hears him.

'You're a long way from home, Colonel.'

The voice seems further away. He waits, ears straining over his own breathing, the engine. The silence screams at him, loaded with menace. The clunk against the bodywork is neither a bullet nor a stone, but something else, a noise familiar yet alien, something his mind cannot process but which his instinct tells him marks the end of an encounter, the completion of the dialogue. He scrambles to open the door, slithers down the high seat onto the ground beneath, begins to grip the ground with his fingernails and pulls himself low and fast through the coarse grass and stony subsoil. He breathes in deeply, prepares to dive forward, finds himself deafened, burning, subsumed into a blinding, agonising fireball that drives the breath from his lungs into the fetid, stinking night air.

★　★　★

He starts awake, consciousness flooding his brain with awareness and panic. He rolls on the ground, seeking to extinguish flames that may be real, struggles to his knees, crawls away from the fire. He falls sideways into the same ditch he had driven the car. He waits inside it until he can focus his thoughts. He checks himself: arms and legs moving, heart beating. Pain thuds through his skull, in time to his quick pulse; the backs of his hands are burned, but he is still alive, still moving, still thinking. He feels again for his weapon, knows that it is long gone. He wonders whether Tony Uys still stands over him; wonders, optimism suddenly flooding his senses, whether perhaps the explosion of the grenade and then, in probability, the car itself, will draw help from the Hawks to him.

He lies still, trying to stifle his heavy breathing, gasping for the oxygen which has been pulled from his lungs. Nothing happens but for the passing of waves of petrol fumes mingling with burning flesh and hair, the occasional current of cooler, purer air, the incessant cricket calls, the crackling of the fire. If there are footsteps above him, he cannot hear them. If the barrel of a gun is pointing at him, he is defenceless. He thinks he hears a car accelerate; he does not know, cannot know. A sudden calm falls over him: there is nothing to do now.

★ ★ ★

The Hawks arrive sometime later. One of them squats by the ditch and speaks. De Vries does not hear the words but mumbles back, forms words, shouts them. He sees Ben Thwala

352

looming over him, his face expanding at he leans over him.

'Can you move, Colonel?'

De Vries raises his right arm. '*Ja.*'

'Do you think you have broken bones?'

'No.'

Thwala bends, puts his arms under De Vries, pulls gently. At first, De Vries panics, grimaces, cries out, but no extra pain manifests itself.

'Go on. It's okay. Get me up. Get me up.'

Thwala pulls him free of the ditch, half lifts, half drags him to the track, hauls him upright, supports him. De Vries's legs are weak, but he locks himself into position.

'It was Uys. He got away.'

'We'll find him.'

De Vries does not recognize the voice, but the tone is readily identifiable, certainty defying reality: Hawk-speak. 'You got everyone else?'

'*Ja,*' Thwala says. 'Everything as planned.'

'Except this.' The same voice; the same blinkered hubris.

De Vries forces his neck back, faces the man, sufficient energy to wax sarcastically. 'Except Tony Uys. The leader. Everything except him.'

★   ★   ★

By the time De Vries and Thwala arrive back at the main lodge, a car from Skukusa and other nearby SAPS units have arrived. Captain Molewa runs over to him, eyes bulging. 'You are all right, Colonel, sir?'

'*Ja.*'

'What have you done, Colonel?'

'What I said I would. We've cut them down. All of them.'

'All except the White Mamba . . . '

'He has nowhere to go.'

'I hope not, sir.'

'When it all comes out, if there is trouble for you, you ask for me.'

Molewa nods eagerly.

'What have they told you to do?'

'I am to take the guests into Bushbuckridge. There is the hotel there. They are to be guarded until questioning.'

'Good. Most of them won't know anything, but if there are Thais, Vietnamese, they're likely to be smugglers. Make an example of them. I want them interrogated until we have contacts and names of buyers in their own countries. You understand?'

A uniformed officer brings De Vries a bottle of water. He grabs it, unscrews the top, gulps.

'You need medical attention?' Molewa asks.

He holds up a rusty, scarred hand.

'Later.'

One of the Hawks' officers approaches, asks De Vries to accompany him to Major Ntuli. He leads him away from the main courtyard, now lined with staff members, trackers, rangers sitting cross-legged on the ground, to a Land Rover. The vehicle sets off rapidly around the main lodge and rondavels, out into the bush. De Vries feels some strength return to him, but his head is blistered and he is still covered with dried blood. Three or four kilometres down the largely straight track, the road splits. They take the left fork, heading for a more thickly forested area and a broad granite tor, some thirty metres tall, next to which stands a large, new corrugated-iron barn. From afar, De Vries sees spot-lights to the side of the building, a small group of vehicles.

They park, walk around the building to the far side. As he turns the corner, De Vries is overwhelmed by a stench that turns his stomach, the incessant buzzing of flies, swarms of moths flying around and into the two arc lights set up to illuminate the scene. Delicate wings burn and smoke, the odour acrid and intense.

Major Ntuli steps out of the building towards De Vries. 'You were lucky, Colonel, but I am glad to see you still with us.'

'I should have waited for backup, but I thought he'd be gone.'

'We will find Mr Uys in due course. Meantime, you were right about this place. It is the worst I have seen. There are two men from SANParks on their way, more from government bodies.'

'What is it?'

'As you know, most of the rhino horn trade is controlled by Mozambican organized crime, utilizing men from there and here. Last year, the Mozambique government got tough with the smugglers, closing down entry and exit points for the criminals there. Mr Uys and his people seem to have exploited that.'

'What is this place?'

Ntuli lowers his eyes. 'This place is hell, Colonel.'

He turns, walks briskly across a barn area towards double doors set into the back wall.

'Through the doors on your right, there is a workshop, a laboratory of sorts — a butchery. There is luggage, which has been modified to carry horn as part of its structure — very hard to identify. The horn is enclosed within leather tubing. There is also taxidermy equipment for apparently legal export of trophies.'

He turns back to the far wall, nods at a guard, who pushes open a door. The stench leaches into the main area, De Vries gags. They step through into an anteroom, backed by a thick curtain of heavy-duty plastic. Beyond, they are in a large area of flat, unsurfaced ground, hard up against the side of the granite tor, which rises into the eaves of the building. At its base, the land drops away into a deep gash, like a sinkhole, a wide granite crevasse. Above the cavity, flies swarm, larger insects hover.

'Jesus.'

'We don't know how deep it is. Maybe very deep. But there are animal carcasses there. Many of them.' He points. 'Look at these tracks. They are from the bulldozers and forklifts. The animals are poached, brought in here, horn and other valuable parts removed, the carcass dumped. You can see that the earth is stained with much blood.'

'Why bring the animals here?'

'Because of increased aerial surveillance. We see a tagged animal killed and often we can trace the group responsible. Here, I am thinking they stun the animal from afar, collect it and process it here. Away from the prying eyes of drones and helicopters.'

De Vries looks up into the ceiling of this steel and granite cathedral, sees what he assumes are bats hanging from cross-struts, concentrates on not breathing in the insects which engulf them.

'How did nobody know?'

'The rock blocks any noise from this site to the camp. There is nothing for forty, fifty kilometres. The visitors are probably taken on routes to the south of the lodge — they will see none of this. Just a peaceful game reserve. They go away and tell people just that. That's what they're here for. From the air, from the outside, this might just be maintenance works for the park. Maybe they work at night too.'

De Vries turns, eyes watering at the stench and the frenzied insects, pushes back through the plastic curtaining, mouth and throat dry, his entire respiratory system infested with the reek of old animal flesh, blood. He jogs across the barn, Ntuli at his side, and out into the humid night air.

'You do not want to see the workshops?'

'No.'

'The value of rhino horn,' Ntuli continues, 'is maybe four hundred thousand rand per animal on average. Thirty thousand US dollars. Take it to Vietnam, the wholesale value is maybe five, six times that figure. We have seized the horn from dozens of animals previously.'

'Everyone who worked here, everyone they dealt with, we want them all.'

'Men who were working here may have run

into the bush. It will be a dangerous escape for them. Those off-site will know of our raid. They will disappear back to Mozambique, but they will return when a new concern starts its operations. It is a battle I cannot see being won until no rhino remain.'

'How does Uys set this up?'

'Once he has contacts in Thailand, Vietnam, he can establish a pipeline of couriers. Then he can smuggle anything he wants. Whatever brings the greatest return. We have done well here tonight. Your information and instincts were good, Colonel. This is a fine result in our war.'

'But we don't have Uys.'

'I know you think differently, but we have more than we could have hoped. We can clear this area of the Kruger of undesirables, work hard to maintain it as a safe area for endangered game.'

De Vries sighs deeply. Fatigue is hitting him hard. 'What about the offices at the lodge? Is there a safe?'

'I do not know that now. But we control everything. If there is evidence to be found, we will find it.' He looks at De Vries, seems to recognize that the pain from his injuries must now be setting in. 'I will have a driver take you to a place to rest. Once the Anti-poaching Unit, the investigators, arrive tomorrow, all this will be out of our hands.'

De Vries nods. 'Good work.'

A Land Rover draws up beside him. He steps into the passenger seat, grits his teeth to absorb the jolts as the vehicle heads back towards the lodge.

★ ★ ★

The black officer sweats profusely, his features distorted by his squat nose recoiling from the stench. De Vries looks above him to the black, jagged spires of rock, which reach skywards, bats and vultures circling, darkening the midnight blue sky. 'This,' the man says, 'is where you will be now. It is hell.'

De Vries chokes and splutters, struggles to breathe as the air seems to thicken, saturated by zigzagging particulate, the whining increasing in volume as he feels himself enveloped. He looks over at the officer.

'I will have a driver take you to your place of rest.'

De Vries jolts awake, his left hand gripping the side of the mattress, the back of his head clammy from the wet pillow, sheets twisted away to the opposite side of the bed. He sits up, feels the blood flow from his head as pain floods his arteries. He lies back down, panting, his body cold from fever.

The bedroom is small, curtains cutting out moonlight, outside seemingly silent. He is disorientated — has no idea where he is or, as the room spins, even where in the room the bed is located. He sits up again, drinks from the bottle of water by his bed, blows his nose, smells again the odour of hacked and rotting animal carcasses. He feels nauseous, dizzy, switches pillows, lies back down.

Even as sleep overcomes him, he sees the tall, white-haired figure above him: 'I will find your wife and your pretty daughters . . . '

He moans and tosses, incapable of managing his racing brain, unable to control his failing body, out of control, surrendered to the indefinite care of unconsciousness.

★ ★ ★

De Vries shuts his eyes as a nurse disinfects his cuts, dresses them, bandages his left hand. He dislikes being touched, rejects the tactile greetings of his friends. He has called his ex-wife in Windhoek, waking up the family, asked her to stay with their daughters for a while longer. The instruction was not met with resigned acceptance, more an anger that he is the cause of their exile, that he has not nullified the threat to them. At least, for now, they are in Namibia, away, he hopes, from immediate danger.

There is no news of Tony Uys. Patrols have seen nothing, other units received no reports. Many, still in thrall to him, may have let him escape. He is gone. Nothing else about the operation matters to De Vries now. Only the threat from Uys.

Bweha Bweha is sealed off by police lines.

At the reserve, the driveway is wet with misty morning rain, which sits on leaves and stems, forms a close patchwork of immovable tiny drops on the side and back windows of the car.

The air, when he steps out from the car, is soft

360

and cool, smelling strongly of the earth. The scene is as different from the night before as it could be. He limps towards the lodge entrance, flashes his ID at the officer by the door. Inside, teams of forensic technicians work, while police officers bag and tag evidence, take it out of the building into the waiting vans.

After a few moments, he finds a private office at the back of the building, with windows overlooking the bush. It is decorated in classic safari-lodge style, complete with sepia photographs of hunting safaris, hurricane lamps, a zebra skin on the floor. Behind the leather-covered desk, two technicians are on their knees in front of a safe set into a credenza running along the back of the room. A young black officer, standing over them, turns to De Vries.

'Can I help you, sir?' De Vries holds up his ID. 'What can I do for you?'

'What else have your teams found in here?'

'We have already taken out a desktop PC and the files from the two desk drawers here.'

'That evidence should be withheld. The PC and files are coming with me to Cape Town, along with whatever is in that safe.'

The officer smiles. 'I cannot allow that, sir. They are all part of our evidence.'

De Vries takes a deep breath. Something about the depth of pain in his head has calmed him. 'You can photograph, bag, mark them. But they come with me, Sergeant. This is a joint operation and evidence relating to Tony Uys comes to Cape Town.'

The officer takes a pace back from De Vries,

produces a cellphone, dials, turns his back on the room while he speaks.

In front of him, the technicians seem to be drilling the lock. De Vries is aware of someone entering the room, finds Ben Thwala at his side.

'I have already cleared the Tony Uys evidence to come with us. We have a Land Rover for it, and a flight back to Cape Town with the Hawks unit this afternoon.'

De Vries is grateful. Thwala is a familiar face, a reminder of a time when every centimetre of his body was not burning with pain.

The black officer finishes his call, looks across at De Vries. 'That is all in order, sir.'

De Vries turns back to the safe at the sound of a metallic clink. The now thoroughly drilled door is gouged open. One technician stands, lays a plastic sheet across the surface of the desk, prepares evidence bags. One by one, items are brought out, handed up to him: bundles of euro and dollar banknotes, boxes containing phials of brown liquid and various sizes of syringe, two handguns, with boxes of ammunition, a selection of certificates, legal documents and sealed envelopes.

De Vries puts on plastic gloves to inspect the handguns. They are both old models, seemingly unused for some time. The smaller is a Smith & Wesson, a stubby gun holding what he thinks would be .357 Magnum ammunition; the other is a larger gauge, probably .44, also manufactured by Smith & Wesson.

'This could be the gun Dale Rix claims Uys used to kill Willem Adam.'

It feels heavy in his hand, weighty with significance but, without forensic examination, it could be nothing more than another weapon among dozens discovered on site. He turns to Thwala. 'Keep an eye on all of this. Make sure it's placed in the correct vehicle. No mistakes. I want Dr Ulton examining these tonight.'

He turns away from the office, wonders what else the documents might reveal, whether they might suggest where Uys would run to.

⋆　⋆　⋆

The return journey passes quickly. The men chatter and laugh. They have sustained one minor injury: the thigh of one of the Hawks is badly burned. Otherwise, the operation is classed a major success.

De Vries sits alone towards the front of the passenger section of the aeroplane. He thinks about the chain of events that has brought him to where he is, wonders who among those he has spoken to has been honest. His mind returns to Major Johan Bekker in Johannesburg, the lack of information imparted, that which he must surely have known but withheld. He recalls Bekker's actions on the day of Lulu's abduction, wonders whether his impotence was genuine, or whether he was motivated not to act more assertively by a different pressure. This, he reflects, is always the problem with conspiracy. Everyone must fall under suspicion.

A group of Afrikaner men, soldiers, all dismissed suddenly when the war abruptly ends, disillusioned, bitter, angry. Was this the motivation for developing a criminal network over twenty years to exploit the lives of humans and animals alike? And who has backed them? A loose association of sympathetic contacts in all walks of influential life, all linked, tenuously perhaps, by an Afrikaner brotherhood? And how many more were extorted, blackmailed and threatened into co-operation? He is relieved that, if nothing else, what promises to be a lengthy inquiry in the Kruger will be handled by others.

When he thinks about Uys, he feels a cold blade of fear in his chest and stomach that he will never again be able to rely on his family's safety.

He looks out of the small oval porthole at the blank, arid landscape of the Karoo, the brown mountain formations, the perfectly flat line of sky as far as the horizon. Amid such enormity, he is so small.

★   ★   ★

Cape Town, Saturday, 9 January 2016
De Vries receives multiple SMS messages on his cell phone as he drives into town. Most of the South African visitors have returned home after the holidays and the tourists are still sleeping. The freeway around the Mountain is empty. He speeds around Hospital Bend and onto De Waal Drive, taking the corners belligerently, feeling charged both by the developments of his case, and also by the urgency to find information on Tony Uys's whereabouts.

In the lift, he replies to Jack Esterhuysen's message. Esterhuysen, unaware of the events of the previous days, has only one thing on his mind. It reminds him of one misjudged night, momentarily joyous, irrevocably tarnished, regretted:

No one will tell Marc Immelman. We spoke in confidence. Get better.

★   ★   ★

On an otherwise quiet floor, Henrik du Toit's office is bustling. As well as Du Toit, Norman Classon sits behind the desk. Don February, Sally Frazer and Steve Ulton sit on narrow chairs brought in for the conference.

'Close the door, Vaughn.'

De Vries sits next to Don.

'As you know,' Du Toit starts, 'Dr Ulton and his team have been working on the evidence recovered from the Bweha Estate all night.'

'Bweha Bweha,' Classon says.

Du Toit glances at him. 'As I say, all night. I'm going to paraphrase now because Dr Ulton will provide the detail. The computer and files retrieved from the office of Tony Uys refer only to the operations of the concession. They will be passed back to Jo'burg where they may form part of their investigation into the activities there. However, we have had more luck with the weapons retrieved from the safe. Steve.'

'The first of the two weapons, the Smith & Wesson .357, has been linked to previous crimes, but the information in the system is corrupted. Put it this way: the weapon is known to us, and is significant. We're just having difficulties with context right now. The larger pistol is a .44, also manufactured by Smith & Wesson. Having compared striations on the ammunition following test firings, the weapon is a match to that used in the killing of Willem Adam in Durban on the fourteenth of October 1994.'

'That's extraordinary,' Du Toit says. 'You have DNA or fingerprint evidence?'

Ulton smiles nervously. 'This crime is over twenty-one years old. The duration of a readable print is usually determined by multiple facts: the 'matrix', that is to say, the chemical composition of the substance that was transferred to the surface the 'substrate', or surface on which the print was deposited and, most importantly, the environment in which the item was stored, everything from subsequent use to temperature, humidity, even altitude. In this case, despite the weapon being kept sealed, DNA testing has produced no results and the fingerprints remaining are degraded but not unmatchable. There are partial matches both to impressions provided for us by Dale Rix, and to prints taken from Tony Uys's office, which we understand, purely for investigative, and not court purposes, to be exemplars of his own.'

'My God.'

'Rix proved a reliable witness,' De Vries says. 'And he guessed right, as far as Uys's likely actions concerning the gun — keeping it as insurance against later claims. But we still have only Rix's word that it was Uys who pulled the trigger.'

'There's nothing to guide us there, Steve?' Du Toit says.

'No. It's unlikely the trigger would have yielded any kind of discernible print or even DNA. Certainly, after all this time, there isn't anything.'

'But we have the weapon and we have a statement.'

Du Toit turns to Don February. 'In your opinion, Warrant Officer, do you believe what Dale Rix has stated is reliable testimony? Your instinct?'

'I think, sir,' Don says quietly, choosing his words carefully, 'that Mr Rix was in a highly disturbed state, something like a breakdown. If he had fired the weapon that night, I think that he would have told me.'

'On top of everything else,' De Vries says, 'we must find Tony Uys for questioning regarding the murder of Willem Adam.'

Du Toit nods.

Norman Classon says, 'A court is unlikely to accept Dale Rix's testimony unsubstantiated. The investigation at the time found nothing whatsoever to suggest the identity of the culprit or culprits. The rain washed away most physical evidence, and there was no witness evidence recorded either.'

'Rix's story makes sense.' De Vries says.

'But it doesn't make a case.'

'The investigation was tainted by the prevailing political imperatives of the time.'

Classon stares at him. 'That statement is unlikely to endear you to anyone.'

'I don't care.'

Du Toit holds up his hand. 'All right. You both make valid points. I, for one, am happy to say that our unit has identified the prime suspect in the murder of Willem Adam, and is now seeking to question him.' He glances at Classon. 'I assume that is uncontroversial?'

'In as much as it is means nothing, it's fine.'

Du Toit rolls his eyes.

De Vries grinds his teeth. He loathes the political public relations of South African policing, has energy only for the chase. 'No matter what sounds good,' he snaps, 'I have an intensely pressing reason to want Uys located and arrested.' He stands. 'May I get on with that, sir?'

* * *

'Tony Uys flew out of Jo'burg airport on an afternoon flight to Dar es Salaam.'

Don stands in the doorway to De Vries's office.

'How is that even possible?'

Don shrugs.

'It is a busy place. Someone made an oversight . . . ?'

'Or someone was sympathetic to the cause. He in Dar es Salaam now?'

Don steps into the office, closes the door behind him.

'Dale Rix mentioned that Uys had made a lot of money, lay on the beach at his house on Zanzibar. Maybe that is where he is.'

'Dar es Salaam is the obvious gateway. Rix tell you any more about his place there?'

'It was a passing comment only. The others in the group had not done so well, but Uys had money.'

'I bet he did. Can you track flights out of Dar?'

Don laughs. 'No. And I do not think that a polite request would help, however official. In any case, he could take a ferry, a private boat. It is not that far.'

'He say where on Zanzibar?'

'Outside Stone Town, I think. I do not know for sure.'

De Vries leans back in his chair, rights himself before the arc takes him off balance. 'Anyone we talk to in Stone Town could tip him off. If he doesn't know that we know he's there, we have one advantage.'

'Sir?'

'I'm thinking aloud, Don. He's in Tanzania, but he's not in Tanzania. Zanzibar is a political, diplomatic, policing nightmare.'

'Then he is in the wind?'

'He is,' De Vries muses. 'But at least we know the direction it's blowing . . . '

★   ★   ★

Deputy Assistant Provincial Commander Thulani's office is kept icy cold, perhaps purely for his comfort or, possibly, to ensure the brevity of unwanted interviews. Henrik du Toit and De Vries both wear jackets and ties, sit reluctantly

369

around his enormous desk. Two sharp-suited minions stand to one side, taking copious notes. De Vries knows immediately that they are not cops, instinctively senses the machinations of SAPS public relations. A twenty-year-old crime solved.

'It was Warrant Officer February's work. He knew something wasn't right about Dale Rix. He has good instincts. He applied pressure at just the right moment, and Rix gave it up.'

'I'm sure Brigadier du Toit will note your commendation.' He nods at Du Toit, smirking. 'And it shows there are, and always have been, terrorist groups of every kind.'

'If you mean every colour, then, yes, sir, there are.'

'We in the SAPS are colour-blind, Colonel.'

'We are, sir, but since our unit is sometimes referred to as 'White Crimes', I think each of these inquiries has proved that we must have elite teams for every eventuality.'

Thulani glances at the note-takers, waves a thick wrist dismissively. 'As I have explained to Brigadier du Toit, I made contact with my opposite number in Tanzania regarding information on Mr Tony Uys. We take every threat against one of our officers and his family very seriously. You have liaised with Johannesburg?'

'Liaised? Yes, sir.'

'Good. Your family are safe?'

'For the time being.'

'Good. A new case now?'

De Vries's smile remains intact. Thulani has done what he needs to be seen to have done, what he will tell his superiors when De Vries and his family are killed.

'Absolutely.'

★   ★   ★

'As a matter of fact, I do.'

'Who?'

Marantz squeezes his eyes shut. 'I'm assuming he's still alive. He was one of Caro's parents' friends, a kind of uncle to her. Gay. Lived out in East Africa most of his life, went back to Zanzibar.'

'I didn't think they liked gays.'

'They probably don't, but Freddie Mercury was born there. There's a bar in Stone Town. A bit of a shrine.'

'You been?'

'No.'

'Want to come?'

Marantz studies him, says slowly, 'Who is on Zanzibar and why do you want to know if I have any contacts there?'

'Tony Uys.'

'How do you know?'

'I don't, but there's a chance. Don picked up something a witness told him. He has, or had, a house there. He flew from here to Dar es Salaam — that would be the gateway. You said it yourself, John, while he's free I can't relax. Suzanne called me this afternoon. They want to go home. They've got jobs and study. If they go back, what can I do? I'm fifteen hundred Ks from them.'

'You already know how I feel about protecting family ... If Uys is there, will the police co-operate?'

'No. Tanzania is hard enough to work with, but Zanzibar is semi-autonomous. Besides, this man is an expert in surrounding himself — one way or another — with informers and supporters. The police there are very happy to be paid by private supporters. I doubt they even need much persuasion. He'll have them tied up nice and tight. You can rely on it.'

Marantz shakes his head. 'I don't get it, Vaughn. There has to be a plan. We go there. We have no weapons, no authority. The police are antagonistic. You want to gawp at him in his compound?'

'I don't know, John. But I tell you this: nothing will come from diplomacy or seeking co-operation. Uys will stay there till he wants to set up shop somewhere else. I've closed down his operation in the Kruger, the pipeline for smuggling to Thailand. And he's made his threat. He said, 'I'll find your wife and your lovely daughters.' I keep hearing those words over and over again. For all I know, whoever works for him in Jo'burg is finding out where they are now. That puts Suzanne's mother and her boyfriend at risk as well. I can't let it lie. It's impossible.'

Marantz sits still, eyes scanning his high-ceilinged living room. 'I should go. He doesn't know me.'

'No. It's both of us, or no one.'

'We'd have nothing, Vaughn. Even if we could get weapons, Uys could be tipped off. We could be walking into a trap.'

'I know, I know. But if that's what he thinks, then he won't expect us.'

'That's desperate talk.'

'I am desperate.'

'There's a line, Vaughn.'

'I'm right there.'

Marantz sighs. 'Cyril, Caro's uncle of sorts, I bet he's connected to everything and everyone. Eccentric Englishman living in Stone Town. It might be worth talking to him. Let me find him, see what he knows about this Uys guy . . . '

'Do it,' De Vries tells him. 'I've taken three days' leave.'

Marantz stares at him; logic and madness are converging.

★ ★ ★

Cape Town, Sunday, 10 January 2016
He has not slept, kept awake by the thought of his daughters on Jo'burg streets. His brain races. He wonders whether he can find someone to guard them, decides that he must. He knows that the threat will never diminish until the cause is annulled.

He should not have involved Marantz. His approach was a sign of his own weakness — that, alone, he is afraid. His friend is still in shock, grieving yet driven, stoked by his own loss to take abnormal risk.

His stomach somersaults, his leg jolts. A moment's thought about Kate and Lulu, even Suzanne, disappearing, gone until one day their bodies are discovered.

He swings out of bed, thankful that it is light outside.

★ ★ ★

At eleven thirty, Don February and Sally Frazer watch Charles Adam return from Mass in a white Rolls-Royce Silver Shadow. Don waits ten minutes before turning into their driveway, pulling up in the gravelled courtyard behind the car.

The servant, Joseph, avoids eye contact as they pass him into the dark, cool hallway. He guides them to the drawing room, closes the door behind him.

'I thought that everything had been concluded, Officer. Why are you here, in my home, yet again?' Charles Adam stands, elbow resting on the mantelpiece above the ornate fireplace, patrician, strained.

'I have a piece of property that may have belonged to Chantal, sir. I wanted to show it to you.' Don produces a small gold ring, set with tiny diamonds surrounding a pale sapphire. He holds it out to Adam in the palm of his hand.

Adam glances at it, returns to his pose. 'I don't recognize it.'

'It seems old, sir. It is not a family piece you gave to Chantal some time ago?'

Adam looks down at the ring, to Don. 'It is a cheap piece of jewellery of poor quality. Wherever it came from, it was not this house.'

'Perhaps your wife would recognize it.'

Adam shudders. His voice is low, impatient. 'I've told you before. Chantal left this house six years ago. She left us. I've had no dealings with her since. This item is not something any of us would associate with her, or us.'

In the distance, beyond the dining room, they hear a frustrated sigh, a stifled groan, the sound of sharp footsteps coming towards them. The far door to the drawing room opens and a woman in her mid-sixties appears, dark hair swept up and back from a tight, smooth face.

'Is it them again, Charles?'

Adam holds up his hands. 'It's fine, my dear. Just leave it to me. It's all resolved. It's over.'

The woman approaches Frazer. 'Who are you?'

'Sergeant Sally Frazer, Special Crimes Unit.'

'Well, Sergeant,' her voice is clipped, haughty, 'I want to know why you are here again. This is harassment, and I will not stand for it.'

'Warrant Officer February,' Frazer indicates towards Don, 'is merely checking whether some property found in Chantal's lodgings belonged to her.'

Mrs Adam glances at him, returns to Frazer. 'I'm sure it does not and, frankly, even if it did, we would want nothing to do with it.'

Don holds out the ring in his hand in front of her. She flicks out her hand, slaps it away, does not even watch it fly across the room to land and roll away from them, first silently on the thick carpet, then clattering across the polished wood floor.

'Lillian, please. There is no need . . . '

'There is every need,' Lillian Adam says, turning back to Frazer. 'That girl was given everything. Everything our own children were blessed to have. A good education, servants to wait on her, a wonderful estate to grow up on. And how did she thank us? She made up a story about Charles, the man who had always been loyal to her. We had been married thirty-five years. Do you think I would take the word of a stranger over my own husband?'

'What story?' Frazer asks quietly.

'That's irrelevant.'

Lillian Adam glares at her husband. 'She claimed he tried to seduce her. That he came to her room and locked the door. She had read a story in a magazine and she tried to blackmail us. After that, I wanted nothing to do with her. I encouraged her to leave, and when the chance came for her to go, I welcomed it. We all did. We had put ourselves out, but what she demanded of us was beyond the call of duty. She was a greedy child and what happened to her came as no surprise to me.'

Don walks slowly across the room towards the ring, bends down on one knee, retrieves it from under a chintz sofa. 'I will return this ring to where it was found.'

'Inform your superiors,' Lillian Adam says, 'that no further effort need be expended on this matter. You are not to bother Charles, or me, or our servants, with any more questions. Are you clear on this?'

'Quite clear, madam.'

She leans towards a button on the wall, almost

376

indistinguishable in the same paint colour, presses it. The door opens and Joseph appears. 'Show these people out, Joseph.'

She turns briskly, walks to the back of the room, lets herself out. Again, they hear her footsteps, this time diminishing, until she reaches carpet once more.

Don glances up at Charles Adam, his hands now in his trouser pockets, lips pouting.

'Thank you, sir,' Don says respectfully, 'for answering my last question.'

He turns, walks with Sally Frazer to the door, ignoring Joseph, through the hallway and out into the warm, fresh air of a Constantia afternoon. Joseph closes the front door without looking for them.

At the car, Don turns back to the house, looks up at its magnificent façade surrounded by the ancient oaks.

'It is what De Vries always says ... ' He glances at Frazer. 'Whenever he sees beauty, in a person, or a house, or a family. He says, 'It is only the skin. Inside, there are always secrets.''

'And the ring?'

He pulls it from his pocket, looks at it. It is small and light, the gold of the ring tarnished and worn.

'I will put it back in my box at home.' He looks back at Frazer. 'It was my mother's engagement ring from my father, forty-two years ago.'

★   ★   ★

377

Stone Town, Zanzibar, Tanzania, Sunday, 10 January 2016

Stone Town is forty degrees centigrade, the light so bright that the white paint on the walls, even the soft coral hues on the buildings, make his eyes water. The taxi is ramshackle and hot, the dusty roads potholed and without markings. The heat rises from the road, occasionally seasoned with spice, freshly cut herbs, animal dung.

By the time De Vries hits the seafront Mizingani Road, modernity has overtaken the town yet, to his left, a dhow with a cinnamon sail drifts by. They have flown together to Dar es Salaam, then taken separate flights to Zanzibar, one small precaution against attracting attention.

He is dropped a few moments' walk from the Palace Museum, feels immediately alone, marked as an uncertain tourist. He spots a gleaming white bell-tower, walks towards it purposefully.

The Sultan's Palace is a church-like building, enveloped in three layers of balconies and verandas, framed by old acacia trees. With its dazzling white exterior, grand entrance and bell tower, it might be a relic of French or English colonialism, yet there are Moorish details on the iron balustrades, an incongruous Victorian street-lamp of European origin.

At the entrance, a man in dusty robes scrutinizes him, cranes his neck upwards, gesticulating, says: 'You meet the two gentlemen? First floor, first floor.'

The man averts his eyes. De Vries walks

378

inside, the interior cooler and dim, finds the staircase to the next floor, walks out onto the deserted balcony. As he turns the corner, glances back down the side of the building, he sees Marantz sitting with an elderly man at a brass tray table. Marantz sees him, waves him forward.

'Here is the friend I am helping.' He presents the man. 'This is Mr Cyril Cheyne.'

Cheyne pushes himself off the upright wooden chair, offers his hand.

'Vaughn de Vries.'

From inside the building, a boy brings a third chair, offers tea, disappears back into the cool, dark rooms.

'Are we the only ones taking tea?' De Vries says, sitting, facing Cheyne.

'I am afraid that it is the privilege of familiarity. I live in a fine coral house, but I have no more than a tiny courtyard. If I want to meet friends, I come here. They spoil me — not because I am a scholar but, only, I fear, because I am a benefactor.'

His voice is upper-class English, accented from perhaps Kenya or mainland Tanzania. His almost bare scalp is blemished by decades under the sun, his clothes loose, yet tailored and smart.

'Unlike most of the family members, I was privy to the career of Johnathan Marantz — read into that what you will. Like Caroline, I understood the risk. I was telling John that, to her, it wasn't a burden. It was part of the man she loved. He must not blame himself for the evil others do.'

379

Marantz sits very still, his expression unchanging.

'You never met Caroline?'

'No,' De Vries says. 'I met John a year or so after he came to Cape Town.'

He picks up his cup, brings it to his mouth, retracts it as the heat from the tea reaches the handle.

Cheyne glances to his side, then beyond De Vries. The veranda is very peaceful, the traffic from the coast road still audible, but muted. Within the branches of the gnarled trees, there almost seems a breeze. He speaks quietly, only his hands gesticulating extravagantly.

'I don't know what you're doing here, but since John has already asked me about Tony Uys, I think it is better that I don't find out.' He sits back in the chair, still upright, his little belly swollen. 'Everybody knows Tony here. They know, but they have never met. They know, but they have no wish to know more. Some act for him. The rest of us hope that his malevolent gaze will not fall upon us.'

'Why?'

'A man like him. How would they have said it? With no discernible means of support. Those of us who have been here a while understand from where such money emanates — and it is not to be spoken of.'

'He threatened me, my daughters, my ex-wife. He told me he would kill them.'

Cheyne retrieves his tea from the table, balances the saucer on his belly, lifts the cup to his lips, sips genteelly. He places it back on the saucer, holds it against him.

'So I understand.'

'You'll help us?'

'I already know what you want. It is in hand. A man who says he owes me a favour — I think he says that merely to induce a situation whereby I am in his debt — will obtain the items you require.'

'That's good.'

'I was so pleased to see John,' Cheyne says wistfully. 'I could hardly believe it.' He turns to Marantz, still stony-faced, silent. 'But I am not so naïve as to imagine that there would be no cost.'

Marantz shakes his head, murmurs, 'I'm sorry.'

Cheyne touches his shoulder lightly.

'I asked him to help me,' De Vries says. 'Any blame is on me.'

'And I am not a child,' Cheyne states. 'I'm quite capable of saying no, especially to such a ridiculous request.'

Marantz turns his fingers into a gun.

'Anything that might happen to Tony will not be unwelcome but, I am bound to tell you, it is more likely that he will prevail.'

'Is he here? When did he get back?'

'I have no idea. If John told you that I was some kind of bush telegraph, then I'm afraid you will be disappointed. I am just a moderately well-off old man, who is happy enough to pay for company with generosity. But that does not make me a confidante.'

'But you know where he lives?'

'It's no secret. I've driven past the property on occasion. It is ostentatious and inappropriate except, perhaps, for a man such as he.'

'He has servants? Guards?'

'I have no idea, but he could purchase both with ease.'

'Could we get into his property?'

Cheyne takes a deep breath, glances at Marantz, who says, 'That's our business. Even sitting here with Cyril endangers him. We should go.'

'Finish your tea,' Cheyne says. 'No one will bother us. The other door is locked.' He stares along the veranda, through the acacia trees towards the sea, a narrow plane, almost indistinguishable from the sky. He turns to Marantz. 'It is perhaps better if only you call in later on.' He smiles at De Vries. 'I think people would know you're not my type.'

De Vries grins. 'More and more people are saying that.'

★ ★ ★

They dine at their hotel on Kelele Square in the heart of Stone Town. The modest Beyt Al Salaam is busy with tourists of varying ages, full of conversation and excitement, pink from the sun, drunk on cheap lager. Waiting for Marantz, De Vries takes a stool at the quaint orange-painted bar, nurses a series of beers of varying temperatures. After almost two hours, he slips off the stool, ambles casually towards the front entrance, out onto the tree-lined avenue. The streets seem quiet, although there are still groups of tourists walking in the warm night air, followed or ambushed by hawkers and beggars. The night sky is clouded, the moon absent. There is no sign of Marantz so he wanders back inside. There is a tropical, yet African, smell in the air, which reminds him that he is not on home territory, that the inferences he draws from unexpected movements, strange sounds, a change in atmosphere, are unreliable. The flights, the heat, the crowds; his intense, unfocused drive within to an unknown end: they have all taken their toll. His temples throb, his half-closed eyes watch his fellow drinkers bobbing gently in time to the sensation in his head.

He looks up to see Marantz in the hallway, a parcel beneath his arm. He raises his glass to him. Marantz points at the glass, then to himself, walks out of view. De Vries orders a soda and another beer, carries the glasses into the dark wood-panelled hallway, past the dimly illumi-nated reception desk under two glimmering Moroccan pressed-metal lanterns, up the stair-way.

Marantz's room overlooks the narrow street. Over the acacia trees, between two white castellated buildings and a palm tree, he can see a narrow vertical strip of view: the ocean, dark and heavy, illuminated by lights from the properties; the sky, bulging with huge white clouds dimly glowing as they pass.

De Vries closes the door, passes Marantz the soda. 'Why so long?'

'Cyril wanted to talk.'

'About your family?'

'About you. What you were doing. What *we* are doing.'

De Vries takes a long draft from his beer. 'I don't want to think too much. I want this to end.'

Marantz opens the parcel, wrapped in brown paper. It contains a shoebox, sealed with tape. From inside, he withdraws two handguns, a selection of ammunition. De Vries picks up the smaller of the two. 'Jesus. What does Cyril's friend do? Work in a museum?'

'We need to test these.' Marantz is taciturn, examining the weapons and ammunition, checking the chamber.

'There's oil in the barrel. I don't like oil there. It hides imperfections.'

De Vries places the other gun back on the bed, drains his glass. 'I'm going to bed. You want to knock on my door tomorrow?'

'Stay in your room, swim, whatever. I'm going to take a drive across the island. His house is somewhere on the coast between . . . ' He fumbles a note out of his jacket. 'Pongwe and Gulioni. There's the Kiwengwa Forest inland, a dirt track to his house. Cyril has a young friend who works in one of the resorts on the east coast. He says locals know not to go near the place.'

'Why?'

'Why do you think? Because unpleasant things result.'

'You don't need me?'

'I'm going alone because he knows you. Stay

384

here, keep your head down. I'll be back by lunchtime. We'll talk then.'

De Vries nods numbly. Marantz turns back to the guns, does not look up as De Vries lets himself out of the room and the door slowly closes itself, clicks shut.

★ ★ ★

Stone Town, Zanzibar, Monday, 11 January 2016
He wakes once, early, hears the call to prayer from a distant minaret, falls back into a depth of sleep he has scarcely ever experienced. The fact that, as he lies in bed, a friend is progressing his cause, keeps his mind from firing. His overriding sensation of momentary thought: his head is extraordinarily heavy.

By ten o'clock, he has showered and dressed, taken a banana from a fruit bowl, tried one cup of weak coffee in the hotel. In sunglasses and baseball cap, he wanders towards the sea, finding a coffee kiosk midway, using gestures to order a huge espresso. At the sea-wall, he looks left and right in from a calm blue sea, to the pale pink of the old coral buildings, the soulless new hotels, decaying modern houses. There is terracotta tile and rusting corrugated iron on the roofs; traffic noise drowns out the lapping waves but for a few short pauses when the breeze hits his face and the sea envelopes his brain. He finds a bench, sits head in hands, occasionally glancing up at a passing fishing boat, his mind seemingly empty but for the beat of his pulse.

When the sun overwhelms him, he idles in a wide semi-circle to return to the Beyt Al Salaam, strolling shady side-streets, batting away the hawking children.

★ ★ ★

At lunchtime, Marantz returns, takes him down to his cooler, larger bedroom, opens a map of the island and begins to brief him. Marantz's recall of detail astounds him, as does the minuscule writing in a tiny hardbound notebook.

'Off the main road, there are dozens of turnings, most of them unmarked. Took me a while, even once I identified the property, to work out which one is his. About half a kilometre down the track, there are two substantial stone gateposts, electric gates, with an entry-phone and video. A fence marks his boundaries, and a deep ditch, but anyone could climb over it. You just couldn't get a vehicle there.'

A knock at the door makes De Vries start. Marantz answers it, thanks the waiter, takes a tray from him. He sweeps the map from the table, places cutlery wrapped in napkins in front of De Vries, presents him with a plate of fresh fish and vegetables.

'We've got to eat. You have breakfast?'

'Banana.'

'Impressive.'

'But this, John.' He stares at the plate. 'This isn't what I need.'

'It's exactly what you need. We have a long day ahead.'

De Vries begins to pick at the fish. His appetite is shot.

'You could walk along the beach from the nearest resort,' Marantz says, 'but it must be four or five kilometres. Whoever owns the plots there has kept them large, even though most of the houses are small.'

'Even Uys's?'

'It's not huge, but it's grand.'

'Is he there, John?'

'I don't know. I wasn't going to get any further than the gate. Not then. There's forest by the roads, but precious little cover after that. A few bushes, low trees. The ground is very rough. But there is a brand new light blue Land Rover outside, not parked as such, just there. That, apparently, is what he drives.'

'You see anyone?'

'No. And no one came down the track either. I had my bases covered if they did. It's very quiet around there once you're away from the development.'

'Can we reach it from the beach?'

'I don't know, but we may not have to.'

De Vries drains his coffee cup, feels grounds in his mouth, splutters.

'Why not?' He sticks his tongue out, picks at it.

'Because just inside the gate, about twenty-five metres on, there's a junction box, and that is where the power lines meet the property. I'm thinking if we disrupt them, someone — maybe even Uys himself — will have to come out to see what's happening.'

'Uys? A man like that? He'll have staff, kids working for him.'

'Maybe. But, even so, we may get to see who he has there, and whether he's guarded.'

De Vries nods, turns towards the open window, stretches his neck, invites the light sea breeze to blow down his collar. 'Why is today so busy?'

'Because the forecast is for heavy cloud tonight, maybe even rain. If we want to get to that house, we'll need darkness.'

'I'm ready to move whenever we have to.'

They sit silently, Marantz glancing at the map, De Vries lost in thought.

'We haven't discussed the endgame,' Marantz says, modulating his voice. 'What you want from this. I'm assuming one of two things. You meet him, you tell him that your family's off-limits, that if anything happens to them, you'll hunt him down but, if he stays out of SA, the matter's closed.'

De Vries shakes his head. 'Or you find some way, with two old weapons, to dispose of Tony Uys without leaving any evidence, and we make our escape via a traceable car, with our real passports, either by air or by sea.'

'You don't have to be involved.'

'I am involved, Vaughn. I'm involved and I want to be. I've fired the guns, both function — I tested them discreetly in a bog, somewhere over there.' He points at the map. 'I know what it is to lose family, and how, in a moment, your life can change. You talk about Uys like I've never heard you talk about a perpetrator, an enemy, before.

You're afraid for your family, and I know you. Nothing will go away. I'm just saying: you have to know what you want.'

★ ★ ★

As cloud begins to blow in from the north, the atmosphere of the town changes. The air is still warm, but the humidity, even in a place surrounded by sea, intensifies. Children withdraw from the beach walls, tourists settle into bars or return to their hotels. The streets begin to empty.

Marantz returns from another excursion, with a holdall containing black clothes. 'Tracksuits. Nike rip-offs. Perfect for us.'

De Vries handles the clothes, frowns.

'Heavy-duty hammer, duct tape, some other provisions. If they can't see us, maybe we can get close. It wasn't exactly exhaustive surveillance, but there are no obvious cameras.'

'Why are you doing this?' De Vries asks.

Marantz sits down, faces him. 'Because I couldn't protect my own family. Because my career with the British government is officially over, and I'm very much on my own now. I have plans but I hate unfinished business. Can't relax when something needs doing. It's the way I've always been.'

'You don't owe me anything.'

'We're friends. I don't keep tally. If something goes wrong, I'm off the radar. No one knows my name. I think Tony Uys comes here, to his own fiefdom, to relax, and I think we're going to get him because he just doesn't think we're coming.'

'If we're lucky,' De Vries says, 'he's marked me as dead already.'

★ ★ ★

The sun sets, officially, at 18.44, but the low, scudding cloud, thick and heavy, has made it seem dark long before. The lights in the windows of homes and hotels seem unfocused through the rain-spattered car windows. They leave Stone Town in a squall of fine mist.

As they drive into the interior of the island, the roads deteriorate. There are no streetlights, darkness encroaches around them. An occasional light shines greyly between rough scrub and scattered trees; convenience stores lit by fluorescent tubes in villages with names ending in I and O cast a sickly white pall, refracted in their rain-beaded windows. The thoroughfares are potholed and cracking, cyclists weave across the road, the occasional broken-down vehicle stands at the side of the fast-diminishing tarmac covering.

At the island's centre, the road narrows further. Closely planted trees, ancient and overgrown, line the street, casting heavy droplets onto the car's tinny roof. Marantz drives, focused and unyielding, fifty to sixty kilometres per hour at most.

When they see mountains in the distance, they are vague grey forms against an almost black sky, starless and cold. They pass through Koani and Mpapa. The land flattens, agriculture invades, the road widens. At the crossroads, they lower their windows, smell the sea ahead.

'We're on the east coast,' Marantz tells him. 'You'll see developments everywhere.'

He turns left, heading north. Pongwe is an elongated village, a mixture of poor dwellings with modern shops and businesses. To their right, they glimpse the occasional light from beachfront hotels, but otherwise the road is dark and quiet, modern enough to boast painted lines up the middle of the surface. Either side, there are grassy verges only a few metres deep, beside low woodland.

Around five kilometres out of Pongwe, Marantz slows, peers at the tachometer on the dashboard, measures out three hundred metres, pulls onto the verge, lights off, engine idling. 'The turning onto the Uys compound is over there.' He points with his chin. De Vries can see nothing. Although the rain has stopped, there is almost no light from the sky, not even a distant glow from the coastline.

'I'm going to park in the forest. We'll walk just inside the treeline to ensure that passing cars don't pick us out in their headlights.' Marantz slowly steers the vehicle over a shallow ditch, turns, reverses into the woods between two overhanging trees until they feel the car's bumper hit a trunk.

They exit the vehicle, take rucksacks from the boot, drop down to their knees, survey their route ahead.

De Vries is shaking, legs cramped from the journey, eyes wide, straining to make out features in the blank darkness. He wonders whether his eyes have deteriorated, whether Marantz is seeing more than he can. He follows him as they trudge over soft, shifting ground. A single group of cars passes. They step deeper inside the pitch black close-growing trees, wait for the cones of light to brighten, broaden, suddenly disappear, replaced by the red glow of their tail-lights.

It takes almost fifteen minutes to reach an unmarked driveway. They skirt the track for the first fifty metres, keeping to the edge of the woods but, when the trees end, they see heavy gateposts and iron gates. Occasionally, a gust carries the sound of waves crashing onto the coral lagoon along the east coast but, for the most part, other than the wind in the trees, there is silence.

De Vries holds up a pair of binoculars, points them towards the coast.

'I can see the house. There's some light.' He scans their surroundings. 'If there's anyone out there, I can't see them.'

'If there's anyone out there, we're fucked.'

Keeping low, they cross open ground to the wire fence, traverse a deep, dry ditch. Marantz uses an old pair of rusting wire cutters to form two foothold steps, and De Vries clambers over, Marantz following. From there, they move diagonally to the right of the gateway, until a cylindrical metal junction box appears in the gloom. Above, telegraph poles carry wires, then drop down into the unit.

Close up, they discover that the box is made from heavy-duty metal, painted olive green. The structure is already degrading. Marantz prises open a rusted corner, reaches in and opens the locking mechanism manually. The contents are old, to De Vries intimidating, a low hum emanating from them.

'You know what you're doing?'

Marantz glances back at him. 'Physics O level only. That, and my childhood destructive tendencies.' He studies the interior by the light of a pen torch, reaches into his rucksack and produces a small box of firelighters. He lays half a dozen at the base of the box, drops a lighted match onto them, backs away.

The fire blazes brightly, illuminating oily black smoke, the scrubby surroundings. They lie flat on the ground some twenty metres away. After almost four minutes, there is a dull, vibrating thud. The box jolts and a shower of sparks loops from it, like a cheap firework.

De Vries raises his head, positions the binoculars to his eyes, points them in the direction of the house. 'No lights.'

'Good. Keep the binoculars down. Don't let a headlamp catch them.'

De Vries pockets them, watches Marantz run low and fast around the junction box so that he is on the opposite side of the track, hidden in a clump of spiny bushes. Behind him, a single car races past on the coast road, its exhaust raucous in the cool night breeze. As the sound fades, he can hear nothing. No birds, no animals, just the distant roar of the unending waves.

After five minutes, De Vries sees two headlamps moving towards them down the track from the house. He feels his pulse quicken, anticipating that it could be Uys himself.

It is only when the vehicle is slowing beside the junction box that he sees it is an old *bakkie*, driven by a middle-aged black guy. The man jumps from the van, turns on a torch, points it at the box. Marantz is approaching behind him. When he raises his gun, De Vries stands.

'Stop what you're doing.'

The man jumps, the torch slipping from his grasp onto the dirt track, illuminating his boots. He lifts his hands quickly, face taut, eyes wide.

De Vries gestures with his gun. 'Walk to the gates. You do as you're told, nothing bad happens. You try to run, make a move, we shoot.'

The man walks slowly along the track to the gateposts, waits. Covered by Marantz, De Vries searches him, finds nothing in his pockets but an old-model cell phone. He takes out the battery, throws it in one direction, hurls the handset the other way into long grass.

'Sit on the ground. Keep your hands up.'

De Vries grabs his left wrist, pushes it down to ground level, pulls a heavy duty plastic cable out of his rucksack, ties it around the man's wrist, attaches it to the bottom rung of the iron gate, tightens it, pinning the man's shoulder to the ground. 'How many people are in the house?'

The man looks up at him pitifully, uncomprehending, frightened features exaggerated in the shadows cast by the penlight.

'I know you speak English,' De Vries says. 'I know Mr Uys. I know what he expects. Don't fuck with me.' He brandishes the gun in the man's face.

'Four . . . There are four. Four more than me.'

De Vries takes duct tape from the rucksack, tears a length from the roll, prepares to place it over the man's mouth.

'Wait.' Marantz stands over the man, studies his eyes. The man looks away. Marantz kicks him, regains his attention. 'If you lie, I will kill you on the way out. How many people? Men and women. How many?'

The man's pulse throbs in his neck. His face is sweating. 'There are two guards in the shed at the front.'

'Two guards?'

He nods. 'Two cooks, one man, one woman, in the kitchen in the basement. Two servants. I am one. Another is there.'

De Vries says, 'Is Uys there?'

The man nods again. 'He is there.'

De Vries wraps the duct tape around the man's head, bites it off, wraps a second, longer piece around his torso, pinning his free arm to his body. They climb into the *bakkie*, reverse it onto the grass, then drive slowly up the track towards the house.

De Vries turns to Marantz. 'He's there.'

'Keep it cool. As we planned.' A hundred metres short of the low stone wall around the perimeter of the house, he slows to walking pace, De Vries jumps out; Marantz drives on.

De Vries struggles to keep up with the *bakkie*, running along the rough grassy verge. He follows it through the gap in the wall, then races towards the large, dimly illuminated shed to the right of the building. Marantz edges the vehicle in a circle around the wide courtyard, sees another under cover in an open-fronted wooden building, drives towards it, parks facing outwards. In his rear-view mirror, he focuses on the shed. A man at the entrance is smoking, silhouetted against flickering light, perhaps from a paraffin lamp, inside the tiny building. Beyond the shed, he can make out De Vries moving across his line of vision.

Marantz opens the door, calls to the guard unintelligibly, watches him amble across the yard towards him. At the moment the guard might be able to make him out, Marantz steps forward, weapon pointing. The guard freezes. Marantz advances, grabs him by the arm, frisks him, retrieves a revolver.

'Stay calm, you live. Hands up. Walk back to the shed.'

Beyond the man, Marantz sees De Vries skirt the shed, his silhouette momentarily appearing in the doorway. Moments later, he backs out, gun drawn. Marantz guides his guard inside to join the other.

The interior of the shed is basic: two wooden chairs, a narrow table with empty Fanta cans, a full ashtray, an old radio-cassette player. Marantz examines a rotary phone, tugs the lead from the wall. While De Vries continues to stand over the guards, Marantz searches the second, removes his phone, a large flick-knife. He secures their wrists and ankles with cable ties, winds duct tape around their heads, over their mouths, cuts it with the knife. The men do nothing. They sit still and unmoving, retaining eye contact with Marantz throughout.

'Stay here, do nothing and live. Get clever, you die. Understand?'

Both men nod.

De Vries backs out. Marantz scans the room once more, steps outside, closes the wooden door.

De Vries whispers, 'No fight in them.'

Against his ear, Marantz replies, 'One servant, two cooks, and Uys. Be fucking careful.'

He runs to the front of the house, stands with his back to the white stone wall beside the door, waits.

De Vries looks up at Tony Uys's house, its white classical façade visible in the gloom. It has neo-classical pillars at either side of stone steps leading up to the grand front door, two sets of Georgian-style windows on each of the two floors, an apparently flat roof with castellation on all four plains. It is a simple rectangular design, a coastal fortress in miniature. A single, elongated palm tree stands to the right, its brittle leaves whistling in the breeze.

He jogs towards the tree, struck by the intensity of the wind coming off the sea now that he is overlooking the beach and, beyond it, the lagoon. He cannot see the water, but the back lawn, which slopes towards it, is dimly illuminated from inside the house. He backs against the side wall, slides along it as far as a high narrow window, stretches his neck to peer inside.

397

Within, he sees a hallway and staircase, both dimly lit, apparently empty. He ducks beneath the ledge, continues to the corner of the building. His hearing is polluted by the low roar of the waves but, within the soft cacophony, he thinks he hears a car engine, muffled calls. He dismisses it. He looks up at the sky, the huge shredded palm leaves taut and crackling.

Flat against the wall, he eases around the corner, sees a row of French doors overlooking the beach and lagoon. Inside the broad reception room, there are four hurricane lamps on a central table, a paraffin lamp at the far end. He gingerly tries the first doorway, turning the handle slowly, taken aback that the old-fashioned mechanism clicks and releases, the door pulling away from him in the wind off the sea. He edges inside.

The room is more imposing than it seemed from outside. The floor is broad stone slabs, the white walls sparsely decorated with dark oil paintings beneath unlit brass picture lights. The furniture is huge and solid, made of indigenous wood, hand-carved. The high-ceilinged room runs the breadth of the building, culminating in a huge stone fireplace. De Vries stands perfectly still, listening for movement. He hears the scrape of a shoe against a flagstone, more distant sounds, undecipherable to him over the wind against the windows, the waves.

The dimly lit doorway darkens. Shadow precedes him: Tony Uys strides into the room, sees De Vries, his weapon held out in front of him, stops.

'I'd say what the fuck are you doing here, but I guess I know.'

His voice is loud and strident, utterly without fear.

'You took my daughter. You threatened my family. That was a mistake.'

Uys smiles.

'So you come all this way to take me in — on your own?'

'I'm not alone.'

Uys turns casually to his left, gazes down the length of his living room.

'And I haven't come to arrest you.'

Uys stares at the gun, still nonchalant. 'You think killing me ends this? Who do you think scooped your daughter off the street?'

'You tell me.'

Uys walks towards him. 'I don't think so.'

'Stop. Stop now.' De Vries focuses his eye down the barrel of the pistol. 'Put your hands up.'

Uys stops, smirks at him, hands at his sides. 'All you're doing is betraying your family's name. You should have more sense.'

'My name has nothing to do with who I am. You're a murderous crook, not a patriot.'

Uys stretches his shoulders. 'You're naïve. Every war demands money. I'm a treasurer. What I do is for a greater cause.' He steps forward again.

De Vries backs away towards the corner of the room. 'What you do ends now.'

Uys laughs. 'That's not up to you.'

De Vries stares at him. Behind him, he sees the

light flicker in the hallway through the door. He hears footsteps, wonders whether it is Marantz. He looks back to Uys, who seems closer to him. His hands sweat in his gloves, the gun feels heavy.

There are three sharp shots from outside the room. De Vries drops to his knee, looks back at Uys, sees blood pouring from him, his hands at his neck, legs bowing, the great trunk falls.

Beyond him, De Vries sees multiple shadows. He pushes himself back from his position, grabs at the door handle to the French doors through which he came, falls through the door, rolls to one side. Above him now, inside the house, he hears two more shots. Ankles and calves burning, he thrusts himself around the side of the house, scrambles, torso raised but almost on all fours, towards the cover of bushes and the thicker grasses. He hears the metal door slam shut, assumes he is being followed.

His vision is restricted to little more than a couple of metres, beyond which the blackness is disorienting. He wonders whether to fall and freeze, hoping he is not discovered, but instinct tells him to run. He estimates the forest begins a few hundred metres inland and ahead of him, their car at its edge by the main road.

He wonders about Marantz; he heard no other shot before the ones that hit Uys, yet nothing makes sense. He stumbles on, his chest tight and sore. He stops, squats in the grasses, listens. His ears ring. He hears nothing but hollowness. He raises his head, sees the house in the distance. A figure runs around the side, between the wall and the palm tree. He gulps air, holds his breath. Still nothing. He gives himself thirty seconds, gauges his position to the beginning of the forest, sets off slowly, determined, utterly bewildered.

Even with the pen-torch, finding a path through the forest is almost impossible. He renavigates himself when he hears a car pass in the distance, stumbling on, despite his fatigue. Suddenly, he sees a flash of lights through the trees, realizes that the road must be close.

He comes out of the forest onto the scrubby verge, staggers onto the tarmac, sees headlights, lurches back towards the forest. The car passes, blue lights flashing — police. He sits against a tree in the dark forest, swings his rucksack onto his lap, finds his cell phone. He takes off his gloves, switches it on. There is one SMS: *WTF! At car, will wait. 150m from turn-off.*

De Vries messages back, fingers numb and clumsy, pockets the phone, staggers to the edge of the trees, continues to walk back up the road. Two more police cars pass, other vehicles, in greater numbers than before. Each time, he ducks back into the total cover of the trees.

After half an hour, he hears a voice: 'Vaughn?'

'Ja.'

He steps past a fallen branch, sees Marantz.

'We've got to go.'

They throw the rucksacks into the back of the car, open the front doors, get in.

'Jesus,' De Vries says. 'What was that?'

'Two guys. Looked like army, special forces. Pros for sure. I ran upstairs.'

'They took Uys down, right in front of me. Don't know whether they saw me; probably heard us talking.'

Marantz starts the engine. 'Why were you talking?' He puts the car into reverse, looks in his rear-view mirror. Already the headlights are reflecting in it, blinding him. 'Shit.'

De Vries turns around. A police car is at the edge of the road, officers already jumping out.

'Shit. You dump everything?'

'Yes.'

De Vries swallows. 'I still have the pistol, tape, ties . . . Shit.' They open the doors, step slowly out of the car, hands aloft.

The police officers start shouting, ordering them to the ground. De Vries hears them in his damaged ears as tinny, distant cries; his back cracks loudly as he sinks down.

★ ★ ★

Stone Town, Zanzibar, Tuesday,
12 January 2016
He has fallen asleep, eventually, with the impression of bars burned into his eyes. He wakes to find them fill his field of vision. Momentarily afraid, he rubs his eyes, focuses. They are black against grey, dividing his world into tiny quadrants. He stretches, grimaces as his back spasms, the concrete ledge hard on sore hips. He sits up, sees Marantz across the cell from him, horizontal, eyes open.

'You slept.'

'I was fucked.' De Vries says, his voice hoarse.

Marantz laughs. 'It's eight o'clock, maybe. No breakfast.'

'Can't get the staff.'

'Still, luxury digs. Suite to ourselves. There's the drunk and disorderlies somewhere down there.'

'Any bright ideas in the night?'

'According to my brief research prior to our visit, the Tanzania Police have a reputation for brutality and a propensity to accept money over the upholding of the law. Our officers last night showed little appetite for either.'

'I'm conflicted.'

Marantz laughs. De Vries wonders why, when they are in trouble, helpless, Marantz seems more relaxed.

'If they don't discover who you are, you'll have to decide which cards to show. The pistol they found on you, you're sure you didn't fire it?'

'Positive.'

'Then let's hope they don't have an expert who matches shots from that gun to the bullet-riddled body of Tony Uys.'

De Vries knows how evidence can be concealed, reformed, constructed.

They wait.

★ ★ ★

He catches a glimpse of a wall clock that tells him it is eleven twenty. The corridors smell of shit, masked by bleach. Two officers escort them, without cuffs, to an office, knock, let them in, back out.

'Good morning, gentlemen. Sit down. Sit down, please.'

They sit in front of his desk, behind which tatty blinds offer glimpses of the street beyond the confines of the Kijito Upele police station.

'I am Captain Felix Suleiman Khalifa.' He is young, probably in his mid-thirties, tall and very slim, wearing 1960s-style horn-rimmed spectacles, his English perfect. He remains standing behind his desk, his mouth a straight line. 'I know who you are, Colonel Vaughn de Vries of the South African Police Service. But you, sir, Mr Johnathan Marantz, I do not know you.'

He sits down, lightly balled fists resting on the desk in front of him. 'So, last night, two armed men disable the electricity supply to the house of one of our residents, break into his property, immobilize his security staff. The owner is fatally shot four times, twice from point-blank range, probably when he was lying on the floor. They make their escape. My officers apprehend you at the roadside, barely one hundred metres from the entrance to the property. Two rucksacks are confiscated, one of which contains an Italian Beretta 70 pistol, a knife, tape and cable ties identical to those used to restrain the staff.'

'The weapon was mine,' De Vries says. 'It wasn't fired.'

Khalifa smiles. 'I know that. But the fact remains that a capital offence has been committed and we can place you at the scene.'

'You interested in evidence?'

'That is my job.'

'Do you want to know what happened?'

'No.'

'No?'

'No, Colonel. I know what happened. You are sitting in my office this morning only so that I can decide what I will do with you.'

'We didn't kill Tony Uys. He threatened me and my family. He was behind the abduction of my daughter in Johannesburg less than a week ago —'

Khalifa holds up his hand. 'I told you. I do not wish to hear your story.' He sits back, still calm, his voice steady and confident. 'If you had been apprehended not even six months ago, you would have been arrested and put on trial. You would have confessed, and the evidence would have supported your confession. Believe me, I know how things work in Tanzania, especially, perhaps, here on Zanzibar. But you are fortunate. We have certain men in government who seek to make our society a better place. So, I am in command here, on Zanzibar.'

De Vries glances at Marantz, who is silent and still.

'So, Colonel, what did you do to make an enemy of Mr Tony Uys?'

'He was the prime suspect as the head of a criminal gang of men and women involved in the smuggling of human beings, drugs, ivory and rhino horn from South Africa, predominantly to the Far East. We shut down his trafficking operation in the Western and Eastern Capes, raided his headquarters on the outskirts of Kruger Park, where we found evidence of his activities and a mass grave of endangered species.'

'That was good work.'

'You knew Uys was involved in criminal activity, but he was allowed to reside here?'

'Until I arrived, Colonel, Zanzibar was a refuge for many undesirables. Deals were discussed, bargains made, blind eyes turned. But, you should know, Tony Uys made no such deals here.'

'No?'

'No. When you were on that man's property, I believe you witnessed a sanctioned attack on Mr Tony Uys by members of an elite unit of the Tanzania People's Defence Force — our army.'

' 'Sanctioned'?'

'The attack was ordered . . . from within our government.'

'Why?'

Khalifa takes off his spectacles, wipes his eyes. 'Because he had failed.'

De Vries shakes his head.

'You rested downstairs this morning so I could have time to assemble what information could be gleaned. From my contacts, yesterday I had received word that there were government operatives on Zanzibar. I knew that Mr Tony Uys was protected from high up. If that protection were to end, it would do so at the behest of those who had granted it in the first place. There are those in positions of power — I am sure throughout Africa — who use it to enrich themselves and to undermine individuals and institutions, even foreign governments. I believe that Tony Uys was sponsored by one of these groups within, or close to, our own government. When he lost his grip, he became a liability.'

There is silence in the office. Through the blinds, there is a slight breeze, the honk of an old car horn and an exhaust sputtering.

'I was only trying to protect my family.'

Khalifa stares at De Vries. 'I am going to say this to you, Colonel, out of respect. My men have retrieved several weapons from outside the Uys compound, quite different from the modern tools found inside, on his security guards — a nasty-looking knife, other . . . equipment. It cannot be linked with you. So, contrary to what you have most certainly read about our police force here on Zanzibar, this is what I propose. I will have you driven to the airport. You will fly to Dar es Salaam and, from there, you will take the first available flight back to South Africa. If you come to Tanzania again, I expect you to contact me.' He leans forward, opens a small ebony box on his desk, passes De Vries a card. 'If I should require assistance in South Africa, I trust that you will make yourself available.'

'I don't have a card, but yes.'

'Well,' Khalifa says, 'I will be able to locate you, wherever you are.' He stands up, glances at his gold wrist watch, waits for De Vries and Marantz also to stand, offers his hand to each man. 'I trust you have both enjoyed your brief visit to Zanzibar?'

They nod. The office door opens, and the two policemen who escorted them from the cells lead them out of the ornate glazed doors, down the

407

steps of the 1960s Kijito Upele Police station, into the car park. They do not hold open the doors to the car, but get into the front, wait for De Vries and Marantz to climb onto the back seat, and they set off with a jolt.

★ ★ ★

They scarcely speak until they reach the business lounge in Julius Nyerere International Airport in Dar es Salaam. De Vries takes a bottle of wine from the complimentary bar, sits in a corner with his back to the largely empty room. 'You asked me why I was talking with Uys.'

Marantz shrugs. 'You don't have to tell me.'

'I wanted him to know . . . but also . . . ' He puts his glass on the table. 'Also . . . I wasn't sure. I didn't know . . . '

'You didn't know if you could kill him,' Marantz says softly. 'It's all right.'

'No, it isn't. My family depend on me. I don't know why I hesitated. I don't know why I didn't pull the trigger.'

'You didn't need to.'

'But if I had . . . ' He picks up his glass, his hand shaking, downs the liquid, pours again.

'That's why I said I would do it,' Marantz says. 'You like to think you're a renegade, but you're not. You know there's a line. You prefer to believe that you don't see it, but you do. You might walk right up to it, toes touching, lean over, grab what you can, but you never cross it. I did — and now it's as if the line was never there.'

'That's not good, John.'

Marantz sits back, suddenly nonchalant. 'It's over now, what I was in the past, the life I led. This was it. Everything starts anew. It has to.'

'Good.'

'And neither of us need look back on what happened on Zanzibar and be anything other than grateful that we found an honest cop who recognized another.'

De Vries nods, coughs, stands and turns back to the bar. When he returns to their corner, Marantz has his head down over his phone, typing.

★ ★ ★

Cape Town, Wednesday, 13 January 2016
'Chantal Adam's chance to speak about what her uncle had done had passed. She knew that people in South Africa had followed her career in America, had read about the drugs, and sex, and alcohol.' Don February looks up from his notes, finds his audience attentive. 'When she came back, she wanted nothing her adoptive parents could offer, which was maybe no more than money, perhaps even to buy her silence. Her mother did not even believe her. I think she came home hoping her old friends would support her, help her rebuild her life, but anyone associated with the Adams was unwilling to come forward and her school friends had moved on. Probably her only friend was Dale Rix, the man who had nearly shot her father, who had been there on the day he died.'

He looks at Brigadier du Toit, De Vries, and

wonders whether the emotion in his voice is unprofessional. When he had first been part of a group who met in Brigadier du Toit's office, the door shut, blinds lowered, he had felt honoured. Now, it is merely his job, the conclusion of his investigation.

'However privileged her childhood, I do not think Chantal Adam received much love. Charles Adam said they had been 'compelled' to look after her, and his wife described her as a 'stranger'. If the story about her adoptive father coming to her room is true, it would explain why she refused ever to go back there, even to take their money.'

''I can't go back,'' De Vries says.

'What?'

He turns to Du Toit. 'What she tried to write in that godforsaken motel room. On the paper found inside her stomach.'

'We know,' Don says, 'that she had a disagreement, an argument, with Angela Cole, the woman who took her in and in whose home she left her possessions. She spent time with some Australian tourists, perhaps one man in particular, in the Rucksack Rooms off Long Street, but he and they disappeared without telling her. The manager said she seemed shocked and upset when she returned there asking for them. Maybe she thought she had found someone to protect her, to love her.

'How she was recruited by Diane Kemmel, I could not discover. It is not possible that she knew who Ray Rossouw and Jan de Mueller were — associates of the man who killed her father. Perhaps she thought that she could start a new life in Thailand, that this was an opportunity — but whatever happened in that room made her desperate to escape.'

'But why not await rescue?' Du Toit says.

'Maybe Leon Barker threatened her sexually,' De Vries says. 'We can't know what was going through the mind of a girl in so much trauma. She was drugged. We know they did that to the girls to disorient and subdue them. She had a stomach full of cocaine. Perhaps she thought we'd arrest her. Perhaps she was just tired of a life seemingly out of her control . . . '

Du Toit leans back in his chair. 'You've managed to find a theory, if not necessarily proof, to support Chantal's actions. I can't see how we can proceed against Charles Adam, but at least we have an insight.'

'Adam . . . ' De Vries says. 'The word of one dead girl against his. You can bet that, if what she claimed was true, it won't have been the first time. It was probably the decision to get away from him, maybe to try to expose him, that cost her everything.'

'Abusers seem untouchable at the time,' Du Toit says. 'They have an aura about them. By the time people accept what happened to them, it's too late.'

'Everything we do,' De Vries says, 'every act we investigate, stems from a decision at a moment in time. It could be something totally unimportant, unacknowledged. It might be the moment when a neuron fires in anger, a hand lashes out, a finger pulls a trigger, or it may

411

germinate from an event years before, the act itself contemplated for decades. To deal with the result, you have to understand the cause.'

'Very philosophical.'

'I'm not interested in the result, the statistics. You and General Thulani may think this job is all about success rates and league tables, how it's perceived, but I want to know the truth, the answer. That's all.'

'I think of how many times you don't find a reason,' Du Toit says. 'So much crime is mindless.'

De Vries turns to Don. 'What did you find out about the girls who reached Bangkok?'

'Not much. I informed you that we had contacted the embassy in Bangkok, that they were unhelpful. I asked the brigadier to bring pressure . . . ' He trails off.

'General Thulani signed the official request,' Du Toit says. 'He came back to me a couple of days later. No information available. Officially.'

'What does that mean?'

'I don't know, and neither did he, but the response is sanctioned by the foreign ministry. We are, it seems, unable to obtain information on this subject.'

'That's ridiculous. We need to find out how many SA citizens have been arrested, tried, imprisoned. We need to work for their release or, at least, repatriation.'

Du Toit looks towards his window. 'Off the record, I think that's the point. They don't want them repatriated, serving their sentences in prison here. There's no space, no money. It's a problem best left off radar, off budget, out of the media.'

'Our own government? The Constitution . . . '

Du Toit holds up his hand. 'I've argued the case already.' He points upwards. 'Deaf ears. This is why we do what we do here. Why we need to keep on doing it. Whatever else happens, we have justice at the forefront of our minds.'

There is silence. De Vries says, 'Don here solved a twenty-year-old murder: Willem Adam, a precursor to the new South Africa. That is, at least, justice done. Surely that will please General Thulani and his ilk. When Tony Uys is found and arrested, we'll get the story from him.'

He feels no remorse for misleading his colleagues. To practise obfuscation, to embrace the disingenuous: these are necessary for him to function in this environment. He checks himself, acknowledges that it is for no higher purpose than self-preservation.

'General Thulani is conflicted, Vaughn.' Du Toit glances at Don February, aware that he has dropped his usual formality in front of a junior officer. 'You have caused many problems for Major Ngcuka at the Organized Crime and Drug Unit. Colonel Wertner is threatening to investigate your relationship with Warrant Officer Heyns. You have overspent every budget he controls. I think a low profile is called for. A case, perhaps, away from Cape Town?'

'Yes, sir.'

★   ★   ★

De Vries calls his daughters, tells them to take precautions in public, to travel with friends. He knows that nothing can protect anybody, that invulnerability is impossible. His reassurance is convincing, but devoid of conviction; he's afraid that cells within Uys's group could still operate alone. Yet, without Uys, what would be the motivation to hurt him, to harm his family?

He drinks late into the night, meditating on the theme, recalling his emotion as he stood before Uys, gun primed, pointing it without the will to fire the shot. He wonders, had he not been interrupted, what he would have done, wonders whether Marantz's talk of lines not crossed merely veils his weakness.

When he goes to bed, his limbs heavy on the old staircase, he leaves the curtains open, the street lights muffled by branches on the pepper trees, Devil's Peak silhouetted against a bright silver-blue sky, and he thinks about Lee-Ann Heyns.

Ambition, an obsession, perhaps psychosis, drove everything else in her life away. To be acknowledged as an equal, as a superior, within a career whose prospects for women like her are diminishing until almost non-existent. What a life it had led her to live.

He lies on his back, exhausted and awake, understands everything she did, realizes that, in front of him, around him, because of him, she had gone to her death.

He turns over, remembers his first drive with her on Christmas Day, from the Adam house back around the Mountain, down towards

414

Kirstenbosch Botanical Gardens, how she had admired the lush wooded mountain slopes stretching for kilometre after kilometre above the city, that this was her favourite view. He had proposed then the drink, at his house: a decision at a moment in time, something totally unimportant, unacknowledged. Something fatal.

★   ★   ★

Cape Town, Friday, 15 January 2016
His new investigation will take him a little over a hundred and fifty kilometres from Cape Town, beyond mountains, around circuitous roads. He will feel disassociated from his home city.

He hardly ever calls Marantz before he visits him, reasoning that if he is out — which he rarely is — there is either the Foresters Arms or Barrister's restaurant in Newlands for a steak and a beer. He may argue to himself that he is checking on him after his return from London, but he knows that he has no one else with whom he can share the terror of his weakness, the magnitude of each tiny decision.

This year, the agapanthus under the oak trees that line Newlands Avenue seem unwilling to flower. He still loves this road, an almost perfect tunnel of green, dark cocooning. He crosses the freeway onto Rhodes Drive and takes Vineyard Street up the side of the Mountain, joins Vineyard Heights — the very highest road — climbs the hill to its peak, freewheels towards Marantz's house.

He parks under the overhanging shrubs of the

next-door house, many of the homes in the area still empty for another day or two before their wealthy owners return from Plettenberg Bay or abroad. He takes off his seatbelt, pulls out his cigarettes, lights up. As he extinguishes his lighter, he sees the garage doors slide open, the headlamps from a car beam across the street, Marantz's old ivory Mercedes pull out and turn. De Vries slides a little lower in his seat, sees Marantz smiling, a red-haired girl in the passenger seat.

Whether or not he sees De Vries's car — maybe he chooses not to — John Marantz drives past up the hill. De Vries stays low; watches the tail-lights in his mirror suddenly brighten as the car brakes cresting the summit, before it, and the two red lights disappear.

Epilogue

Durban Daily News, *17 October 1994*

Former Cabinet Member Assassinated
Willem Fourie Adam was one of the architects of the National Party group that lobbied internally for a peaceful handover of power and for free elections, yet the very peace for which he fought has eluded him in his private life. Just eight months into retirement from the political scene, Adam, 49, was gunned down in his car in the Chatsworth area of the city. Police are still appealing for witnesses to the evening attack on the former NP minister.

Adam resigned his place in government to spend time with his wife, Daphne, who was recently diagnosed with a serious degenerative illness. In the back of the car with Adam was his three-year-old daughter, Chantal. Police say that the toddler was bloodied but unharmed. An eminent child psychiatrist told the *Daily News* that, as a young child, witnessing an event as shocking as the assassination of her father is likely to leave scars which could last a lifetime.

Acknowledgements

Many thanks to my editors, Krystyna Green and Martin Fletcher, who have persuaded me to streamline, clarify, delete and expand, ultimately vastly improving the final manuscript.

My police adviser, Captain Mariaan Steyn, is absolved of all blame for my inaccuracies, since she advises me on the protocols of the real SAPS and not the imagined elite units of my stories.

Many people have contributed ideas, both consciously and otherwise: Kate Birch gave me *Dead Cows for Piranhas* to read; many other Cape Town friends contributed anecdotes and images which lend many new angles to my vision of Cape Town.

Thanks to Robert, Tania, the Birch clan, Dickie/Chris, and many others.

Gareth Hughes once again read the early drafts, providing a crucial objectivity and his usual apposite comments.

★   ★   ★

Many links online have been squinted at and sometimes absorbed.

I highly recommend Hazel Friedman's *Dead Cows for Piranhas* — her investigations prove the inhumanity of the drug trade and cast suspicion of duplicity on those who should be protecting their people. Thanks to Gary Baines's

'South Africa's Forgotten War', published in *History Today*, vol. 59, I was able to understand a conflict, and its abrupt termination, that had been previously unknown to me.

We do hope that you have enjoyed reading this large print book.

Did you know that all of our titles are available for purchase?

We publish a wide range of high quality large print books including:
**Romances, Mysteries, Classics
General Fiction
Non Fiction and Westerns**

Special interest titles available in large print are:
**The Little Oxford Dictionary
Music Book
Song Book
Hymn Book
Service Book**

Also available from us courtesy of Oxford University Press:
**Young Readers' Dictionary
(large print edition)
Young Readers' Thesaurus
(large print edition)**

For further information or a free brochure, please contact us at:
**Ulverscroft Large Print Books Ltd.,
The Green, Bradgate Road, Anstey,
Leicester, LE7 7FU, England.
Tel:** (00 44) 0116 236 4325
Fax: (00 44) 0116 234 0205

Other titles published by Ulverscroft:

THE SERPENTINE ROAD

Paul Mendelson

South Africa, 1994: Even after the release of Nelson Mandela and the promise of free elections, extremist groups terrorise the country. Captain Vaughn de Vries finds himself in pursuit of the suspects of a fatal bombing in his precinct, under the command of one of the most feared white police officers of the time: Major Kobus Nel. Out of radio communication and without clear evidence, the South African Police Service barges into a township and sets off a chain of events that will resonate for nearly a quarter of a century . . . Cape Town, 2015: Six men are murdered, each with a connection to a point in the past that de Vries would sooner forget. Old wounds, hidden in history, are exposed, and a mysterious killer approaches, whom no one seems to be able to stop . . .

THE FIRST RULE OF SURVIVAL

Paul Mendelson

Seven years ago in Cape Town, three young South African schoolboys were abducted in broad daylight on consecutive days. They were never seen again. Now, a new case for the unorthodox Colonel Vaughn de Vries casts a light on the original enquiry, which he is convinced was a personal failure on his part; the abductions have haunted him for those seven years, costing him his marriage and peace of mind. Struggling in a mire of departmental and racial rivalry, de Vries seeks the whole truth and unravels a complex history of abuse, deception and murder — and in the process discovers he is no longer sure who his friends and enemies are . . .